little black dress
· IT'S A GIRL THING ·

Dear Little Black Dress Reader,

Thanks for picking up this Little Black Dress book, one of the great new titles from our series of fun, page-turning romance novels. Lucky you – you're about to have a fantastic romantic read that we know you won't be able to put down!

Why don't you make your Little Black Dress experience even better by logging on to

www.littleblackdressbooks.com

where you can:

♥ Enter our **monthly competitions** to win **gorgeous** prizes

♥ Get **hot-off-the-press** news about our latest titles

♥ Read **exclusive** preview chapters both from your **favourite** authors and from brilliant new writing talent

♥ Buy **up-and-coming** books online

♥ Sign up for an essential slice of romance via our **fortnightly email** newsletter

We love nothing more than to curl up and indulge in an addictive romance, and so we're delighted to welcome you into the Little Black Dress club!

With love

The *little*

Five interesting things about Allie Spencer:

1. Four years at university gave me the skills necessary to roll a Hula Hoop across the floor of the college bar with my nose.

2. I have a secret ambition to be a stand-up comedian.

3. The first rule of life is: if you love it – buy it. I'm still thinking about the orange silk fifties cocktail dress I saw in a vintage shop ten years ago . . . sigh.

4. I have a total soft spot for men in glasses (and I keep nagging my husband to wear his more often).

5. I once had a cat that used to eat chillies covered in vindaloo curry sauce.

By Allie Spencer

Tug of Love
The Not-So-Secret Diary of a City Girl

The Not-So-Secret Diary of a City Girl

Allie Spencer

little
black
dress

First published in 2010
by LITTLE BLACK DRESS
An imprint of HEADLINE PUBLISHING GROUP

A LITTLE BLACK DRESS paperback

2

Cataloguing in Publication Data is available from the British Library

ISBN 978 0 7553 5294 4

Typeset in Transit511BT by Avon DataSet Ltd,
Bidford-on-Avon, Warwickshire

Printed and bound in Great Britain by
Clays Ltd, St Ives plc

Headline's policy is to use papers that are natural, renewable and
recyclable products and made from wood grown in sustainable forests.
The logging and manufacturing processes are expected to conform to the
environmental regulations of the country of origin.

HEADLINE PUBLISHING GROUP
An Hachette UK Company
338 Euston Road
London NW1 3BH

www.littleblackdressbooks.com
www.headline.co.uk
www.hachette.co.uk

To Isla (my real sister) and Grace, Nancy and Sarah Jane (my fake sisters), you are the best a girl could wish for!

Acknowledgements

As always, this book feels more like a team effort than a solo venture and I would like to express my gratitude to everyone who has helped to take it from the first glimmering of an idea into a published novel. First among these are of course Claire, Sara and everyone else at Little Black Dress who have been so wonderful over the past few months, together with my agent, Teresa Chris, who has been equally fantastic. There are also many, many others who have read the book and given feedback, provided childcare, helped with publicity, provided me with factual information about the banking sector and much more besides – thank you from the bottom of my heart, I couldn't have done it without you. In particular I would like to mention: Liz and Jake, Matthew, Sarah Jane, Nancy, Lee-Anne, Caz, Clive, Claire, Struan, Grace, Jane, Julie, Jill, Kaye, Alison, Sam, Karen – and my cousin Isabel for letting me borrow her name – even if I did spell it differently! I would also like to wish the Romantic Novelists' Association all the very best as they celebrate their Golden Jubilee in 2010; and, last but by no means least, there's Chris, my husband: thank you and I love you.

Prologue

I am sitting in the saloon bar of the Rose and Crown in my home town of Bournebridge, Wiltshire.

Well, that's not strictly accurate.

When I say 'town', I mean 'sleepy village halfway up the back-arse of nowhere'; and when I say 'saloon bar', I'm talking about the half of the pub that doesn't have sawdust strewn underneath the bar to catch the broken glass on a Saturday night. There is another pub a short jaunt along the high street, but as the drinks are twice the price *and* the landlord knows my parents, I'm better off roughing it down at the Rosie.

Besides, it's not just me who drinks here.

Right now it's half past four on a Friday afternoon in April and the place is heaving. There are a couple of old geezers in cloth caps over in the public bar nursing halves of stout and arguing over the odds for the four forty-five at Sandown, but the rest of the demographic is quite clearly on the younger side.

In fact, most of it is quite clearly on the younger side of eighteen – but as long as you're not actually *wearing* a school uniform and you don't try to pay for your drinks with Monopoly money, the staff here don't seem to mind. So, casting my eye around the room, I can see my mate Caroline and her boyfriend Robbie (both Lower Sixth like me), plus there's quite a few in from the boys' grammar in the next village, drinking halves of sweet cider and trying to pretend they don't give a monkey's about their upcoming exams.

I, however, do.

I care very much.

In fact, I am so desperate to conjure up some good exam grades and use them to grapple my way out of rural Wiltshire and away from my family that right now I'm drinking Diet Coke and doing my best to learn my French vocabulary, despite being deafened by the mating cries of the lesser-spotted English adolescent.

Or greater-spotted, if you're talking about Robbie's mate Kev.

No, I'm here because my mum and dad have just had another almighty row about Dad's business – their third this week. I'd just come in from school and walked into the kitchen to see my mother in a state that could only be described as 'core meltdown' over my father's failure to chase up an invoice for ten thousand pounds. My father protested that the cheque was on its way, while my mothered countered forcefully that she'd believe it when she saw it.

They didn't even realise I was there.

So, needing to get away and with my escape routes limited to the Rose and Crown or hiding out upstairs (where my sister Mel was testing the strength of the floor joists with her deafening music), I picked up my purse and went straight back out again, leaving the parentals to slug it out amongst the windowsill-top pots of herbs and the Le Creuset.

I look up as the door to the pub creaks open and spews another gobbet of grammar-school boys out into the room. You can always tell the St Peter's crowd – they slap on far too much aftershave, wear a lot of black leather and stare at girls in a slightly scary way. There's one in particular, with deep brown eyes and a gob permanently on fast-forward, who seems fixated with me. Sometimes I can feel his eyes burning through my mad curly dark hair right into the back of my neck and – oh yes, there we go! Even though I'm looking in the opposite direction, I know that he's right behind me, and I can feel his gaze like a shaft of sunlight focusing through a magnifying glass as it bores its way in between my shoulder blades.

But I'm not interested.

Right now I'm on a mission with my French vocab and so, even though he *is* on the hotter side of cute, I do what I always do: ignore him and go back to my books.

Until—

'Oi,' I say. 'Watch what you're doing!'

Strange Staring Man has bumped into my table sending a good half of my Diet Coke flowing freely across my French exercise book.

'Sorry,' he mutters (ironically, for the first time in his life unable to make proper eye contact with me). 'I wanted to give you this.'

And he drops a small, neatly folded square of paper down on to the table before walking quickly over to the other side of the bar and disappearing into the fold of a dozen more or less identical gangly teenage boys.

I dab at the Coke spillage with a beer mat (not very effective) and then do the same with the corner of a nearby curtain (rather more effective but it gets me a dirty look from the barmaid). Then, crisis averted, I put my soggy book back in my bag and pick up Mr Starey's piece of paper.

For a moment I consider *not* opening it; but then I think, what the hell, and peel back the corners to reveal, in all its spidery glory, the handwritten invitation: *Will you go for a drink with me?*

Er, no. I don't think so. Even though my stomach does a secret little flip at the thought.

I roll my eyes in exasperation (just in case he's looking – which he probably is, given the way the hairs on the back of my neck are standing on end) and then crumple the note up in my hand. I'm about to chuck it on the floor but the barmaid glowers at me again, so I shove it inside the little diary I always carry in my bag, stand up and make my way through the throng to the door of the pub.

I'm just about to step out into the spring sunshine when I feel the weight of his stare yet again and turn round. He gives me a smile so dazzling they could probably use it to illuminate Wembley Stadium – but for a million bazillion reasons I'm simply not in the mood. Returning his grin with a Grade 1 thermonuclear scowl, I lift the latch on the door and make my way home to see if peace has broken out in the old family homestead, tossing his screwed-up note into the kichen bin when I arrive.

And that is the last I see of him, and his scribbled invitation for drinkies *à deux*.

Or so I think . . .

But fate, as usual, has other ideas. Including the less-than-brilliant one that the best time to reintroduce us will be ten years later, in the middle of one of the biggest financial scandals the City has ever seen, just when my sister Mel is about to pitch up on my doorstep on the run from her home in Bristol with a bunch of West Country heavies hot on her trail.

All that, however, is in the future. First I need to go to uni, get a dullsville job as an analyst with the Chiltern Bank, buy a hideously overpriced two-bedroomed flat in Hammersmith, and hook up with Tom, a hotshot trader who possesses a body your average Greek god would kill for, but who doesn't realise that the phrase 'going out with' refers to me, his girlfriend, and not getting beered up with the rest of the lads at work. Finally, I have to get fantastically drunk at an impromptu birthday party and wake up at stupid o'clock on a Thursday morning in dire need of a vat of black coffee with a large helping of Alka-seltzers on the side.

So let's fast-forward a decade to half past five in the middle of March – and if I'm not much mistaken, the alarm is about to go off . . .

A sound like an incoming missile alert sliced through the air and threw me into a state of confusion. Up until then I'd been asleep and dreaming about a man hitting me on the back of the head with a sledgehammer; now, however, even though I was awake, my dream not only seemed to be carrying on but the pain was also getting worse.

I groaned.

Loudly.

What was going on?

'For God's sake turn the bloody alarm clock off!' muttered a voice next to me, half muffled by the duvet.

I reached an arm out from under the covers and smacked the clock hard. So hard, in fact, that it shot off my bedside table and into the outer darkness over by the wardrobe.

I groaned again and tried to open my eyes, only to find that they were glued shut by a combination of excess alcohol consumption, extreme sleep deprivation and Lash-a-bility – *the mascara that keeps on working while you party!*

'If you don't turn the alarm clock off,' the voice next to me said, 'I shall do it myself. And after that, I shall be forced to execute *you* for crimes against humanity.'

Frankly, death seemed pretty appealing right then (as

opposed to the 'death warmed up' option, which I was currently experiencing). However, I was never one to shirk my duty, so I threw back the covers, crawled on my hands and knees towards the noise (which now seemed to have an added pneumatic drill-like quality to it), picked up my hairdryer and aimed it at the offending timepiece. There was an almighty crack – one that felt as though it had sliced the top of my skull open – and then peace, blessed peace, reigned supreme.

Exhausted, I lay down with my head on the carpet and the throbbing in my temples subsided slightly.

'What time is it?' muttered the occupant of my bed.

'I don't know,' I said. 'I can't actually open my eyes.'

'Are you all right?'

'So long as I lie down flat it's okay,' I said. 'If I try to stand up, I feel as though I'm going to slide off the floor. How about you?'

I prised one eyelid open with my fingers and was rewarded by the sight of Polly, my friend and work colleague, draped over the edge of the bed with her normally sleek black hair standing up on end.

'I was well and truly mugged by the beer gorilla last night,' she whispered.

'You mean the Long Island Iced Tea gorilla,' I reminded her, rolling on to my back to see if that helped at all, 'who was accompanied by his cousins the Chardonnay chimpanzee and the Tequila Slammer orang-utan.'

Polly groaned and put a pillow over her head.

'I hate you,' she said. 'It's all your fault; it was your birthday.'

'It couldn't have been,' I said, wondering who'd turned up the wattage on the street light outside my window and wishing I could reach my sunglasses. 'My birthday's on a Wednesday this year. We would never have got this drunk on a week night.'

'But it *was* your birthday.' Polly struggled up briefly on to her elbows before collapsing back on to the mattress. 'I know that because we all went to the pub after work and then you invited everyone back here after last orders.'

Vague, swimmy recollections of catching the tube to Hammersmith with fifteen of my closest friends and co-workers swam into my addled brain.

'Oh God,' I mumbled. 'Are they all still here?'

'No, you sent them home.'

'So why are *you* here?'

'Because I spilled tequila on my shoes and put them under the shower for half an hour to clean them off. They were wringing.'

'And why are you in my bed?'

'You said I wasn't allowed to sleep in the spare room because I had to stop you calling Tom in the middle of the night and yelling at him.'

'Why, what had he done?' Yelling at anyone was certainly not my usual MO; I must have been pretty far gone even to have contemplated it.

'He'd— Oh, fuckadoodle, Laura! Have you seen the time – we are *so* dead!'

I peeled open my other eyelid just in time to see Polly drop my mobile phone on to the bedside table as though it had scalded her and sprint into the bathroom.

'It's Thursday!' she yelled, her words cutting through me like the blade on a scythe, 'Thursday the tenth of March, and we're late for work.'

'Shit!' I murmured and staggered after her, pausing only briefly to throw a couple of Nurofens and half a pint of water down my gullet.

Thursday the tenth of March was not the day to be late. Thursday the tenth of March was not the day to be turning up at work with a raging hangover. Thursday the tenth of March was the day they were announcing redundancies in the analysis department of the Chiltern Bank, and the last thing either of us wanted to do was give the powers-that-be any encouragement to send the Curse of the Job Centre in our direction.

Three quarters of an hour later, with our arms linked together to keep us vertical and each clutching a bottle of mineral water, Polly and I lurched up Cornhill in the City of London, before hanging a right into St Andrewgate, where the Chiltern's head office was situated. Five years ago, this street had contained nothing to mark it out from any other City thoroughfare (some low-rise, low-grade office buildings; a white, slightly scary Hawkswood church at one end and a couple of take-away sandwich shops); but now, thanks to the profits made by our bank (*the bank that wants to make you smile!*) during the boom years, it was home to the Screwdriver – the newest and biggest super-skyscraper in town. We rounded a corner and found ourselves squinting as the spring sunlight bounced energetically off its glass and chrome structure. Considerably fatter at the base, its angular sides tapered thirty-five floors later to a rounded point that would have had Sigmund Freud rubbing his hands together in glee, it was so striking and cutting-edge that it made every other building around look as though it needn't have bothered turning up.

I always felt a little thrill of excitement as I trotted up the four pale Yorkstone steps that flowed out from the base of the building like ripples on a pond. I might not earn as much as Tom on his trading desk; I might secretly think that churning out endless reports on company performances and share movements was not the most exciting job in the world; sometimes I might even dream of doing something really off the wall like being a big-game warden or monitoring dolphin numbers in the

Bahamas – but I totally loved the fact that I got to work in the hottest building in town.

No, scratch that.

The hottest building in *the world*.

People applied for transfers from our New York offices just so that they could work at the Screwdriver. The guys in the Paris office said *mais non* to the Left Bank and begged to be allowed to work amongst *les rosbifs* here in London. Applications were also up from Tokyo, Singapore and Hong Kong, the kudos of the Screwdriver outweighing the charms of life in the Far East; and even the Aussies were queuing up in droves to leave sunny Sydney so that they could work in the British rain at the 'Screwy'.

As for me, a country girl from a no-mark village in darkest Wiltshire, it was so awesome I felt as though I was doing something vaguely illegal sneaking in here every day.

'Morning, Dennis,' I croaked to the man in a deep claret-red morning suit and top hat who was standing at the top of the steps next to the automatic door.

'Morning, Laura!' Our doorman deftly tipped his hat a quarter of an inch in our direction. 'Morning, Polly. Passes?'

We waved our laminated security passes in his general direction and he pushed the revolving door open, allowing us to glide into the cool (and mercifully shady) marbled expanse of the foyer. We gingerly click-clacked our way across the polished floor, past a desk so huge it had to be staffed by three receptionists, and into one of the glass-and-chrome lifts that shuttled up and down the see-through frontage of the first twenty-five floors of the building.

I leaned my still-pounding head against one of the cool steel ribs that encased the elevator pod and closed my eyes.

'Remind me why I'm here,' I muttered, 'and not at home sleeping it off.'

Polly mumbled, 'Floor twenty,' into the lift's voice-activated control panel, before trotting out our departmental mission statement: 'Because we not only deliver the best – we are the best.'

'Bollocks,' I said, clutching my temples as the lift rocketed upwards, leaving my stomach behind somewhere between floors ten and eleven.

'Okay,' she conceded, 'we're actually here because if we call in sick we'll get redundancy for sure; and if *that* happens we'll never get another job ever again because everyone now thinks that bankers are the Antichrist and we'll be forced to move back in with our parents until we finally die in our old pink bedrooms with peeling posters of Robbie Williams and Damon Albarn on the walls. That's why.'

I shivered. The idea of going home to the bosom of my family (or my mother, anyway; my parents had divorced not long after my dad's business had disappeared down the U-bend) was enough to convince me of the importance of dragging myself into work come hell or a hangover. In fact, I would even have been willing to wear the bilious lime-green Chiltern baseball cap and T-shirt to client meetings around town if it gained me any Brownie points with the HR department.

'You're all right,' I said mournfully. 'You could always shack up with Archie. If I lose my job and I can't pay the mortgage I'll *have* to move home.'

The sound of Polly choking came from somewhere over by the lift door.

'Oh God,' she said in a strangled voice. 'Ohgodohgodohgod. Are you serious? Me? With *Archie*?'

I opened one eye and saw her having some sort of seizure. Archie was a tall, thin chap in our department who had had a thing for Polly since the moment he'd first walked through the doors of our office and seen her lovely face illuminated by the light of the photocopier.

'After you put your shoes in the shower, you spent the rest of the evening playing tonsil tennis with Archie in the kitchen,' I informed her.

'Floor twenty,' announced the lift in a voice that sounded almost like Professor Stephen Hawking, and we crawled out of our glass pod.

We found ourselves on a carpeted corridor bounded on one side by huge glass panels held together by a spiderwebbed network of chrome frames and on the other by a seemingly endless curving white wall containing a number of identical doors. Polly leaned against the latter and put her head in her hands.

'Oh God,' she breathed again. 'That's why there were ten messages from him on my voicemail this morning.'

She looked up at me, obviously expecting the worst.

'I didn't – tell me I didn't – with him – with Archie?'

'After I'd turned off the shower and put your shoes in the airing cupboard, I found you asleep in the hall under the coat rack fully clothed,' I reassured her. 'Your virtue remains intact.'

Polly closed her eyes with relief.

'But you still haven't told me why I wanted to yell at Tom,' I added, thinking that yelling at anyone right now would have serious consequences for my headache.

'Because he— Oh, shit, Laura, it's gone eight o'clock. Get moving.'

Ignoring the impressive cityscape pooling out below me through the glass panels, I scurried off along the corridor behind Polly, feeling like a twenty-first-century Alice in Wonderland heading down the rabbit hole. We passed door after door after door, some with brass nameplates announcing the occupants to be 'Smithers and Company, Insurance Brokers', or 'Carridan and Lacey, Solicitors', until we stopped at one with the Chiltern's logo on it, swiped our passes through an electronic card-reader and walked into a large office area. Croaking hello to various colleagues, we made our way through rows of desks topped with computer monitors, in-trays and telephones, hung a left down a wide corridor lined with photocopiers and then turned right through a pair of double doors. This was our patch, our home territory. It consisted of a small open-plan room containing fifteen identical workstations separated by brown desk dividers a foot or so in height, a small kitchen area and, on the far wall, two very large flat-screen televisions respectively blasting out Bloomberg and the less well-known, but eerily prescient, Financial News Today. The latter broadcast from a small set of studios two streets away from the Screwdriver but were often in there with the breaking stuff before the big boys at the BBC or Sky had time to reshuffle their scripts.

I found my desk, dumped my bag and coat, then shoved off to the kitchen to concoct the super-strength, forty-thousand-volt espresso that was needed if I was going to manage anything more productive than lying with my head on the desk, drooling out of the corner of my mouth.

A phone started to ring.

My temples throbbed.

Nobody picked the phone up, so it carried on ringing.

My headache got a hundred times worse.

It didn't stop.

I began to hate the person who owned the phone.

Still it continued.

I put my hands over my ears.

Another phone joined in.

I screwed my face up to try and block out the sound and . . .

. . . realised that my jacket pocket was vibrating.

Sheepishly I put my hand into my pocket and pulled out both the mobile I used for personal calls and the BlackBerry I had for work.

The screens told me that both callers were Tom.

The fuddled state of my brain found this difficult to understand, but nevertheless I gamely pressed a phone to each ear.

'Tom?' I said. 'What are you doing ringing me twice? In fact, *how* are you ringing me twice?'

'I rang your mobile with my mobile but you weren't answering so I called your BlackBerry with *my* BlackBerry and waited to see which one you picked up first.'

I realised that I could only hear his voice in my left ear so I switched my mobile off and stuffed it back into my pocket.

'Okay,' I said, having very little idea of what he'd just said but being profoundly grateful that the ringing noise had abated. 'What can I do for you?'

'I wondered whether you liked it?'

Oh shit: my birthday present.

It all came flooding back to me: *that* was why I'd wanted to ring him at one o'clock in the morning.

'It was a man's watch, Tom,' I said with remarkable composure.

'No it wasn't; it just had a few gadgety bits on it. It's the last word in Swiss design and it cost me an arm and a bloody leg.'

'Tom, listen to me: it was a man's underwater watch capable of telling me the depth of dive, water pressure per square metre and temperature, and it came with an optional shark-proof reading light attachment. When, exactly, in my hectic life of spreadsheets and City finance did you think I was going to use it?'

'I don't know – couldn't you use it to start conversations with important clients at drinks parties?'

I took a very deep breath.

'The strap is so big the whole thing keeps sliding off my wrist, and anyway you know perfectly well analysts don't get invited to any client drinks parties.'

'Okay, fine,' replied Tom wearily. 'I was in such a rush when I picked it out I must have gone for the wrong thing. Sorry.'

Last year my present had been a ticket for a World Cup rugby match at Twickenham – in the stands; none of your corporate-hospitality-with-free-champagne-and-a-three-course-lunch malarkey. At least with jewellery he was heading in the right general direction, even if he couldn't quite manage the gender specifics.

'Go on then,' he continued, as though he was doing me an enormous favour. 'Keep the refund and get yourself something else.'

I bit my lip. Choosing my own present with a refund from a useless watch wasn't as romantic as having my boyfriend lovingly select the perfect gift to celebrate my twenty-seventh birthday – but it was probably the best I was going to get.

'All right. I'll meet you after work and you can give me the receipt. Then you can buy me a belated birthday drink to make up for not coming out with us last night – and what about a belated birthday candlelit dinner for two whilst you're about it?' I suggested hopefully.

Tom had texted yesterday to say he had to pass on my party because of an emergency team meeting at work. A journalist at Financial News Today had broken a story about the investment bank Tom worked for, Davis Butler, having massive undeclared losses. Their share price had fallen like a stone and it was currently touch and go as to whether they would survive.

From the other end of the phone came a silence so uncomfortable it might have been wearing jeans three sizes too small.

'The thing is, Laura, I'm going to be a bit busy.'

'Yeeees?' He'd better have a bloody good excuse . . .

'It's England versus South Africa tonight, so me and a few of the lads were going to catch it on the big screen at the Lamb and Flag,' he concluded sheepishly.

'But you missed my birthday party!' I protested. 'You owe me a night out.'

'I know and I'm really sorry about it. How about tomorrow? Seven-thirty at— Oh, shit! Laura, I've got to go; the boss wants to see me. Later!'

And he rang off.

I shoved my BlackBerry back into my pocket and turned to see Polly leaning against the fridge.

'What?' I barked, busying myself with the coffee machine.

Polly raised her hands in submission. 'Hey, I didn't say a word.'

'He said he was sorry about blowing me out last night,' I said, slamming cups around and then cringing as the noise reignited my thumping headache. 'And you know things are difficult for him at the moment after that news story broke: they're still talking about massive redundancies. Oh, and he didn't mean to buy me a crap present, he was just stressed out.'

Polly's visage softened – but only marginally.

'So he's taking you out to the Ivy to make up for it?' she asked, opening a tin of biscuits and shoving two chocolate digestives in her mouth at once.

'No.'

'Whisking you away for a romantic weekend in Florence?'

'No.'

'Replacing that stupid watch with an engagement ring and suggesting that the pair of you start house-hunting first thing Saturday morning?'

'Don't be daft. You know he's living with his mum and dad till he's got enough money saved for a deposit.'

Polly frowned. 'That boy could afford a down-payment on Windsor Castle, but there you go. So when are you actually going to see him?'

'I'm calling in briefly to the Lamb and Flag to throw the diver's watch at his head at about a quarter to seven this evening. After that it's all rather up in the air – soon, anyway.'

Polly's eyebrows shot skywards and she helped herself to another digestive.

'I don't know why you put up with it,' she mumbled through a mouthful of biscuity mush. 'You can't have seen each other properly for ages.'

I shrugged and picked out a custard cream.

'It won't be like this for ever,' I said. 'It's a phase. A blip. We're both flat out at work and we have a healthy range of interests outside our relationship.'

Polly gave me a look piercing enough to open a can of beans at fifty paces.

'You need a healthy range of interests *inside* your relationship too,' she reminded me. 'When you first got together he couldn't leave you alone for five minutes – texts, phone calls, flowers, the whole nine yards. Now you're lucky if you see him from one week's end to the next.'

'It'll be fine,' I said. 'Like I said, it's not for ever, and anyway, we've been together for over a year now; part of it's probably our relationship moving on to the next stage

– you know, less of the uncontrollable passion, more of the need to make sure the bills get paid and the suits get picked up from the dry-cleaner's.'

And I looked away and fiddled with the filter on the coffee machine for a bit.

It was true what I said – well, almost true. Over the past few months Tom and I had been spending less and less time together, but I'd sort of blocked it out. To be honest, I couldn't think of a night in the last six weeks when we'd actually been together, but it wasn't as though I'd spent our time apart sitting alone at home in my pyjamas, drinking Chardonnay and sobbing into a tissue.

Well, the sobbing into a tissue bit, anyway.

However, apart from being crap at present-buying, Tom pretty much ticked every box I could think of (and even a few that I couldn't). Not only was he tall, fair and so achingly gorgeous both in a suit and out of one that my knees still went a bit bendy when I saw him, but he was also financially secure and came from a pretty much together, traditional family – both things that had been painfully absent from my own upbringing. So I told myself that it would all be okay as I smoothed over the missed dates and the forgotten phone calls; forgave him when he almost always needed to work late; and reassured him that I understood the pressures that came with his job. After all, this was me, remember: the girl who would rather run a mile than have a stand-up row and who could win the Nobel Prize for Biting Her Tongue.

I fished a jammy dodger out of the tin and turned back to Polly.

'Oh, what do I know anyway?' She gave a big, heartfelt sigh. 'I haven't had a boyfriend in so long, I probably qualify as some sort of neo-virgin.'

'There's always Archie,' I reminded her, pouring her

cappuccino and switching the function to espresso for myself. 'He's nuts about you.'

Polly shrugged. 'Yeah, but he's – well, he's Archie, isn't he? He's sweet enough, but he jumps about like an overenthusiastic Labrador puppy with its tongue hanging out and I don't know if I could handle that *full time*.'

'It's only because he's nervous,' I replied, putting my mug under the hissing spout of the machine. 'Anyway, I think you should try it; he might just give you a pleasant surprise.'

Polly took a sip of scalding coffee and fanned her mouth violently.

'Oooh-er, missus,' she replied. 'Anyway, we'd better get back in there. The firing squad are due down in five.'

We walked back out to the office area, took our seats and booted up our computers so that it would look as though we were doing something vaguely constructive when the posse from HR made their appearance. We knew the form from the whispered tales that wound their way from department to department like quick-growing jungle creeper: a small number of Human Resources staff would appear; there would be a general announcement about the 'rationalisation of staff numbers' and the need for 'downsizing' given the 'non-advantageous economic climate'; then the name of the first victim would be read out and they would slope off to a small, soundproof office with Sophie Spink, our Head of Personnel, to be given their marching orders. After that another name would be called and the pattern repeated until the cull was finished. It was a horrible, degrading process and it always made me think of us, the powerless employees, as a herd of trembling wildebeest, with a pack of Human Resources lions prowling round the outside, picking off as many as they could get away with.

We didn't have to wait long. Before I'd even been able

to get Spider Solitaire up on to my screen, the double doors burst open and in marched Sophie in a tight tailored suit and heels so high and spiky you could have used them to harpoon whales.

We all sat bolt upright at our workstations and a terrified hush descended on the room. Eyes darted from colleague to colleague and then back again to Sophie as we tried to second-guess who would be first up for the walk to the scaffold.

Despite the fact that she seemed to be operating without her usual entourage of minions, Sophie didn't waste any time in getting to the point.

'You all know why I'm here,' she said, each syllable issuing from her mouth like the crack of a bullet exiting a gun barrel. 'But I am pleased to tell you that there has been a slight change of plan.'

Gary down at the end gave a whooping cheer, but Sophie silenced him instantly with a scorching glare.

'We have obtained four voluntary redundancies from the private client department,' she continued, her tone of voice making it sound as though she'd extracted those personally through the use of thumbscrews and a torture rack. 'And therefore the disruption to Analysis will be minimal.'

The collective fear of fifteen people that had been cresting above us like a huge dark cloud rolled away and the sun shone once again: we were saved! We all lived to work another day!

Sophie stood regarding our palpable relief with a steely gaze; she hadn't quite finished.

'So if Laura McGregor would like to follow me, please, the rest of you can get on with your work.'

And she twisted her mouth into something that, on Planet Spink, might have passed for a smile.

At that moment, I swear that my blood turned to

ice. In fact, if you had severed one of my arteries, tiny red ice crystals would have come clunking out and spilled over my desk. I sat rigid with disbelief, my right hand still gripping my mouse and my left lying comatose in my lap.

Sophie shot me a gimlet-eyed look.

'If Laura McGregor would like to follow me,' she repeated, slightly louder than before, 'the rest of you can get on with your work.'

Somehow my body managed to raise itself up out of its seat and take the five steps across the carpet to join her. I could feel the stares of my colleagues – pitying, relieved, even genuinely distressed – boring into my flesh as Sophie and I then made our way over towards a tiny room situated next to the kitchen.

Once inside, she shut the door, pulled down the blinds and gestured for me to take a seat. However, I found I couldn't actually make my knees bend and my bottom place itself on the low plastic chair positioned opposite hers. My pulse was thumping in my throat and my palms were beginning to sweat. Sophie shrugged and pulled up a chair for herself before slapping down a large beige envelope on the teeny tiny table between us: it was my personnel file.

'Right, Laura,' she began, her tone of voice indicating that our meeting represented a rather tedious low moment in her otherwise action-packed schedule of personnel management. 'Let's get to the point.'

I closed my eyes and tried to resign myself to my worst nightmare: I was about to lose my job. Without my job I would lose the preferential mortgage rate the Chiltern offered its employees, and without *that* I would probably have to sell the flat. It might take months – if not a year or two – to get another job in finance; and in the meantime all I would have to live on would be a dwindling pot of money from the sale of my home and whatever the bank decided to cough up as my severance package. Polly's scaresville scenario might even come true and I'd have to move home with my mother.

However, before I could get round to grappling Sophie to the ground and using one of her dagger-like heels to slice open my wrists, I became aware that she was still speaking.

This struck me as odd; I mean, if all she had to tell me was to put my stuff in a box and make sure I was out of the building by nine o'clock, she was being rather long-winded about it. Maybe . . . perhaps . . . possibly . . .

'If I might . . . just . . . for one moment,' I began tentatively.

Sophie gave me a withering look.

'Yes?' she snapped, sounding as though she would rather eat live spiders than give me the right of reply. (Although to be honest, I wouldn't be that surprised if they used that sort of thing as a training technique to keep them mean 'n' focused up in HR.)

'I have been with the bank since graduation,' I said, fear of my grisly fate giving me little option but to put the case for the defence, 'and in that time I have become one of the most profitable members of my department. My line manager comments favourably on my work and I have always exceeded my performance targets by a margin of at least thirty per cent. I would suggest that given those performance indicators, I am not the obvious choice for redundancy within my department.'

Blimey! Had that been me? Had I really just opened my mouth and made those particular words come out? I was impressed. The question was, would Sophie be too?

'Is that all?' she said, unblinking.

My spirits sank. She might as well have said 'So?' or 'Whatever!'; her voice told me that her mind was already made up. I was doomed. Doooooooomed, d'you hear?

I took a deep breath and waited for the ritual humiliation of the handing-over of the P45.

'As I was saying,' Sophie resumed pointedly, 'you are to report to Will Barton in SunSpot Hedge Funds. You will be working with him for the next few weeks in addition to your usual role.'

'I'm sorry,' I said. 'Would you repeat that, please?'

I was totally convinced that what she had actually said was 'Please ensure you leave by the main doors and surrender your pass to Reception,' but it hadn't sounded like that.

'Really, Laura,' Sophie grumbled, 'you need to pay more attention. I've told you to report to Will Barton at SunSpot. There's a new hedge fund coming online in a couple of months and Will needs someone for a few weeks to oversee the data that's going to go into the prospectus and help with various bits and pieces. There will be some analyst duties but it's basically a bit of a mixed bag – still, I'm sure you will rise to the challenge.'

For about ten seconds, I forgot to breathe.

'Will Barton?' I gasped, feeling as though I had somehow died and gone to heaven.

'Will Barton,' Sophie confirmed brusquely, lining up her papers and tapping them together on the top of the table. 'He's expecting you for a preliminary meeting at a quarter to nine. He can answer any questions you might have then. That will be all.'

And she stalked out of the little room on her harpoon heels, leaving me staring moronically after her.

'Will Barton,' I breathed once again, still unable to process this piece of information.

Will Barton was a legend in his own (and everyone else's) lunchtime. A hugely successful hedge fund manager in New York, he had been lured across the pond four months ago to be head of the Chiltern's 'alternative investment portfolio' – aka more hedge funds – with a transfer package that would have made Alex Ferguson wince. While other banks had been jettisoning hedges faster than you could say 'the market may go down as well as up', it seemed that anything Will Barton touched turned – almost literally – to gold. The boy could do no wrong.

And I got to work for him!

As soon as I regained the use of my legs, I walked back to my desk and sat down heavily. Polly rushed over.

'You okay?' she whispered.

I nodded dumbly.

'I've got a friend at the Royal Bank of Wales,' she whispered. 'There's a maternity leave position coming up in the analysts' department. Do you want me to ring her?'

I shook my head.

'It wasn't the sack,' I breathed. 'It was Will Barton; he's my new line manager.'

Polly's eyes grew as wide as trendy bistro pasta bowls.

'You get to work with Will Barton?' she said. 'You jammy cow.'

The envy in her voice was almost tangible.

'That would be "work with him", Polly,' I reminded her, 'not "go out for lots of dinner dates with him", and he wants to see me in – shit – he *wanted* to see me two minutes ago.'

I scrambled out of my seat clutching at a pad of paper, a biro and my bag.

'Good luck,' Polly called after me, 'and if he needs a plus one for any of his posh corporate functions, you can give him my number.'

I legged it over to one of the lifts situated on the interior of the building and pressed the button to open the doors.

'Floor eighteen,' I panted into the voice-operated thingy – and we were away, my stomach left thirty feet above me on floor twenty and my mind racing as I tried to envisage what life in the world of hedge funds was going to involve.

2

Will's fame was such that I knew exactly where to find him. Once the lift had regurgitated me on to floor eighteen and I had swiped my pass to let me back into the Chiltern-controlled parts of the building, I hurried along a series of windowless corridors, past rooms full of men like Tom who spent their days shouting numbers into telephones and finally through a set of beech-veneer double doors that led into a medium-sized office area similar to my own. There I headed towards a young woman whose scowl and pinched expression suggested that she spent her spare moments chewing wasps, but who occupied a larger workstation than everyone else and therefore presumably enjoyed some sort of superior status. Her name, which was written on a little plastic bar on her desk, announced itself to be Melody Byrd.

'Laura McGregor,' I said, 'to see Mr Barton. Could you tell me where his secretary sits, please?'

She gave me a look that would have caused a lesser analyst to crumble into dust, but given what I'd already had to overcome in the way of trauma that morning, it merely made me feel a trifle put out.

'That would be me,' she replied loftily, 'but he's on a conference call at the moment, so you'll have to wait.'

My mind wandered back upstairs to some unfinished

work in my in-tray. Even if I had been seconded to SunSpot, I couldn't just ignore my outstanding reports. I didn't want the Spink firing me in two weeks' time because there'd been a barrage of complaints about me being a total slacker.

'Maybe I should come back later?' I suggested, thinking I could use the time to crack on. 'When would be convenient?'

'Mr Barton will see you as soon as he is at liberty,' she announced as though he was royalty (which in the wacky world of hedge funds I suppose he was). 'Meanwhile, you are to wait in the meeting room.'

Melody nodded in the direction of a pale wooden door over on the far side of the office, throwing in an extra, bonus scowl as she did so.

'Fine,' I said, deciding not to risk annoying Will on my first day and resigning myself to working late instead. 'Anywhere I could make myself a coffee?'

'No,' said Melody gracelessly, and turned back to her computer.

As I don't have a highly developed masochistic streak, I decided not to bother engaging her in further conversation, so I made my way over to the meeting room and opened the door. It revealed itself as a large, airy space containing a few bucket-shaped plastic chairs, a large paper flip-pad propped up on a wooden easel, a table and, to my surprise, a man.

He was sitting with his back towards me, swinging on his plastic chair like a schoolboy and typing away rather painfully on a laptop with two fingers.

'Hello?' I ventured, wondering if I was in some sort of queue, and if so, how long I was going to be kept hanging around.

There was no response.

'Hello?' A little louder.

Still no acknowledgement of my presence.

'Excuse me,' I called, walking round to the other side of the table and putting my face right down to his level, 'Are you waiting to see Will Barton?'

The man looked up, gave a loud cry of surprise and then promptly overbalanced, disappearing backwards on to the floor.

'Oh God.' I rushed round to the other side of the table to make sure he hadn't brained himself. 'I'm sorry, I didn't mean to scare the living daylights out of you.'

'No, no, it's quite all right.' The man scrambled to his feet and pulled a couple of earpieces out of his ears.

'IPod,' he explained. 'I had it on shuffle. I didn't hear you come in.'

He was tall, slightly over six foot, and on the wiry side of slim, with dark brown hair that had been gently spiked towards the front, giving him a nicely tousled appearance. He was wearing a charcoal-grey suit, which (to my trained eye) looked rather expensive, but its effect was marred by the fact that one of his shirt-tails was hanging out over his belt and his tie was a bit skew whiff.

He hastily tucked in his shirt, grinned a grin that lit up the room like an exploding firework and extended a hand in my direction.

I shook it.

However, as our hands locked round one another in that time-honoured platonic greeting used by professional people the world over, something rather unusual happened. My knees, which until then had been happily doing their usual job of keeping me upright and enabling my legs to move, suddenly felt as though they were having some sort of orgasm: a thrilling, tingly, pulsing, wobbly feeling overtook them and for a moment I wondered whether I was going to be able to remain vertical.

'I'm Laura,' I said, fighting hard to keep it together. 'Laura McGregor.'

'Alex Hodder,' he replied, not showing any signs of letting my hand go. 'Alex.'

'Alex,' I repeated distractedly, conscious that my face was growing hotter and hotter. 'I'm Laura McGregor.'

'Laura,' he echoed, still grasping my hand. 'Yes, Laura. Right. Of course. Er, hello, Laura!'

I never knew quite what it was, but something – his tone of voice, his choice of words, perhaps the way his smile seemed to radiate out from his eyes as much as his mouth – tripped a switch somewhere deep inside my brain. And then there was his name: Hodder. Hmmm . . . Hodder . . . it was bafflingly familiar.

'Alex *Hodder*,' I murmured, half to myself, half to the man standing in front of me clutching my hand. 'I know this must sound like a bit of an odd question, but haven't we met before?'

Something flickered over his face for a second or two – then disappeared. He liberated my hand from his and his grin slid down the scale from 'wildly iridescent' to 'a little bit sheepish'.

'Um, maybe,' he said, giving an almost imperceptible shrug. 'Normally I'm a business correspondent for Financial News Today and I do bits and pieces for camera.'

'Oh,' I said, still able to feel the phantom pressure where his hand had grasped mine. 'Oh, right.'

I hastily smoothed down my skirt and told myself to get a grip: I was at *work*, for goodness' sake; this sort of thing didn't happen at *work*. And especially not at *my* work.

Alex gave an awkward cough and looked at his shoes.

'Don't tell my boss,' he said, 'but I'm actually here today to do a freelance piece on Will Barton – the man whose reputation is rising as fast as his profits, that sort of thing. Although God knows if I'll ever be able to sell it. Everyone's fed up to the back teeth with finance and the economy right now; what producers sell their souls for are stories about skateboarding parrots or hamsters that can sing the national anthem.'

He looked at me hopefully and tilted his head slightly to one side.

'You wouldn't happen to have a parrot I could borrow for a bit, would you?'

'Sorry – what?' I boggled at him. Was he was seriously expecting an answer?

'A parrot. Or a macaw will do – I'm not fussy. Possibly even a canary, although I have to say it wouldn't look quite as impressive on the screen. The only bird-life I can't consider is a duck; they did that once on *Nationwide* and it is still spoken of in hushed tones through the hallowed halls of family television. I need to be seen to be cutting a fresh swathe and not raking over old ground – although hopefully not mixing my metaphors quite as much as that on the voice-over commentary. So what have you got on you avian-wise? Go on, surprise me!'

He was, you know.

'Um, nothing,' I replied, my burning face cooling down for a moment only to flare up once again in the heat of his smile. 'I'm afraid I left the house this morning completely bird-free.'

Despite my hot little cheeks, I was grinning back instinctively. Whoever he was, he was nuts. Pleasant and amiable perhaps, but definitely nuts.

'Oh well.' He shoved his hands into his trouser pockets. 'It was worth a try.'

I ran my eye over him one more time. Even though we usually had FNT on one of the tellies in the office, I had a niggling feeling that I had not simply clocked him while he was reading out the market reports. The niche he had in my brain was much more significant than that and I tried racking it one last time, but to no avail. Even though he was rather easy on the eye (particularly for a journalist who specialised in spare prices and company mergers), reason told me that this had no bearing on whether or not we'd met before. Lucy Stephens, one of the girls I'd known at university, had once been similarly mistaken and spent half an hour in a nightclub trying to convince Prince Harry that they'd been at school together.

Best just forget about it and move on.

'So,' Alex twinkled at me, 'that's me – what about you?'

'Me?' I shrugged. 'I work here. In fact, I work for Will – or I will do after we've had a meeting and he's told me what the job entails.'

'Interesting.' Alex perched on the edge of the table and leaned in towards me inquisitorially. 'So you're a Barton Babe, then?'

'I'm a *what?*'

The easy-going, dare I say it *flirty* atmosphere that had been building up between us wavered slightly. Whilst I wouldn't have known a Barton Babe if one had waved a bunch of blue-chip share certificates under my nose, I was pretty certain it wasn't anything I would aspire to. It sounded far too much like a plastic doll with blonde hair and improbable contours – and the world was definitely not ready for Investment Banker Barbie.

'You *know*,' he said in a voice that meant I couldn't tell whether or not he was being serious, 'one of the City girls gagging to get into the hedge-fund business because Will Barton is heading up the team.'

This suggestion was so completely outrageous that I had to pick my chin up off the floor and reinsert it into my jaw socket.

'That is the biggest load of crap I have ever heard,' I snorted. 'Why do you men always assume that women are incapable of making informed, professional judgements about their career choices? Just because you spend every six seconds – or is it three? – thinking about sex doesn't mean we have to, too.'

I may even have added a bark of derisive laughter for good measure. Alex, however, just grinned good-naturedly and slid off the table, leaving me feeling bizarrely self-conscious at having mentioned the word 'sex'.

This would *not* do! Now I was just being ridiculous. Knee-orgasms notwithstanding, of *course* I didn't find him attractive. I already had a rather handsome boyfriend, thank you very much, and any journos I might happen to meet were *definitely* surplus to requirements.

Thankfully Alex chose not to pursue the point. Instead he bent over, picked his plastic chair up off the floor and sat down again, stretching his long legs out in front of him, putting his hands behind his head and leaning back nonchalantly as if he owned the joint.

'So, if you don't work in investments, what do you do?' he asked.

'I'm an analyst,' I replied, deciding to wrest some dignity back out of the situation and pull up a chair too. 'I look at trends, study world affairs, dissect company performances, crunch numbers and my work is used to advise the bank's clients – including some of the biggest corporate investors in the world. So you'd better be nice to me, Alex Hodder, because the performance of your pension fund could depend on whether or not I'm having a good day.'

'And are you?'

'Am I what?'

'Having a good day?'

Even though his voice sounded relaxed – teasing even – his eyes told a different story. They were dark and serious and flickered intently over my face as though he was, quite literally, trying to read it.

'Might be,' I replied cagily and glanced at him out of the corner of my eye.

This was probably the worst thing I could possibly have done: our eyes crashed together and my earlier knee-orgasm was knocked somewhere into the middle of next week. It was as though al-Qaeda had detonated a sort of sight-based explosive in the room and I experienced a physical sensation so intense that I was surprised to find that I was still sitting on my chair and hadn't been blown through into the office next door. My head was thumping, my ears were ringing, and my heart was pounding so hard it was touch and go whether it was actually going to break out of my ribcage.

I gulped, blinked and stared at him in horror. This wasn't me getting all star-struck over a minor celeb; this was something else entirely, and as my eyes skittered over his astonished face, I knew that he'd experienced it too.

But worse, much worse was to come.

As the metaphorical smoke cleared, I suddenly realised where I'd seen him before: Alex Hodder wasn't some tuppeny-ha'penny journalist reading out the odd bit of news while he waited for his first big break to come along – that break had already happened. He was the man who had scooped the story about Tom's bank; a story that had not only put my boyfriend's job under threat, but had also led to a massive drop in Davis Butler's share price and caused so much concern amongst its wealthy clients that it had lost millions in deposits within hours of the story going out on the air. *And*, in case that wasn't enough, it had also been the reason why Tom had had to spend the evening of my birthday buttering up his boss and not dancing the tequila-filled night away at my party.

What I did next was really quite spectacular.

'It was you!' I leapt so far out of my chair I almost dented the polystyrene ceiling tiles. 'You were the one who ran that story about Davis Butler and almost ruined them single-handedly! Just because you wanted to get your face plastered over as many TV screens as possible, you went with some irresponsible, half-baked story and caused nothing but chaos.'

Suffocating embarrassment over our explosive reaction to each other, fears for Tom's job, and a fair amount of wrath that Alex, however tangentially, had managed to stuff up my birthday all conspired to produce the angry words that exited my mouth faster than Jenson Button pulling out of the pitlane.

To my surprise, however, my companion did not leap up indignantly to defend himself. Instead he looked at me for a moment or two and pressed his fingertips together thoughtfully, almost as if he found my point of view intriguing.

'That's quite an accusation,' he replied lightly. 'To suggest that I would deliberately manipulate the facts of a story for my own ends.'

But I was far too agitated to get stuck into an intellectual discussion on the ethics of broadcast journalism.

'It's not an accusation,' I told him, my arms folded and a scowl that Melody Byrd would have been proud of plastered over my face. 'That's exactly what people like you do for a living. Does that make you feel good about yourself, Alex – the fact that you personally caused hundreds of people to lose a great deal of money and thousands more to lose their jobs? Does it – hmmm?

Because frankly, if it was me I wouldn't be able to sleep at night!'

As I watched (possibly with a bit of lip-curling thrown in for good measure), a slight spasm passed over his face. I instantly felt terrible. Oh God – I'd overdone it! I'd actually upset him! I was a nanosecond away from doing the decent thing and mumbling an apology when I realised, on closer inspection, that he was doing his best to rein in a smile.

'It was a close call,' he said at last, unable to keep it under wraps any longer and allowing a wicked grin to spread across his face, 'deciding whether to use my super-powers for good or evil.'

My contrition vanished and I stared at him in disbelief: *was he for real?*

Picking up my bag and shoving it on my shoulder, I began to make my way over to the door. Despite my orders from Melody, I'd wait for Will somewhere else; if I didn't, there was a very real risk I was going to go insane.

Or possibly be arrested for GBH with a flip-pad easel.

However, to my surprise, Alex didn't simply raise his hand in farewell as I made a dignified, if haughty, exit. Instead he leapt from his chair and positioned himself firmly between me and the door.

'Mr Hodder,' I said, my voice lowering itself to an angry rumble, 'please get out of my way.'

'Not before we sort this out,' he replied, all vestiges of amusement wiped from his face. 'I am not going to let you walk out that door thinking that I ran that story purely for my own personal advancement and without being very, *very* sure of my facts.'

I drew myself up to my full height of five foot four and wished I'd put higher heels on that morning.

'Oh, don't be so ridiculous,' I snapped, meeting his

gaze head on – and noticing for the first time that his eyes were exactly the same rich colour as a bar of Bournville.

'No, I'm completely serious.'

He was too, you know.

I could sense real determination in his voice. He stood in front of me frowning, with his hands thrust deep into his trouser pockets.

'We are going to sort this out over a drink,' he continued. 'No, even better – over dinner. You and I are going to have a full and frank discussion and I will convince you that not only did I tell the truth about Davis Butler, but also that the story was so important it had to be made public.'

Dinner? With him? Now I was more convinced than ever that I needed to run far and run fast. I tried to dodge for the door, but he was too quick and blocked my path once again.

'Plus, you never know,' his eyes suddenly twinkled with interested amusement, 'you might even enjoy yourself.'

I gave him a scowl so scorching you could have used it to weld a ship together and made another break for the exit. This time I was too quick for him and it was with an enormous sense of triumph that my fingers closed round the door handle.

'Actually, I don't think I would,' I replied, elated that freedom was now (quite literally) within my grasp. 'And more to the point, Alex, I already *have* a boyfriend, and he certainly wouldn't appreciate me going out for dinner with the journalist who has spent most of this week trying to make him unemployed!'

Ha! That would tell him! Whatever our-eyes-met-across-a-crowded-room shenanigans might have happened in the meeting room behind us, he'd now get the message and *back off*.

Annoyingly though, Alex didn't quite see it like that.

'Well, don't bother with him tonight,' he persisted pleasantly. 'Meet me instead and explain how I manage to get away with peddling these obscene untruths on national television without ending up in court. Besides, I'm sure your boyfriend will understand – my guess is he'd rather be watching the rugby on a big screen somewhere with a pint in his hand.'

His arrogance – not to mention his beyond spooky accuracy – sprang the strange new fiery me back out of its box before you could say 'swing low, sweet chariot'.

'Er, excuse *me*,' I cried. 'Do you seriously think I would to stand up my own boyfriend in favour of a dirt-digging journalist whose only motivation in asking me out is to get the next spurious story to further his career?'

'How do you know I want to further my career?' Alex asked innocently. 'I might *actually* want to take you to dinner because I find you intriguing, scintillating, utterly arresting and ultimately want to woo you away from this boyfriend of yours.'

The gob-smacking audacity of this made my breath catch in my throat and I found myself hiccoughing in a decidedly unattractive manner. As payback, I gave Alex another ferocious stare, but was shocked to find there was no trace of amusement in his Cadbury-brown eyes. In fact, the seriousness of his gaze hit me with the force of a freight train and I quickly looked away again.

'Get this, Alex.' I finally recovered the power of speech and decided to use it to disabuse him of any misconceptions he might still be harbouring, 'I am *not* going to have dinner with you, or lunch, or breakfast, or, for that matter, high tea or even a kebab after closing time. In fact, if I ever see you again it will be several lifetimes too soon.'

Stepping over the threshold, I turned to face him for what I fully intended would be the last time.

'Oh, and if you so much as *think* about screwing the Chiltern or SunSpot on that TV channel of yours, I personally will make you wish you'd never been born. Is that clear?'

Alex produced a smile so enthusiastic I might as well have just promised to nominate him for Journalist of the Year.

'As crystal, Laura McGregor.'

And then I turned on my kitten heel and pulled the door shut – very firmly – behind me.

It was well after lunchtime before I'd finally had my meeting with Will. In fact I'd almost given up hope of seeing him at all that day. After leaving the meeting room, I'd hung around for an hour or so near Melody's desk reading the *Financial Times*, I'd been shooed back to my own workstation, where I'd finished off a report about German manufacturing output, accepted delivery of a large bunch of roses from Tom, anxious to make amends for his diving-watch bloomer, and then watched intrigued as Polly opened a series of e-mails from Archie and blushed and giggled appreciatively in his direction. *Methinks the lady doth protest too much!*

Then, at half past two, as I was considering my next report (Far Eastern emerging markets) and wishing I'd bought some painkillers during lunch, my phone rang.

'Good afternoon, Laura McGregor, the Chiltern Bank analysis department,' I said, rubbing my temples.

'Hi, Laura.' A deep male American voice wafted over the airwaves. 'This is Will Barton. I'm sorry I was unavailable this morning – I had a conference call with an old client of mine who wants to invest big bucks in a SunSpot fund; and then after that there was a media type to deal with – and, well, you know how it is, the morning essentially disappeared up its own ass.'

Given what I'd been through that day, this was soothing stuff. Will's voice was so rich and smooth that it was the aural equivalent of watching golden syrup slide over clotted cream; each syllable made me feel as though my headache was receding and that a calm equilibrium was being restored to my life.

'It's not a problem,' I replied. 'When would you like to reschedule?'

'How about now? Is now good for you?'

'Now is fine.'

The emerging markets could wait. They'd still be emerging in a few weeks' time after the new SunSpot fund had been fired off into the financial stratosphere.

'Great, I'll see you in five.'

In fact I made it in three. This time there was no lengthy wait in a meeting room haunted by unnerving journalists; instead Melody merely gave me a low-grade scowl before phoning Will to let him know I had arrived, and two seconds later the door to his room was flung open and I found myself in the hallowed presence of Willoughby Barton.

He was a young, broad-shouldered man of average height, with short fair hair and a fringe that flopped over his forehead in a preppy manner. His eyes were, I noted, dark blue and the tan level of his skin spoke of yachts in the Bahamas rather than rainy days in the Square Mile. Without wanting to sound as though I am stating the obvious, you need to know he was the most emphatically, quintessentially *male* being I have ever come across and I wouldn't have been surprised to see actual testosterone leaching from his pores.

He shook my hand firmly, gave me a smile so blinding that a pair of snow-goggles would have come in handy, then, to my utter surprise, kissed me enthusiastically on both cheeks.

I made a mental note to reconsider my position on Barton Babes.

I sat down on an obscenely comfortable leather chair positioned in front of a huge oak desk, and Will seated himself in a swivel chair on the opposite side, pulling out one of the desk drawers and resting his feet – crossed at the ankles – on its edge. He acted like he owned the place, which, given what he was rumoured to achieve in profits on a regular basis, was probably not far wrong.

'So, Laura,' he gave me Part Two of the radiant smile, 'how do you feel about becoming part of the SunSpot team?'

I looked round the room in which we were seated and nodded enthusiastically. Unlike my plain, functional office upstairs, this was obviously the lair of one of the bigger beasts in the financial jungle. As well as the ridiculously comfortable chair I was currently parked in (which I now loved with all the fervour of a mother for her first-born child), the rest of the room was interspersed with elegant and obviously expensive pieces: a shelf unit, a table surrounded by four low black-leather armchairs, and, on the far wall, a built-in audio-visual system, currently screening CNN with the sound off. On two of the other walls hung abstract modern paintings and on the fourth, lit by a thin strip lamp, was— I blinked and looked again – could it be?

Well, if it wasn't actually an *original* Monet, it was a damn good imitation.

Will followed the line of my gaze.

'Fine art,' he said, 'one of the safest investments around.'

'It's amazing,' I murmured.

Will nodded his assent.

'You can say that again,' he replied. 'It's doubled its

value three times in the past two years. That's pretty amazing in anyone's book.'

Not quite what I meant, but still . . .

I did my best to drag my attention back to the matter in hand.

'So, what exactly will my function be within the team?' I said coolly.

Bloody hell! A Monet – a real Monet, not four feet away from me! How cool was that?

'We've got a new fund called Dresda coming on stream very soon, and whilst most of the groundwork has been done, one of my team screwed his leg skiing at the weekend and is a write-off for at least two months. I need someone to keep an eye on things whilst he's gone. Plus, because a lot of the analysis has already been taken care of, I may need you to do some other stuff such as liaising with Marketing, that sort of thing. I know it's not your usual bag, but are you up for it?'

So, it was basically a watching brief with a bit of advertising spin thrown in for good measure; I could handle that.

I nodded my assent.

'Now, Laura,' he continued, 'I've seen your résumé and I know you've been with the Chiltern a long time, but I wanna make it clear that unlike some of the British bosses here, the only thing I'm interested in is results. If you can't give me those – you're out. No old-boy networks here.'

He was regarding me with such intense scrutiny, I was half surprised not to feel scorch marks appearing on my face.

'Fine by me – seeing as I'm not an old boy,' I said emphatically.

Will let out a snort of appreciative laughter.

'I had noticed,' he said. 'Any experience working with a hedge fund like us?'

For a moment I considered a bit of creative exaggeration but swiftly changed my mind. Apart from the fact that he had read my CV, I didn't want him to think I was a pro and then make some stupid slip-up that anybody who had been in the game for twenty milliseconds would have avoided. Unemployment was too close for comfort as it was, without me waving my arms and shouting 'Oi you – over here!' and generally drawing attention to myself.

'Not as such, no,' I confessed. 'Although of course I'm au fait with the basic principles. Plus I'm aware that the hedge funds you managed in the US have outperformed not only the market but also every other alternative investment vehicle over the past five years. No doubt the board is expecting you to provide an encore this side of the Atlantic!'

Will grinned a lopsided grin.

'You do your homework, Laura, I'll give you that. Okay, so here's where we are right now: I have a couple funds maturing in a month or so and what I need to do is to get those clients – plus their profits – signed up to Dresda. Your mission – should you choose to accept it – is to produce the figures to show that the new fund totally rocks. Those guys have to be on their damn knees *begging* us for the chance to be a part of it. Dresda is the Big One – right? It is the Beatles, the Jimmy Hendrix, the Elvis fucking Presley of hedge funds and the whole world needs to know about it. Can you do that?'

His charisma and enthusiasm were not just infectious – they were positively explosive. I felt like selling my flat, cashing in my pension and bunging the proceeds straight into Dresda. In fact, if Will had turned round at that moment and told me to put everything I owned on the three forty-five at Kempton Park, I'd probably have gone right along with it, no questions asked.

Instead, however, I managed a more restrained: 'You betcha!'

Will yanked his feet out of the drawer, leapt off his chair and leaned over the desk, his hand outstretched.

'Then welcome aboard, Laura. I think you and I are going to get along just fine.'

'Good,' I said, shaking his huge paw of a hand as vigorously as I could manage. 'I mean, cool.'

'Okay.' Will nodded briskly. 'Go get a password from IT and spend the rest of the day acquainting yourself with how our systems work and reading up on our past performance. I want you to be able to give me chapter and verse tomorrow morning. Meeting at seven thirty a.m. See you then.'

The injection of enthusiasm delivered by Will could not, however, override my lingering hangover, and after spending a brain-aching afternoon trying to make head or tail of the SunSpot programs (written by Will himself – an IT whizz as well as a financial guru and a sex god), I was happy to arrive home and close my front door on the big bad world.

I loved my flat. It was the ground floor of a small-ish Victorian terrace, which I had bought as a rat-infested shell that looked as though it would have been more at home in bombed-out Beirut than west London, and slowly nursed back to health. Although I shared a front door and a hallway with my upstairs neighbours, I had two bedrooms, a living room, kitchen and bathroom as well as a small back yard to call my own, and after years of dodgy house-shares (not to mention the war zone that had constituted my childhood home), it was the first place I had ever lived where I felt absolutely safe.

Once inside, I plonked my flowers in a vase, poured myself a glass of water and bunged a ready-meal into the microwave. Then I curled up on the sofa and watched a painfully unfunny sitcom set in a bank, called *Whoops, There Goes My Bonus*. It was so hilarious that I fell asleep after about twenty minutes and only woke up when the intercom buzzer on the front door rang an hour and a half later.

Twice.

Extremely loudly.

After I'd climbed back down from the ceiling and soothed my jangling nerves with a couple of deep breaths, I made my way cautiously to the door wondering who on earth would be calling round at nine o'clock at night. No one (not even Polly) would bother coming all the way to Hammersmith without ringing first; unless – a wave of hope flowed over me – unless it was Tom, so desperate to get down to a bit of birthday kissing and making up that he had left the pub early and forgotten to phone.

I pushed the intercom button, praying that it wouldn't just be a pizza delivery boy with a bad sense of direction.

'Hello?' I ventured. 'Tom?'

'Of course it's not Tom,' barked a female voice. 'Hurry up and let me in, it's bollock freezing out here.'

I buzzed the front door open and then turned the lock on the inner door that led from the communal hallway into my ground-floor abode. There before me, rather than the five foot ten of handsome equity trader I had been hoping for, stood a five-foot-nothing blonde girl wearing a black leather biker jacket, what looked to be a pair of Russell Brand's cast-off jeans and a scowl that could have curdled milk – had there been any in my hallway at the time.

I blinked at her.

She raised her eyes heavenwards and made a sort of tetchy ticking noise with her tongue.

'So do I, like, actually have to *ask* you if I can come in?' she said.

It was my sister Mel.

My younger sister Mel.

My younger sister Mel who, when grace, decorum and propriety were being handed out, was hanging around at the end of the queue drinking alcopops and trying to cadge a cigarette out of anyone who looked mug enough to give her one.

'What on earth are you doing here?' I said, my jaw flapping open with astonishment.

'There's no need to be like that,' replied Mel shirtily, taking off the biker jacket and dumping it on the floor next to a large holdall. 'And besides, I *texted* you.'

'No you didn't.'

'Well, I must have rung.'

I shook my head.

'E-mailed then.'

'You don't have a computer.'

'I might.' She narrowed her eyes defiantly.

'Mel, you haven't voluntarily been in touch with me since last year when you tried to get a loan out of me so that you and Gareth—'

'Gobshite,' Mel corrected me.

She slid a finger through her pale corkscrew curls.

'Whatever. So that you and Gobshite could go to Glastonbury.'

'Which you *totally* blew me out on by the way.'

'Too right! Because I don't have piles of spare cash hanging around that I can just dole out to you whenever you ask for it, that's why.'

Mel repeated her tsk-tsking noise and I could feel the familiar side effects of a conversation with my sister beginning to build: the blood pumping loudly in my head, my fists clenching involuntarily, steam leaking out of my ears, etc. etc. I made myself take a very deep breath.

'All right,' Mel continued, as though it was a matter of

very little consequence, 'maybe I didn't *actually* contact you – but I meant to!'

She bent down to pick up the holdall.

'Excuse me,' I said, 'but where do you think you're going?'

'The spare room.'

As far as Mel was concerned, this was obviously a no-brainer.

'You can't just do that,' I cried.

'Oh?' She dropped her bag back down on to the floor. I closed my eyes as the zip dug a gouge in the laminate flooring. 'Why not?'

'Well . . .' I searched round for a zingy, pithy reason – but sadly drew a blank. 'I – er – might have someone else staying.'

'Do you?'

I shifted uncomfortably.

'Um, no, actually,' I admitted.

Mel immediately leapt upon this as a sign of assent.

'Cool!' She grinned at me, left her holdall where it lay and made her way into the kitchen.

I followed her, glowering at her bag as I went past.

'So,' I said, leaning against the cooker with my arms folded, 'to what do I owe the honour?'

But Mel didn't bother to reply. Instead she reached down a plate, opened my fridge and helped herself to the remains of a roast chicken and some cold potatoes.

'I thought you were vegan,' I said.

'I am *mostly*.' Her voice was muffled as she stuck her head back inside the refrigerator in case there were delicacies she had overlooked the first time. 'But I reckon my iron levels are low due to stress. Glass of wine?'

She pulled an open bottle of white from the bottom shelf and waggled it at me.

'Oh, go on then, why not?' I sighed and reached two glasses down from the cupboard above my head.

Mel was already foraging in the bread bin. Then she found herself a knife and proceeded to slather butter, followed by large amounts of chicken liver pâté, on to a roll. If she was indeed a vegan, her enthusiastic consumption of animal products put her on a new, experimental wing of the movement.

Finally, with her spoils in hand, she wandered through to the living room. I trailed bemusedly in her wake carrying the wine bottle.

'Mel,' I asked again, 'why are you here?'

Mel chewed a large mouthful of chicken and spuds, swallowed and gave me an ingratiating look.

'Well,' she began, 'I know we've had our differences in the past, but I thought we should try and support each other as a family a bit more – so I thought you and I should spend some quality time together.'

'How thoughtful of you,' I murmured, watching as she bit into her pâtéd roll in a manner reminiscent of Stone Age man ripping off a mouthful of wild boar. 'So you wouldn't be after any money, then?'

Mel had permanent money hassle; this was mainly because Mum/the DSS/I didn't respect her human right to never do a stroke of paid work. On Planet Mel, the reason for this was that she was an *artist*, and being forced to sully her hands would kill her creative spirit. The fact that she had never yet produced anything more artistic than a map of how to get to her house didn't seem to bother her in the least.

'Not money.' She avoided my gaze.

'Well what is it, then?' I didn't buy into this 'quality family time' rubbish for a moment. 'And please note that any answers involving delayed giros, music festivals or karmic cleansing won't wash.'

Mel chased a crumb round her plate with a bit of a distracted air.

'I needed to get away for a bit – a week. Or two. Or something. Anyway, you've got bags of room. You won't even know I'm here.'

I was just about to open my mouth and give her a long list of reasons why I *would* know she was there when something – call it a sixth sense, or sisterly intuition – whispered that there was more to this than Mel's normal scrounge-meister behaviour. There was something slight and frail about her appearance, and the dark circles under her eyes told of a string of sleepless nights. I couldn't simply turf her out on to the streets.

But equally, unsympathetic as it might sound, I knew that neither could I put myself in the position of offering her an inch and my sister then (inevitably) taking a mile. Even though I'd got myself a temporary reprieve at SunSpot, there was no telling whether further redundancies were on the cards, and if that *was* the case, there was no way I would be able to afford to support the pair of us long term.

'Look,' I said, 'I'm potentially in a spot of bother.'

Her blue eyes flashed across at me, her normal languid curiosity mixed with something that might just have been real concern.

'You're not pregnant, are you?' she asked slowly.

'You've got to be joking,' I said, rather taken aback. 'Tom and I have both been so busy we haven't seen each other for weeks, and as far as I'm aware, sleeping in separate beds on opposite sides of London isn't known for maximizing the chances of conception.'

Mel took a large gulp of wine and muttered something under her breath. My anti-capitalist, neo hippy sister and my hotshot, career-obsessed boyfriend were each other's worst nightmares; and the subsequent simmering tensions made the occasions when they did coincide about as relaxing as a UN-patrolled Peacekeeping Zone (with yours truly invariably wearing the blue helmet).

'But it's cool,' I added quickly, trying to avoid a lecture on Tom's manifold shortcomings. 'I'm seeing him tomorrow and it will be fine.

'*It*', said Mel loftily, 'isn't the problem; *he* is. He takes you for granted – except when he wants you to bail him out because he's got himself into a hole at work. You need to dump him, or even better,' her eyes glittered enthusiastically, 'let me dump him for you.'

'No,' I said firmly, shaking the last few drops of wine into my glass.

'Oh, please,' Mel wheedled. 'I'd do ever such a good job. He'd never bother you again.'

'I said no,' I cried, a little nervous as to what she had in mind. 'Anyway, as far as boyfriends are concerned, there is no way you are claiming the moral high ground – you can say what you want about him, but at least Tom isn't a fully grown adult still deluding himself he's going to make it as a rock star.'

'Actually,' Mel went a trifle pale, 'Gobshite and I aren't together any more.'

'Gareth,' I reminded her.

For once my sister didn't rise to the bait. Instead she put her plate down and stared hard at the toes of her scruffy baseball boots.

'Mel,' I nudged her leg with my elbow. 'Mel, are you okay?'

Her gaze snapped defiantly back on to my face.

''Course I am,' she said.

'Do you want to talk about it?' I offered.

'No,' she said, before adding, 'Except to tell you that he's a cheating, double-crossing, two-faced, lying, fuckwitted bastard, and if I ever see him again, I'm going to smack him so hard he'll spend the next six months looking for his teeth.'

'Right.' I nodded.

'Anyway,' her eyes narrowed, 'I thought it was your life we were discussing, not mine. Go on, Laura – spit it out.'

I took a deep breath.

'Well, there are a few problems at work – what with the credit crunch and so on – and there's a risk I might lose my job. So it might mean I have to think about other ways of making a bit of cash – like possibly putting a lodger in the spare room.'

Mel looked incredulous.

'But you – you always have money. I mean, you're *Laura*.'

She said my name as though it was synonymous with Howard Hughes or George Soros.

I sighed. 'Yeah, but there's no such thing as a job for life. You'll find that out for yourself one day.'

'But you're a *banker*,' she persisted. 'The City – bonuses – all that malarkey.'

'Okay, first up I'm an analyst not a banker; second up, even when I do get a bonus, it's nothing like the ones you hear about on the news; and third up I have an outrageous mortgage, student loans, household bills and a couple of credit cards to pay off. Like I said, I don't have a lot of money to throw around.'

Mel whistled softly through her teeth as the idea began to sink in that her sister was not, in fact, a bloated City fat cat.

'So anyway,' I continued, 'you can stay for a bit – but I'll need you to chip in with the food; plus, if it looks at all long term, some of your Earth pounds are going to have to be forthcoming in the form of rent.'

Mel looked as though she was considering all her

options – even though they pretty much amounted to 'pay Laura to stay here' or 'go home and face the music with Gobshite'.

'Okay,' she said at last, managing to make it sound as though *she* were doing me the favour by moving in, 'you're on. But here's the deal: if Gobshite calls, you have to tell him you have no idea where I am – do you get that? You haven't seen or heard from me— Ooh!' She suddenly sounded excited. 'Except when I rang to say I was having a gap year in India.'

She looked so chuffed that I couldn't bring myself to remind her that a gap year implied some sort of productive activity either side of it.

'Fine,' I said, a fresh wave of exhaustion breaking over me. 'Well, the duvet cover and spare sheets are in the airing cupboard, and the house rules are: no drugs, no tobacco and if you touch any of the booze without asking I'll strangle you with my bare hands.'

'Great.' Mel leapt to her feet and began making her way out to the hall and her holdall.

'Er – excuse me,' I called, pointing to the detritus of her late-night snack. 'Plate! Glass! Or were you expecting the dishwasher fairies to pick up your slack?'

Mel humphed good-naturedly and cleared up her dirty dishes. As she did so, however, a thought struck me.

'Mel, you know what you said about Gobshite calling?'

At the sound of his name, I saw her flinch slightly.

'Yeees?'

'How would he know my number?'

Mel busied herself rinsing the dirty plate under the tap before stacking it neatly in the dishwasher. Wonders would obviously never cease.

'Um, I might have left my mobile back home in Bristol. Your number is in my contacts list.'

I suddenly felt a bit uneasy. She'd obviously scarpered

pretty smartish if she'd forgotten to take her phone with her.

'Mel, does Gobshite have this address?' I asked tentatively.

Mel shook her head.

'He knows you live in London, but nothing more than that.'

'Okay,' I said trying to lighten the atmosphere a tad, 'just so long as I don't need to sleep with a baseball bat under my pillow.'

Mel flinched again, and despite the fact that she tried to hide them in her pockets, I noticed that her hands were shaking.

Something was very definitely UP.

'Melissa McGregor,' I said in a warning sort of voice, 'is there something you want to tell me?'

'No.' Her jaw jutted out defiantly and her eyes were steely and resolute. 'Now if you'll excuse me, I think I have a bed to make.'

And, head held high, she swept past me and out into the hall.

Thoughtfully I put my own glass in the dishwasher and then followed her out of the kitchen. Leaning under the coat rack was a cricket bat of Tom's that had been languishing there since the last match of the season. I picked it up: it was solid and heavy and I could wield it with just the right amount of clout.

I put it back down.

No, that was ridiculous. I couldn't start taking weapons to bed. Before I knew it, I would become one of those scary pro-gun people who don't feel safe in their own homes unless they have three automatic rifles, some hand grenades and a couple of ground-to-air missile launchers loaded and primed to deal with any nocturnal intruders.

But then again . . . something had obviously gone

horribly wrong between Mel and Gobshite. Plus, he was a good six foot three and looked as though he numbered a couple of brick privies among his recent ancestors.

I picked the bat up, put it under my arm and made my way down the corridor to my own room, where I shoved the bat under the bed.

I had a funny feeling things were about to get very interesting indeed.

I was rudely awakened the next morning by the sound of Mel making herself a bacon sandwich. In fact it was only the smell of sizzling rashers winding its way down the hall and seeping under my bedroom door that told me there was actual food involved and she wasn't simply banging the frying pan repeatedly against the stove-top.

Rolling over to look at the clock, I got my second nasty shock of the day – shit! Half past six! I needed to be at work by seven thirty for my meeting with Will. At this rate I'd be lucky to get in before the markets opened at eight.

Pausing only to trip over the handle of the cricket bat, I whizzed though the shower, whizzed into a dark, sober suit, which I teamed up with a new, rather low-cut top, and then whizzed into the kitchen on a quest to find my mobile and my work BlackBerry before I left for the station.

'Oh, it's you,' said Mel, a bacon sandwich poised midway to her mouth; she sounded genuinely surprised to see me.

I wondered if there was some sort of benefit I could claim for having to look after a hopeless sister.

'Yes, it's me,' I confirmed, looking in the bread bin and then under the kettle for my errant pieces of technology.

'What are you doing up at this time? I'd have thought for you it's still practically the middle of last night.'

I watched as she peeled back the top layer of her sandwich and squirted a large amount of brown sauce inside.

'I thought I'd get an early start,' she announced through a mouthful of breakfast, 'and anyway, this thing started ringing and woke me up.'

She reached into the pocket of her jeans and slapped my BlackBerry down on to the kitchen table.

'Careful!' I cried, gathering it up in my arms like an overprotective mother. 'That cost a lot of money!'

Mel eyed me with bored superiority.

'You shouldn't clutter up your life with the physical manifestations of an oppressive capitalist ideology,' she opined. 'It's bad for your aura.'

'Well, it's an oppressive capitalist ideology that's bailed you out on more occasions than I care to mention,' I reminded her, flicking through my calls register to try and find out who'd been trying to contact me so early.

'I can save you the bother.' Mel finished her sandwich and put another couple of slices of bread into the toaster. 'It was some bloke called Alex wanting to know if you could meet him in Islington at eight o'clock tonight.'

I stared at her, my hands frozen to the buttons on the BlackBerry: Alex *Hodder*? What the hell was Alex Hodder doing calling me at half past six in the morning?

Or indeed, at all?

Mel's baby-blue eyes twinkled wickedly at me.

'So,' she said, 'things between you and Tom not as exclusive as they used to be? Or are you just trying out the competition before you finally give Trader Boy his marching orders?'

'Neither,' I replied tetchily, stuffing a yogurt and a museli bar into my handbag to eat after my meeting with

Will. 'Alex is business – and what's more, *my* business, not yours.'

Mel's eyebrows shot upwards in perfect synch with the toast in the toaster.

'Then why the guilty blushes, oh sister of mine?'

'I'm not guilty.'

Surprised and pissed off maybe, but certainly not guilty: at twenty-seven years old I reckoned I knew the difference.

'I *said*, I am not guilty,' I repeated.

Mel sniggered and began to cover her toast with butter.

'Anyway,' she paused mid-slather, 'I said "yes" and he said "brilliant" and I said "where" and he said "outside the Design Centre on Upper Street" and I said—'

'Wait, wait, wait.' I held my hand up, wondering if smoke was actually issuing from my ears or whether it just felt like it. 'You pretended to be me and fixed up a meeting with this – this . . .' I struggled to articulate the word in relation to Alex. 'This *man*?'

My sister nodded and bit into her first slice.

'He sounded really nice – especially when he apologised for his behaviour yesterday.'

I covered my face with my hands: did she have no shame?

'He said,' Mel frowned as she tried to recall Alex's actual words, 'that he wouldn't want the fact that he had allowed his feelings to run away with him yesterday to prevent the pair of you having a long and mutually advantageous relationship.'

I looked at her through my fingers.

'And you said . . . ?'

'That it was all fine and dandy and I – or you, or whoever we're talking about – would be counting the minutes till eight o'clock tonight. Oh, and he said that if you got there early, he lives at number six Duncan Road so do feel free to knock.'

'Arghhhhhh!' I muffled a scream.

'What?' asked Mel innocently. 'Did I say something wrong?'

'If he ever calls again,' I growled, 'just save yourself a lot of time and tell him to go to hell. Or even better, keep him company and go there yourself!'

And I snatched the slice of buttered toast out of her hands and slammed my way out of the front door.

Thankfully, Will was busy on a long telephone call with the Tokyo office when I arrived so he didn't realise I was fifteen minutes late. I waited for him as before in the meeting room – keeping my eyes peeled for scary stalker-type journalists as I did so – and ate my muesli bar. Of course, I had absolutely no intention of meeting Alex at the Design Centre and even less of ringing him to let him know I wasn't going to be turning up. Today was Friday and I was determined that tonight I would finally get to spend some quality time with my boyfriend come hell, high water or Alex Hodder.

When I was eventually ushered into Will's hallowed presence, the meeting itself was fairly straightforward. He asked me how I had got on the day before and I confessed that the accounts didn't really look like anything else I'd ever come across.

Will grinned and ran a hand through his floppy white-blond fringe.

'It'll make more sense if you can put the numbers in some sort of context,' he said. 'I'll e-mail you a database of all the closing figures, profits and payouts for the last four years. I want you to write a report to show which investment sectors have served us best in the past.'

'No problem.'

Well, it sounded simple enough, didn't it?

'Any more questions?' asked Will, turning up the sound on his end-of-office telly so that we could both watch the market opening.

The only one I could think of was 'will I still have a job this time next year?' but as even Will's Renaissance Man capabilities probably didn't stretch to clairvoyance, I shook my head.

'I'll get cracking then,' I said.

Reluctantly I heaved myself out of the chair and made for the door. Just as I was about to exit, Will swung round.

'Just one more thing.'

'Yes?'

Will focused on his computer screen and started fiddling with the mouse.

'You're having dinner tonight with Alex Hodder from Financial News Today.'

'I'm sorry,' I said, battling with an overwhelming urge to check both my ears were still in place. 'What did you just say?'

Will looked up from his computer screen, mild annoyance etched across his otherwise Hollywood-perfect face.

'Alex Hodder, the economics correspondent for FNT, is taking you out for dinner tonight. I spoke to him yesterday and he mentioned that he wanted an industry insider viewpoint on a couple of stories. I said you'd do it and gave him your BlackBerry number. He should be paying, but if you need cabs and things, keep the receipts and put it through on expenses. Here's his card if you need to get in touch.'

I had heard of the phenomenon known as 'spontaneous human combustion' before, but had never considered that such a thing might be physically possible – until now, that was.

I was literally speechless with indignation: how dare Alex Hodder manipulate my boss into giving him the dinner date he'd been unable to extract from me personally? What was it about him that he simply couldn't shrug, mutter something about not winning them all, and slope off back to his desk to plot his next scandalous scoop? Then I thought about Tom's likely reaction to the news that I was about to spend the evening breaking bread with his personal nemesis – and the whole scenario slid into a fresh circle of hell.

I wouldn't go. It was a simple as that: I just wouldn't go.

Will rummaged through a tray on his desk and then held a business card out towards me. However, the idea of coming into contact with *anything* that had once been in Alex's pocket was so appalling that I simply stared at it in horror.

'C'mon, Laura.' Will waggled the card at me impatiently. 'Take the damn thing already. I've got things to do.'

'Me and Alex,' I said at last, 'it's – ah – difficult.'

Will gave me a stare so cutting it would have felt at home in a hairdressing salon.

'Laura, I think you might be confusing me with someone who gives a damn!'

Reluctantly I reached over and removed the oblong of thick embossed paper from his fingers.

Think! *Think!*

As I stood there like a stuffed lemon, willing my brain to come up with a decent excuse, my boss rubbed a hand across his face, suddenly looking as though all the woes of the Square Mile were resting on his impressively broad shoulders.

'Laura, this is a fantastic opportunity for us to get some exposure for Dresda ahead of the big launch.

Hodder wanted to meet me, but I have to be in the States this weekend so I thought it would be the ideal opportunity for you to show me what you're made of by being my stand-in. Are you telling me you're not up to this?'

The atmosphere in the room suddenly switched gear and determination flashed through me like sunlight glinting off cold, clean steel: if I wasn't up to it, would that mean I was heading for the chop? Did I really think a dinner with Alex was worth losing my job over?

'No,' I said hurriedly. 'Of course I'll do it. Just tell me this, Will: what if he twists what I say to create a story like he did at Davis Butler? They nearly went under because of him.'

Will didn't look impressed by this last-ditch attempt to save myself from Alex Hodder's dastardly clutches and folded his arms.

'Last night I went out for a meal and I had sea bass,' he said cryptically, 'and you know why that fish was there on my plate and not hanging out under the ocean somewhere?'

'No,' I murmured, wondering where the heck this one was going.

'Because it opened its damn mouth!' said Will. 'You just tell Hodder what we want him to hear and nothing more, get it? Debrief here, seven thirty a.m. Monday – okay?'

'Okay!' I said, stuffing Alex's card into my bag and noticing that my hands had already left damp finger marks on its pristine cream surface. 'I'll go and confirm him now.'

'Good,' said Will, flashing a smile in my direction. 'And as he's paying, remember to go for the caviar, the lobster and the vintage champagne.'

I left Will focusing on his PC screen and stomped my way back to the lifts. I was seething. Even though I didn't think for a moment that Alex had sidled up to my boss, thrust a wad of folded-up tenners into his top pocket and whispered, *Any chance you can fix me up with that hot new analyst of yours*, I still felt as though I had been somehow outmanoeuvred. Above all, I found myself dreading what I was going to say to Tom, and as I knew that the words 'Oh hello, darling, you don't mind if I pop out for a meal with the man who almost got you the sack, do you?' weren't going to cut it, I found myself craving a bit of head space to plan exactly how I was going to tackle the subject. So I scheduled a meeting with a triple-strength-no-decaff-full-power-aviation-fuel espresso and prepared to conjure up the delicate balance of words necessary to keep Tom happy.

Or at least to stop him from turning up at the FNT television studios and shouting the odds at Alex live on air during the one o'clock news.

However, just as I pressed the elevator button, my BlackBerry went off.

'Hi? I mean, good morning, Laura McGregor, Chiltern—'

'Laura?' Julie, one of our receptionists, cut across my telephone mantra. 'There's a Tom Harper in the foyer asking for you. He says you're not expecting him but it's urgent.'

To say that I was staggered by this news was putting it mildly; in fact, if she'd rung to inform me that Will had a second career gigging as a cabaret drag act in New York, I wouldn't have been more astonished. Tom was the archetypal City boy who happily spent fourteen hours a day glued to his desk, and I simply couldn't imagine what he was doing hanging around the Screwdriver's reception area when he could be shouting 'buy' and 'sell' into his phone and generally conjuring large amounts of money out of thin air.

And, more to the point, I hadn't even begun to work out what was I going to tell him about Alex.

'Sure,' I said bravely, 'tell him I'm on my way.'

When I arrived at the ground floor, Julie looked up from her computer screen and nodded towards a horseshoe of easy chairs in the far corner where my beloved was slumped, staring doggedly at the floor. He was not a pretty sight: his normally impeccable hair was all over the place, his tie was out of kilter, he wasn't wearing a jacket and one of his cufflinks was missing. He looked so rough that for a moment I had to fight the urge to spit on a tissue and tidy him up a bit.

'Can we use Room B at the back there for a couple of minutes?' I asked Julie, thinking that whatever he had to impart was probably best done away from flapping ears.

Julie tapped at her keyboard.

'Done,' she said. 'Anything else?'

'If Will Barton needs me, buzz him through on my BlackBerry; I'll leave it on vibrate. Anyone else – anyone at all – is to leave a message on my desk voicemail and I'll get back to them.'

This was an important precaution: the last thing I needed was Alex ringing whilst I was closeted with Tom and the whole thing descending into bad-tempered chaos before I'd had a chance to explain myself.

'Tom,' I said brightly, making my way across the marble floor towards him, 'how's things?'

He stood up and gave me a weak half-smile.

'Shit,' he said bleakly, as I steered him towards Room B, a small, nondescript office positioned between two of the elevator shafts and containing not much more than a tiny table and three chairs. 'Things are pretty much shit.'

And they weren't going to get any better once he found out about Alex, I thought grimly.

'Oh,' I said, reminding myself that Tom's life lurched between the twin peaks of 'shit' and 'awesome' on a pretty regular basis. 'Any particular reason?'

Tom had the look of a spaniel that had just lost its favourite chew toy down the back of the sofa, all big eyes and a lot of patheticness, and I hoped against hope that he hadn't come to tell me he was now unemployed.

'I've arsed up,' he told me, sitting down on the far side of the table and burying his head in his hands. 'I've majorly arsed up.'

Then his eyes focused on my low-necked top and he frowned slightly.

'Isn't that a bit, well, *revealing* for work?'

I stared down at my chest and tried to quantify what an acceptable volume of workplace cleavage should look like.

'Other people liked it,' I said defensively, rearranging the collar and thinking of an approving remark from Polly earlier that morning. 'Anyway, tell me what happened to you.'

Tom put his head back into his hands. His countenance had deteriorated from that of an unhappy pooch to something more closely resembling a dying duck in a thunderstorm – whatever it was was clearly a Big Deal.

'I had a position – an awesome one,' he told me. 'I bought in on one of the American car manufacturers that everyone knows is toast, betting that the share price would fall – but instead of it going down like it should have done, it rose. It fucking went through the fucking roof because some Korean company now wants to take it over.'

I knew exactly what he was talking about – we had discussed it last week as being a good move when Tom had rung asking for my opinion on some investment strategies. The company had been teetering on the brink of insolvency for months now and today had been earmarked as the day they would either file for bankruptcy or the clouds would part, stirring music play and they would miraculously find a buyer. And against all the odds, it seemed the latter had happened (minus the celestial choir, naturally).

I opened my mouth to tell Tom *I* wouldn't have believed it either when my BlackBerry started to vibrate, making me jump a good two feet into the air. Sneaking it out of my pocket under the cover of the table, I had a quick look at the display. Damn! It was an e-mail from Will entitled 'urgent'.

'But you had a stop loss set up, didn't you?' I soothed, trying to sneak a glance at the message without him noticing. 'A trigger for an automatic sale of the shares so you wouldn't lose too much money?'

'There wasn't any point,' Tom informed me in a dull voice. 'The whole thing was a dead cert.'

My mouth gaped open and all thoughts of Will, Alex and anything else fled my mind. *He hadn't bothered with a stop loss?* That was like – that was like (my brain groped around for a suitably suicidal analogy) going bungee-jumping but not really being fussed about whether or not you fixed the rope on properly.

Tom put his arms on the table and buried his head in them.

'I'm down a million smackers,' he mumbled. 'The final redundancies are being announced on Monday and if I don't pull off something pretty bloody spectacular, I'm going to be one of them. What am I going to do? Tell me what I'm going to do, Laura!'

I was glad he wasn't able to see my face. *A million pounds sterling?*

'Okay,' I said, yanking my thinking hat firmly down over my ears, 'who knows you've lost this much money?'

'No one. I haven't filed the paperwork yet. I reckon I've got till close of play tonight.'

'Fine.' My brain was racing, my mental Rolodex of current market statistics flicking over at lightning speed. 'Here's what you'll do: don't try and get it back in one big hit – there are a whole raft of company profits statements due out this afternoon. Run with some of those and build it up bit by bit – Zeta Oil should be a good one; British American Airways is another. Plus the Royal Bank of Wales is looking to take over one of their Chinese competitors.'

My BlackBerry went off again. It was beginning to sound pissed off and I had a nasty feeling Will would be too if I left it much longer before getting back to him.

I pulled it out of my pocket as far as I dared and checked my inbox: *Urgent – Sender william.barton @chilternbank.com.*

'Tom – do you mind if I get this?' I said. 'It's another one from Will.'

Tom shook his head.

'Be my guest,' he said. 'Who's Will anyway?'

'Barton,' I muttered, fiddling with the buttons. 'I've been seconded to SunSpot.'

Tom wound his hand round my wrist and forced it down on to the table; the BlackBerry slithered from my grasp.

'You're working for Will Barton?' he gasped. '*The* Will Barton?'

'Yes,' I said, retrieving my hardware and opening the e-mail, '*the* Will Barton.'

'Holy shit,' breathed Tom reverentially. 'That man – he's *beyond* amazing.'

He was practically salivating on to the table.

'As far as I'm aware,' I wasn't quite sure what to make of Tom's new, boundless enthusiasm for all things Barton,

'Will cannot walk on water, raise the dead or bring about world peace. He's just a guy who happens to be good at his job.'

'Good at his job?' Tom echoed, leaping forward from his chair and grabbing me by the shoulders. 'That man has a perfect investment record – he is a legend. Laura – you've got to get me in there; it would be *beyond* awesome. I could tell Davis Butler to stick their rotten trading desk up their rotten—'

'Tom,' I said sternly whilst disentangling myself from his vice-like grip, 'listen to yourself. I'm not Derren Brown: I can't just walk into Will's office, get him to look into my eyes and magic you a job at SunSpot. Why don't you send him your CV and then call him in a couple of weeks to see if there's anything suitable? I'll give you his direct dial if you like, but I don't think there's much more I can do to help.'

Tom, however, was miles away in some weird trader fantasy.

'You know,' he said, gazing somewhere into the middle distance, 'I've always felt there's this sort of *connection* between me and Barton.'

'You've never met him,' I objected. 'Do you even know what he *looks* like?'

'No – but that's irrelevant,' my erstwhile super-rational boyfriend continued. 'Me and him together – man, the pair of us would be on fire; we'd be the dream team! You've got to get me on board, Laura; you've got to swing this one for me.'

I ran my fingers supportively along the back of his hand.

'Tom, I don't really see what I can do to help; and anyway I'm up to my eyes with work and . . .'

Tom looked at me with his puppy-dog eyes and I'm pretty certain his bottom lip was jutting out just a tad.

'Go on then, e-mail your CV over to me first and I'll check it through for you,' I sighed.

Tom punched the air and then, as an afterthought, leaned over the table and kissed me.

'Thanks, Laura. You're the best.'

I glowed. Briefly.

'I owe you a thank-you too, Tom, for the roses.'

He gave me a still-suffering half-grin.

'Well I couldn't risk you waltzing off into the arms of another bloke because you were annoyed with me, now could I?'

I felt as though a lightning bolt had zipped through me. *Oh God, another bloke – Alex!*

'I know this is probably not a good time, Tom,' I said softly. 'But something's come up and I'm not going to be able to see you after work like we'd planned. I was wondering, could we maybe leave it till tomorrow? Or you could come round later tonight when I'm back home? I'm sorry to do this to you, especially after the trade went wrong and everything, but . . . Tom? Tom? Are you listening?'

His focus snapped back on to me.

'Of course I'm listening.' He sounded offended. 'And I was going to say that tonight would be bad for me too. Me and the lads have been thinking we might spend this weekend in Dublin. Lance found some one-pound flights on the net this morning and we decided we could neck back a bit of Guinness, explore the town and head back on Sunday. What's not to like?'

Er, I could have told him what was not to like. He'd double-booked me with a drinking weekend in the Emerald Isle and he hadn't thought to mention it?

'What about you and me?' I asked incredulously. 'What about us spending some time together?'

Tom shrugged. 'Well, I suppose you could come if you

really wanted to, but I don't think you'd enjoy it. Anyway, you're the one who's cancelling this time; don't get your knickers in a twist with me over it.'

Even though he was technically correct, the wise words of my best friend (and, even though I hated to admit it, my sister) echoed through my mind and resonated deep inside. This wasn't healthy independence; this was something else – something that, despite the roses and the flirty texts and the 'love you babe' e-mails, might gobble up our unsuspecting relationship and leave me with nothing but a string of missed dates and broken promises.

'Tom,' I said, taking a deep breath and asking the question before I could think better of it. 'I have to know – is there anything wrong?'

He stared at me as though I'd gone completely mad.

'Of course there is – I've just lost a million quid – I told you.'

'No, not about work; about you and me.' I took an even deeper breath. 'We used to be a couple, Tom; we used to have fun – good grief, we actually used to *talk* to each other. Now the most meaningful conversation we've had for ages was the one a moment ago about how cool you reckon my boss is.'

'Work is mental, Laura; you know that. In fact you're just as bad as me with your business meeting tonight or whatever it is.'

'Point taken – but at least I was hoping to reschedule for tomorrow. What I want to know is when will your work *stop* being mental – not to mention your mates; or the footie, or the rugby or the test match? Every time we have arranged to meet up in the past two months – a whopping twenty dates – you have blown me out. I miss you, Tom – I miss *us*. When are we going to get back to how things were?'

But to my amazement, Tom had pushed his chair back and was making his way over to the door.

'Thanks for the advice on the trade,' he said. 'Call me and let me know what Barton says about vacancies and I'll e-mail my CV over for you to have a look at.'

He hadn't listened to a word I'd been saying.

'No,' I said, pushing past him angrily. 'You call me. But not before you've decided whether you actually want a girlfriend, or whether some combination of recruitment consultant and trading troubleshooter would suit you better.'

'Laura,' he had the gall to sound upset, 'don't be like that. I love you – of course I do.'

'Then you'd better start acting like it,' I hissed, letting the door slam behind me as I stalked out of the room and into the lift next door.

By one o'clock that afternoon, I'd decided to cancel the dinner and rearrange my meeting with Alex at work, because anything that even remotely resembled a date with him made me feel hideously uneasy.

By four, I'd decided I might as well go – it would take my mind off my problems with Tom, and more importantly, I didn't want Alex thinking I was chickening out.

By six, after a box of chocolates had arrived from Tom together with a note telling me that I was the girl of his dreams, I'd decided the whole thing was madness, and that even if Will was happy to sack me on the spot, the last thing I should do was have dinner with a borderline insane (if admittedly attractive) man who had designs upon my person. However, by half past six, when I'd tried and failed to get hold of Alex on both his work number and his mobile five times, I thought sod it and started deciding what I was going to wear.

It would be fine, I told myself. Alex hadn't actually wanted to meet *me* in the first place; he knew that the position of Laura's Boyfriend was currently occupied; and his grovelling apology to Mel that morning indicated that even if he *did* fancy me, he wasn't about to plant a smacker on my lips and suggest we rode off into the sunset together.

'So, where's he taking you?' asked Mel as I came out

of my bedroom for the fifth time to scrutinise my reflection in the full-length mirror next to the coatstand in the hall.

'Dunno,' I said non-committally, glancing over my shoulder and pulling my skirt down so that it skimmed below my knees rather than showcased them.

'Well,' Mel continued, 'I hope you have a good time. If Tom really has blown you out and buggered off to Dublin, I reckon you're entitled to see how the other fish in the sea perform. You never know – it could be the start of a beautiful friendship.'

At the sound of Tom's name, my stomach gave an unhappy little flip. I had spent most of the afternoon – when not dithering over Alex or trying to puzzle out Will's accounts – worrying about what was going to become of us. I accepted that we were adrift and that things couldn't go on as they were, but short of telling him that if he didn't pull his Calvin Klein socks up then he and I were deader than a cremated dodo, I didn't quite know what to do for the best.

And despite my fears, I refused to believe that we were at that stage yet.

'Listen, Mel, if my boss hadn't told me to do this, then believe me, wild horses wouldn't be able to drag me over to the Design Centre tonight,' I said firmly. 'Alex Hodder is a low-down, despicable toad who puts his own personal advancement before the needs of others.'

Mel put her index finger to her lips and frowned in a show of staged puzzlement.

'And that makes him different from Tom . . . how?' she asked innocently.

I focused on rearranging my necklace rather than defending my boyfriend's manifold shortcomings.

'Dear Pot, thank you so much for your observations – love Kettle,' I replied.

'The difference is,' Mel produced a bottle of nail polish (mine) from the pocket of the cardigan she was wearing (mine) and began shaking it vigorously, 'I left my despicable toad; you're still lumbered with yours.'

Leave it, Mel; for goodness' sake just leave it!

'Which reminds me,' I took a lipstick from my bag and began applying it, 'I want a bit of a chat with you. If I'm supposed to be covering for you, I need to know what happened between you and Gobshite.'

Mel's gaze darted upwards and met mine in the mirror. She had the look of a chicken that has just spotted a fox trying to sneak its way into the coop.

'No you don't,' she replied. 'One: we're over; and two: he must not know where I am. Those are the only two pieces of information you require.'

'But last night you were scared.' I protested. 'C'mon, Mel, we might not be joined at the hip, but I'm your sister and I care about you.'

'Then you'll drop it,' she growled. 'Leave it alone! Don't go there.'

Now I was more convinced than ever that some sort of four-act drama had been playing out in Bristol.

'Tell me.' I gave it another go.

'Bloody hell, Laura, what part of the word "no" do you not get?' she replied.

For about five seconds she looked as though she might be about to cry and I decided to do as she said and leave it. For now at any rate.

'So, do I look all right?' I asked, turning round to face her.

She nodded, reached over and pulled my neckline down slightly; I immediately pulled it back up again. If Alex wasn't getting knees, he *certainly* wasn't getting any décolletage. A grin broke through on Mel's pale, troubled face.

'You must fancy him pretty badly if you're nervous about showing off a bit of cleavage,' she said.

'I don't fancy him at all,' I said, wondering if wearing a scarf to cover up my entire neck/chest danger zone would be bordering on the neurotic.

'Yeah, right.' Mel leaned nonchalantly against the wall. 'What do you want me to tell Tom when he rings?'

'Tom won't ring.' I was on pretty safe ground with that one. 'And even if he does – this is business.'

Mel threw me my coat.

'You look great,' she said. 'Now – go, before he decides you've stood him up.' She grinned wickedly. 'And don't do anything I wouldn't do!'

Admittedly, that left the field pretty much wide open, but as I had no intention of doing anything at all apart from putting some food in my mouth, not saying very much and then scarpering as soon as was polite, I didn't give her suggestion a lot of thought.

As I wandered up Upper Street towards the domed façade of the Design Centre, I wondered which high-end eatery we would be patronising that evening. I was pretty confident that with a television budget and a desire to impress urging Alex on, tonight would be about fiddly food, expensive wine and a lot of hot air.

So when I heard his voice and turned round to see him standing in front of me wearing a knee-length overcoat with the hood of a sweatshirt pulled out over the collar, jeans and a pair of rather tatty red Converse boots, I had to blink once or twice before I could reply.

'Hi.' His voice was soft and a little (surely not?) *hesitant*. 'I wasn't actually sure if you were going to come.'

'Neither was I,' I replied. 'But this is a business meeting, and what I might or might not want doesn't come into it. Besides, it was my sister you spoke to this morning and she more or less set me up.'

'A fine, right-thinking sort of girl, obviously.' He grinned at me, although a slower, lazier grin than I remembered. 'I must thank her when we meet.'

'Who says you're going to meet her?' I had been in his presence for no more than thirty seconds and already I was indignant.

'Sorry!' He held his hands up in mock surrender. 'I apologise; business it is. Now, partly because I know how much you like Turkish food – but also because I was so sure you weren't going to show up that I didn't risk booking anything – I thought we could go to my favourite ever restaurant.'

My spirits fell. I should have gathered from his less-than-formal dress that anything involving a Michelin star was not on the cards – but even so . . . a measly kebab? If it had been Will attending as originally planned, I didn't think for one moment Alex would have suggested a main course that was traditionally served in a paper wrapper with chips and a tub of coleslaw on the side.

'Actually, you're wrong, I don't like Turkish food,' I said, wondering if I should suggest a curry instead.

'Of course you do.' Alex set a brisk pace up the road, leaving me trotting along behind.

'Excuse me!' It's hard to sound pissed off when you're out of breath but I gave it my best shot. 'I think I'm in command of my own mind enough to know what I do and do not like.'

'Trust me,' he grabbed my hand and ushered me across the street, 'you'll love it.'

'Don't say that.' I wrenched my hand free. 'You know nothing about me, least of all whether or not I like chunks of grilled meat cooked on a skewer. I could be vegan for all you know – like my wretched sister.'

'Are you?'

'No, but—'

'I didn't think so.'

'You didn't – *what*?'

I was so indignant that my mouth opened and closed like a hyperventilating goldfish. Before I could recover the power of speech, Alex had pushed open the door of what I had assumed was a small terraced house and ushered me inside. I was immediately hit by the chatter, the colour, the laughter, the flickering candlelight and an irresistible, delicious smell that made my stomach rumble.

'Mr Hodder!' A waiter with a big bushy moustache pushed his way through the tables towards us with a broad, welcoming smile on his face.

'How wonderful to see you! Please, this way; we have one table left' – he indicated a small, rickety-looking wooden contraption lit by a flickering votive candle in a jam jar – 'but if table two is not to your satisfaction, table fifteen will be leaving shortly, and if you would like to wait at the bar, I will bring you drinks on the house.'

I looked round the crowded room, amazed that they could fit fifteen tables into such a tiny space.

'No thanks.' Alex nodded enthusiastically. 'This will be great, won't it, Laura?'

I nodded, and as I did so, the weird feeling spread over me again that I *knew* Alex from somewhere – really knew him. In a suit and tie, he had simply been the man from the telly – but in his hoodie and jeans he looked like . . . but then it was gone again.

'Can I get you and your lovely lady something to drink?' The waiter clapped his hands together loudly and a younger version of himself appeared holding a pad of paper and a pen.

I was about to point out emphatically that I was *not* Alex's lady, lovely or otherwise, when I noticed the head waiter standing behind me with his arms outstretched ready to take my coat, and closed my mouth again.

'Bottle of house red, please,' Alex said. 'If that's okay with you, Laura?'

I normally drank white – preferably fizz if I could get it – but right at that particular moment it seemed to me that red wine was the only drink worth having.

'I don't normally do red,' I said, slipping into the chair being held out for me by a third waiter and smiling at a fourth who was depositing a basket of fabulous-smelling, still-warm flatbread on the table in front of me. 'But I'm willing to be flexible.'

'Your menus.' The head waiter was back once again, putting dishes of olives and long green chillies on the table and pouring wine into Alex's glass.

Alex swilled the wine round the bowl of the glass, sipped it and pronounced it delicious, and my glass too was duly filled with a sweet-scented ruby liquid that radiated warmth and well-being from my tongue down into my tummy and out through my veins to the tips of my fingers. Feeling well disposed towards the world in general, I ran my eye down my menu. Alex gave his the briefest of glances before placing it neatly on top of his napkin and attacking the food already before us.

'Go on,' he nodded at the dish of chillies, 'try one.'

I shook my head. 'I don't . . .'

'. . . do chillies?'

He finished my sentence for me and my feeling of well-being diminished slightly. *Why* did he have to keep second-guessing me? It was very irritating.

'These aren't hot,' he informed me. 'At least, not very.'

He picked up a chilli from the dish and held it out. I

went to take it from his fingers, but he tightly grasped the stump of a stalk at the far end and refused to let go. I gave him an annoyed frown, selected my own from the dish and bit the tip off: it was sweet, sour, crunchy and tangy and it exploded in my mouth like a firework.

'You said it wasn't hot,' I muttered accusingly.

Alex's eyes twinkled – or that might just have been a trick of the candlelight.

'Have a mouthful of wine,' he suggested. 'Chilli is alcohol-soluble. Great, though, wasn't it?'

I nodded grudgingly and, refusing to be branded in Alex's memory as the Girl Who Was Afraid Of Chillis, took another bite, making sure I kept eye contact with him as I crunched through its shiny green skin.

'Very Freudian,' said Alex approvingly, causing me to gulp it down the wrong way and cough violently.

'No random Freud references,' I told him as I wiped my paws on my napkin. 'In fact whilst we're at it, the ground rules for this evening are: no smiling, no winking, no touching, no grinning, no talking about anything that isn't one hundred per cent to do with SunSpot and absolutely, completely no more of this "let's patronise Laura by telling her what she does or doesn't like" thing you've got going on.'

Alex had the decency to look taken aback.

'I'm sorry,' he said with a sincerity that impressed me. 'That was never my intention.'

The head waiter materialised at Alex's elbow clutching his notepad.

'Are you ready to order, Mr Hodder, sir?'

Alex handed back both our menus and, without even so much as a glance in my direction, ordered a selection of little starters and two portions of a complicated-sounding dish involving lamb and aubergines. My annoyance gauge ratcheted up about fifteen points.

'Excuse me,' I hissed, 'don't I get a say in what I eat?'
Alex bit his lip and looked apologetic.

'Sure,' he said, 'sorry. I got carried away.'

I took my menu back and scanned it. Damn him! He
had gone and ordered *exactly* what I was going to choose
for myself. Grrrrrrr.

'Actually, that looks fine,' I said testily, handing the
menu back to the waiter. 'Although can I have calamari for
the starter as well.'

'Make that for two. The calamari's awesome.'

The waiter beamed and nodded and then vanished.

'So then, Mr Hodder,' I said, confidently snapping the
head off another chilli and washing it down with a large
swig of wine, 'what can I do for you?'

'A tempting offer,' he replied, completely deadpan,
pushing the flatbread towards me, 'but in view of the fact
I have to pretend you are Will Barton, I think we should
stick to matters of a purely professional nature.'

I thought about kicking him under the table but, not
wanting my intentions to be misinterpreted, tore off a
piece of bread instead. I examined it briefly for any
potential Freudian interpretations and then popped it
whole into my mouth. It was gorgeous.

'Sorry,' he said, doing much the same, 'that was an old
joke, but this probably wasn't the time or the place.'

'Do you come here a lot?' I asked, changing the
subject and tugging off another helping of bread. 'They
seem to know you.'

As I spoke, the atmosphere on Alex's side of the table
changed. It was as if an orchestra had struck up behind
him with a loud minor chord.

'I used to,' he said, picking up the wine bottle and
recharging our glasses, 'but then something happened
and I kind of avoided it for a while. I thought tonight
would be a good chance to see it in a fresh light.'

'Oh?' I was intrigued. 'Do you mean "something" or "someone"?'

Our starters arrived.

'I thought we weren't supposed to talk about anything other than SunSpot.' He gave me an inscrutable look.

Interesting . . . Perhaps Alex wasn't the self-assured smoothie I had him down as.

'So anyway, Will, back to business,' he continued, offering me a calamari ring on the end of his fork. 'How do you account for your phenomenal success in such a volatile market?'

'Well,' I said, pulling the ring off the prongs and popping it into my mouth, 'the fact that I keep my head, plan my strategies and do my research. Oh, and I have the best team of analysts anywhere in the City.'

Alex grinned and helped himself to a filo pastry parcel. I ran my eye down over his tousled dark hair, his clear complexion, his dark eyes and generous mouth and noted, to my amusement, that looking at him was a rather pleasant experience.

'And your forecast for the rest of the year?' he asked, spearing the last calamari piece with his fork and offering it to me.

'Continued volatility but with some big gains in sectors that have been unaffected by the downturn,' I said confidently. 'Home entertainments, supermarkets, pizza delivery companies and so on. Possibly also in the alternative energy sector as people aim to negate fuel price increases.'

I removed the ring with my fingers, tore it in two and offered him half back. He nodded, opened his mouth and took it from my fingers. As his mouth closed, his upper lip caught the edge of my nail and about twenty thousand volts whizzed down my spine. I looked away and wiped my hands vigorously on my napkin, trying to ignore the electric aftershocks still snapping through my nervous system.

Think business, think SunSpot, think how much he annoys you, for goodness' sake!

'And Dresda?' Alex gave me a strange sideways look. 'Which area would you be recommending they invest in?'

'That's easy,' I replied with a grin, as our main courses accompanied by a fresh bottle of wine clattered down on to the table. 'The one that is going to make us an obscene amount of profit, of course.'

'No free share tips, then?' He smiled back and topped my glass up.

Despite my fears, this was in serious danger of turning into a pleasant evening. Well, anyway, more pleasant than sitting at home trying to watch *Emmerdale* while Mel informed me I was a bloated capitalist parasite living off the sweat of the downtrodden poor.

'Not from me,' I replied. 'I crunch the numbers but I don't want the responsibility of putting someone else's money where my mouth is. Will and his trading desk make that call.'

Alex put his fork down and leaned in over the table, his voice low and suddenly urgent.

'Be honest with me, Laura. Does everything Will Barton touch really turn to gold? Any electroplated fake nuggets lying around that you want to tell me about?'

The matey atmosphere that had been putting in a tentative appearance at table two vanished abruptly. Was this his game? Soften me up with a couple of glasses of the red stuff and then squeeze me for his next big story? I suddenly felt as though he'd played me for a fool: as far as he was concerned, I was nothing more than a big fat sea bass that he was keen to hook on the end of his duplicitous little line.

'Don't even go there, Hodder.' I angrily speared the

last of the pastry parcels before he could get his hands on it. 'I did not give up my Friday night so that you could try and get your next half-baked exposé out of me.'

'Hey!' Alex shrugged as though this were of no consequence and popped an olive in his mouth. 'I'm just asking. Will hinted that he had something on his mind and I took a wild stab in the dark, that's all.'

'Listen,' I said, not understanding why it should matter so much to me if Alex saw me purely as the source of his next scoop, but only knowing that it did, 'even if I had proof that Will was siphoning off twenty per cent from every deal he did and investing it in an offshore account in the Bahamas, I wouldn't tell you. Hell, I wouldn't say anything if we had a room in the Screwdriver where we tortured sweet little fluffy kittens, and neither would Will. His future – my future – depends on the continued success of the bank. The last thing we would do is give you any ammunition to run a scare story on us like you did for Davis Butler.'

Alex leaned in over the table towards me. His voice was low and urgent and there was – could I be imagining it? – something that looked like real concern in his eyes.

'For the last time, Laura, I did *not* make that up as some sort of publicity stunt. It was a story – a bloody good story – and I am a journalist. Of *course* I was going to report it.'

'And sod the consequences?' I replied defiantly.

'*Think* about it.' Alex was struggling to remain calm; for some reason convincing me of his integrity obviously meant a great deal to him. 'The fact that I broke the story when I did meant that the bank could be saved from total collapse – how on earth was that irresponsible? Come on, Laura, your job requires you to analyse the money markets – what if those markets were skewed because of the Davis Butler scandal but you didn't know? How would that affect your calculations, your clients – your job, even? You benefited from that story as much as anyone.'

He was right – of course he was: even though fraud and dodgy accounting practices were illegal, the smell of money in the City occasionally attracted con men in the same way that blood under the sea attracted sharks. Rules and regulations meant nothing to them – and sometimes, even though I would rather have stabbed myself in the arm with a pudding fork than admit it to him, it needed people like Alex to uncover the truth.

I glanced up and met his eye. Only rather than the inquisitorial scrutiny I had been expecting, I saw a deep, honest compassion that threw me rather off guard.

'It's not really about Davis Butler, Alex,' I said, the words somehow falling out of my mouth before they'd been vetted by my brain. 'You have no idea what it's like to work in the City at the moment: the redundancies, the rumours, the cutbacks. Every day you wake up and think it might be you, and every evening you go to bed and wonder if you're going to cop it tomorrow instead.'

'I know.' I noticed that he had put his cutlery down and was resting his chin on his hands. 'Believe me, I know. For the last four years I've lived on a series of six-month contracts and it scares the hell out of me. But I love my job; for me, the gains outweigh the risk. Maybe you don't feel the same?'

His gaze was so intense I could almost feel it nudging me off my seat.

'It's kind of swallowed me up.' It felt as though it was somebody else speaking. 'I've been there since gradu-ation, it's the "good steady job" my mother always went on about, it takes up most of my waking hours – and sometimes I think that if I left I wouldn't have a clue who I actually was.'

Oh God! I started to cringe. Had I honestly just opened my mouth and allowed those particular words to spout out? I had never – *never* – said anything like that to another human being in my life! I wasn't even sure if I'd admitted it to myself – so why should I choose to start baring my soul to Alex bloody Hodder, of all people, in the middle of a heaving restaurant? A wave of acute embarrassment swept over me: he would now think I was a few share certificates short of a portfolio and probably discuss this opinion with Will first thing on Monday morning, and then—

But, just at the exact moment I was floundering around trying to formulate some sort of witty, intelligent comment, his knee came to rest against mine under the table. In my addled state, normal restaurant etiquette temporarily eluded me and I took this as an act of war.

'Kindly keep your legs to yourself!' I cried. 'Get this one into your head, Alex Hodder: I do not fancy you, I do not want to go out with you, and if, by some hideous twist of fate, you were the only man left alive on earth, I would have no hesitation in declaring myself a lesbian!'

I froze; the restaurant around us had become eerily still. You could have heard a kebab drop.

I studied the floor intently, my cheeks blazing. Maybe if I stared at the tiles hard enough, a handy trapdoor would materialise and I could slip through it. For methods of escaping my current situation, it was currently beating the idea of impaling myself on the butter knife only by a very short head.

'Coffee, Mr Hodder?' The head waiter appeared as though from nowhere to pour (Turkish olive?) oil on the troubled waters at table two. 'Or maybe dessert?'

Alex raised his eyebrows questioningly in my direction.

'No thank you,' I muttered, unable to look either of

them in the eye.

I couldn't believe what I had just done. I had allowed my personal agenda to hijack an important business meeting, and whatever his crimes, Alex certainly hadn't deserved that shot about lesbians to be delivered forcefully to a packed and attentive house.

'I apologise,' I said. 'That was out of order. Your knee caught me at a bad moment.'

I prayed again silently that he wouldn't be on the phone to Will first thing Monday morning to tell him all about it. For a moment Alex regarded me with a level gaze across the tea light before a broad grin broke over his features.

'I'm sorry too.' To my amazement he sounded genuinely contrite. 'I probably deserved it – after all, I had no business prying into your feelings about your job. Look, I'll get the bill and then I'll walk you to the tube.'

'There's really no need,' I replied, thinking there was no point in prolonging the agony of the evening beyond the restaurant door.

'I insist,' said Alex, scribbling his signature on a credit slip and offering me one of the mint imperials rolling round the saucer on which the bill had arrived. 'It's late, you've drunk most of a bottle of wine and I want to make sure you get there all right.'

I was about to protest further, but as we left the fragrant atmosphere of the restaurant, the cold of the night air hit me like a forehand jab from Lennox Lewis and I found myself groping for something to keep me perpendicular. Instinctively Alex lifted his elbow and I watched with a strange disengagement as my hand slid into the gap between his arm and the concave dip of his waist. Then we set off down the street, pretty much cocooned in our own thoughts.

'At least it wasn't as bad as last time,' Alex said

cheerfully as we left Upper Street and made our way through the Friday-night throng down towards Angel.

'Pardon?' My brain was a fuzzy blank registering only the effects of the wine, the satisfaction of a full stomach, and the warmth of his body where it pressed against my forearm. Conversation felt like an unnecessary, challenging extra.

'The restaurant. Last time I had dinner there with a member of the opposite sex, there were crockery casualties.'

'Really?' I stared at him, the fuzziness dissipating. 'If that had been me, I wouldn't have dared show my face again.'

Alex gave a rueful little shrug.

'I'd been a regular there for years before it happened, and more importantly, we had to go there tonight so that you would discover your love of Turkish food.'

'Because you would know a thing like that?'

'Evidently, yes.'

I nudged him in the ribs with my elbow and he laughed. I'd never met a man whose mouth was as busy as his: he was either smiling, laughing or talking, in complete contrast to Tom, whose default setting was 'seriously harassed'. I had a weird pang of regret that the evening was drawing to a close.

We had arrived at the brightly lit entrance to Angel tube station. I slid my arm out of his and began delving in my handbag for my Oyster card.

'Will you be all right getting home?' he asked.

'Of course,' I replied automatically.

'If you wanted me to see you to your door . . .' he began.

I might have mellowed towards him, but that didn't mean I wanted him trailing all the way to Hammersmith with me. So to stop him finishing this unwanted offer (and also to indicate that there were no remaining hard feelings), I reached up to his face – intending to plant a hasty 'mwhah-mwhah!' farewell kiss on his cheek and then vanish into the night.

Only I was so hasty that I missed.

I missed by quite a lot.

In fact I missed by so much that I got his mouth instead.

I saw Alex's eyes pop open and his eyebrows shoot almost off his forehead entirely. I would have disentangled myself and legged it down the escalator, only at that moment something rather debilitating happened to my knees and my entire body seemed to crumple like a piece of waste paper into his waiting arms.

I removed my mouth from his and found myself looking up into his face.

'That was a mistake,' I gasped.

'I know.' Alex's voice was strangely breathless too.

My heart was thundering away faster than the hooves of a Derby winner, my brain was begging me to make a move and wriggle free of his grasp, but at the same time the rest of my body was adamant that this would be a crazy-mad thing to do and refused to toe the line.

Alex swallowed hard. Somewhere along the lines of a snake trying to gulp down an egg.

'You'd better get off home then,' he said, not moving a millimetre.

'Yes,' I agreed enthusiastically, remaining exactly where I was. 'I better had.'

I would like to be able to report at this point that I got a very firm grip on myself, shook him warmly by the hand and thanked him for a pleasant evening.

Only I didn't.

Instead I stood transfixed in front of him, like a rabbit staring at some dangerously attractive headlights that were heading its way. I could feel his breath on my cheek; smell the clean, slightly musky scent of his skin; and from somewhere a pulse was reverberating through my body, only for the life of me I couldn't have told you which one of us it belonged to.

Then slowly, very slowly, he traced the line of my jaw from just under my ear lobe down to my chin with the tip of his index finger, making my blood pressure shoot up with both fear and anticipation. I'm not entirely sure what happened next, because I closed my eyes, but I do remember his lips brushing mine, my knees providing an encore of their buckling performance and his lips approaching mine, and then – BAM! A hand slapped me hard on the back and I cannoned forward, almost sending Alex crashing to the ground.

'Hey!' cried Mel's voice. 'Fancy meeting you here.'

I felt as though I'd been skewered by an electric cattle prod. I leapt away from Alex (who was doing a fair bit of leaping himself) and boggled at her.

'What the . . . ?'

'I decided to go to a stand-up comedy thing at the King's Head with my mate Karen,' she said nonchalantly before nodding to my fellow kisser. 'She lives round here and— Oh, hello, I didn't see you there. You must be Alex – I'm Mel, Laura's sister.'

I was too jumpy, however, to bother with formal introductions.

'Look, Mel,' I said, anxious to distance myself from whatever had just happened between us, 'he walked me to the station and now he's going. There's nothing to get excited about. No wild tempestuous affairs or anything.'

Bother! *Why* had I gone and mentioned tempestuous affairs? Why put the idea into her head?

Mel, however, was scrutinising Alex too closely to take

any notice.

'Don't I know you?' she said at last, titling her head on one side as if this would give her a better idea of where she'd seen him previously.

'He's on telly,' I said, 'an economics correspondent.'

'No,' she shook her head, 'somewhere else; somewhere in real life.'

My heart sank. Mel was not known for her reserve and inhibition when it came to members of the opposite sex. Had he been an old conquest of hers that I had merely remembered in passing?

'Oh no,' I said. 'Oh, *no*! You haven't? Not with him?'

Mel rolled her eyes. 'You've got to be joking,' she said, less than graciously in my opinion. 'No, Alex, I give up. Your secret lives to fight another day.'

Alex opened his mouth as though he were about to enlighten us, then thought better of it and closed it again.

For a split second, a connection too formed in my beleagured brain, the same one that had been troubling me in the Meeting Room: Alex *Hodder* . . . Before – *bang* – it vanished into the other once again.

'Anyway,' Mel turned to me, 'I have an urgent message for you from Tom. He rang to tell you that he decided not to go to Dublin and would you mind calling him back before ten o'clock, please, so that he can let his mum know for definite that he'll be getting hot and sweaty under the duvet with you.'

She shot a sly look at Alex.

'That is, if you *want* him to get hot and sweaty with you . . .'

'Tom said that?' I was reeling from the combined shock of having kissed a man who was not my boyfriend; being seen doing so by my meddling sister; and then being told by her in front of said man that my boyfriend wanted to spend a romantic night with me. It was like a scene from *Neighbours*.

Mel grinned. 'Well, he didn't actually use the words "hot and sweaty", but that was the gist of it, yes.'

I felt as though I'd just fallen out of the guilty tree and hit every guilty branch on the way down.

'If Tom wanted to talk to me, why on earth didn't he ring on my mobile?' I asked guiltily.

Mel looked a bit sheepish.

'He did,' she said awkwardly, 'but the reason you didn't *know* he had was that I might have sort of borrowed your phone, seeing as I left mine in Bristol and you've got that BlackCurrant thing as a back-up.'

She offered me the telephonic communication device in question and I snatched it back and stuffed it into my bag.

Honestly, it was like sharing a flat with the Artful Dodger.

'And what time is it now?' I demanded, looking round the station concourse for a clock.

'Twenty to eleven,' Alex piped up helpfully.

Mel's face fell.

'Oh, rats. He said not to bother phoning if it was after half ten, because he'd be on the train home to Wimbledon. But,' she added, 'look on the bright side, sis: I've saved you spending a whole night with him, so actually it's a real plus!'

I glowered at her – and then at Alex, who was doing a bad job of trying to disguise a smirk. My glower, however, had little effect on Mel. She shook her head, jutted her chin out in customary defiance, and made her way sedately through the ticket barrier, halting at the top of the escalator to wait for me.

As soon as she had gone, Alex stepped forward, his brow furrowed and an awkward look on his face. He went to take my hands in his but I pulled them back out of reach, stuffing them deep into the pockets of my coat.

'Look, Laura,' he said, his voice low and a little strained, 'I know that you're already in a relationship, and what you said earlier in the restaurant about us and the lesbians is pretty much engraved on my brain, but back there – just now, before Mel appeared – please don't try and pretend you didn't want to kiss me.'

I looked him squarely in the eye and prepared to hold my ground. Whilst I couldn't explain what had just happened with Alex, I did know that Tom had forgone the chance of a weekend's boozing in Dublin to be with me. That was enough, in my opinion, to indicate that our relationship still had a fighting chance of survival.

All other bets were off.

'Like I said, Alex, I'm already with someone,' I told him, anxiously looking over my shoulder at Mel, who was drumming her fingers on the escalator handrail and obviously wanting me to hurry up. 'Besides, you and me – well, I think it would be an incredibly bad idea.'

I reached out and ran a finger down the sleeve of his coat. The faintest echo of a knee-orgasm shivered down my legs.

'Thanks for dinner,' I said, 'and you were right about the chillies.'

And then, without waiting for a reply, I turned and walked through the ticket barrier, linked arms with Mel and together we disappeared down into the bowels of the Northern Line, leaving Alex standing forlornly under the harsh glow of the overhead lighting, being buffeted by the bustling throng of Friday-night travellers.

That final image I had of Alex, of him standing stock-still amid a swirling melee of Friday-night travellers, played on my mind for the rest of the weekend. It popped up at random times and places — whilst I was cleaning my teeth; wondering what to cook for supper; or as I ploughed my way through the pages and pages of SunSpot investment data I'd brought home from the office. There was something about leaving him there by himself that bothered me – a forlorn quality, possibly even a loneliness, that seemed to belong to me just as much as to him – but I couldn't quite put my finger on it. So in the end, I did what I always did: I wrote the episode up as my daily diary entry (a diary which I now kept on my laptop rather than in a little book) and did my best to put it behind me.

My feelings of guilt eased slightly because I didn't have to face Tom that weekend after all. I phoned him on Saturday morning intending to invite him over for dinner, only to be told by his mother that some family friends had turned up unexpectedly and it would be more convenient for *her* if she could 'borrow' him for a couple of days. True to form, I didn't even bother to protest. My time as Tom's girlfriend had taught me that his mother pretty much called the shots, and unless and until I got him to slip a ring on my finger and mutter something in front of our assembled friends and relations about having and holding, it wasn't worth the hassle.

However, given the lack of Tom and the strange cocktail of emotions I was experiencing in relation to Alex, I can't say I was that disappointed when the alarm went off at half five on Monday morning and I had a day full of distractions at work to look forward to. In fact, as I zoomed up the side of the Screwdriver in the see-through space-age elevator-pod to rendezvous with Will, I felt as though I was leaving my worries hanging around at street level like a sort of depressive fog, whilst I headed towards the clear blue skies and sunshine of a day in the office.

And let's be honest, it isn't often you feel that good about going to work, is it?

'Good morning, Melody,' I smiled, presenting myself at her desk. 'Isn't it a lovely day?'

She scowled at me with such vigour you would have thought I'd interrupted her just as she was just about to crack the secrets of cold nuclear fusion.

'Did you actually *want* anything?' she asked, tetchily tapping the top of her desk with her pen.

'Just trying to be pleasant.' I smiled again and then turned and knocked on Will's door.

'Come in.' Will's voice was as rich and soothing as ever.

I pushed open the door and saw he was on the phone, with his back to me, looking out over the panoramic vista of the City below.

'... I've gotten some, but nowhere near enough.' There was a pause. 'Of course I did! Are you suggesting I schlepped all the way over to Wall Street and then spent the weekend with my feet on the desk eating pretzels? Right then. Yes, I *did* go sailing; it was with three guys from Morton's interested in corporate investment in Dresda. That's right – they're thinking about it. Look,' he glanced at me, 'I gotta go – yeah, sure. Sure I will. Bye.'

And he hung up.

For a millisecond, Alex's words about Will having something he wanted to get off his chest sprang into my brain, but I quickly dismissed them. Will wouldn't be having a conversation about anything dodgy on a main phone line – not when he knew as well as I did that the Chiltern recorded its employees' telephone calls for security purposes. No, it was probably just a routine debrief with his line manager, or even something less exciting than that. At the Chiltern we didn't do scandals; we just did staid and boring. The arrival of a new cappuccino machine in Reception was the most exciting thing to have happened to us for months.

'Laura!' He beamed at me as though I was the answer to his most fervent prayers.

'How was New York?' I asked tentatively.

Will's grin didn't diminish by a single watt.

'Oh, same old, same old,' he said. 'Bunch of half-dead guys in suits telling me you can't make money in a volatile market. But I took in La Traviata at the Met, which more than made up for it. I tell you, Verdi is my homeboy! You'd have loved it – hey, next time, how about you come along?'

'Okay!'

Wow! New York! The Empire State, the Statue of Liberty, the pretty much endless duty-free shopping opportunities . . . Suddenly the idea of a stint in New York felt very appealing. I'd always been so busy leaping through the next hoop in my ongoing quest for stability and security that I'd never seriously considered doing anything slightly wacky like moving abroad. Hey! Maybe SunSpot would be my ticket to widening my horizons? I could see if Will would set me up with a secondment and . . . hmmm, let me see . . . I could let the flat, and as for Tom . . . well, he always talked about Wall Street as if it was some sort of mother ship, so he'd probably come too . . . and—

'Now, Laura, how was your weekend?'

My mind was jerked away from thoughts of parading down Broadway with Tom (wearing a pair of red braces) on one arm and a couple of Macy's bags slung over the other and snapped back to the paroxysm of embarrassment that constituted my evening with Alex. Suddenly the poisonous smog of troubles I'd left down at ground level seemed to be pouring in through Reception, thronging round the lift shafts, and pressing the buttons for floor eighteen.

'Well. . .' I began, wondering how to phrase this in the most neutral way possible. 'I, um, had that meeting you requested.'

Will snapped his fingers together in recollection.

'Of course – and Hodder sent me a text this morning to say it had been a frank and profitable discussion covering SunSpot's product range. Good work, Laura.'

A profound sense of relief washed over me, although I did manage not to gasp *thank God for that!* out loud.

'Cheers,' I said, aiming my gratitude as much at Alex as at Will. 'I've completed the initial assessment you asked for in your e-mail on Friday.'

I put a CD-ROM with my homework on it down on his desk and allowed myself a small sigh of relief. My troubles seemed to have given up the chase and were sloping back off down the fire escape, muttering under their breath.

'Good. Right, now, a couple of things.' Will gestured down to the other end of the office where a blonde girl of about my own age was seated at the round table. 'Talking of Marketing, this is Isobel Norland. She's been involved in the project for a while now, mainly liaising with existing clients we are hoping will roll over their profits into Dresda. I've got a big function coming up at Middle Temple on Friday, and in view of the excellent work you did on Friday with Alex Hodder, I want you to come along and press the flesh with me and Isobel.'

As I watched, Isobel uncrossed what looked to be about three and a half metres of perfectly honed leg and stood up, extending a hand towards me. Despite the fact that I had deliberately dressed in my smartest suit and most expensive shoes in order to bolster my flagging ego, I immediately felt as though I'd spent the last three years living under Waterloo Bridge in a cardboard box. Her dress, her attitude, her movements all whispered 'City Success Story'; and when she spoke, her clipped consonants and polished vowels suggested that the world of gilt-edged securities and government bonds ran through her to the point of being imprinted upon her DNA.

'Isobel,' reminding myself I was every bit as good as she was, I walked over to her and grasped the proffered palm, 'how lovely to meet you.'

Will stood behind us, one hand on his hip, the other clutching a large cup of coffee in a brushed-chrome holder.

'Isobel joined us about a year ago,' he said. 'Even though we are outsourcing most of the publicity to an external company, I thought it would be useful for her to be aware of your role in case she needs to liaise with you leading up to the launch.'

'Fine,' I said. 'Great.'

Isobel smiled and revealed a row of teeth so

dazzlingly white she could have used them to guide aircraft in to land at night.

'*Such* a pleasure,' she replied, '*so* looking forward to it.'

'Okay, now, Laura, I want you to fill Isobel in on the type of investments we have previously used in SunSpot products – and make sure she has the closing balances for every fund that wound up in the past twelve months. I'll get the relevant files e-mailed over to you. All clear? Good. Let's go make some money!'

'Well, well, well.' To my surprise, Isobel slipped an arm through mine as we walked out of the room. 'Our Mr Barton seems rather taken with you.'

'You reckon?' I said. 'I mean – thanks.'

Isobel gave me an inquisitive look with her pale blue, slightly buggy eyes.

'Bad luck poor old George busting his knee at Klosters, but if it gives you a leg-up maybe it's not so bad – you have no idea what it's like day in day out for me with no one but men to talk to.'

She made it sound as though the male species was, as a whole, beneath her notice.

'Aren't there any other girls in your department?' I queried, thinking I'd seen one or two of them flitting round the place. Isobel pulled a face.

'Well *technically*, yes.'

Technically? I was intrigued: was she about to let on about a mass sex-change experiment down on the tenth floor? But Isobel had veered off on to a completely different tangent.

'Not that I'm complaining about Mr Barton.' She drew me into a little alcove by a water cooler and lowered her head towards mine. 'Isn't he to *die for*? Plus he gives me fabby little treats like theatre tickets and free trips to New York; I mean, where *bonuses* are concerned, money is all right as far as it goes but it gets boring after a while, don't you find?'

I opened my mouth to say that not enough of it came my way for tedium to have set in, but Isobel was already off into conversational pastures new.

'Anyway, I'm here because I play to my strengths,' she informed me, 'and my strengths are, essentially, having lunch with people and telling them how super SunSpot is. I'm not really into the numbery, figuresy side of things. Ha!'

She laughed a laugh that sounded like an air bubble stuck in a central-heating pipe.

'Did you know that before I started out with the lovely Will, I thought that a hedge fund was some sort of grant for farmers to keep their fields looking pretty! I told him that once, and he was so shocked, he dropped the cup of coffee he had in his hand all over his computer keyboard! What a hoot – the whole thing exploded! He still thinks I was having him on.'

I didn't know whether I should be impressed that she still had a job, or very, *very* afraid.

'So you don't think that a grasp of the figures would help you to sell the products, then?' I suggested.

Isobel squealed with laughter at the very idea.

'Good *Lord*, no,' she gushed. 'Of course, I learn the script – what the returns are, what the competitors are up to, yadda yadda – but I simply couldn't bear to be one of those little people who have to spend day in day out staring at a screen and trying to work out if we are half a per cent better or worse off than we were yesterday. That would simply be *beyond* tedious.'

'Like me?' I challenged.

She looked me up and down with a pitying glance and then reached over and tweaked my collar.

'Never mind, sweetie.' She threw another thousand-watt smile in my direction. 'It's hardly your fault. Oh, and before I forget,' she lowered her voice conspiratorially, 'kitten heels, darling – they're over and *really are never coming back.*'

It was like being mugged by Trinny and Susannah.

'Right!' I nodded sagely and decided that for the sake of both my job and my sanity I was going to have to make a conscious effort to find her amusing rather than irritating beyond belief. 'Look, I'll get that stuff Will was asking for over to you this afternoon, okay?'

'Of course.' Isobel gave a little girlie shake and grinned winsomely in my direction. 'Anyway, I can't stand around here chatting all morning: my manicurist is due at nine and I have to decide what I'm wearing for my lunch meeting so that she can match the nail colour to my dress. *So* lovely to meet you, Leonora.'

'Laura,' I corrected her.

'You're welcome.'

Then she air-kissed me loudly on both cheeks and sashayed her way towards the lifts in a cloud of Chanel perfume.

I decided to take the stairs.

Back at base, I booted up the computer, ran my eyes down the latest figures, watched the Bloomberg ticker do a full circuit at the bottom of the telly screen on the wall to make sure I was up to date with the news and then logged on to my e-mails.

The first one was from Polly.

To: laura.mcgregor@chilternbank.com
From: polly.marchant@chilternbank.com
Subject: Personal Development
How was ur weekend? Archie Boy wants to do drinks Thursday – yikes! Any chance of a foursome with you and Tom?
P xxxxxxxxxxx

I looked across the office at her. She was on the phone but kept glancing in Archie's direction, where he was busy building a tower of Post-it note blocks to try and impress her. Awww, sweet: young hearts in the springtime of their love, etc. etc.

I e-mailed her back.

To: polly.marchant@chilternbank.com
From: laura.mcgregor@chilternbank.com
Subject: Personal Development
Tom being elusive this week but I could always paint my face green and masquerade as a gooseberry if you're desperate!
I xxxx
Ps Mel staying – have so far managed not to kill her

For a moment I thought about mentioning my close encounters with Alex and getting Polly's take on them, but I quickly changed my mind. Even though I knew she'd never do so on purpose, I feared that in the brain-lite state brought on by the early stages of infatuation, she might accidentally gabble out his name and Tom would discover that I'd spent the evening with a man he would love to run over in his car. Besides, as far as my personal life was concerned, the big question was never going to be 'Shall I date Alex?' (the answer to which was 'I don't think so'), but 'What am I going to do about Tom?' (the answer to which I hadn't quite worked out yet).

I glanced back over at Polly, who was unable to keep her eyes on the screen for more than twenty seconds before she looked up, caught Archie's answering gaze and blushed. I'd felt like that about Tom once, the whole 'I can't keep my thoughts off you, *let alone* my hands' thing, and I missed it badly.

Clicking on the e-mail Will had sent me so that I could

check out his trading accounts, I continued to roll the Tom conundrum round my mind. There had to be some way that we could juggle our work and our social lives and still have time for one another. Between us we clocked up two degrees and a mountain of banking exams – a little thing like relationship logistics couldn't be *that* difficult, surely?

As I waited for the information to load, I had my brilliant idea. In fact it wasn't so much brilliant as spectacular, and it took my breath away to the extent that I dropped my mouse with a clatter and made Claire at the workstation next to mine shush me loudly. What if – I was almost hyperventilating with excitement – what if Tom moved in with *me*? It was perfect! It would get him untangled from his mother's apron strings; he and I would have endless evenings together without needing to arrange them in advance; *and* it might even turn into a trial run for buying a place of our own!

It had no down sides, no hidden catches – it was totally, one hundred per cent win-win. In fact, it was *so* win-win that Ladbrokes would have refused to give me odds on it.

Feeling extremely chuffed with myself, I sent Tom a text asking him to call me, got rid of my Chiltern screen-saver (*the bank that wants to make you smile!*) and turned my attention to the SunSpot accounts.

Even though I wasn't a trader, I knew more or less what to expect – you couldn't be Tom Harper's girlfriend without receiving regular, in-depth tutorials about the health of his portfolio and the rigours of maintaining it at peak form – but the SunSpot books looked even more impressive than I'd bargained for. Despite the recent economic climate being more treacherous than an icy mountain pass, the company had achieved almost embarrassing levels of success: virtually every fund had outperformed its rivals by at least five percentage points, whilst the ones that hadn't were consistently as good as their closest competitors. The thing Will and his traders were especially strong on was the actual business of 'hedging', whereby they would 'go long' on one stock – say Asda (meaning that they would buy shares in the expectation of them going up in value); but reduce the risk of the venture failing by 'going short' on a rival supermarket and betting that *their* shares would fall. It was a case of heads we win; tails you lose.

Only Will never, ever seemed to do any of the losing.

I was flicking my eye across the figures, half focusing on them and half floating on a fluffy pink cloud dreaming about life with Tom as my live-in lover (hmmm . . . his 'n' hers monogrammed bathrobes – were they the way forward?), when I noticed something strange.

I was looking at the records of the individual trades on one of the funds, Gisela, which had matured about three months ago – and saw something that made me do a double-take: one of the deals was registering a profit.

So what, I hear you cry, of course it is! This is Will Barton and his über-team of managers and traders – what else are they going to be doing *except* making money hand over fist?

But this was different.

You see, for a report I had written two months ago, I had been looking at the same sector and I knew – *I knew* – that on the fifteenth of August last year British American Airlines stock had fallen because of the threat of another war in the Middle East and the fear that this would impact upon fuel prices. The whole thing had blown over within twenty-four hours and by now everybody had forgotten it.

Apart from me, obviously.

But there it was: staring me in the face and trying to convince me its stock hadn't totally tanked.

I glanced at the clock on my computer screen: half past ten. I didn't have time for this. Whatever might be going on, I needed to stop messing around with Gisela and get on with giving Isobel the data she needed to work her black arts with. The phantom trade would probably turn out to be nothing. Someone would have stuck in a plus sign rather than a minus or simply forgotten to file their paperwork when they should have and bunged it in a few days late. For all the computerisation of the modern trading desk, cock-ups like this were still inevitable. It wasn't even worth mentioning it to Will.

Now, back to Dresda. Hmm . . . what was currently undervalued?

Renewables? Software?

I opened a new window on my computer. Let's see now . . . Zeta Oil was looking promising – just as I'd told Tom the week before. And some twelve-year-old in America had invented a new sort of search engine that suggested the answer before you'd even asked the question and gave you vouchers for free cola . . . interesting . . .

The phone rang. It was Julie from Reception.

'Someone to see you, Laura,' she said.

My heart sank faster than the Stock Market on Black Wednesday. Was it Tom, here to tell me that he hadn't been able to turn last week's turkey trade around and he'd been given his marching orders?

'It's a girl,' Julie continued. 'She says her name is Mel. Do you want me to send her up?'

With this bit of news it's possible my heart sank *even* further. At least with Tom I had a fair idea of the disaster zone I would be dealing with – but with Mel, the field was wide open. Had she burnt the flat down? Been arrested? Caused an international diplomatic incident? I dreaded to think.

I dashed off to the lifts and went groundwards as fast as the technology would allow.

As soon as the doors pinged open, I ran out into the marble and chrome magnificence of the reception area.

'Mel?' I yelled, causing several men wearing expensive silk suits with flashy linings to turn their heads in unison and glower at me. 'Mel? Where are you?'

Julie, who was busy transferring a call, jabbed her pencil in the direction of an overpadded cream seat situated behind a clump of potted banana palms.

'Mel?' I demanded, running in the direction of the jabbing and almost coming to grief on the glass-like floor. 'What's going on?'

Slowly – very slowly – a copy of the *Financial Times* was lowered and a small, blonde, curly head peeked out over the top. It could have been Mel, but equally it could have been a shy creature of the woods wearing wraparound sunglasses and with the collar of its coat – or should I say *my* coat turned up to the level of its nose.

'Shhhh,' she hissed, and glanced round her anxiously.

'What's going on?' I asked, sitting down next to her and watching in astonishment as she sort of shrank into me. 'Are you okay?' Mel didn't reply. 'Is it Tom, then?' I was suddenly filled with panic that his losses might have doubled and in despair he'd hurled himself from the window of the trading room.

'Tom's an arse,' Mel replied, 'but if you're not counting that, I'm not aware there's anything the matter with him.'

'Thank God,' I said, remembering that his trading room didn't have any windows. 'What is it, then? In case you hadn't noticed, I'm at work – and before you ask, I am *not* lending you twenty quid.'

'I was just out and about and thought I'd see how things were hanging with my big sister,' she replied.

'Things are cool,' I informed her. 'Now scram!'

She didn't scram. Instead she gave a frightened little half-gasp and shrank down inside her newspaper once again.

'Mel,' I said, trying in vain to pull the front page down a bit so that I could speak to her. 'You can't stay here. I have an urgent piece of work to complete for my new boss and . . .'

But she wasn't listening to a word I said. Instead her eyes were locked on to a scruffy individual wearing a helmet and battered motorbike leathers who had entered the foyer via the revolving glass doors.

'Shit,' she muttered and slid back as far as she could into her chair, her face shielded by the front page of the *FT*.

Unable to take any more of this weirdness, and worried in case one of Will's clients walked in and saw me shouting at a banana palm, I grabbed her by the elbow and, with her newspaper still placed firmly in front of her face, marched her over to the nearest lift.

'Floor twenty,' I announced, and we were whizzed skywards at Mach 4. Mel gawped as a consequence of both the G-force and the spectacular panoramic view.

'Now,' I said, 'before I open the secret trapdoor in the floor and send you plummeting down on to the pavement below, kindly tell me what the hell is going on.'

Mel swallowed heavily.

'I went in to town to look around – to the National Portrait Gallery, actually. And I saw him.'

'Saw who? Alex?'

What? *Whaaaat?!* Why was Alex Hodder's the first name that leapt into my brain?

'You think I'd be in this state if I'd seen Alex? No, it was Gobshite.'

'Oh Mel,' I replied. 'Of course it wasn't Gobshite. He's a feckless layabout, not James Bond – there's no way he'd have the nous to stalk you through central London. Besides, it's only just gone half past ten and you told me he never gets up till four in the afternoon.'

The lift reached floor twenty and we both stepped out. I glanced nervously in the direction of my office and prayed no one I knew would come past.

'But he was *here*.' Mel had started to get a bit hysterical. 'He was here in this building – at Reception. You *saw* him.'

'Mel,' I put a hand on her arm and discovered it was trembling, 'that wasn't Gobshite; that was a motorbike courier.'

'But – but . . .' Mel wrenched her arm free and stared at me, her face pale. 'I *did* see him, I really did. Back in Trafalgar Square. He yelled at me and I legged it on to the nearest bus. I got off at Cheapside but I thought I spotted him behind me again in the crowd so I ran. I ran until I saw this place. Then I came in to look for you – I didn't think he'd follow me in here, and even if he did, I knew you'd be able to sort him out.'

The last few words trailed off into a mumble, and against the white backdrop of the internal wall, I could see that she was still shaking. This wasn't Mel playing silly beggars; this was serious. Whatever the threat Gobshite posed, it didn't sound like something she was going to be able to handle on her own.

But in my go-getter, time-off-is-for-wimps workplace, with the HR posse stalking round the building, there was very little I could do about it.

'Look,' I said awkwardly, 'I believe that you saw him and I will help you with this – whatever it is – but right now I have to go back to work. Go downstairs and I'll get Julie to give you a coffee and you can collect your thoughts. We'll sort this when I get home tonight – okay?'

A look of complete and utter panic flew across her features.

'Please,' she said in a squeaky voice that sounded more like one of the mice from *Bagpuss* than my devil-may-care sibling, 'please take me home. Take me home now. I'll be safe in the flat.'

'I can't, Mel.' I glanced guiltily down the corridor, half expecting to see Sophie Spink standing there tapping her watch. 'I can't just take half a day off like that.'

'Fine.' She slumped against the wall. 'Then I'll wait here till you've finished.'

'Melissa!' I looked around desperately for inspiration. 'It's half ten and I won't be leaving till six at the earliest. You can't simply hang round in corridors for seven and a half hours. You'll get arrested or something.'

She had gone whiter than a snowball in a bucket of bleach, and as I watched, a tear slipped out of the corner of her eye and trickled down her cheek.

'I can't go back down there,' she whispered. 'I just can't.'

Then the thing I had been dreading actually happened: the lift door behind us opened and Will stepped out carrying a huge sheaf of papers.

'Laura?' he said, his voice matter-of-fact and (thankfully) not angry. 'I need a word. Something's come up on the Dresda project and you weren't answering your phone.'

Mel sniffed loudly and wiped her nose on the cuff of my coat.

'Hey,' Will frowned at me, 'who's this?'

My heart sank – not just into my boots, but probably back down as far as the reception area.

I did the introductions.

'Will, this is my sister Mel; Mel, this is my boss, Will Barton.'

I emphasised the word 'boss' as much as I dared. I was also tempted to add the words 'who can fire me any time he chooses', but as I didn't actually want to put any ideas into his head, I held my peace.

Will grinned at Mel, who bit her lip and blinked tearfully up at him. Then the grin disappeared from Will's face and he beckoned us to follow him down the corridor.

'I think you'd better come in for a moment or two,' he said, and escorted me and Mel through the security door that led to my office and then into the little meeting room next door to the kitchen.

'Right.' He pulled out a chair for us both, put the papers down on the table and then walked back over towards the door. 'I'm going to fix some coffee. Meantime, you two have the room to yourselves.'

Mel managed a watery smile, which Will acknowledged with a nod of his head.

'If there's one thing I hate more than weeping women,' he said, 'it's women weeping outside my offices. It does nothing for my reputation.'

'So,' I turned to Mel as the door closed behind him, 'spit it out.'

Her lip wobbled and for a second she looked as though she was closing in fast on core meltdown.

'Come on, Mel.' I pushed my chair back and walked over to the window. 'Whether you like it or not, I am your sister and I am involved. You need to tell me what it is that I am involved *in*.'

Mel looked up and muttered something almost entirely inaudible.

'What?' I demanded.

'Money,' she repeated, only slightly louder.

Why didn't this surprise me?

'You owe Gobshite money?' I echoed. 'How much?'

Mel was silent.

'I said, how much?' I repeated as loudly as I dared, remembering that the office partition was only flimsy prefab and the last thing I wanted was to broadcast our family drama to everyone on floor twenty, most of whom would probably already be hovering round outside with their ears pinned back ready to pick up whatever they could.

'I don't owe him anything,' she stuttered.

I pushed my hands against my temples in despair.

'Well, what *is* it then?'

'It's – it's other people.'

'What other people? What's it got to do with them?'

'Debts,' she said, her sound levels back down to the almost – but not quite – inaudible. '*We* owe money.'

'Okay.' My panic subsided slightly. Money. Loans. That sort of thing could be sorted out. 'So he's after you because you walked out on a pile of debt?'

Mel turned her face away and I decided to take that as a yes.

'All right,' I touched her hand, 'how much do you owe?'

Mel looked up at me through long, dark, tear-stained lashes.

'Nine,' she said.

I breathed a sigh of relief.

'It's fine,' I said, reaching over and squeezing her arm, 'nine hundred is nothing. If you could see my mortgage you'd understand—'

'Not nine hundred.' Mel's head had dropped back down again. 'Nine thousand.'

I swear my chin actually hit the carpet tiles.

'*Nine thousand pounds!*' I echoed in disbelief. 'Are you sure they haven't put a couple of noughts on the end by mistake? Or could they have worked it out in roubles or Mexican pesos or something in error?'

I sat down heavily on the free chair and stared at her.

'Who in their right mind would lend you nine thousand pounds?'

'My bank for a start,' said Mel, putting her feet on the chair and hugging her knees in tightly to her chest. 'They let me have an overdraft – and then their credit-card company offered me a card. Then I got *another* card offer from a different bank and maxed out on that one too. Then I applied for a third one online and after that I got some store credit and—'

'But you don't have a job,' I protested, wondering when she was going to leap up and yell 'Ha ha fooled you!' and we could get back to reality. 'Why would they think you were good to make the repayments?'

'I worked in a pub five nights a week,' said Mel, 'a cash-in-hand type thing, but that was enough as far as they were concerned.'

'Bloody hell!' I put my head in my hands. Of course I knew in theory that this sort of irresponsible lending went on; I just didn't expect the consequences of it to turn up at my place of work in tears expecting me to sort it all out.

'I didn't actually set out to borrow nine thousand,' Mel went on. 'It was a grand here and a grand there. But I could never afford to make anything other than the minimum payments, and in the end that didn't even cover the interest. The whole thing spiralled out of control.'

I rubbed my face with my hands.

'No shit,' I murmured. 'But why, Mel? You don't have a family to feed or a mortgage to bankroll – why did you put yourself in this position?'

'Gobshite needed equipment for the band, so we put that on the first card.' The story came tumbling out.

'Then his van got written off when Slasher hit a lamp post trying to avoid a dog, so that was the second card. Then I had to take the third out to buy food and stuff because most of my wages were going on repayments for the other two.'

I lifted my head and looked despairingly at her.

'And Gobshite and Slasher?' I asked. 'What were they doing to help you meet your financial commitments?'

Mel's previously ghostly face went bright red.

'They were gigging with the band,' she said. 'All their money went on petrol and stuff for that.'

I could imagine the scenario only too well. Mel might be a sisterly pain in my arse, but she could be as loyal as she was stubborn. If her beloved had the chance to break into the big time she would have done everything she could to help.

'And let me guess – international stardom is still eluding them? The megabucks for the stadium tour never materialised?'

She nodded and looked back down at her scruffy baseball boots.

There was a gentle knock on the door.

'Come in!' I heaved myself back off my chair and watched as the door opened and Will appeared with his chrome coffee holder in his hand.

'All sorted?' he asked, looking expectantly from me to Mel and back again.

Yeah, of course it was . . . if you counted 'sorted' as your sister being completely and utterly up the proverbial wazoo, not just without a paddle but probably minus the canoe as well.

'Let's just say I know what I'm dealing with now.' This was the most positive take on the situation I could come up with.

My eyes slid from Will – commanding, well dressed

and obviously wealthy – over to Mel – tiny, vulnerable and without a penny to her name. The contrast couldn't have been more profound. Even I, with my student loans, heart-stopping mortgage and various credit cards, was in a place of financial security that she could only dream of.

'Were any of the credit cards from the Chiltern?' The question slipped out before I even knew it had formed in my brain.

Mel nodded, and I suddenly felt extremely uneasy that my employer was at least partially responsible for her plight.

'Look,' she said, 'please don't tell Mum; she'll go into orbit, you know what she's like. I just need a bit of time to lie low and figure out what to do, that's all.'

It was as if she'd forgotten Will was in the room. But I hadn't.

'Mel, I'm sorry, but I have to get back to work,' I said softly, conscious of his gaze focused like a laser beam between my shoulder blades. 'We'll talk about it when I get home tonight. There has to be some way through.'

'But if I go out there . . .' Mel started to fill up once more. 'What if he finds me?'

'He won't,' I said as comfortingly as I could. 'This is a city of seven and a half million people. You'll be fine.'

'Or,' Will walked over to the table and indicated the enormous pile of papers on it, 'you can stay and do my photocopying. The office junior on one of the trading teams just cried off with a migraine and there isn't time to send it out to the print shop. Are you up for that?'

Mel wasn't really in any position to argue. She nodded and wiped away one last stray tear.

'Photocopiers are round the corner on the left,' he said. 'Use my ID code to access the machines. Here.'

He scribbled something on to a green Post-it and slapped it down on the top sheet.

'I want three copies of everything, all in date order and nicely bound.'

Mel leapt to her feet.

'Sir, yes sir!' she cried.

'Six pounds an hour, cash in hand. Deal?'

'Deal.'

And she was out the door before you could say 'international capitalist conspiracy'.

We spoke again that night, and after a flash of genius on my part – and some initial resistance on Mel's – I made her an appointment to see one of the debt counsellors at the excellent Citizens' Advice Bureau. She trundled down there the next day and they helped her work out the exact amount she owed and then began the slow and painful job of approaching her creditors and trying to renegotiate her repayments. Despite a lingering jumpiness and a belief that Gobshite was still lurking round every available corner waiting to grab her, my little sis was delighted with this outcome. She even swore blind that she would get a job and pay me back for the first few instalments I made on her behalf – leaving me to wonder whether hell had truly frozen over.

If I was being honest, part of my willingness to stump up a bit of cash in Mel's favour came as much from my regret that the Chiltern had been one of the institutions to lend her money she couldn't pay back as it did from a sense of sisterly solidarity. Even though I had never processed a credit-card application or sent anyone a letter telling them that they too could borrow thousands of pounds at a once-in-a-lifetime introductory rate, my employer had.

And somehow, somewhere along the line, I felt implicated.

On a happier note, Tom texted to say he was intrigued

by my mystery proposal and wanted to meet up on Thursday (*Go Laura! Go Laura!*). The down side was that because his parents were away on holiday that week, he couldn't come over to my flat because he had to feed the cat – but still, a sizzling hot date *was* a sizzling hot date, and I spent most of the morning planning my line of attack so carefully that by the time I'd finished, he'd be on his knees begging to be my roomie.

When Thursday arrived, I left work on time for once. I showered, changed into something much less comfortable but with a heavy emphasis on plunging necklines and push-up bras, then booted up my laptop to quickly write up my daily diary instalment.

'Coffee, Laura?' Mel swung into the flat. 'Oh, Mum rang – she's up in London tomorrow for a teachers' training thingy and wants to stay over here. I'll sleep at Karen's if you like.'

'Fine,' I said without even looking up. I wasn't ecstatic at the idea of having Mum to stay – she was too much like Mel for one thing, and having the pair of them in the flat bemoaning their woes would be like being followed round by my own private Greek chorus – but still, she *was* my mother and it had been a long time since we'd coincided.

Mel ground to a halt in the living-room doorway and watched me with interest.

'Wassat?' she asked.

'Diary,' I mumbled, 'I write a diary.'

'Still?' She sat down heavily on the sofa and squashed up against me, trying to see the screen.

'Yes, *still*,' I said, re-angling the machine so she couldn't see it.

'You used to do that when you were a teenager,' she said, as though this was something I might have been previously unaware of.

'I know.' I paused in the middle of typing in my password. 'I was the one doing the writing, remember?'

There was a pause while the diary software I'd installed on the laptop loaded up. It was great: everything was recorded in nice, automatically dated chunks and you could even upload directly on to the internet if you wanted to in the form of a blog. However, as the idea of my personal thoughts and feelings being available for the whole world to giggle over was so appalling, I'd rather have paraded naked down Oxford Street than use that particular feature.

'Those journals were fantastic,' Mel enthused. 'I used to love them.'

I stared at her in horror.

'But they were private!' I cried. 'You mean you actually read my diary?'

'Of course!' Mel sounded astonished that I should be unaware of this.

'But . . . but . . . how?'

'Simple – I waited until you went out, crept upstairs, got the book out of your underwear drawer – not a very original hiding place, I must say – and read it. Josie thought they were hot too.'

'*You read them to your best friend?*' I was beyond incredulous.

'It was quality entertainment,' grinned Mel before sprawling back against the sofa cushions and resting her hand melodramatically on her forehead. '*I think I love him – but we are both so young; how can I know for sure? When he kissed me last night, I was in ecstasies of rapture. What will I do when he goes to university next term and leaves me all alone in dullsville Wiltshire? I don't know if I can cope.* What was he called now – something tedious. Sid? Ted? No – Ed, Ed Forster. The brainy one with the glasses. Wonder what happened to him?'

'Bollocks,' I said firmly. 'I would never write guff like that.'

Mel grinned. 'My rendition was true to the spirit of the original, and you definitely had a thing for old Eddie. But moving on to the present – do you write about you and Tom, then?'

'I might,' I said guardedly.

'How about Alex?' Mel's eyes lit up. 'Have you written about him yet?'

'Shut up about Alex,' I replied moodily.

'We're taking that as a yes, then.' Mel nodded sagely. 'Oooh – what about me? Am I in there?'

'Yup.' I let out a big sigh. 'I wrote about you. Now stop hassling me and go and make that coffee – or are you waiting for the beans to be flown in especially before you make a start?'

Mel was still hovering.

'Can I have a look?'

'No,' I said firmly, wishing I'd never brought the laptop out from its hiding place, 'you can't. It's private and I'd like you to drop the subject now.'

'Please?'

'No.'

'Go on – you know you want to really.'

'No I don't – and if you don't stop bugging me, I'll throw you out on your ear and you'll have to move back in with Mum and tell her all about your debts.'

'That was a low-down, mean thing to say,' she told me. 'I'm only showing a proper sisterly interest in your life – and your love life.'

She grinned hopefully at me, but the little quip about my love life made me remember I hadn't yet told her about Operation Cohabitation. Placing the laptop on the floor, I folded the screen over to hide it from prying eyes, and prepared to bite the bullet.

'Look, Mel, I need a word with you.'

'If it's about the repayments, you'll be glad to hear I've got a couple of job interviews lined up.'

'Good for you – but no, it's not that. You see, I'm going round to Tom's tonight, and when I get there I'm going to be—'

She cut me off.

'Laura, I don't actually *want* to know what you're going to do to the bloke. Just the thought of you kissing him makes me go all horrible and icky. Anything else is way too much information.'

I sighed. I just *knew* she wasn't going to take this well.

'What I mean is – Mel, I'm going to ask him to move in with me.'

I waited for her to explode with anger, but instead she roared with laughter.

'Oh Laura,' she giggled, 'that was so funny! You know for a minute there I thought you said you were going to ask Tom to move in with you!'

'I did.'

'No you *didn't*.' Mel slapped her thigh to demonstrate her stratospheric levels of amusement.

'Watch my lips, Mel: tonight, after I have mellowed him up with a couple of glasses of fizz I, Laura Elinor McGregor, will ask Thomas Andrew Harper if he wants to live with me.'

Mel stopped mid-guffaw.

'Are you crazy?' she asked.

I raised my hand against any further protest.

'I acknowledge that things haven't been at their best between us for a while, but I've given it a lot of thought and it basically comes down to a problem of time.'

'Yeah, like he doesn't have any for you – or would that be respect I'm thinking of?'

'Shut it, Mel. You don't know him like I do.'

'Good thing too, because I'd have given him a slap round the face and told him to get lost a long time ago.'

I put my hands over my ears.

'I am not LISTENING!' I cried. 'I cannot HEAR you!'

'And I cannot believe I'm in the presence of a grown woman DOING THAT WITH HER EARS!' Mel bellowed back.

We glowered at each other, but I did condescend to remove the hands.

'As I was saying,' I went on, 'the real issue with us is that our work schedules mean we never get to see each other. If he's living here that problem disappears. Bingo!'

Mel muttered something about the real issue being that Tom was an arse, but I chose not to react.

'I know you don't approve, but that's the way it is, Mel,' I said firmly. 'So when you get your job, you might like to start thinking of finding yourself somewhere else to live. It could get a bit crowded with three of us.'

Mel scowled. 'Believe me, if Tom moves in, I won't be hanging around to find out whether or not it feels a bit crowded.'

'Fine by me!'

'Good!'

'Good!'

And she stomped off to go and make a loud noise in the kitchen.

Thankful for the respite, I entered my password and began typing.

I still don't feel entirely comfortable about the idea of asking Tom to move in and I'm not sure why. The bottom line, however, is that things cannot go on as they are and having thought about very little else I am pretty sure that I love Alex, so asking him to—

Huh?????!!!!!! What had I just written? Quick – get rid of it!

'Coffee, sis.'

But before I could hit the delete button, Mel had slapped a mug down on the table next to me and splashed my hand with boiling beverage.

She squinted at the screen and panic rose inside me.

'No!' I yelled. 'You do NOT read my diary! Not now, not ever. Is that clear?'

I switched the computer off and shoved it under a chair before stalking out into the hall and putting on my coat. A night away at Tom's was going to do all three of us a power of good.

It was two hours later. I was sitting on the sofa in a nineteen thirties semi-detached house with Tom on one side and an overweight ginger moggy (who was concentrating on transferring as much hair as possible on to my new black skirt) on the other. The living room around me was a rather chintzy affair, with floral chair covers and pelmets, a swirly pub-type carpet and some stretch velour thrown in here and there for good measure. The overall effect left me in no doubt that the fact that we had the lights down as low as they could possibly go was a Very Good Thing.

For some reason, however, I couldn't chill. No matter how much I tried to think 'mellow' and 'seductive' and enjoy the feeling of Tom's arm round my shoulders and my cheek resting on his chest, I ended up feeling like a nervous schoolgirl wondering if she'd read enough kissing tips in *Just Seventeen* to impress her first big date.

'Drink?' I suggested, thinking that this might assist the chilling process, and indicated the bottle of Moët I'd brought with me from Hammersmith to toast our new status as cohabitees.

Not that Tom *knew* about our new status as cohabitees yet, but I liked to think I always came prepared.

'In a minute.' My soon-to-be in-house amoroso shifted his position so that we were looking deep into each other's eyes.

I found my gaze skimming across his skin and saw . . . a small scar at the edge of his lip that I swear hadn't been there the last time we'd got this close . . . not to mention a couple of fine lines at the edges of his eyes. Had I just not noticed them before or had he been busy changing during the time we'd spent apart?

And if he had, did that mean I'd been too?

'Tom,' I murmured, thinking of a conversation I'd had in a Turkish restaurant seven days previously, 'do you know who I am?'

'Is this some sort of trick question?' He planted a kiss on my mouth and hooked a stray curl away behind my ear. 'You're Laura McGregor, star analyst at SunSpot hedge funds and my gorgeous, sexy girlfriend.'

'No,' I said, kissing him back, 'not *what* I am, but *who* I am. I think somewhere along the line I might have forgotten.'

'Don't start going all bloody weird on me,' said Tom. 'You'll sound like your sister. And right now I'm not interested in who you are but what you're about to do for me.'

He lifted my face up towards his, brushed a crumb away from the corner of my mouth and planted a long, lingering kiss on my lips. To my utter horror, the first thing that popped into my brain was not the pleasant anticipatory tingle of a night wrapped in my loverrrr's arms (not to mention his duvet) but a full technicolour-with-added-surround-sound-close-up of me snogging Alex.

I gave a small, involuntary squeal, which I managed to turn into a cough.

'Bit of pizza crust,' I gasped, hoping that Tom would interpret my flaming cheeks as a sign of oxygen deprivation, 'got caught in my throat.'

I commanded all thoughts of Alex to bugger off and tried once more to relax into Tom's embrace. The evening was turning out rather well, I reminded myself. I'd only had to wait fifteen minutes outside the front door for Tom to turn up; he'd paid the pizza delivery boy *without* asking me for a contribution; and he had only mentioned work twice.

Even though I said so myself, the omens were good.

'Mmmmm.' Our lips parted and he smiled a lazy smile. 'I've missed that.'

I smiled a lazy smile back. He'd missed me! Ha – hear it and weep, Alex! In about an hour from now, not only would I have a gorgeous boyfriend, but I would have a gorgeous boyfriend who had *agreed to live in my flat.*

I rested my head on his shoulder and sighed contentedly as the future metamorphosed into a soft-focus fantasy. It would be perfect! We would take the tube into the City together every morning and share his 'n' hers cappuccinos – maybe even playfully dabbing a blob of coffee foam on each other's noses (hilarious!); we would go shopping at Waitrose on the King's Road every Saturday and take it in turns to push the trolley loaded with grown-up food like butternut squash and couscous; we'd spend hours and hours and hours having hot and cold running sex; and best of all, we would never have to *plan* any of this again – it would just happen naturally!

God, I was brilliant.

My mobile started to ring but I ignored it. Instead I reached over and fiddled with the buttons at the top of Tom's shirt, focusing on my soon-to-be-live-in-lover as he traced a line of kisses down the side of my face, along my jaw and then down my neck. Just as I was expecting him to continue down into my artfully arranged cleavage, he stopped.

'Laura,' he stared at my hands, which had now got as far as the fifth button on his shirt, 'what's happened to your nails?'

I glanced down at my fingers. Inspired by Isobel and her on-site manicure, I'd painted my nails Rouge Noir in honour of the occasion.

'It looks sophisticated,' I informed him.

'Hmmmm.' Tom considered this. 'And your hair? What have you done to your hair?'

I ran a finger through one of my curls.

'Just a few highlights,' I said. 'I had them done yesterday. I fancied a change.'

'I don't know that I did,' muttered Tom. 'Maybe I will have that drink after all.'

As he slit the foil and eased the cork out of the bottle, I put his opinions on my grooming choices behind me and pondered the best way in which to introduce the subject of the flat-share. Obviously going in there with a hale and hearty 'So, Tom, you and me moving in together: how about it?' wasn't likely to swing it for me. I was going to have to use all my cunning feminine wiles to bait the hook so that he simply had to bite.

I surreptitiously undid another button on my blouse.

'How's work?' I asked, hoping that he'd bounced back from his loss and was feeling a bit more positive. 'Did you sort it all out?'

Tom poured us both a glass of fizz and took a deep draught of his, putting his feet leisurely up on top of the coffee table as he did so.

'Yup – I expanded the old portfolio quite a bit. I even went over my trading limit on Tuesday to get in on a real dead cert – and came out laughing. You are looking at a twenty-four-carat, A-star winner here, Laura.'

I stared at him. I had an awful feeling I was looking at a twenty-four-carat, A-star idiot.

He had recouped his losses, fair enough – but to achieve that, he had spent more than he was allowed to by his bank. We were on the verge of Nick Leeson territory.

'You went over your trading limit?' I whispered. 'What if they find out?'

Tom grinned. 'They won't; and if they do, I made enough on that deal so that they won't care. You've got to speculate to accumulate, Laura; that's what you analysts don't understand! Besides,' he added gleefully, 'as soon as Will Barton hires me, I'm out of there.'

I closed my eyes and groaned inwardly. I'd completely forgotten to mention anything about Tom to Will – or even read his blasted CV.

'Laura?' There was a warning note in his voice. 'You have *spoken* to Barton, haven't you?'

'Well . . .' Er, how was I going to put this? 'Will's been rather busy, you know, with the new fund and trips to New York and everything; and I've been flat out with work; and Mel's hit the skids in quite an impressive way and—'

My beloved let out a tetchy little sigh.

'But in your text you said you wanted to see me because you had something important to tell me,' he grumbled.

I put my glass down and encircled him with my arms. 'Oh I do, Tom; believe me, I do.'

'And it's got nothing to do with SunSpot?'

Would the man shut *up* about SunSpot already?

'No,' I said, lifting up my face and looking into his in an attempt to conjure up a more intimate mood. 'It's more personal than that. A wonderful surprise!'

To my astonishment, his face fell faster than a skydiver with a faulty parachute.

'Oh God, Laura, you've not gone and got yourself pregnant?' he cried, leaping out of my embrace.

Arrgghh! Yet again my carefully orchestrated seductive atmosphere turned tail and galloped off into the sunset.

'What do you mean, got myself pregnant?' I asked indignantly, giving him a dirty look to ensure he was in no doubt as to my displeasure. 'As far as I know, that's not biologically possible.'

Tom put his glass down and covered his face with his hands.

'You bloody are, aren't you?'

'No,' I said, folding my arms in front of me and hrrrrumphing in the traditional 'I am extremely annoyed with you' attitude women have used for millennia to signal displeasure to their mates. 'I am not pregnant – possibly because, Tom, you actually need to have sex for that to happen, and as far as I'm aware, the last time we did it was over six weeks ago.'

Tom responded by reaching for his champagne and downing it in one.

'Well, thank the Lord for that,' he replied, before reaching for the bottle of Moët and topping up both our glasses. 'So what was it you wanted to tell me?'

I took a long, cool sip and felt the tension begin to ease out of me as the tiny bubbles made their way down my throat. There was no point in getting agitated; I needed him calm and relaxed if my master plan was going to work – and that required *me* to be calm and relaxed as well.

'All right.' Tom's hands encircled my waist and he looked down into my eyes. 'I'm sorry, that didn't come out very well; you know how I feel about babies and *that* sort of thing. Anyway, what was so important that you had to come and see me on a school night?'

I kissed him.

'Maybe I'd like to see more of you?' I said.

Tom's hand ran down my back and in under the edge of my blouse, stroking the skin at the base of my spine. This was good; this was so much better than brushing lips with Alex Hodder in a draughty tube station.

For the love of God, Alex, just leave me alone, will you!

'And how much more of me would you like to see?' he enquired teasingly.

'Oh, I don't know . . .' I kissed him again and undid another button on his shirt. 'A lot. In fact, how does "all of you" sound?'

'It could be arranged. And when would you like to see me?'

'Ooooh – how about now?'

'Now sounds good.'

'Come on, then.' I pushed the cat out of the way, leaned back on the cushions and pulled him down gently on top of me. 'Put your money where your mouth is, trader boy.'

Tom undid a couple more of my buttons and ran his hand up my leg, hunching my skirt round my hips before pushing my knees apart with his.

'I love you,' I murmured in between kisses, wanting to check his reaction before I made my move.

'Mmmmm,' he replied.

I took that as a sound of assent. It seemed like now was as good a time as any to come out with it.

'Tom,' I said, throwing his tie on the floor and running my hand along inside his shirt, 'what would you say to the idea of moving into the flat with me?'

Despite the fact that his mouth was currently in the vicinity of my collarbone, his reply was perfectly audible.

'And why would I want to do a thing like that?' he chuckled.

Um, this wasn't supposed to happen.

I untangled my neck from his lips and prepared to think fast and think smart.

'Because we haven't seen each other – properly – for ages, and last weekend had the kibosh put on it because your mum wanted you to stay home. I was thinking that if we actually lived together it wouldn't be so difficult for us to . . . well, you know, spend a bit of quality time together.'

I ran my hand round the top of his trousers and toyed with the button on his fly to emphasise my point.

'Come on, it would be fun! Nothing would change with regard to work or friends or the rugby or any of it. It just means we get to do this every single night.'

But rather than melting into a helpless heap of acquiescent male jelly as I had hoped, Tom slithered out of my clutches, did his fly button up again and plonked himself back on his side of the sofa. It was all going rather annoyingly off-script.

I reached out to stroke his hand, but Tom clenched his fist in an agitated fashion and frowned at me.

'I thought you were different, Laura,' he said slowly. 'I didn't think you were into all this joined-at-the-hip commitment stuff.'

Although I was beginning to reconcile myself to the fact that he might not be moving in first thing Monday morning, this one came rather out of left field and I found myself reeling. There was a sting in his choice of words that took me aback. I had been with the man for more than a year through some pretty trying circumstances – what was that if it wasn't commitment?

'Tom,' I said, still doing my best to stay calm and reasonable, 'don't push this back on to me. This is about both of us – and the fact that if things continue as they are, we won't *have* a relationship, just a series of random, ad hoc couplings!'

Tom looked as though he was struggling to find the down side to this scenario.

'So?' He shrugged. 'Maybe that's where we are right now; maybe we just need to accept things as they are and get on with them.'

It was only thanks to great personal restraint (and my internationally renowned conflict-avoidance abilities) that I didn't actually scream at this point. Instead, I leapt off the sofa and stood there quivering with frustration and trying to pull my skirt back down to a respectable level.

'Well, I think you're wrong,' I replied, my teeth firmly on the gritted side.

Tom slid off the sofa too, and he definitely wasn't a happy camper.

'Fine. And if I don't move in with you, then what? You'll do something pathetic like ending it?' He picked his tie off the floor and angrily stuffed it into his trouser pocket.

Actually, I hadn't given any thought to what I'd do if he turned down the once-in-a-lifetime, never-to-be-repeated special offer of living in sin with yours truly; it had been such a brilliant idea, what need had I for a Plan B? Instead of him sulkily picking fluff off one of the chair covers as he was doing now, he should have been rushing immediately to pack his toothbrush and leave his mother a note asking her to forward his mail.

But he wasn't.

And with my heartbeat picking up and my palms starting to feel a little bit sweaty, I looked at my options and found that I could count them on the fingers of one hand – and still be left with three digits to spare.

'Well it can't go on like this,' I replied, suddenly feeling bolder.

For about two seconds Tom looked as though I'd just biffed him round the face; he'd obviously been calling my bluff. Then he snapped out of it, put his angry head back on again and started doing his shirt buttons up with a great play of annoyance.

'Fine,' he replied.

'*Fine!*' I echoed back, determined that if he was going to play hardball, then so was I.

It was all getting rather stand-offish and there was some huffing and puffing going on when, without warning, the shrill tone of my mobile cut through the tension between us, making me jump a good couple of feet into the air. Tom glowered at me, his hands on his hips, as though this interruption, too, was entirely my fault.

'Well?' he growled. 'Aren't you going to get it?'

'It's probably Mel,' I replied, thinking I now had nothing left to lose by telling him my sis was already in residence. 'I didn't mention it before, but she's moved in to the spare room for a bit.'

He reacted pretty much as though I'd announced that I'd discovered a time portal in my boiler cupboard and invited Genghis Khan and his ravaging Mongolian hordes to stay for a couple of months as my lodgers.

'*Mel is going to be living there too?*' he said incredulously. 'Are you mad? In which lifetime did you think I was ever going to agree to share a flat with your loony sister?'

My mood blackened by several shades and I could feel my blood pressure start to rise. Even though she might annoy the hell out of me eighty per cent of the time, Mel was still family, and Tom should know by now that if he was rude about her, he was walking on seriously dangerous ground.

'I told you earlier,' I replied, trying to keep my tone brisk and businesslike. 'She's in trouble, she needs my help – it's not a permanent arrangement.'

'She needs help all right,' he agreed, 'preferably psychiatric and if possible involving large amounts of sedative drugs! Did I tell you that last time we met, she called me a selfish pig?'

This display of self-centred superiority was the last straw. A sense of protectiveness towards Mel surged through me, and any desire to have Tom as a flatmate disappeared. For the first time in our relationship, I opened my mouth and actually yelled at him.

'Yes you did!' I exploded. 'You went on about it for at least three weeks after the event, and you know what? After your performance this evening, I'm beginning to think she was right – you are a pig. In fact, all I'd need would be two slices of bread and some tomato ketchup and I could turn you into a *bacon sandwich*!'

Tom took a step back and stared. He'd never seen me in full-on row mode before, and I think it came as a bit of a shock.

'Hey!' he said, obviously put out, 'You can't talk to me like that!'

But before I could get my act together and tell him I jolly well could if I wanted to, my phone went again.

Exasperated, I rummaged through the detritus at the bottom of my bag, intending to switch the damn thing off, but as I pulled it out into the open I glanced at the caller display – and almost dropped it again in horror.

You see, it wasn't Mel on line one ringing to tell me Gobshite was trying to make off with my telly to cover the debts; or my mum calling to check it was still okay for her to crash at the flat tomorrow night; or even Will telling me I needed to come in early to double-check some figures for him.

It was Alex.

The last man – for a million bazillion reasons – I would want Tom to know was ringing me. However, right at that precise moment I lost the plot and, crucially, the power of internal monologue.

'Oh shit,' I breathed, 'it's Alex.'

I immediately felt my cheeks catch fire and I clapped my free hand across my mouth in case any more incriminating words snuck out. I couldn't have looked any guiltier if I'd tried.

Tom suddenly looked like a particularly fierce tracker dog who'd sniffed out a fugitive. I swear his ears actually pricked up as I spoke.

'Who's Alex?' he asked.

I froze, phone in hand, unable to speak – or indeed to manage anything other than breathing and not falling over.

'I *said*, who's Alex?' Tom repeated, his face darker than cumulonimbus building up for a thunderstorm.

What the hell was I going to tell him?

'He's just someone from work,' I managed at last. 'Someone Will knows.'

My stomach was churning and my heart felt as though it was trying to crawl out of my chest cavity via my windpipe.

'Laura,' said Tom in a low, eerily calm voice, 'I know you, and what's more, I know when you're not telling the truth. Look at you – your nails, your hair; all this crap about us needing to deepen our relationship – there's something weird going on.'

He paused for a moment and then delivered his killer blow.

'You've been having an affair, haven't you?'

As the words came out of his mouth, I suddenly experienced a wave of pure blessed relief breaking over me. For the first couple of microseconds I assumed this was because he had not made the connection between the name Alex and the journalist who had nearly cost him his job.

But I was wrong.

As I stared at Tom, standing in front of me with his hands on his hips and an expression of pure disgust etched across his features, it suddenly dawned on me what this lightness of being actually was: we were *over*. His final, triumphant piece of arsewittage about me having an affair had severed whatever it was that had kept me bound to him over the past few months.

And it felt pretty damn good.

I threw the mobile into my bag and decided it was time to inform Tom of his new status as a single person.

'Yeah, right!' I said, my voice angry but low and controlled. 'Because if I was having an affair, that would be the ideal time for me to ask you to move in with me! How *dare* you, Tom! How dare you accuse me of sleeping with someone else when I have done everything I humanly could to keep this relationship going! I have put up with you standing me up, cancelling our dates so that you could go to the pub with your mates, and whingeing non-stop about your work; I have put you first time and time again – and you know what? I'm sick of *it*, I am sick of *you*, and I am sick of the person *I* have become because of it. You are the biggest, most repulsive, piggiest pig I have ever met and I wouldn't move in with you if you had the last house on the planet!'

For a moment Tom looked as though he was going to shout back; then he thought better of it, his eyes narrowed and he threw a glance at me that was loaded with pure contempt.

'You've changed, Laura, do you know that?' he spat. 'And what's more, I don't like what I'm seeing.'

A week before, a day before, even possibly an *hour* before, the force of his words would have had me floundering around for a conciliatory response. Now, however, I found myself taking a very deep breath and looking him dead in the eye. It was as if the mask he had been wearing had finally slipped, allowing me to see him for who he really was. Yes, he was still tall; yes, he was good-looking; yes, he was well dressed and highly driven, but as Mel had always pointed out, he was also undoubtedly an arse, and I couldn't believe I'd gone so long without realising it.

'I think you're right, Tom,' I replied, feeling the burden of our failing relationship being lifted from my shoulders once and for all. 'I have changed. And speaking as the new, improved Laura, I'd like to announce that you and I are over. Do you get that? O.V.E.R. Finished, through, history, *finito*! And it feels fan-fucking-tastic!'

Tom's mouth gaped open in a gratifyingly unflattering way, whilst a small smile of triumph played around mine. Then, before he could say anything that might mar my moment of ascendancy, I turned on my heel and strode off out the door and down the garden path.

Twenty hours later, I trotted up the four semicircular stone steps that led to Middle Temple Hall and in through a pair of huge black wrought-iron gates emblazoned with the insignia of the Lamb and Flag. I was feeling unaccountably nervous. Despite squeezing myself into the blackest of little black dresses and the most vertiginous of high heels (and remembering to ask Mel to drop off the spare key at Mum's conference venue before she went over to Karen's), I had an eerie feeling that I was in for a bit of a weird one, mainly because I had inside information that Tom was going to be there too.

'Relax,' Polly said as I got changed in the ladies' after work. 'You're probably still in shock after what happened last night; the pair of you had been together a long time and a break-up is going to take a bit of getting used to.'

'I suppose so, Pols,' I said, layering on the mascara, 'but he was in such a strange mood – I mean, accusing me of having an affair? What was that all about?'

'Do you think he might be having one himself?' Polly's eyes grew to the size of saucers. 'What if he brings a "plus one" to the do this evening?'

I shrugged and blotted my lipstick.

'If he hasn't got time for one relationship, I doubt he can manage two. But in case he does start acting strangely tonight, I'm planning on sticking close to Will. Tom is desperate to work for him, so there's no way he'd do or say anything in Will's presence that might jeopardise his chances.'

'Good thinking, Bat Girl.' Polly nodded approvingly. 'Remember – it's a work function; what can possibly go wrong at a work function?'

What indeed?

'Ticket please, miss.' A man in a porter's uniform checked my invitation and pointed towards a flight of wooden steps on the left. 'Ladies' cloakroom is up there and sherry is being served either in the Minstrels' Gallery or the Parliament Chamber.'

I did as I was told and climbed the clattery stairs. I checked my coat in, reapplied my lipstick and then paused: Parliament Chamber or Minstrels' Gallery? Hoping that there might be real minstrels involved, I opted for the latter and walked up yet another flight of steps and out on to a broad wooden balcony that stretched the entire width of the hall.

I helped myself to a glass of sherry and went to gawp down through the intricately carved screen on to the rest of the hall. It was like something out of a fairy tale: candlelight twinkled off the silver place-settings that were laid out on four long rows of tables running from one end of the room to the other. On a dais at the far side stood a high table, even more stunningly bedecked. The panelled walls were decorated with coats of arms and large, impressive portraits; and arching over me was an incredible hammer-beamed roof. I craned my neck to try and get a better view of it – and stumbled backwards into another function-goer, spilling sherry down myself in the process.

'I am so sorry,' I gasped, unsure whether I should first try to placate the person I had bumped into or mop up the alcohol spillage that was busy creating an embarrassing wet patch down the front of my new dress.

'Here, take this.'

A large white handkerchief hove into my peripheral vision and I froze. Bugger, bugger, *bugger*! Of all the people in all the banking functions in all the world . . .

'Thank you, Alex,' I said stiffly, looking around quickly for a means of escape and finding none. 'But that won't be necessary.'

'Don't be ridiculous.' He waggled it at me. 'You look like you've been scuba-diving.'

'Whatever.'

Why did this man keep turning up in my life? *Why?* Did I send out some sort of homing signal?

I hesitated for a moment and allowed my eyes to slide from his polished shoes up through a perfectly creased trouser leg, a dinner jacket, a starched dress shirt, a slightly floppy bow tie and finally to his face, which appeared rather pale and pensive.

My stomach gave an unexpected and appreciative flip at the sight of him. You know, sometimes you can really hate your stomach . . .

'You're looking nice,' he offered.

'I know.' I sniffed, dabbed at my wet patch with his hanky and ran my gaze down the length of his body for a second time.

My stomach flipped again. It was beginning to annoy me.

He looked completely stunning, and even though I defy any but the most unattractive male specimen to look un-yummy in a black tie, there was something about him that evening that made my breath catch in my throat and my knees do quite a bit of thrumming.

Naturally, though, I chose not to inform him of this and looked away quickly before the flipping/catching/thrumming thing got any worse.

'Not that you don't look nice at other times,' Alex said nervously. 'Can I get you a refill?'

'No thanks,' I said firmly and handed back the hanky. 'I can get my own drinks, thank you, Alex.'

'Um,' he said, 'um, about the phone call last night. I wanted to let you know I was going to be here in order to avoid any – um – awkwardness.'

'Great,' I said, awkwardly. 'I mean, it's fine. I mean, look at us – not awkward at all. In fact – awkwardness? What's that?'

I gave a strangulated laugh. There was another short pause during which I edged away slightly.

'Look,' Alex ran a hand through his hair, 'about Friday . . .'

Suddenly, to my immense relief, through a gap in the carved wood of the screen I spotted Will peering at the place settings downstairs. He was accompanied by Isobel, who was wearing an exuberant and obviously expensive scarlet dress with matching shoes.

The spell was broken.

'I'm sorry, Alex, I really have to go,' I said, and before he could protest, I'd slipped past him and was off down the stairs.

The dinner itself passed pleasantly enough. I chatted to the colleagues and competitors seated in our vicinity; the food was good, the wine even nicer; and under Will's approving gaze I even managed to slip out a few tantalising titbits of information about Dresda that had people nodding with interest and programming the launch date into their electronic diaries. After the port and the speeches, the tables and benches were pushed back and a jazz band set up on the dais underneath a humongous portrait of Charles I. Fearing a second onslaught from Alex during the mingling, I stuck to Will like an industrial-strength limpet – a tactic that not only seemed to work re Hodder-avoidance, but also allowed Will to manoeuvre me through a throng of journalists, financiers and minor politicians, effecting introductions as he went.

I even began to enjoy myself.

It quickly became clear why SunSpot had Isobel on the payroll. For all her imperious comments about my wardrobe and her self-confessed confusion over hedge funds, the girl could work a room like no one I had ever seen. A combination of long legs, a dazzling smile and the ability to never take no for an answer meant that she could charm the birds from the trees – and would surely have done so, had there been any feathered life forms present.

After a while, though, she was swallowed up by the crowd and for a minute or two I completely lost sight of her vivid scarlet dress. Then, just as I was in the middle of discussing investment returns with a man from a pension company who had six chins and a hideous laugh, I saw a flash of red out of the corner of my eye. It was the woman herself – and next to her, looking like a rabbit facing down an oncoming juggernaut, stood Alex.

My first thought was 'Ha!', closely followed by 'Serves him right'; but as my gaze darted between Isobel and her unwilling captive, I saw her reach out a forefinger and run it along the side of Alex's hand. It only took a split second; it was a gesture that, had I looked round at any other time, I would have missed entirely, but, for some unknown reason, it made me feel as though a giant hand had reached down and swivelled my world through one hundred and eighty degrees, leaving me dizzy and confused and unable to work out which way was up.

I took a large mouthful of wine and forced myself to look in the opposite direction. *This was ridiculous.*

'. . . so of course the punters are getting a bit restless,' my companion continued, his voice sounding like the whine of a mosquito, 'and who can blame them? With their funds falling in real terms year on year . . . '

I tuned him out. To my dismay, I found myself unable to concentrate on anything other than the mini-drama that had unfolded a few feet to my left. I didn't understand: was Isobel on the pull, or was she simply using her considerable charms to give us some free publicity?

'. . . in some cases, of course, it's a handy vehicle to play the markets, but for other poor buggers it's all they're going to have once they retire . . . '

Without warning, my mind suddenly made a series of rather unwelcome leaps. When we had been at the restaurant Alex had mentioned an acrimonious break-up – could the saucer-smashing villainess be Isobel herself? Completely unable to stop myself, I glanced in their direction once again.

They were still standing next to each other, still engaged in conversation, but to my utter (and still inexplicable) relief, Alex's demeanour was not that of a man desperate to reunite himself with a lost love. In fact, he looked more like a man who wanted to yell 'Hey! What's that over there?' and make a bolt for the door. Despite Isobel fluttering her eyelash extensions at him with the energy of a hyperactive butterfly, Alex seemed resolutely unmoved. I watched as he shrugged in a non-committal fashion and then spent quite a long time looking at his shoes.

'. . . and with company pension schemes folding faster than you can shake a stick at . . . ' My pension man droned on, oblivious to my lack of interest.

Then it happened.

Just when I'd convinced myself that their intimacy was purely a product of Isobel's imagination, Alex reached over and tucked a strand of her blonde hair behind her ear. Then he dipped his head in towards her and kissed her lightly on the corner of her mouth.

For a moment I thought I was going to choke: my breath imploded painfully in my chest and I produced a nasty hiccoughing noise – so much so that the pension man stopped talking about fund transfer values and patted me on the back. As I looked up mid-gasp, I met Alex's gaze. Isobel had drifted off and he raised his hand in greeting, smiled a cheery smile and started to make his way over. Panic rose within me. Even though I didn't understand the wave of powerful emotions that had been sloshing around during the past two minutes, I was pretty certain that chatting with Alex was not going to improve matters. For the second time that evening I looked wildly around for a way out, and also for the second time, I found myself hemmed in on all sides by the great and the good of the Square Mile.

Then, just at the moment when I had given up all hope of deliverance, a number of quite extraordinary things occurred in rather quick succession.

The first was that Will appeared at my side and slid his hand into mine preparatory to leading me off to meet another contact; it felt warm and solid and comforting and caused the Hodder-induced confusion to slowly trickle out of me. However, about a millisecond after our fingers interlocked, I was conscious of a shout from nearby, followed by running footsteps and the smack of a fist connecting with a jaw. Will staggered back, bumping against my right arm and making me disperse the contents of my glass down the front of my dress yet again.

'Oh no!' A very unwelcome voice rang out round the panelled walls and bounced off the stained-glass windows. 'It's you – it's Will Barton. Oh God – I didn't think – I didn't know . . .'

The chatter in the room disintegrated into one of

those silences that make you feel you want to be somewhere else.

Anywhere else.

Immediately.

Will yanked his hand out of mine and pressed it up against his jaw. I could see a red mark emerging between his fingers.

'I don't have a fucking clue who you are or what you're talking about,' he growled, 'but I'll damn well make sure I see you in court.'

'I don't believe it,' said Tom, looking from me to Will and back again. 'I don't bloody believe it. Did you kiss him? Did you actually kiss Will Barton?'

'Tom,' I cried, wondering which one of us was going mad, 'are you insane? I've never kissed Will. I've never even *considered* it – no offence there, Will. This man is my *boss*, Tom; the one *you* were getting your knickers in a twist over wanting to work for – remember?'

'You know this guy?' Will stared at me, his eyes wide and disbelieving.

My cheeks blazed bright red.

'He, er, we, er . . . he used to be my boyfriend . . .' My voice trailed off under the sheer weight of embarrassment.

Thank God I was at least able to use the past tense.

'Fine. You can give me his details first thing Monday so that my lawyers can sue his ass off.'

'Listen up, Laura.' Even though he was currently being restrained by a couple of burly porters *and* had a writ from Will Barton to look forward to, Tom decided to grab hold of the metaphorical shovel with both hands and dig himself into an even deeper hole. 'Even if it's not Will, I *know* you're having an affair! Don't try and deny it.'

'For the last time, Tom,' I hissed, 'I have not been sleeping with anyone else!'

It was hideous; worse even than one of those dreams where you turn up to work and suddenly discover you're stark naked. I knew that everyone in the room that night (plus all their friends and acquaintances and *their* friends and acquaintances) would forever associate the name 'Laura McGregor' with 'the man who smacked Will Barton round the chops'.

'You wanna add a libel writ from Laura to the assault charge?' Will drew himself up to his full height and towered in an alpha-male manner over Tom (who by now looked not merely like a beta male, but positively omega). 'Because if you don't, I suggest you take the opportunity to fuck off right now.'

Even though it was calm and level, there was something in Will's voice that was truly menacing. If it had been me in Tom's shoes, I think I would have spontaneously combusted out of sheer terror. Instead, as the porters began to drag him away, he let out one last defiant yell.

'It was on the internet,' he cried. 'I read it on that stupid blog you've got on the internet.'

This made no sense at all, and as the doors of the hall closed behind him, I sat down heavily on a nearby bench and put my head in my hands. The jazz band decided to strike back up again with a funky little dance number, and people slowly drifted back into small groups, filling the room with the buzz of chatter.

Most of it about me, I suspected grimly.

In a flurry of lipstick and red silk flounces, Isobel bounded up.

'Will, darling,' she cooed, 'how simply frightful! Is it bad?'

'No.' My boss experimented with a grin and winced slightly. 'Nothing terminal.'

I looked up at him from my bench and wondered idly if he would fire me now or wait until the morning when he could hand me my P45 in person.

'I . . .' I began, but the words simply wouldn't come. 'I – I . . .'

I gave up and slumped back against the table, my fingers over my eyes and the mother of all headaches starting to stake out its territory rather aggressively between my temples.

'So,' Isobel parked herself in front of me, her hands on her hips and her head tilted sideways in an inquisitive manner, 'who exactly was that man?'

I opened my bag to check I had my Oyster card ready for the getaway I was planning as soon as humanly possible.

'Tom Harper,' I muttered. 'He works for Davis Butler on their trading desk, and until recently he used to be my boyfriend.'

As I said the word 'boyfriend', a nasty little shiver made its way down my spine. I couldn't believe I'd put up with his crap for so long.

'Bit of a hunk, though,' Isobel commented in a matter-of-fact tone.

'Whatever.' I popped a couple of painkillers out of a blister pack I'd found at the bottom of my handbag and knocked them back with a random glass of champagne sitting on the table next to me. If I succumbed to some sort of drink 'n' drugs cocktail coma, it would probably be for the best. Then I heaved myself to my feet, mumbled a heartfelt apology to Will, who nodded his acknowledgement as he pressed an ice pack up against his wounded jaw, and went to collect my coat.

After the noise and heat of the party, the silence of the clear, cold March air outside was a blessed relief. I walked down the steps from the hall and across the gravelled courtyard by the fountain before turning up the little lane that would take me out on to Fleet Street. I had no idea how I was going to handle the next few days of my life. As well as a delusional and possibly violent ex-boyfriend on the loose, I was pretty much convinced I was out of a job – and the manner in which it had all happened meant that no one this side of Hong Kong would be thinking of Laura McGregor as a useful new addition to their team. I was humiliated, unemployed and, basically, stuffed.

And there was nothing I could do about any of it.

In sheer frustration, I swung my handbag angrily against the wall of Middle Temple Lane and it burst open, scattering lipsticks, powder, purse, phone and Oyster card to the four winds.

Fuck, fuck, *fuck*!

Getting down on to my hands and knees, I began scrabbling about in the darkness. Rip! My tights caught on the tarmac. Ouch! My hand brushed against something sharp, and – oh no – someone was shouting my name; someone was coming after me; someone who sounded depressingly like Alex.

The image of him kissing Isobel sliced through my brain and, if such a thing was actually possible, made me feel a million times worse.

'Go away,' I yelled, hauling myself upright and stuffing the items I'd managed to retrieve back into my bag.

'Are you all right?' He skidded to a halt just in front of me.

'Fan-bloody-tastic. Now, there are a hundred reasons why I don't want to talk you right now – or, in fact, ever – so if you'll just excuse me . . .'

'I'm going to see you home.'

'You are not.'

'Yes I am.'

With a cry of annoyance, I turned away from him and, as fast as my high heels would carry me, marched up the lane in the direction of Fleet Street. Alex followed. I stopped; he stopped. I took a step; he did exactly the same. It was turning into a bad-tempered game of Grandmother's Footsteps.

'Go back to the party,' I hissed. 'I have had more than enough idiotic men to last me a lifetime, and that includes you!'

'You're upset.'

'Too bloody right I'm upset.' I set off up the road once more. 'What I need is some time alone to get my head straight – so do me a favour and sod off.'

'No.' Alex was now level with me, and opening the little door that led from the lane out on to the glare and noise of Fleet Street. 'I won't. Taxi!'

'I am not getting into a cab with you,' I protested, but Alex was already opening the door and I found myself giving the driver my address.

'This is completely out of order,' I added, as I allowed myself to sink on to the back seat of the cab and loosen my shoes with something approaching relief. 'And I want you to know I am not happy about it *one little bit!*'

Alex clambered in after me and pulled the door shut, and we sat for a while in stony silence. At least, it was stony on my part; Alex was busy emanating quiet concern – but that only made me feel even more annoyed with him. I had no idea what had been going on between him and Isobel and I had even less of an idea why the thought of their fleeting caress was still making my heart race and my stomach churn. What I *did* know was that my top concern (both emotionally and professionally) was self-preservation – and if Alex thought he was in with some sort of chance with me, he was sorely mistaken.

'Don't think you're coming in,' I informed him, just in case either of us had any ideas to the contrary. 'My mother's staying and the last thing I need is to have to explain why some man who isn't my boyfriend has brought me home. I've got enough of my own problems – not to mention Mel's – without having to explain it all to her at eleven o'clock at night.'

'What's up with Mel?' asked Alex.

'Debt.' I rubbed my exhausted face. 'Thousands and thousands of pounds' worth of debt. She can't pay it, I can't pay it and I don't want my mum being hassled with it – not that she's got any money either: we come from a broken, bankrupted home. It's pathetic really. You could do a *Panorama Special* on us.'

Alex glanced out of the window and a troubled expression flickered across his face. Then he stretched out his long legs and turned back to look at me.

'Mel wouldn't want to do an interview for me, I suppose?' he suggested casually. 'We'd pay a fee – nothing extortionate, but it might help her cash flow.'

'Oh for goodness' sake, Alex,' I snapped. 'This is private family business, not another opportunity for you to raise your journalistic profile. What I told you goes no further than the doors of this cab, and if you breathe a word to *anyone*, I will personally push you in front of a tube train.'

The cab went over a speed bump and our knees crashed together. Without warning, the voltage output of a large electricity substation zoomed up my legs, through my body and exploded into my brain. I gave a small involuntary gasp and closed my eyes as the charge ricocheted through my limbs and bounced off several vital organs.

Alex too paused for a moment, but when he came back, he did so with all guns blazing. I had obviously pushed a significant button.

'Why do you always assume that I'm only out for what I can get?' he demanded angrily. 'I do the one thing I can to try and alleviate Mel's situation and you go and bite my head off.'

We took a sharp left, which sent me careering down the back seat on a direct collision course with him. His hand inadvertently slid under my dress, touching the back of my thigh and making me shudder violently as my nervous system threatened to go into full meltdown.

'And you know why?' I cried, clinging on grimly to the strap above the door to prevent any more slippages. 'Because I don't *need* your help. I can cope perfectly well by myself – and even if I couldn't, the last person I would ask is – is—'

To my utter astonishment, I had been about to finish my sentence with the words: 'the man who kissed Isobel' – but I stopped myself just in time. That was crazy talk: Alex and I were not together, and apart from anything else, I had only just split up with my boyfriend and was most definitely *not* on the market. What should I care if Alex went round snogging every single woman he could get his wandering hands on?

He swung towards me in his seat, and even in the murky orange twilight that passed for darkness in west London, I could see that he was annoyed. When he spoke, his voice was low and gravelly and I could feel it reverberating up through my body like an earthquake tremor.

'Laura, for Christ's sake – haven't we had this argument enough times? I broke the Davis Butler story and I'm glad I did. If some people suffered in the fallout then I'm genuinely sorry, but what exactly do you want me to do about it? Hitch a ride back in the Tardis and do things differently? Take out a full-page ad in *The Times* apologising for any unforeseen consequences? Walk through the streets of London whipping myself as a penance?'

'Yes! No! I don't know!' I cried, wishing I could book myself in for a brain upgrade, since mine clearly couldn't cope with everything currently being thrown at it.

He threw himself angrily back into his seat and we rattled through the streets of Hammersmith, a heady cocktail of animosity, frustration and intense physical chemistry pulsing round us, until the cab mercifully drew up outside my front door.

I leapt out, closely followed by Alex, who pulled out his wallet to pay the fare. I, however, elbowed him roughly out of the way and shoved some cash in through the driver's window.

'And I don't need you to pay my taxi fares, thank you very much!' I cried as I stalked up the path and pulled my key out of my bag. 'In fact, what is it that I need you for again, Alex? Oh yes, that's right – *nothing*.'

'Good grief, Laura.' Alex was hot on my heels. 'Are you always this argumentative, or have you been taking lessons?'

'I am *not* argumentative,' I yelled back, my key poised in the lock. 'You're the one who keeps picking fights. Now – are there any more of my personal shortcomings you want to throw at me, or are you just going to *go home*?'

Alex took a deep breath and pulled himself up to a rather impressive six foot two.

'Okay, what about the fact that you're too frightened to acknowledge that last Friday meant something to you?'

The shocking truth of his words made my hand shake so much the key slipped back out of the lock and grazed my thumb.

My mood, consequently, did not improve.

'For the last time, Alex – I got a bit drunk and I kissed you by accident. It was a mistake. Now forget about it and move on.'

The window of the upstairs flat flew open and my neighbour Mrs O'Linehan leaned out.

'For the love of God, will the pair of you keep the noise down! I don't give a tinker's curse if you kissed me Laddo there or not – but don't go waking me up over it!'

'Sorry!' I called.

I grabbed Alex by the arm, dragged him inside the flat and shut the door.

'I thought I wasn't allowed in,' he observed, a trifle too smugly for my liking.

'It's only because when I murder you and bury the body under the floorboards I don't want that woman upstairs hearing your dying cries of agony and telling the police,' I hissed. 'Do not look upon this as encouragement in any shape, manner or form.'

Alex took me gently by the elbows and peered into my face, giving me very little option but to peer back. At that moment, with a bewildered intensity in his brown eyes and his lips just a fraction parted, he was so knicker-wettingly gorgeous that the physical effort involved in not simply throwing myself into his arms was phenomenal.

Not that I had *any* intention of doing any throwing, you understand.

'What about me?' he whispered. 'Doesn't it matter what I feel?'

With superhuman strength I extricated myself from his grasp.

'No,' I replied, 'it doesn't. And you know why? Because this is a free country and I am allowed not to fancy you!'

'I don't believe you!'

'Well you'd better start trying!'

My heart was thumping away harder than a heavy-weight boxer and my face felt as though it was about to burst into flames. I told myself again and again that all I had to do was walk away; tell him to leave; break whatever spell was keeping me transfixed to this indefatigable, infuriating man: but no matter how hard I tried, I couldn't. My body was refusing to take any orders from my brain – and what was more, it had suddenly acquired its own agenda.

Alex's lips – dry, warm and shockingly unexpected – brushed mine.

'Don't you dare kiss me!' I shrieked, prompting a loud thumping on the ceiling from Mrs O'Linehan. 'Or I swear to God I really will call the police!'

'I didn't kiss you.' Alex looked equally shocked and rather indignant.

'Well who the hell was it, then?' I cried. 'Because unless I am very much mistaken, there are only the two of us here and I don't think it's physically possible for me to have kissed myself!'

'You kissed me.' To my annoyance, his tone had the cheek to be accusing rather than appreciative.

'Don't be ridiculous.'

'Yes you did.'

'No I didn't.'

He scowled at me.

'Oh for goodness' sake, Laura; if I'd kissed you, it would have felt like this.'

His fingers skittered down across my shoulders and a second later his mouth was moving forcefully against mine – which seemed more than happy to go with the flow and join in. The thudding of my heart went up by several notches and I felt my knees turn into something with the consistency of trifle.

Dammit! He was right: it must have been me! I could have kicked myself (only I was still wearing my stiletto heels and probably I'd have given myself a nasty puncture wound).

Alex pulled away and we stood with our faces millimetres away from each other, his breath hot on my cheek.

'See?' he murmured. 'Totally different.'

I could still sense the pressure of his fingers on my arms; the touch of his dinner jacket against my waist; the feel of his leg where it brushed against mine – and at every point of contact between us, there was enough chemistry whizzing off into the atmosphere to keep the scientists down at ICI busy for the next couple of years.

Enough! My brain suddenly re-engaged. *Put the man down. Move away from the man.*

But I couldn't.

Or maybe that should be 'I wouldn't'.

But whichever it was, just when I should have been making my excuses, pushing him out the front door and slamming it behind him, I forgot all about my anger, all about my mother staying, all about Davis Butler, and moved my head a couple of degrees to the right. Then I opened my mouth, planted my lips on his and kissed him as though my life depended on it.

I remember thinking: this is utter madness, why am I kissing him? Why? And whilst we're on the subject, how come I also want to run my hands down his back and up under his shirt and . . . Oh! Aaahhhh! Mmmmmm! Bloody hell, Alex, how dare you be this irresistible?

Swish! His jacket came off and draped itself over the leopard-print broom I kept in the hallway by the coat rack – but neither of us really cared. By now, he wasn't just confining his lips to my mouth but had widened his attention to my neck, my jaw and my throat. As he did so, one of his fingers traced a lazy line along the palm of my hand and up over my wrist, and suddenly – yet again – came the image of him kissing Isobel in the crush of the crowd in Middle Temple Hall.

'Isobel,' I spluttered, pulling my mouth away from his collarbone (which I had accessed by pulling off his bow tie and undoing the top three buttons of his shirt). 'What about Isobel?'

Alex, his eyes closed, ran his hands through my hair and took my ear lobe fleetingly into his mouth.

I almost passed out.

'Isobel Schmisobel,' he said. 'Someone I knew about a thousand years ago; someone I have no intention of spending time with again if I can help it.'

Thank you, God!

His hand ran down the curve of my waist and he murmured: 'Tom?'

'Over,' I said. 'You knew that. You knew it before I did.'

'You and me?' His mouth was so close to my ear that I felt, rather than heard, his words.

'A bad idea.' I caught my breath as his leg nudged in between my knees. 'A very bad idea. All this kissing has to stop, right now, then you should go home, make yourself some cocoa or whatever it is you do after a night out, and we should never see each other again.'

Just to reinforce this point, I slipped a hand inside his shirt. Alex made a sort of gulping noise and I felt his leg wobble slightly.

'You really believe that?' he said, his lips now on my eyelids. *My eyelids!*

'Examine the evidence rationally.' I was forced by powers beyond my control to undo three more buttons on his shirt. 'We've only just met; we are totally unsuited; all we do is shout at each other, and if we make any more noise, my neighbour upstairs will kill you – and after that she'll do the same to me.'

'But apart from that?' His hand was sneaking up my back and gently tugging at my zip.

'Apart from that, I think you are the sexiest, most annoying, most gorgeous, most infuriatingly persistent man I have ever met, and . . .' I felt him slip the sleeves of my dress down over my arms and bury his face in my shoulder. 'Oh, for goodness' sake, just pull the whole thing off!'

For once in his life, Alex actually did as he was told and manoeuvred my dress down as far as my waist. Not wanting to be outdone, I pawed at the few remaining buttons on his shirt before triumphantly throwing it on to the ground next to the radiator.

What followed next was almost more than I could bear. Alex somehow managed to be urgent, gentle, passionate and considerate all at the same time, and after a year of Tom (who thought that seductive foreplay was a matter of remembering to remove his socks), I suddenly realised what all the fuss was about.

With a less-than-seamless grace, we stumbled over a pair of Mel's shoes before cannoning into the coat rack and sending its contents crashing on to the laminate beneath. Next we bumped against the bathroom door; and finally (more by good luck than design) we fell into my bedroom and landed heavily on top of my duvet – where Alex proceeded to whack his head hard against the wooden bedstead, making the walls judder and Mrs O'Linehan pound on the ceiling yet again. Then, to take his mind off the bruise that was rapidly appearing on his right temple, I undid the buttons on his trouser waistband and slid my hand inside the zip.

Even though I say so myself, his reaction was impressive. And after that?

I confess I wasn't really aware of anything apart from me, Alex and the fact that I wanted him more than I had wanted anything before in the whole of my life. The loser-shaped hole that was all that was left of Tom; my worries about Mel; my fears for the future of my career – it all vanished. It was as though the entire cosmos, with its billions of star systems and all the infinite possibilities of creation, had contracted down to the two of us, a thirteen-tog duvet and a John Lewis king-sized divan.

'Laura?' Alex rolled over and ran his hand softly over my breastbone, my naked stomach and down across the top of my thigh, making me shiver with delight.

'Mmmm?' I twisted my body around his and propped myself up on his chest.

'You know what you said about me not coming into your flat?'

'Uh-huh?' Had that been me? It felt like a lifetime – not to mention several alternative universes – ago.

'Only if you want to pretend that I *didn't*, I've got about fifteen minutes till the last tube leaves.'

'I see,' I said slowly. 'And what if I've changed my mind?'

'Then we've got' – he glanced at my bedside clock – 'about seven hours to go until breakfast.'

'That's quite a long time,' I murmured.

Alex lifted his face and kissed me, and I sensed a subtle change in the chemistry between us.

'It *is* a long time,' he replied, and slid his arms round my waist, pulling me back down on top of the naked warmth of his body. 'Although something tells me it's not going to be long enough.'

'Then we'd better make the most of it, hadn't we?'

And that's exactly what we did.

I woke up the next morning with a big fat smile on my face. For a bleary-eyed moment or two I wasn't sure why I was feeling this upbeat, but then came a rustle from the other side of the bed and I felt a mouth plant itself on the nape of my neck whilst a tall, muscular body dove-tailed around mine.

'Good morning, you.' Alex's voice was thick and heavy with sleep.

My smile wavered as the full implications of what had happened the night before swam into my pheromone-saturated brain.

I had slept with Alex Hodder, investigative journalist.

In fact, I had not merely slept with him, but enthu-siastically dragged him into my bed and kept him there, fully occupied, for a whole eight hours. This couldn't be explained away as a simple mistake, or youthful exuber-ance, or one too many glasses of wine the night before. This was something else – and as yet, I wasn't entirely sure what.

Whilst I was pondering my fate, Alex's hand wandered up my thigh and I caught my breath.

'Sleep well?' I asked, opting for some small talk, given that every other size of talk seemed to have temporarily deserted me.

'Eventually.'

He had a grin the size of Bedfordshire plastered over his face; there was no need to ask if he'd enjoyed himself.

'You know——' I began and then stopped.

Out of nowhere, a wave of heart-stopping vulnerability broke over me. The urgency of the night before had vanished and I now felt – literally and metaphorically – totally exposed. It was as though somewhere along the line I'd forgotten to put my skin on and I was running the risk of Alex being able to look right down into the depths of my soul, just as I could into his.

But before I could analyse where all this had come from, something else happened: far from continuing his exploration of my anatomy and reducing me to the gibbering mush of femininity that he had the night before, Alex cleared his throat nervously.

'I'm afraid something's come up,' he said.

There was a pause.

'It's all got a bit complicated.'

I turned my face away to try and hide my disappointment.

Oh no, I thought. He's about to tell me this was all a colossal mistake.

'You see,' he stroked my cheek and I held my breath, waiting for him to deliver the final blow, 'you see, Laura, I hate to mention it, but . . .'

He looked away and my heart sank still further, while a million unhappy predictions of what he was about to say careered round my head: he'd done it for a dare; he'd done it for a joke; he'd thought I was *a different* Laura McGregor with three porches, a Lear Jet and an island in the Caribbean; he'd——

But no!

'. . . I think I'm in love with you. I think I have been since you started yelling at me about lesbians in the restaurant.'

'Love?' I echoed faintly.

'I know, I know.' He shifted uneasily. 'And before you say it for me – I don't *do* love; at least I didn't used to. But you – I don't know – everything is just different. Overwhelming. Unnerving. Honest. Really quite scary. It took every ounce of courage I had to get into the cab with you last night.'

Well, I would never have guessed *that*.

So this was new, slightly uncertain territory for him as well. Sinking back against him, I rested my cheek on his shoulder.

'That makes two of us,' I said. 'This feels different, Alex, very different.'

His lips ran lightly along the dip between my jaw and my neck and his hand slid in between my thighs. My whole body fizzed and tingled like bubbles in a glass of champagne.

'The question is, Laura – is it good different or bad different?'

I rolled over and faced him, putting my arms round his neck.

'I think,' I said slowly, 'I think I'd say that different is good.'

'Different is bloody fantastic,' murmured Alex and shifted on to his side, pulling my body in against his. 'And I intend to enjoy being different for a very long time to come.'

He kissed me, a kiss that seemed to involve every single part of my body, from the soles of my feet up to the crown of my head. Then he gently ran a hand along the curve of my back, from my shoulder blades down as far as the tops of my legs, and that was it – I was a goner: once again, it was as if nothing else in the entire world existed apart from me, him and—

A little further down the hallway, a door opened.

Oh, shit! My mum!

My mum, who wasn't aware that I'd dumped Tom and spent the night in bed with a man I've only known for thirty seconds; my mum, who had her own key to the flat and could have let herself in *at any point* during the preceding night.

I pulled myself out of Alex's arms and scrambled out of bed.

'Laura?' He sat up and stared at me. 'What's the matter?'

'Um, nothing,' I said, dragging my dressing gown off its hook on the back of the door and shoving my feet into my slippers. 'Just need to go to the loo, that's all. I'll get you a cup of tea while I'm up.'

Bugger! I glanced at the clock. Nine thirty! Mum was a notoriously early riser and would probably have spent the last two hours wondering where the hell I was.

Alex grabbed my hand and tried to pull me back down on to the bed.

'I don't want tea,' he said in a firm, matter-of-fact voice. 'I want you. Preferably without any clothes on and preferably now.'

For a moment I wavered – then there was the sound of footsteps. I had to go – I had to!

'Pill,' I said, pulling my hand back as inspiration struck. 'I need to take my pill after last night I don't think we ought to be leaving anything to chance!'

Alex looked questioningly at the empty condom packet lying on the floor and then back at me.

'You can never be too careful,' I said, then pecked him on the cheek and disappeared out the door.

There were making-breakfast-type noises coming from the direction of the kitchen. However, as they were within the normal decibel range for such activities, I correctly deduced this was not Mel back early from Karen's.

'Oh, hello, darling.'

My mum was standing at the counter pouring boiling water into a couple of mugs. She was wearing the old dressing gown I kept in the spare room, but her own slippers. Her normally tidy bobbed hair looked as though she'd been letting the class hamster nest in it.

Something was *not quite right*.

Still, I mused, she'd had a late one at the conference – she was probably knackered and hung-over too. Takes one to know one.

'For me?' I asked, taking one of the mugs.

Mum's little round face looked startled.

'Oh yes,' she said, as though the idea had only just occurred to her. 'Yes, I made it for you.'

I frowned at her.

'If you did earmark it for Mel, then I can easily brew up another,' I said, thinking that I might be able to sneak back in to Alex whilst the kettle was boiling and explain that we found ourselves on Parent Alert Code Red.

'Mel?' my mother asked vacantly.

'Yes, your other daughter. She stayed over at her mate Karen's so that you could have the spare room.'

'Oh,' said Mum, her grasp on reality suddenly recrystallising. 'No, I haven't seen her. I don't think she's back yet.'

My tummy rumbled loudly and I wondered how many calories I'd burnt up during the night with Alex's help.

'Would you like a slice of toast?' I asked.

'What?'

'Toast,' I said, wondering if she was having some sort of prolonged Senior Moment. 'Hot, crunchy bread traditionally eaten at breakfast and served with butter and a variety of different condiments.'

'Um, no, no.' She looked round with a worried expression on her face. 'I'm not hungry.'

'Mum,' I threw two slices of wholemeal into the toaster and folded my arms, 'what is going on?'

'I don't know what you mean, darling.'

'Well,' I gestured at her, 'look at you: in nothing but a dressing gown, all jumpy, not wanting any breakfast . . . Something's the matter. Are you feeling poorly?'

My mother's expression brightened quite considerably.

'Yes,' she said, 'that's it. I'm not very well – up in the night, you know. I hope I didn't wake you.'

Bugger, bugger! If she'd been up and about, had she heard something?

'Um,' I said as casually as I could, 'did you – er – hear any funny noises last night?'

My mother looked positively horrified.

'No,' she said in a strange, tight little voice, 'I didn't hear anything. Nothing at all.'

Arggghhhhhhhhh. She had! She was just saying that to be polite! The idea that she might have inadvertently eavesdropped on me and Alex was so completely awful that I wanted to die on the spot.

'You see,' I stammered (I was such a crappy liar), 'there have been noises – um – from upstairs . . . the neighbours – Mr and Mrs O'Linehan. It's really embarrassing and I don't quite know how to tackle them over it.'

Even though the idea of Mr and Mrs O'Linehan getting down to a bit of mattress-surfing made me cringe like mad, the ruse worked and my mother let out a huge sigh of relief.

'Yes, of course, the noises must have been your neighbours. I hope they didn't wake you too.'

As my face was already scarlet from the exertion of lying so much in such a short space of time, I decided that one more wasn't going to make any difference.

'No,' I said firmly, 'I'm used to it. I slept. All night. Like a log.

'On my own,' I added, just for good measure.

'Right.' My mother nodded and then froze.

I followed the direction of her gaze and saw a jacket.

A man's jacket.

A man's dinner jacket draped over the handle of the leopard-spotted broom where it had been flung the night before.

I leapt like a gazelle in the direction of the offending clothing and clutched it to my bosom. Then I spotted Alex's dress shirt a little further down the hallway and scooped that up too. I tried to stuff it inside the lapel of my dressing gown but it just made me look strangely lumpy, so I took it out again.

'Um, it's a dinner jacket,' I said to Mum, whose mouth had zoomed into a 'now-then-young-missy-you'd-better-have-a-good-explanation-for-this' sort of pout. 'I wore one to the function last night – with a bow tie,' I added, not being able to remember at what point Alex had discarded his. 'It was fancy dress. In a cross-dressing kind of way.'

I cringed again. The idea of spending the evening with a bunch of transvestite bankers was even less palatable than the image of Mr and Mrs O'L getting frisky.

Mum regarded me through narrowed eyes.

'Really?' she said disapprovingly. 'I'd assumed the jacket was Tom's.'

'Ah,' I said. 'Ah, yes, Tom.'

Despite the fact that we'd been together for ages, Mum didn't seem particularly happy with the idea that Tom might have spent the night in my bedroom. I'd hoped that she would have guessed that at the grand old age of twenty-seven I was not still looking forward innocently to the magic of my wedding night – but apparently that was not the case.

Damn. That was going to make the subject of Alex all the more tricky to bring up.

'Mum,' I said boldly, deciding to break with recent tradition and tell the truth, 'Tom and I split up.'

Mum's narrowed eyes widened into concern.

'Oh darling,' she said, 'I'm so sorry. When did that happen?'

I let her give me a hug and a pat on the head.

'Thursday. And then last night he punched my boss in the face because he thought I was having an affair. Not that I am, of course,' I added hastily.

My mother's embrace tightened protectively round me.

'He seemed like such a nice boy,' she said sadly. 'Although, dear, you need to remember that all men are cads and bounders and the ones who pretend to be nice are usually the worst of the lot.'

'Er, thanks,' I said, wondering if any of this was supposed to apply to my dad.

'You know what they say, a woman needs a man like a fish needs a—'

She suddenly froze mid-sentence: it was as if someone had pressed the pause button – I couldn't even be sure she was still breathing.

Then I heard it too.

With its usual hideous creak, the bathroom door had opened and footsteps were making their way down the hall towards the kitchen.

Shit! Shit! *Shit!*

Gradually introducing my mother to the idea of me having a new boyfriend was one thing – for her to meet Alex out of the blue at nine forty-five on a Saturday morning while she was still in her dressing gown and he was probably wearing considerably less than that was quite another.

I put my hands over my face and prayed he'd had enough sense to put some clothes on.

As if in slow motion, the footsteps drew nearer.

Despite the fact that I was almost on my knees with panic, I forced myself to open my fingers a crack, and saw—

'Good grief! Who the heck are you?' I demanded.

A middle-aged man was standing in the kitchen doorway, my mother's familiar flowery dressing gown stretched protestingly over his pot belly.

The man smiled a ghastly smile.

'I'm Gerald,' he said, extending a podgy hand in a half-hearted sort of way. 'You must be Laura. I've heard ever so much about you.'

'Right,' I replied, trying desperately to remember the correct social etiquette for the occasion when your mother invites her lover back to your flat without warning you first.

My eyes were drawn helplessly to the inadequate coverage offered by the Japanese-style silk dressing gown. It was like a slow-motion car crash in a kimono.

'Good to meet you in the flesh – I mean . . . Right. Yes.'

I turned to my parent, who was trying her best to hide behind the fridge.

'Mum?' I asked weakly.

'Gerald and I – um – we've known each other since he became deputy head at my school three years ago. I sort of forgot to mention it.'

She trailed off into a shrug.

'Ah,' I said. 'Well. Yes. Of course . . .'

In that moment, I decided that the only thing worse than knowing that your parents had sex was finding out that they weren't having it with each other – and promptly slumped against the wall for support.

My slump, however, proved short-lived, as a loud rustling noise from my own room made me leap up as though I'd been stabbed with an electric cattle prod.

'What was that?' Mum asked.

'Birds,' I said quickly, all but sprinting down the hallway towards my room and praying I got there before Alex could make the gathering in the kitchen into a foursome. 'Or mice. In fact, I have a problem with both. The birds chase the mice and they make a rustling noise. Just like that, in fact.'

My mother and Gerald were looking blankly at me.

'I left the window open,' I cried, 'and they all got in. Stupid or what?'

'What sort of birds?' Gerald was following me down the hall. 'Must be pretty big ones if they're after the mice. You ought to get it seen to.'

'Yes,' I said, 'thank you. It's in the process of being investigated by the pest control people and—'

I dived into my room at the precise moment Alex was about to open the door.

'What's up?' he asked, hand outstretched towards the handle. 'I heard voices.'

He was wrapped in a towel that covered him from just below his waist to a fraction above his knees, and the moment I clapped eyes upon him, a series of seriously indecent thoughts sprang into my mind and my legs went wobbly.

'Nothing,' I cried, doing my best to bundle the thoughts away again. 'It's just . . . it's just – nothing, except – look, I didn't tell you last night, but my mother's staying.'

'Great!' Alex grinned. 'I'll have a shower, get dressed and then you can introduce me.'

'No,' I said, my head whirling as I remembered the special bonus horror that was Gerald in the dressing gown. 'Not right now; believe me – it's not a good moment.'

Alex's face fell.

'Why not?' he asked. 'We're all grown-ups. I'm sure it won't be as bad as you're imagining.'

'It will be fine.' I kissed him on the nose. 'It's – it's just a logistical thing. Give me a moment and I'll sort it out, I promise; but please stay in here for the time being.'

'You're not having second thoughts, are you?' he asked. 'I mean, of course you can if you want, but I'm not going to pretend it wouldn't hurt if you didn't feel the same.'

I shook my head and kissed him again. He was right; of course he was right: we were all fully consenting adults; there was nothing for me to worry about. It would just be better to do the explanations and introductions with everyone awake and fully dressed and my home not resembling the set of a Carry On film.

'So!' I walked breezily back towards the olds, who had taken refuge in the living room.

Think positive. Think politeness. Think how awkward they must be feeling. Make a pot of coffee so that we can all sit down and talk things over in a civilised manner.

'Anyone like a drink?' I asked.

As I stepped over the threshold, my mother and Gerald leapt apart and sat huddled at opposite ends of the sofa like a pair of guilty teenagers. However, he was now wearing a pair of trousers and a T-shirt (I was in a place where I needed to be thankful for small mercies), and I managed to force a smile.

'Coffee?' I said weakly.

'I've already made some.' My mother's grin was about as rictus as my own. 'Milk?'

I was saved the trouble of replying by an enormous bang, followed by a crash and a muffled oath.

'What was that?' my mother cried in alarm.

'Excuse me!' I legged it out the door, with Gerald once again hot on my heels.

'That's not birds,' he hissed, 'that's a burglar! He must have seen you leave your bedroom and then climbed in through the window. You can't go in there on your own.

Here.' He passed me the leopard broom and picked up a wrought-iron doorstop for himself. 'Take this and keep behind me.'

'No!' I cried. *Think fast; think really fast.* 'No – it'll be Mel. She does this sometimes. She has – ah – an irrational fear of doors. Much happier with a window – in fact, show her an open one and she's away trying to climb through before you know what's happening.'

Gerald's face was ashen.

'Is she having help?'

'Oh yes,' I said, realising the implications of the malady I had just foisted upon my only sister, 'therapy and stuff. She's much better than she was – now it's only houses where she knows the owners. But before' – I gave a hideous laugh – 'it was a nightmare!'

I slipped inside and shut the door quickly behind me. Alex was sitting on the edge of the bed rubbing his head.

'Boxer shorts.' He looked up towards the ceiling light, where the offending item of clothing was draped artistically round the flex. 'I fell off the bed and hit my head on that chair.'

'Poor Alex.' I kissed his increasingly bruised forehead and poked the shorts back down to earth with the end of my broom handle.

'Have you spoken to her?' Alex began to dress himself. 'Am I persona grata yet?'

'Give me a moment,' I replied, 'and you will be.'

Alex, in his pants, socks and a half-buttoned shirt, stood up and pulled me towards him. I inhaled the beautiful scent of his skin and felt his hand wander up inside the lapel of my dressing gown.

'In a minute,' I promised. 'Really.'

And I left the room. Once again.

Right! This time I couldn't put it off any longer. I was

going to march right on in there and tell Mum about Alex, and if she disapproved – well, bring it on.

Not that she had a leg to stand on, mind you, but a little thing like Gerald wouldn't necessarily stop her from speaking her *Daily Mail*-reading mind.

'Laura?' My mother's voice accosted me as I entered the living room. 'What's all this about Mel having a door phobia?'

'Oh, that,' I said. 'Can we talk about that later, only there's something I need to tell you and it's really important and—'

There was the clattering sound of a key in the lock and Mel, fresh as a daisy and showing no signs of her lately acquired door-based issues, waltzed into the room.

'Hey, Mum!' she called and then stopped dead. 'Uncle Gerald – what are you doing here?'

I watched as her eye ran to my mother's hand, which was now resting on Uncle Gerald's thigh.

'Oh fuck,' she muttered and collapsed into a chair.

'Language, Melissa,' warned my mother.

'You mean you knew about this and you didn't tell me?' I hissed.

Mel looked as though someone had just whacked her on the back of the head with a large plank of wood.

'I knew he came to unblock the sink and help Mum with her marking; I didn't know it was, well, all up close and personal.'

'I wasn't intending to bring Gerald back,' my mother said guiltily. 'But we both had a lot to drink at the course dinner last night and he saw me home and then we got a bit carried away. You know how it is.'

I could feel my face lighting up like a Belisha beacon as the words 'pot' and 'kettle' rattled round my head like bullets.

'So,' I seized the cafetière, 'anybody want a quick

one? I mean a quick *cup* – of coffee, obviously. Unless you've all had who you want – I mean *what* you want.' I paused; this was getting ridiculous. 'Gerald, what do you fancy?'

'Obviously he fancies our mother,' muttered Mel, a little unnecessarily in my opinion.

I was about to make my way into the kitchen, where I was planning to kill myself in private, when a voice stopped me in my tracks.

'I'd love a coffee.'

All heads swivelled round towards the doorway. It was Alex. Ruffled and looking a bit sheepish, with two of his shirt buttons missing and his hair all over the place.

My mother leapt off the sofa and backed away from him as though he was Banquo's ghost. Mel whistled under her breath and I almost dropped the coffee pot on to the cream carpet. The smile vanished from Alex's face and he gave me an odd sideways glance.

'You didn't tell her, then.'

'Tell me what?' squawked my mother. Pretty bad form, I thought, seeing as I'd had to deal with her boyfriend when he was wearing nothing but a hairy chest and a couple of yards of flowered silk.

'This is Alex,' I stammered. 'Alex Hodder.'

'I know that,' said my mother. 'The question is, what is he doing in your living room?'

'He's here because—' I began, before realising the full implications of her words. 'How on earth do you know who he is?'

My mother folded her arms and looked from me to Alex and back again. Her gaze was so stony you could have used it to tarmac a road.

'He's Tony Hodder's son. Ten years ago his father was supposed to drop off a cheque for ten thousand pounds from Tony that would have stopped *your* father's business from going under – only he didn't till it was too late. Do you think I'd forget a thing like that?'

I stared at Alex. Oh fuckadoodle – she was right. He had the same brown hair, the same dark eyes I remembered from the Rose and Crown a decade ago. How on earth could I not have made the connection?

'Alexander went to Oxford a couple of months later and I never saw him again – until now,' my mother continued. 'But I'd recognise him anywhere; he hasn't changed much.'

She said this as though it was a Very Bad Thing.

Alex swallowed nervously and shot me a glance.

'I meant to tell you,' he said. 'I was going to tell you.'

'I . . .' The ability to produce coherent thoughts and express them in the form of speech temporarily deserted me. 'I – ah – oh shit.'

The whole room was waiting expectantly for me to get a grip.

Only I didn't.

Firstly because my brain simply refused to absorb the information that Alex's family were (at least partially) responsible for the collapse of my father's business; and secondly because at that moment the doorbell went and Mel leapt from her ringside seat to answer it. I waited, my head reeling, to see who else would be adding their extra complications to the heady mix we already had going on.

'Oh, hello.' Tom wandered into the living room and scratched his nose thoughtfully. 'Maybe this isn't a good time to call.'

'Tom.' My mother flopped weakly down onto the sofa. 'What are you doing here?'

'Mrs McGregor,' he nodded at her, 'and Gerald.'

Did everyone know of this man's existence apart from me?

Tom turned to me.

'Gerald and I met on the golf course last time I went down to Wiltshire with you and – anyway, I came to apologise for that, um, small unpleasantness last night.' He paused for a moment and cleared his throat. 'I also wanted to tell you that I'm going to marry you.'

This time I did actually drop the coffee pot.

'Marry me?' I repeated, my gob feeling well and truly smacked. 'You want a *wedding*?'

'That's right,' he replied, slightly tetchily. 'I'll move in here like you said and we'll get married. Next summer, I thought, June or July – I'm easy.'

I boggled at him.

There were so many reasons why I wouldn't be marrying Tom in *either* June or July that I found it difficult to select just one.

'I can see how you might have been a bit upset about Will,' Tom continued, 'and to be honest I'm pretty gutted myself, because it means my chances of a job at SunSpot have been scuppered; but the important thing is that I'm willing to give you and me another go, don't you agree?'

'What if Laura doesn't want to give it another go?' Alex's voice cut through the stunned collective silence that followed Tom's declaration of intent.

'Don't be ridiculous,' Tom replied gruffly. 'Of course she wants to marry me. And anyway, who said you could stick your oar in?'

'Let's just say I'm an interested party,' Alex replied affably. 'Now, are you going to leave quietly or shall Gerald and I escort you to the door?'

Now it was Tom's turn to boggle: first at Alex; then at me; and then, when he saw I wasn't going to stick up for him, at my mum.

Thankfully he didn't seem to have placed Alex as the journalist who almost got him the sack.

'Tell him,' he commanded my mother, 'tell this man who I am.'

I managed to reconnect my brain to my tongue.

'You are my *ex*-boyfriend,' I said clearly and slowly in case he had any trouble understanding the concept. 'And I would like you to go away, please, and never ever come back.'

'But I've just proposed to you!'

'You have indeed – and the answer is no. I've come to my senses, Tom, and you and I are more over than spandex. Now do as you are told and leave.'

Suddenly Tom's face changed. He had been staring disbelievingly at Alex for a while, and now he went white and then pink and then puce, all in the space of about ten seconds, before he pointed an accusatory finger in the latter's direction.

'It's you!' he cried. 'It's you! The bloke off the telly – you did the piece that nearly sank Davis Butler. You're called Alex something – Alex Hodder!'

Then he went green and his voice dropped to something near a whisper.

'Bloody hell, *you* were the one on the phone to her on Thursday night!'

Alex nodded stiffly.

'Guilty as charged on both counts,' he said.

There was a pause during which Tom's eyes opened so wide I was amazed they were able to remain in their sockets.

'I don't believe it! Laura, for the love of God, please tell me you haven't been shagging the man who almost cost me my job!'

'Don't be ridiculous, Tom dear.' My mother was still in denial. 'That's Alex Hodder. Of course Laura wouldn't be sleeping with him.'

'Then why's he here?' Tom homed in on the weak spot

in her argument. 'And more to the point, why has he got a pair of her tights hanging out of the top of his trousers?'

As if in slow motion, the entire room focused once again on Alex and then on the offending item of hosiery, which, to be fair to him, was not actually attached to his waistband but was protruding slightly from his left-hand trouser pocket.

'Laura,' said Alex softly, after he'd handed me the tights, 'I think this needs to come from you.'

I looked at the five expectant pairs of eyes one after the other: My ex-lover, my new lover, my mother, my *mother's* lover, and finally my sister, who to her credit was not pointing her finger at me and rolling round on the floor hysterical with laughter.

But I couldn't do it.

I simply couldn't open my mouth and make the words 'I'm in love with Alex' come out of it. The burden of expectation weighed too heavily upon me.

'You know what?' I said instead. 'Right now I'm thinking I could do without the lot of you!'

Tom looked as though he was about to spontaneously combust.

'How could you humiliate me like this?' he blustered. 'I even rang your father in New Zealand to ask for his consent.'

'More fool you,' replied Mel with obvious feeling.

But I wasn't listening. Instead, I was staring at the spot by the door that until a moment ago had contained the man I wanted more than I had wanted anyone in my life, but which was now ominously empty.

I raced to the front door, and then to the door that opened on to the street, and sprinted a few paces down the road hoping to be able to call him back and say what was in my heart – but it was too late: Alex had vanished.

Feeling like a Cinderella who had managed to lose not

one but both of her glass slippers, I walked slowly back inside the flat. The mutual recriminations were just beginning. Mel was accusing Tom of being a capitalist pig and Tom was appealing to my poleaxed mother to try and talk some sense into me.

I didn't even bother to step over the living-room threshold.

Instead I returned to my bedroom, drew the curtains and threw myself under the duvet, wishing with all my heart that the events of this morning had never happened.

'Come in!'

It was seven thirty on Monday morning, and I pushed open the door to Will's office and made my way into the middle of the room. Will looked up from his computer screen and I noted the bruise that began on his chin and stretched halfway across towards his left ear. Immediately, Saturday's *It's My Family – Get Me Out of Here* episode seemed to lose some of its technicolour hideousness as I waited to find out if I was about to make it into the next set of unemployment statistics.

'I thought you'd probably want to see me,' I volunteered, and waited for the expected bollocking to commence.

Will put his hands behind his head and leaned back in his chair.

I put my hands in my pockets and prepared to take it like a man – or like a fast-track graduate member of the analysis team, anyway.

'Yup,' he agreed, 'I did. The feedback I've gotten from the hoedown on Friday says that we're on the right track but not home and dry. We need twice as many potential investors, otherwise we're sunk. Now, I know it's not normal analyst duties, but I want you to go get your head together with Isobel and come up with some ideas for selling this puppy based on what the pair of you dug up on Friday – that is, if she's got anything in that head of hers apart from air and designer perfume samples.'

I stood there, braced for him to mention something – anything – relating to the debacle after dinner and my unfortunate connection with it.

But he didn't.

'Will,' I said, keeping my voice as bold and authoritative as I possibly could, 'be straight with me: is my future here affected because of what Tom did?'

Will gave me a look that was impossible to decode.

'You're asking me if I hold you responsible for something that, as far as I am aware, you knew nothing about and had no control over – correct?'

Just tell me whether I'm going to be fired!!!

Will held my gaze for what felt like several millennia and then turned back to his computer screen.

'I don't,' he said at last. 'But the same doesn't apply to your boyfriend.'

'Ex,' I said through gritted teeth. 'Very, very ex.'

'Glad to hear it.' Something in Will's voice turned my blood positively sub-zero. 'Because if he ever comes within half a mile of me again, I shall personally make sure his life is not worth living. However . . .'

I gulped audibly: *what* was he going to say?

'Between you and me and *nobody* else,' Will's eyes burned blue over the top of his screen, 'if you ever felt you did want to look around for another job, it might pay dividends in the long run.'

Huh?

'Let's just say the picture here at the Chiltern might not be quite what it seems, but' – flames leapt from his eyes once more – 'if you so much as breathe a *word* of that to anyone, I will fire your ass so fast you won't know what hit you.'

He touched his bruise and winced.

'Sorry. Bad analogy. Now go make me some cash and you might not have to worry.'

I exited the office as quickly as I could. I lived to work another day.

As I sat down at my workstation and switched on my computer, I saw Polly coming out of the kitchen with two cups of coffee in her hands. She put one down on Archie's as yet empty desk and I watched as she ran her hand lingeringly over the padded back of his chair.

I waved her over: I hadn't seen her at all on Friday and I wanted the low-down about their date on Thursday.

'So,' I said, nodding in the direction of the steaming mug she'd left further down the room, 'things going well? And by that, I mean things you're not telling your mother about.'

She gave me a coy little grin.

'Actually,' she said, 'I've decided to take things slowly this time – you know, savour each stage as it happens.'

'Wow,' I said, impressed by her un-Polly-like levels of self-restraint. 'The Pope would be proud of you.'

'So he should be, seeing as I'm being a good Catholic girl – at least for now.' She smiled. 'Although I have to say that abstinence is proving even more of a turn-on than actually getting down to it. This celibacy lark is definitely hot stuff.'

'Right,' I said, thinking that maybe next time I'd give it a go.

If there ever was a next time.

If I didn't give men up as a lost cause and become the first nun in history to work in a major international bank.

'In fact,' Polly continued, her voice low and confidential, 'I've spent the past three days thinking about nothing else. And that's not all – watch!'

She sat up and cast her eyes round the room.

'Look,' she whispered, nodding in the direction of one of our younger colleagues. 'Georgia: she got laid over the weekend. And Mike too. Not Toby, though, poor chap – he and Claire must have had another row – but – eugh! No! Gross!'

'What's wrong?' I asked.

'Barney.' She pointed in the direction of our smarmy middle manager with his greasy hair and his shirt hanging out of his trousers. 'He got his leg over too.'

'Surely not?'

She nodded weakly, looking as though she was doing her best not to barf.

'You see, it's freaky, but *I can tell*; right now I am nothing more than one great big pheromone.'

Suddenly, the thought of Mystic Polls being able to sniff out my encounter with Alex made me shrink back into my chair with fear.

'Laura,' she asked, 'Laura, are you okay?'

I nodded weakly and bared my teeth in a sort of grin. Polly stared at me for a moment, her eyes narrowed and focused.

'No,' she said at last, 'not getting any rumpy-pumpy; just picking up dazed and confused.'

Well, it was a fair assessment of my state of mind.

'Oh, Laura.' Polly put her arm round me. 'I'm sorry, of course you're feeling bad about breaking up with Tom, and then I go opening my big mouth and—'

'It's fine.' I pinched the bridge of my nose and made myself take a deep breath. 'It is, really – I'm totally cool about Tom.'

The problem was, I wasn't also totally cool about Alex.

In fact, second only in the worry stakes to the thought that I might be for the high jump at work was the fact that I had rung him five times over the course of the weekend but heard nothing back. At first I'd just put this down to bad luck, but as Saturday night turned into Sunday, and then Sunday metamorphosed into Monday morning and there was *still* no response, things looked very bleak indeed. We had to talk, we had serious issues we needed to discuss – and if he didn't have the guts to pick up the phone and call me, we were pretty much over before we'd even started.

'I'm afraid that things got hideously complicated,' I whispered, deciding I might get some relief from unburdening myself. 'There was this guy at the do on Friday and, well, I discovered my mother hates him because his father was the person who caused *my* father's business to collapse, then Tom turned up and started proposing marriage, and then, after all that, I couldn't say out loud that I was in love with this guy so he buggered off and I haven't heard from him since. Not your ideal pre-Saturday-breakfast time scenario, really.'

'I can't pretend I understood any of what you just said,' Polly gave my hand a comforting squeeze, 'but it does sound horrible. We'll go for a drink later and you can tell me all about it in more detail.'

I nodded and wiped my finger under my lower eyelid to check for mascara leakage.

'Look,' she continued, 'I don't mean to sound flippant, but if this bloke ran away *and* causes trouble between you and your family, do you honestly think he's worth getting upset about?'

I bit my lip; this was the sixty-four-billion-dollar question I'd spent most of the weekend stressing over.

'I hate to say it, Pols, but it didn't feel like a rebound thing; it was bigger than that. It's just with the 'my mother would like to shoot him and mount his head on a plinth in the hall' problem; and the 'me upsetting him and him running off" thing; and then the 'him not calling back' issue, I don't know if it would ever work.'

Polly glanced over her shoulder to where Archie the Magnificent had just seated himself at his desk. He twinkled at her. Polly looked torn.

'Go,' I told her, 'go and be happy. Only remember: no tongues in the office or I'll kill the pair of you with my bare hands.'

Polly slid off the desk.

'Sure you're okay?'

'Sure I'm sure. Now sod off.'

My words to Polly had displayed a bravado that I did not actually feel.

I swallowed hard in order to ward off any lumps in my throat that might feel like putting in an appearance, and then took a large swig out of the coffee Polly had forgotten to take with her.

Alex's absence from my life for forty-eight hours had hit me much harder than I could ever have imagined. It was as though he had removed one of my vital organs during our intimate exchanges on Friday night and taken it with him, leaving an emptiness right at the centre of my being. In contrast, my split with Tom felt strangely trauma-lite; the only side-effect was an overwhelming desire to kick myself for taking so long to get round to dumping him.

What was it that Alex had managed to do in the space of one short night that Tom had failed to achieve in an entire relationship? I simply had no idea.

I picked up my phone and my BlackBerry and checked for messages.

Nothing – apart from a text from my mother thanking me for having her and Gerald to stay; apparently they'd had a really nice time.

At least someone had, I thought grimly.

For the three billionth time since Saturday I sighed heavily. I couldn't go on like this. I'd batted a volley of conciliatory balls into Alex's court and now it was time for him to hit one back; if he didn't, well, then I was simply going to have to accept that this was the end of the line. After all, we'd only spent one night together, and however deep my feelings seemed to run, surely it wouldn't be *that* hard for me to get over him, get over myself and move on?

I pulled out my phone again and double-checked that there were no missed calls or unanswered texts in the four seconds since I'd last looked at it.

Unsurprisingly, there weren't.

I decided to send Alex one final text and tell him that if he didn't get back to me by close of play today then I would consider us well and truly finito.

I pulled out my phone and chose my words very carefully.

Pls call 2day if u want to try and work things out. L

There. Not desperate, not grovelly, not angry.

I put a little 'x' next to the L.

Then I deleted it.

I put the 'x' back once more.

And deleted it again.

Why was this so hard?

Then a thought struck me: what if he was out of the country on a top-secret journalistic mission and didn't get my text till Wednesday? What if he'd dropped his phone under the wheels of the number 73 and had no idea I'd been ringing? What if . . . ?

Oh crap. I couldn't go round issuing ultimatums. Instead, I'd unilaterally give him the week to get back to me, and if I still wanted to give it a go and he came up with a really good excuse for his telephonic silence, then we'd take it from there.

Or maybe we wouldn't.

After all, the fallout from my parents would be unbearable, and was I really sure I wanted a relationship with the son of the man who had ruined my dad?

But then again, wasn't I an adult capable of making my own decisions whether or not they approved? Or maybe . . .

Argghh!

My head started to pound with the effort of it all and I threw my phone back into my bag. Polly was right, the whole thing was truly horrible. What I needed to do was calm down and focus on something that didn't begin with 'a', end in 'x' and have an 'l' and an 'e' in the middle.

As if by magic, a thought sprang into my brain: I was under orders to get in contact with Isobel. As a way of distracting me from Alex, she was of course not ideal, but she was better than nothing. So before I could begin to get worked up over the Middle Temple kiss, I quickly dashed off an e-mail to her as per Will's instructions and then wondered what to do next.

Until she got back to me, I didn't actually have anything outstanding for SunSpot. I did, however, have a report to finish on the growth of economy supermarket ranges within the grocery sector – but as that was so completely tedious that I would rather have eaten my own hair than spend any time on it, I looked around for something else to occupy my one-track mind.

I sneaked another look at my BlackBerry.

Nothing.

I got my phone out of my bag and checked that I had the incoming text alert switched on.

Of course I did.

I drummed my fingers on the desktop, glanced over at Polly, who was laughing loudly at something Archie had just said, and willed Alex to text me back.

Pleasepleasepleasepleaseplease!

Then, out of the blue, I remembered the weird trade I'd seen for the Gisela hedge fund the week before and decided I could kill a few minutes by having another look. This was exactly the sort of thing I needed to divert my brain: figures, numbers and money, all completely rational and one hundred per cent emotionally neutral. I could even pretend it was real work. I clicked on the SunSpot logo, entered my password and in an instant the recent closing figures sprang on to my screen: all extremely impressive stuff.

Of course, Will's profit margins were *supposed* to be good, but I was aware from SunSpot propaganda that this had not come about without some calculated risk-taking. Where other investment companies had looked for a safe harbour amongst the storm-tossed financial seas, SunSpot had hauled up its anchor and set a course for the eye of the hurricane; when others had been issuing profit warnings, SunSpot was uncorking the Krug and flicking through its Ferrari brochure. The continued success was almost unbelievable.

But how?

Had they simply got lucky? Did they have a keen eye for spectacular investments? Or were they secretly more cautious than they liked their competitors to think?

And where, in this picture of unrelenting über-performance, did the trade fit in?

I wanted to know very much indeed.

I clicked on the Gisela fund, and then an icon on the toolbar labelled 'profit and loss'. This, I hoped, would take me back down into the microworld of the fund, where I would be able to see the nitty-gritty of the accounts.

A box appeared on my screen demanding a password.

This hadn't happened last time because Will had e-mailed the files over to me. I went into my inbox, but— Damn! He'd asked me to delete them when I'd finished using the data, and stupidly, I'd done just that.

I turned my attention back to the password box, which was still sitting in the middle of my computer screen. This was now my only way in. Obviously I didn't want to enter my own password – even if I'd thought for a moment that it would grant me access to the inner sanctums of the SunSpot trades. I racked my brains for an alternative – and typed in BARTON.

Nothing happened.

I did a bit more brain-racking. What would Will use as a password? His university – Yale?

No go, amigo.

Then inspiration struck. I remembered his enthusiasm for the Met – now what was it he had seen? Mozart? Puccini? No – *La Traviata.* I typed in 'Verdi' and – ping – I was through.

She shoots! She scores!

Er . . .

Feeling as conspicuous as if I'd jemmied open a safe in full view of everyone in the analysis department, I glanced round. Fortunately, however, the words 'I am snooping around Will Barton's database' did not seem to have been written in large, flashing neon letters across my forehead, and my colleagues were quietly getting on with their own work.

Phew.

I clicked on the same icon I'd used before, and found myself back down on the level of the individual trades. I double-checked the fifteenth of August last year (which was still insisting it had turned a profit) and then randomly skipped forward a couple of months to November to see if anything similar was lurking in the run-up to Christmas. Here I got a second, equally nasty surprise: there was a large profit recorded for a trade on the twenty second of November.

Now, that would have been all fine and dandy, had I not known that the twenty-second of November had been a Saturday. And I was aware of this because it was my mother's birthday and I had spent the day in Bournebridge, refereeing between a self-righteous Tom and a bellicose Mel at her birthday tea.

And that was not all: trawling on through the pages and pages of data, I was able to spot another profit registered for the Sunday after the twenty-second, and one for a Saturday in the middle of January.

One or two might be taken as mistakes, but three? Three was beginning to look a bit too much like a pattern.

I scrolled down the list of other funds, randomly accessing the trading data, and quickly found one or two weekend trades for each of them, plus a couple of deals that I *knew* could not have turned a profit but were listed as having done so.

It wasn't looking good; not good at all.

The way these irregular figures were littered through the accounts told me they weren't innocent mistakes; it was more organised than that. I had a horrible suspicion that they had been deliberately placed to look random, to appear as cock-up rather than conspiracy; and I was beginning to wish I'd never set eyes on them.

I closed the accounts down and sat for a moment staring at the blank screen, my brain buzzing. What the hell was going on?

My immediate instinct was to grab my phone, dial Tom and ask him how his trading accounts worked on a day-to-day basis.

But I wasn't that desperate.

My next idea was again to grab my phone, but this

time contact Alex and ask him what he thought about it all.

But – naturally – that was an even worse idea than ringing Tom.

Instead, I took a deep breath and pulled myself together. I needed to get real. SunSpot was a multi-million-pound company floated on the London Stock Market. It *had* to be all legit and above board: the books would be checked by a million accountants – not to mention the Inland Revenue and goodness only knew who else. Any sign of malpractice would be taken very seriously indeed – and Will was way too experienced to put up with any trouble on his patch.

Then a particularly nasty thought struck me: maybe Will himself was authorising whatever it was that was going on.

I pictured him in his designer office with his Monet and his solid gold Rolex: blond-haired, intense and very determined. Was he a crook?

I shook myself. No, he was an appallingly successful trader and had been so long before he'd arrived at SunSpot. There would be no way he'd jeopardise his reputation for the sake of a few stupid funds; that would clearly be bonkers. And besides, I had no evidence that anything dodgy *was* actually happening – no money seemed to be going out of the funds, only being deposited into them at times when it shouldn't have been. Maybe it was simply down to bad paperwork or inaccurate data management?

But right at the moment when I had just about convinced myself that I could relax, the words that Will had sworn me to secrecy over earlier that day rang through my brain like a clarion call: *the Chiltern might not be quite what it seems*. Could the weirdness in the SunSpot accounts be anything to do with this? I simply didn't know.

So until I had a clue what I could actually *do* about any of this, I made an executive decision to add it to the rapidly expanding list of 'Things Laura Doesn't Want To Think About' and opened up my report on supermarket economy ranges.

By twelve o'clock the next day there was still no word from Alex; and to add insult to injury, I spent the intervening hours of darkness plagued by dreams of him telling me that he was fiddling the SunSpot accounts – and he didn't even have the decency to turn into Robert Pattinson when he'd finished.

I struggled in to work with bags under my eyes the size of shipping crates and the twin problems of AWOL Alex and the SunSpot accounts still batting round my head like moths in a lampshade.

However, on a more positive note, it was Claire's birthday and she'd brought in fresh cream doughnuts, so it wasn't all bad.

I was sitting at my desk mopping up the doughnutty crumbs with the tip of my finger and contemplating a note I'd found that morning half hidden under the communal front doormat at home. It was a scrappy piece of lined paper that looked as though it had been ripped from a school exercise book, and written upon it in thick, uneven capital letters were the words:

WE NOW WERE UR.

I found this puzzling. Not simply due to the many lexicographic incongruities jostling for prominence in such a short sentence, but because I didn't have a clue what it was on about. Who, pray, were 'we'? How could anything be both 'now' and 'were'? Was 'UR' text-speak for 'you are', or was it a reference to the eponymous Sumerian city built five thousand years ago on the banks of the Euphrates river? And if it was the latter, did that mean I was being pursued by a bunch of dyslexic archaeologists?

I turned it upside down and tried to see if it made any more sense.

It didn't.

I folded it up and put it in my handbag and got back to work. Will had passed me a press release for Dresda and asked me to double-check some of the factual details for him (again, not really my bag, but I wasn't about to argue). As my screen was going to be full of numbers anyway, I had decided I would also take the opportunity to have another peek at the SunSpot accounts to see if I could find anything that would put my mind at rest.

I glanced around me – Polly was busy with a deadline, and most of the others were in a meeting. The coast was clear. I went into the SunSpot database, brought up the little password box and had got as far as typing in the letters 'VE' when—

'Hello, Laura.'

My hand hit the 'close' icon faster than you could say 'guilty secret'. It was Isobel.

'Hi,' I said, pulling up a random spreadsheet on to the screen and hoping that she wouldn't quiz me about it. 'How's things?'

'Fabulous, thanks.'

Isobel drew up a chair and tucked her slim, perfect legs demurely underneath. She looked like a cat that had acquired some rather superior cream.

'I had a simply wonderful time at the function,' she continued, giving me a quick sideways glance under half-lowered lashes.

I could tell she was itching to tell me something, but as Friday night was not top of my list of favourite conversation topics, I kept shtum, thinking that if she had any sensitivity, she wouldn't pursue the subject either.

'So tell me again, who was that chap who smacked our darling Will in the chops?' Isobel purred. 'Some star-crossed lover of yours? I have to say he was rather a dish – if a little too handy with his fists.'

Obviously my expectations had been too high.

'Shut up, shut up *now*,' I muttered under my breath, making a great play of adding bits of fake data to my spreadsheet. Then I added out loud: 'Is there anything I can help you with, or did you just drop by to make me a coffee – because if you did, the answer is "yes please, one sugar".'

Isobel giggled a brief but mirthless giggle.

'You are funny,' she informed me. 'Although you do need to understand that I don't *do* kettles.' She picked an imaginary piece of fluff off her immaculate skirt. 'No, I popped over because of our little lunch date, sweetie – don't you remember?'

It all came flooding back. Oh yes, *that* lunch date: it had been me who had requested her presence. I almost felt a bit mean about the coffee jibe.

'Anyway,' Isobel leapt to her Louboutin-clad feet and clapped her hands together like an enthusiastic (but expensively dressed) kindergarten teacher, 'chop-chop, let's go. I'm starving!'

'Really?' My eyes widened with surprise. Isobel had struck me as the slim, willowy type who didn't eat more than once a month. 'I mean, yes – let's!'

I closed down my computer and put my new bag over my shoulder. I had purchased it at the weekend with birthday money from my dad and the guilt money my mother had pressed into my palm just as she was leaving, 'in lieu of paying for a hotel room'.

Isobel surveyed me critically.

'Where did you get that?' she asked, pointing at the bag as though it was some sort of dangerous animal.

'L.K. Bennett,' I said warily, running a protective hand over its precious surface. 'It was in the sale.'

To my astonishment, Isobel's eyes widened enthusiastically.

'Isn't that place *marvellous*?' she cried. 'The clothes are so cheap you can wear them once and then throw them away! I'm a huge fan.'

'Riiiight.' I wasn't particularly thrilled about this endorsement of my beloved shopping location – although I decided it might be to my advantage to find out where she lived and go through her bins every so often.

'Anyway, Lauren,' Isobel continued, 'there's something I need to talk to you about. Come on!'

And she slipped her waif-like arm through mine and steered me over towards the lifts before I could say 'cheese-and-pickle-sarnie.'

The Screwdriver's canteen (oh, the inadequacy of that word!) was situated in the basement. In fact, the entire floor was one big cathedral dedicated to the worshipful consumption of food. Deep beneath St Andrewgate, we had the choice of a Pret A Manger, a Starbucks, a Burger King, a Marks and Spencer, two Benjy's and a Wagamama as well as classic French, Indian, sushi, Chinese and Thai eating areas. There was also a juice bar, a bakery, a place that served delicious-looking salads and a fish and chip restaurant. We even had our own private Belgian chocolate shop. The whole place was of the magnitude that villains in James Bond movies would have needed to build into their secret volcanic island bases to keep their private armies well fed and compliant.

And it was almost – but not quite – free.

My doughnut now only a distant memory, I grabbed a crayfish and rocket sandwich and a smoothie, was given change from a pound coin and then hooked up with Isobel, who was sitting at a table grasping a clear plastic cup with a straw sticking out of the top. It contained a dull greenish-brown liquid that looked as though it had been scraped from the surface of a rugby field.

'Antioxidants,' she explained, taking a small, ladylike sip. 'They increase your life expectancy.'

I smiled politely, deciding that twenty extra years with a free bus pass was inadequate compensation for drinking something that looked as though it had already been through somebody else's digestive tract.

'I know what you said in your e-mail,' Isobel stopped sucking and leapt in before I could finish my mouthful, 'but can we put SunSpot on hold for a while? The most amazing thing has happened and I simply *have* to tell you about it.'

I would rather have eaten a puppy panini in the show-ring at Crufts than listen to Isobel's news, but knew I was cornered and gave in gracefully.

'Shoot, girlfriend,' I said after I'd swallowed my bite, 'tell me how it's hanging.'

Isobel stared at me for a moment as if I'd gone bonkers, and then smoothed down her jacket and leaned in confidentially over the table.

'Well, strictly *entre nous*, of course, it's about a chap. I was with him in an off-and-on sort of a way for a while. We first met at Oxford, although we only got together *properly* a couple of years later.'

'You went to *Oxford*?' This came out with slightly more incredulity than I'd been planning.

'Did I say "at"?' Isobel continued vaguely. 'I meant "in". Anyway, it was all very hush-hush – he had a brilliant mind, terrific prospects, but Mummy was very much against it and said he wasn't good enough for me. In the end, I finished it and he was devastated.'

She sighed loudly, as if the remembrances of dumpings past still weighed heavily upon her.

'Oh,' I said in a small voice.

The idea of another human (even if it *was* Isobel) being upset by the ending of a relationship tugged rather at my heart.

'Well,' she stopped sounding upset and suddenly looked rather animated, 'here's where it gets interesting. I had a call from him out of the blue on Saturday afternoon and we decided to meet up later on that day – and let's just say things got a bit steamy.'

Isobel's eyes glowed briefly as she experienced some sort of uplifting flashback: it was the closest thing I'd seen to her exhibiting a real emotion.

'So you're back together, then?' I asked politely, hoping to steer the conversation as soon as possible on to profit margins and investment histories.

Isobel took an unintentionally loud slurpy-sip of the viscous liquid that constituted her lunch and dabbed the corners of her mouth with a paper napkin.

'Not officially,' she replied, allowing herself a bashful little smile, 'but even though it's early days, I have to say the signs are good. Although I wish he would hurry up and ring me.'

As the words 'ring me' left her mouth, an image of Alex, achingly gorgeous and languidly post-coital, socked me between the eyes and I felt myself swaying slightly in my chair. I looked down and found I was gripping the edge of the table so hard that my knuckles had gone white.

'I'm not boring you, am I?' Isobel slid a solicitous hand across the table and patted my wrist.

'No, no, of course not.'

With enormous effort I removed my hands from their gripping position and readjusted them around my smoothie cup.

'You see,' Isobel was leaning on her elbow, gazing wistfully into the middle distance, 'his feelings for me are powerful – primal – eternal!'

She paused.

'Not that he's actually *used* those words, of course,' her eyelashes fluttered on to her cheeks with the remembrance of that moment, 'but I felt love's destiny between us a long time ago, as he punted me up the Cherwell through the warm twilight of a summer's evening, with the green fingers of the willows dipping into the river and the swallows swooping overhead.'

'But . . . but you said you dumped him?' I put my finger on the fatal flaw in her argument, hoping it would distract her from the swallows, willows and destiny before I threw up all over the table.

Isobel sighed and poked her straw round the pond-slime in her cup.

'Mummy – and myself, obviously – had been concerned that he wasn't really *going places* with his career. And as I'm sure you understand, it is *so* important that one's husband,' she gave a nervous little giggle, 'one's *prospective* husband, is a high-flyer. However, a few weeks ago he had a major breakthrough, and he's now on the fast track to great things. I expect the little talking-to I gave him when we broke up has finally had an effect, and to win me back he's made the necessary adjustments to his life. It's called tough love, you know, Laura.'

The thought that all love involving Isobel was likely to be tough for the recipient skittered across my mind, but I kept my trap shut.

'So this chap, then,' I said, deciding I might as well

request the information she was bound to foist upon me anyway, 'what's his name? I can't keep thinking of him as "Isobel's Mystery Man".'

Isobel let out a deep, heart-rattling sigh.

'His name,' she repeated wistfully, as if it had special talismanic powers, 'his name is Alex. Alex Hodder.'

My right hand (which had been clamped round my smoothie) suddenly lost all of its grasping abilities and the cup slipped out of my lifeless fingers. It slid on to its side, sending a slick of mango and strawberry pulp glooping across the table towards Isobel. She gave a huge shriek and cowered back into her chair as though it was about to bite her.

I watched disconnectedly as the spillage wound its slow but inevitable path round the salt and pepper pots and my sandwich box, consciousness of a cold, numbing darkness working its way up from the depths of my stomach, through most of my vital organs and into my brain.

She was talking about Alex Hodder, the same Alex Hodder who on Saturday had told me he was in love with me. He couldn't be Isobel's long-standing boyfriend, he simply couldn't! Short of me slipping into a parallel dimension or him having a full brain transplant, there was no way he could protest his feelings for yours truly in the morning and then spend the night surrendering to his powerful, primal, eternal passion for her.

Was there?

There had to be some mistake.

'What if he's met someone else?' I blurted out the first remotely coherent thought that entered my mind.

Isobel smiled her cat-like smile.

'Well, I'm sure he hasn't been living like a monk since we broke up, but Alex is a one-woman man, and lucky me' – she stretched her long, perfectly manicured fingers out as she spoke – 'I happen to be that woman. Besides, I want him – and you have to understand, Laura, that I *always* get what I want.'

There was a something in her voice that sent an arctic shiver down my spine. Did she *know* Alex had spent Friday night with me? Did she just suspect? I had no idea.

Then, just when I was beginning to get very freaked out indeed (and my palms were sweating so hard you could have jet-skied across them), a ray of rather twisted hope shot through me. Could she be talking about a different Alex Hodder? After all, the Alex I knew was bold and adventurous and could talk his way out of any situation you cared to mention; he was a million light years away from the human lapdog Isobel's description conjured up.

I took a very deep breath and tried rather hard to make my voice sound like that of a disinterested observer rather than a screeching fishwife on the quay.

'So – this Alex bloke. You met him when you were at – sorry, *in* – Oxford?'

Isobel gave an almighty blush.

'I didn't actually go to university – although for goodness' sake don't tell Will. I might have been the teeniest bit creative with my CV.'

I couldn't care less if she'd awarded herself a PhD in Space Flight Propulsion from Harvard – at that moment, I only cared about Alex.

'But he did?' I stared down at the table, forcing my lungs to inhale air and willing my heart to pump oxygen round my body. 'And you're sure it was Oxford?'

'Yes.'

Okay, I said to myself (continuing to grasp tightly at my tiny straw), this proves nothing: there are probably a million Alex Hodders and some of them will even have degrees from Oxford.

More evidence was needed before I could officially despair.

'And where did he come from originally?' I asked, praying that she would say Aberdeen – or better still, somewhere like Adelaide or Santiago (a different continent would have been good right then).

'Oh, Hampshire or Wiltshire or some such place,' Isobel replied vaguely. 'I went there once and there were cows and fields and *things*. I can't say I paid too much attention.'

'Bournebridge?' I offered, the straw I'd seized upon looking more and more fragile with each passing second.

A light dawned slowly across Isobel's feature.

'Why, yes!' she cried. 'Do you know it?'

'I grew up there.' Getting each syllable out of my mouth took the effort equivalent to pushing a grand piano up Ben Nevis.

Isobel subjected me to a gaze so piercing that it could have lifted the lid off a tin of beans.

'What was your name again?' she asked.

'McGregor,' I mumbled, pretending to cough in order to muffle the syllables. 'Laura McGregor.'

There was a horrible pause that seemed to go on for ever; and then Isobel shook her head.

'No. He never mentioned you. But anyway,' she gave the pool of smoothie another accusing look, 'that's enough about me. What was it about SunSpot that Will wanted us to discuss?'

I found I couldn't respond: my last straw of hope had finally dissolved into dust. The man who had spent Saturday morning lying in my bed and saying he was in love with me had then spent Saturday evening doing pretty much the same thing with Isobel. He had known that the thought of an intimate relationship had frightened me – in fact, he had even 'fessed up to feeling the same way – but had inexplicably flung it back in my face by leaping into another woman's embrace only a few hours later.

The fact that he might or might not share fifty per cent of his DNA with the man who sank my dad paled into nothingness by comparison.

'It wasn't important,' I said, pushing my chair back and preparing to make my getaway. 'I'll send you a memo. Now, if you'll excuse me, Will needed me to finish some work for him by this afternoon, so I'd better crack on.'

'Of course!' Isobel beamed at me. 'Let's do this again soon – in fact, how about next Monday? I'm sure there will have been developments on the Alex front by then and I can fill you in. You know, I've been thinking – maybe this time he and I should just cut straight to the chase and get engaged. What's your opinion? Should I start dropping hints?'

But I had already turned away, biting my lip hard to ensure the pain levels were such that her words had no effect on me.

As I walked over to the lift, utter bewilderment was battling with a sickening feeling of betrayal. I waited for the doors to close, then screamed loudly at the top of my lungs all the way up to floor twenty.

12

I made my way home that evening with my head pounding. I had done my best to immerse myself in work and had ended up staying late to finish some material for a press conference about Dresda – again, way off my job description as a researcher, but essential to my aim of taking my mind off Alex. Only it hadn't worked.

Isobel.

Alex.

Alex and Isobel.

Isobel and Alex.

Whichever way I tried to look at it, the combination made my head swim and my stomach twist painfully.

The hope I'd briefly clung to that there might have been two Alex Hodders roaming across the surface of Planet Earth, and I'd had the good fortune to bump into the one not ensnared in Isobel's tentacle-like clutches, was long gone: her Alex was my Alex – or rather, he'd always been her Alex and never belonged to me in the first place. I was in the uncomfortable position of being the interloper, the Johnny-come-lately, into their long-running romance; and the effort of trying to come to terms with it all was doing my head in.

'Mel?' I called softly as I opened the front door. 'Mel? Are you there?'

No reply.

I went into the kitchen to get myself a large glass of water and a couple of paracetamols and found a note waiting.

At Karen's, it said.

My spirits sank even lower. I had been hoping for another heartbeat around the flat that night. By her own standards Mel had been rather nice to me following the Saturday-morning debacle, and I was contemplating spilling the beans to her about the true depth of my entanglement with Alex and gaining some much-needed sisterly succour.

Instead, it looked like it was just me on my lonesome.

I uncorked a bottle of wine, made a slice of toast for which I had no appetite, booted up my laptop and prepared to unburden myself to my diary. As the program loaded, however, an image of Isobel, all long legs and sleek blonde bob, parked itself right at the forefront of my brain and refused to budge.

I covered my face with my hands and did my best to persuade my mind to stop whirling.

I was angry and upset but overall bewildered. I could understand that Alex might have once fancied Isobel: she was attractive, intelligent (in her own, thankfully unique, way) and rich – in fact most blokes wouldn't even have bothered looking beyond the first of those attributes – but I also had a feeling in my bones that she wasn't the woman for him. Whatever might have propelled him to pick up the phone to her on Saturday afternoon, the thunderbolt realisation that his role in life was to be Isobel's poodle-like consort could not possibly be at the bottom of it.

I thumped the cushion next to me in sheer frustration, but even that didn't help; in fact, all it achieved was to release a cloud of dust, which made me sneeze loudly and drop toast crumbs all over the floor. I took a very large swig of wine, flexed my fingers and began typing away as hard and fast as I could, hoping to draw my feelings out of my mind and trap them in the electronic pages of my journal.

I had no idea what time it was when I actually heard the noise.

After finishing my diary session, I lay for a very long time on the sofa gazing at the ceiling and picking at my fast-disintegrating nail varnish. I must have spent at least a couple of hours in this pick 'n' stare zone as I pondered Alex and Isobel – obviously one of the universe's eternal pairings, up there with Lennon and McCartney, Fred and Ginger and yes, even Ant and Dec – before I realised that if I was to achieve anything constructive the next day, I had better go to bed.

The only problem was, I was too wound up to sleep.

I embarked upon a plan to lure my reluctant body into the land of nod: a shower and a body scrub with a lavender and ylang-ylang concoction of Mel's that boasted almost supernatural levels of slumber-inducing relaxation. That way I would be rested and hopefully able to deal with whatever tomorrow might be planning on flinging in my direction.

I scrubbed and I rinsed and I sang 'Tragedy' by the Bee Gees very loudly indeed, and once the ablutions had been completed, I did feel a little calmer and began to hope I might be at last heading for some shut-eye. In order to clinch the sleep situation, I decided to dry my hair, make myself a cup of hot milk and read a book I had found under the bed called *The Lighter Side of Macroeconomics* until my eyelids couldn't help but close. So there I was, duly cleansed and standing in front of my mirror wearing PJS, dressing gown and fluffy cow-print slippers, and with my hairdryer in my hand – when the front door creaked slightly and then banged open, and a voice somewhere at the other end of the hall breathed a barely audible '*Shit!*'

Bloody Mel, I thought grumpily; couldn't she do anything quietly?

But almost immediately something sixth-sensey kicked in and whispered that things were not as they seemed, and the most enormous shiver erupted from the tips of my toes and rose through my spine until I swear that the hairs on the top of my head were standing on end all by themselves.

I'd turned all the lights in the flat off apart from the small table lamp in my bedroom; but the kitchen light didn't flick on and all hell break loose as my sister made herself a midnight snack. Instead there was the sound of light footfalls making their way tentatively into the living room, then into the kitchen and finally – and terrifyingly – down the hall towards me.

Despite the best efforts of the lavender/ylang-ylang body-scrub combo, I think I was more awake than I had ever been in my entire life, including the time during my A levels when I knocked back a whole packet of ProPlus and didn't sleep for a week. My eyes were virtually out on stalks; my ears were on full alert; and even my skin had become supersensitive – with every breath of a draught, every tiny change in the air pressure around me registering on my goose pimples.

Whoever it was continued down the hallway towards my bedroom.

I held my breath and waited.

The footsteps stopped.

They moved three paces to the right.

Then they stopped again.

Finally, after a pause that could have lasted anything from ten seconds to twenty years, whoever it was turned the handle of Mel's bedroom door. There was an almost imperceptible 'click' as the catch retracted, then silence for a couple of moments, followed by the tiniest sound imaginable as the door swung open on its hinges.

As it did, something snapped inside me.

Even though a millisecond previously I had been frozen with terror, the almost imperceptible noise of the opening door broke the spell, and I felt the angry strength of a lioness defending her territory welling up inside of me.

(Actually, make that two lionesses, or possibly even more – in fact, if there had happened to be any antelope hanging around my bedroom just then, they should have been feeling very anxious indeed.)

With industrial quantities of adrenalin surging through my system, I ripped my hairdryer out of its wall socket and reached under the bed for the cricket bat. Then, in true cop-drama style, I positioned myself behind my bedroom door and aimed the hairdryer, gun-like, round into the hall.

'Halt!' I yelled, momentarily metamorphosing from Charlie's Angel into Robin Hood. 'Who goes there?'

I didn't bother to wait for a reply and rattled my weaponry aggressively against the door.

'I am armed and dangerously insane!' I shouted. 'I am coming out in two seconds and will shoot on sight. All previous intruders have been killed and buried under the floorboards.'

I paused for breath. There was complete silence from the hall.

'I also have a huge dog,' I added and made a scrabbling noise on the inside of the door with my fingernails whilst yelling: 'Down, boy!' as loudly as I could.

Outside Mel's room I heard a thin, weaselly voice cry: 'Oh 'eck!' in a broad Bristol accent, then there was the sound of footsteps running hell for leather back up the hall.

I exited my room in hot pursuit, waving my fake-gun hairdryer at a short, weedy individual who obviously wasn't keen on hanging around to introduce himself. The pair of us sprinted out of the front door of the flat, through the little communal lobby beyond and out into the garden, whereupon (with an athleticism that belied his scrawny build) he vaulted over the low boundary wall and was gone.

I ground to a halt in the space where the front gate should have been (had I ever bothered to get one) and watched him race off into the darkness. For a second or two I contemplated haring after him, but he had too much of a head start for me to ever have a hope of apprehending him. Besides, the night was cold and a strong, squally breeze was whipping off the river a couple of streets away.

Thinking that I needed to get inside as quickly as possible to (a) ward off hypothermia and (b) ring the rozzers, I had turned back to make my way down the path when – bam! An almighty gust of wind seemed to come out of nowhere and the front door slammed shut.

I ran up to it and rattled the handle. Then I tried shouldering it open. Then I inserted one of the pins from the hairdryer plug into the lock and did my best to force it to turn.

After that, admittedly more out of mounting despair than from any rational belief that it would help, I hit the door hard with my cricket bat – several times – which made me feel a bit better but didn't do much for the paintwork.

Finally I threw down my weapons, clenched my fists and yelled in loud frustration at the heavens.

I looked guiltily up at the first-floor flat, expecting to

see Mrs O'Linehan throwing open her window and giving me a piece of her mind— Hey! That was it! Even if it was just to silence my howls, she would come down and let me in. The front door to my flat was open – it was only the communal entrance that was locked.

But despite the fact that I screamed louder than a banshee at a Beatles concert, the O'Linehan residence remained dark and quiet. Rats and double rats! They must have gone away for a few days.

I sank down on the doorstep in despair. I was locked out of my flat with no keys, no phone and no money. My only possessions were a beaten-up cricket bat and a Tesco Value hairdryer, and I was wearing nothing but a fluffy bathrobe, cow-print slippers and Winnie-the-Pooh winceyette pyjamas. And to cap it all, my adrenalin rush was falling away, and my hands were starting to shake.

Things were not looking good.

A piece of litter was blowing round at my feet and I reached out and picked it up. To my astonishment, it was the same cheap paper and laborious handwriting as the note I had discovered half hidden by the doormat earlier.

WE NOW UR HERE GIVE US THE MONEY, it said.

The meaning of this badly constructed sentence smashed into my brain with the force of an intercontinental ballistic missile: it hadn't been meant for me. Sure, I owed money, but this wasn't how the student loans people or my credit-card providers reminded their valued customers to pay up; this was the hard, mean end of the loans market, peopled not so much by the sharks of the financial world as the piranhas, willing to strip their victims of everything they could call their own – sometimes including their lives.

And one of these creatures had just forced his way into my flat at midnight.

For a moment the wild thought struck me that it might

be the O'Linehans he'd been after – but as I knew from the post on our shared front doormat that they had no credit cards and an awful lot of savings accounts, I decided it was unlikely they would have enlisted the services of a usurious and probably violent finance company in order to subsidise their modest lifestyle.

No, the notes had been meant for Mel, and I could have kicked myself for not realising it as soon as I'd found the first one. She'd run away from Bristol not to avoid her Visa bills, but to escape the scary men wanting to rearrange the position of her kneecaps. It also explained why Gobshite was so keen to track her down: they'd obviously paid him a visit too.

And she hadn't told me.

She'd waltzed into my home, raided the fridge and forgot to mention there were men out there who might want to kill her.

At that moment I heard a loud cracking noise that was probably a car backfiring a couple of streets away, but to my frazzled brain it sounded rather too much like gunfire. I leapt up, tripping over my hairdryer in the process, and ran hell for leather in the direction of Fulham Palace Road, the note carefully ensconced in my dressing-gown pocket: if Mel's friends were on the warpath, I didn't want to be sitting around on my front step waiting for them to call back.

With my bravado fading fast and my legs shaking, I ran to the end of my street and looked wildly up and down the main carriageway for a means of escape.

'Taxi!' I screamed, running out into the road and waving my arm hysterically at the oncoming vehicle with an orange light blazing away above its windscreen.

It pulled up and I threw myself into the safety of the back.

'Drive!' I said. 'Please, just drive.'

With a shrug of his shoulders, the cabby pulled out into the stream of traffic flowing west and we hurtled towards the bright lights of civilisation.

I pulled my knees up to my chest and wrapped my arms round them, hugging myself into a tight little ball and staring out of the window at the blur of street-lighting whizzing past. How could she? How could Mel put both of us in so much danger? I didn't think for a moment that her loan-shark buddies would scruple to come after me if they thought I'd be good for a quid or two; and seeing as the chances of my sister actually having the readies to pay them back was about the same as her applying to work for Will as a hedge-fund trader, that meant I was directly in the firing line.

Hmmm . . . bad choice of phrase, I decided and shuddered violently.

'Where to, love?' The cabby interrupted my unhappy thoughts.

We were driving along a street that looked suspiciously like the King's Road, although my state of mind was such that it could have been anywhere north of the river and I wouldn't have noticed. Where to go? Polly? Tom? Will?

'Islington,' I said at last, remembering Mel's note. 'Number six, Duncan Road.'

This sounded familiar. I didn't have any exact recollection of Mel telling me Karen's address, but who else did I know who lived in that part of London?

'Fine.' The cabby gave a deep sigh, did a three-hundred-and-sixty-degree turn to the annoyance of every other motorist on the road, and sped off back the way we had come.

I, however, barely registered the honking horns and angry flashing headlights. Instead I sat huddled on the back seat and wondered what the hell I was going to do.

Although I'd never met any loan sharks before, I was willing to bet they wouldn't be up for a nice little chat with Mel's debt counsellor and then happily accept four pounds fifty a week in part payment. They were much more likely to be interested in smashing my windows and taking my microwave, and if that didn't cover it – well, I didn't really want to think about what they might have in mind as a back-up plan.

However, worse – much worse from my point of view – was the fact that my lovely little flat had been transformed in the blink of an eye from my haven from the big bad world into a place where scary, ruthless men might at any moment pitch up unannounced. Mel had, at a stroke, managed to deprive me of the one piece of security I had worked so hard to provide myself with.

'Duncan Road, love. That'll be twenty pounds.'

The cab drew up beside an unfamiliar pavement. On the far side of it, illuminated by the glow from a wrought-iron street light, was a low wall with black railings, and behind that, a row of elegant Georgian terraced houses. It didn't look like the sort of place any friend of Mel's would have a pad.

'I – I . . .' I clung to the handle above the door. 'I don't know if this is the right address.'

'Twenty pounds, please,' said the cab driver firmly.

'I may have made a mistake,' I bleated.

Where had Mel told me Karen's abode was – Darnborough Street? Duncan Terrace? Darkside Lane?

The cab driver heaved himself out of his seat, came round to the back and opened my door. I was about to be evicted from my taxi out on to the mean streets of Islington without a penny to my name and no proper clothes.

'But I don't have a clue where I am,' I said.

The cabby gave another heavy sigh.

'You're at number six, Duncan Road, like you asked for.'

'But I don't know who lives here!' I was on the verge of tears.

Just then, however, light splashed over the freezing March pavement and I heard the sound of a sash window being thrown open.

'Everything all right?' called a familiar voice.

For a moment I felt utter relief: I was going to be okay!

Then I realised who had spoken, and my spirits sank right back down into my fluffy cow-print slippers.

The window slammed shut, and after a moment or two there was the sound of a front door swinging open and feet pounding up stone steps from basement to ground level. The cabby stepped back and I was forced to look my unwitting saviour in the face.

'Laura!' Alex exclaimed. 'What on earth is going on? What's happened?'

Before I could protest – or, better still, give the cabby directions to turn straight back round and head for Hammersmith – he had thrust a bundle of notes at the driver, hauled me out of the back seat and was leading me down the steps towards his still-open front door. I heard the taxi pull away and my legs almost gave up entirely, threatening to leave me sitting helplessly on the cold stone stairs.

How, exactly, could my life get any worse?

'Can you get me a blanket,' Alex yelled to an unspecified other occupant as we crossed the threshold into a wide tiled hall. 'And stick the kettle on!'

My spirits sank even further – probably down as far as the floor joists. *That* was how it could get worse: I was about to come face to face with Isobel.

For a moment I considered pulling myself free of lex's arms and making a bolt for the door, but as he had a pretty strong grip round my waist and my shoulders, I didn't think I'd be able to pull it off. So instead I allowed myself to be manoeuvred into a large, friendly living room and deposited on a wide, squishy leather sofa.

'Laura.' Alex was on his knees in front of me, holding my shoulders in his hands and staring into my face. 'Are you okay? Has someone hurt you?'

Before I knew it was happening, he slid his thumb gently down the side of my face and kissed me lightly on the cheek. I stared at him as though he'd just suggested we make love on the delicatessen counter at Tesco.

'Sorry,' he muttered, looking embarrassed, 'I didn't do that. Forget I did that.'

Footsteps in the hallway made us both look expectantly up at the door. The thought of seeing Isobel – all post-coital tousled hair and possibly wearing not much more than one of Alex's T-shirts – was something I was profoundly *not* looking forward to, but the footsteps didn't sound very Isobel-esque. They were heavy, and the length of the stride in between them was long even for a girl whose legs started somewhere in the vicinity of her shoulder blades.

An olive-skinned, stubbly *male* face with black sticky-up hair and a faded scar that ran from the corner of his lip to his ear appeared round the door; followed by a thin, lanky body wearing mostly black.

'Here.' The newcomer held out a tartan picnic rug and a glass containing a large helping of amber liquid. 'Blanket and a brandy. Quicker than a cuppa.'

He flashed a dazzlingly white smile in my direction and threw the rug at Alex.

'Cheers, mate.' Alex caught it deftly and tucked it in round me. The man offered me the glass, which I accepted gratefully. If there had ever been a moment when I needed an alcoholic restorative, that moment was now.

'Laura, this is Jules,' said Alex, indicating the tall, skinny man. 'Jules, this is Laura.'

Jules gave me a low, solemn bow and then took my hand, which was lying limply on top of the rug, and pressed it to his lips.

'Enchanted,' he murmured.

This unexpected display of chivalry buoyed me up and I managed a thin smile in return. Alex ran his hand through his characteristically untidy hair and looked at me with concern.

'I'm sorry,' I said, not quite knowing where to direct my eyes and settling on Jules, who was perching nonchalantly on the arm of a chair nearby. 'I didn't mean to pitch up like this. I was in a bit of a state and I must have blurted out your address to the cabby by mistake. I had no idea I'd remembered it.'

'Well,' Alex flopped down on to the sofa next to me and absent-mindedly fiddled with the corner of the rug, 'I'd guessed it was quite an impromptu visit, given your choice of clothing.'

We all looked at my fluffy cow-print slippers, now with most of the dirt from Fulham Palace Road adhering to them.

I took another large sip of brandy.

'Someone broke into my flat,' I said and promptly burst into tears, the hideousness of the past few days finally proving too much for me.

I vaguely felt the brandy glass being prised from my fingers, I thought I heard the front door close, and then all I was aware of for quite a long time was my face being buried in Alex's jumper and every gasp of air I hauled into my lungs bringing with it the delicious scent of him. After goodness only knew how long, I went to rub my eyes but discovered I was trembling so badly that this was impossible. Without a word, Alex folded my hands up inside his own and squeezed them gently.

Slowly, very slowly – as if through the power of his will alone – the shakes died away. He shifted his position slightly, and I realised for the first time that I was no longer sitting on the sofa but was curled up in his arms, his body arcing protectively around mine.

'I'm sorry,' I said again.

'What for?' He tucked my hands in under his jumper to keep them warm, and I could feel the heat from his body flowing up through my fingers and along my arms.

'Disturbing your evening.'

'You did nothing of the sort. In fact, if you must know, Jules and I were working – how sad is that?'

'Working?' I mumbled into his chest, drawing in an extra large helping of eau de Alex.

Alex rearranged his head slightly and rested his chin on my temple.

'We've been talking for years about setting up our own TV production company, so we finally decided to put our money – or rather Jules's money – where our mouths are. But that's not important right now. For God's sake, tell me what happened to you.'

Feeling calmer now that I'd got some of the upset out of my system, I slowly related the events of the break-in. As I did so, Alex neither moved nor spoke, but I could feel pure anger leaching out of him as my tale unfolded.

'Bastards,' he said in a low, dangerous voice when I'd finished. 'Fucking, fucking bastards.'

He reached over and handed me the phone.

'Police,' he said. 'Now.'

At first I hesitated, conscious that I didn't want to spend any longer in Islington than I absolutely had to. However, Alex was calmly forceful in his insistence, so I sniffed my way through a number of connections until I was eventually put through to my local station in

Hammersmith, where a bored-sounding desk sergeant informed me that they had no officers available for non-urgent call-outs at present.

Alex snatched the receiver off me and put it on speakerphone.

'But you heard the woman – someone broke into her flat and left threatening messages. What the hell do you mean, "someone will be round tomorrow"?'

'As I said, sir,' the plod repeated testily, 'the offenders have absconded and no property was removed or damaged; it is a non-urgent situation. Tell the young lady she is not to touch anything and we will take a statement from her in the morning.'

'You're as bad as the bloody burglars!' Alex replied angrily. 'You have a statutory duty to protect the public, and as this lady *is* the public *and* she needs protecting, I suggest you get your arse into gear and send someone out *now!*'

'There is no need for that sort of language, sir. I am merely doing my job,' the policeman chided loftily.

'On the contrary, your job is the one thing you are emphatically *not* doing,' roared Alex and threw the phone down on the sofa in disgust, chuntering loudly as he did so about writing to the Chief Constable. I decided that this would be as good a moment as any to take my leave.

I prised my reluctant body away from the sofa cushions, hauled myself to my feet and smoothed down my dressing gown in a vain attempt to look presentable. It occurred to me that there would have been something nice about going through life with a man who – unlike Tom – actually looked out for my interests. But logic told me that whatever I might want or not want was completely irrelevant: Isobel had staked her claim and Alex had responded enthusiastically to it.

As far as Alex and I were concerned it was game over.

'Everything all right?' asked Alex, looking at me with mild surprise. 'Because if you need the loo, it's—'

I shook my head and wiped my nose on an old tissue I'd found buried in the pocket of my dressing gown.

'No thanks. I ought to be going. I've trespassed on your hospitality for long enough, and it's time I was getting home. If you don't mind, I'll borrow the phone to ring a locksmith and arrange to meet him back at the flat, and then I'll bugger off. I'll post you a cheque to cover the taxi fare you paid earlier.'

Alex stared at me as though I'd just suggested a spot of naked salsa-dancing round Piccadilly Circus.

'This is crazy talk, Laura. You can't go back to Hammersmith!'

'Give me one good reason why not.'

Alex narrowed his eyes.

'Because it's the middle of the night, it's not safe and you haven't even got any proper clothes on!' he replied. 'The only sensible course of action is for you to stay here tonight and I'll drive you home in the morning.'

'Don't be absurd!' I cried.

Was the man nuts? Of course I couldn't spend the night in the flat that Isobel probably regarded as her second home. It said an awful lot about my state of mind that night that I would rather have taken my chances with the Bristol heavies than use a bathroom in which her spare toothbrush might already be installed.

'I'm not being absurd,' he argued back. 'In fact, if anyone round here is, it's you. You are not going home and that's final.'

'Oh yeah?' I countered. 'Well, the last time I checked, the police weren't too happy about men keeping women locked in their houses against their will.'

'It's for your own good, and anyway – the police? You've got to be joking after their no-show earlier.'

I stood my ground and tightened my dressing-gown belt in a show of defiance.

'I'm grateful for everything you've done for me, Alex, truly I am, but if you'll pass me the phone again, I'll make my calls and then leave.'

'Fine.' Alex went over to the mantelpiece, rummaged in a pot and pulled out some car keys. 'If you're determined to be a fathead, then I'll have to go along with it – but the deal is that I'm driving you, and what's more, I'm staying over until the police arrive in the morning.'

Noooo! That was even worse than me bedding down in Islington! The idea of Alex spending the night at my flat and dredging up all the memories of our perfect Friday night together was unbearable. For the first time since I'd found out about him and Isobel, real pain, raw, sharp and overwhelming, stabbed through me, and I covered my face with my hands.

'For goodness' sake, Alex!' I cried. 'I am an adult; I can sort my own life out – I don't need you sticking your interfering oar in!'

'Laura McGregor!' Alex's voice was rising in exasperation. 'Why do you always end up shouting at me?'

Wasn't it obvious?

'Because you're so bloody infuriating!' I replied, my hurt and bewilderment making me fierce. 'What the hell is it to you if I go back to Hammersmith?'

'I care about you, that's what!' Alex thundered. 'And because I do, I am not going to sit back and let you put yourself at this sort of ridiculous risk.'

As this outrageous suggestion left his lips (lips that had no doubt been kissing Isobel recently), I did a double-take.

Was he having a laugh?

'Are you honestly telling me you give a monkey's about what happens to me?' I cried incredulously.

Alex managed to look rather hurt and incredibly irritated at the same time.

'God Almighty, Laura, I would rather cut my own hand off than let you put yourself in danger! You've got to believe me.'

For a split second, the searing honesty in his voice brought me up sharp and I stood there gawping at him, but then the pain broke through once again and I lashed back with venom.

'Okay then! If you're so crazy about me, why did you go and sleep with Isobel?' The words were out of my mouth before I'd even realised they were forming in my brain. 'You don't love me, Alex Hodder. You didn't even have the decency to tell me you'd got it back on with your ex. You are a big fat love-rat and *that's* why I don't need you interfering in my life.'

Alex went very, very pale.

'Who told you that?' he breathed.

'Isobel did!' I yelled, feeling strangely triumphant as I unveiled what I knew of their little liaison. 'She said you called her on Saturday afternoon, you spent the rest of the day getting hot and steamy and that you are now back together. Well congratulations – the pair of you deserve each other and I hope you both rot in hell!'

For a long time neither of us moved nor spoke. Alex did a bit of gawping himself, while I stood there with anger fizzing out of me, willing him to deny it but – equally – knowing he couldn't.

'Isobel?' he said at last.

'Yes, Isobel.' I lowered my voice to a pissed-off rumble. 'You know – the one you first met in Oxford. The one for whom you have a primal, eternal love! The one who thinks you should just cut the crap and get engaged *right now* – her!'

'Laura,' Alex replied slowly, 'I – I don't know what to say.'

'Hold the front page,' I said witheringly. 'Alex Hodder is officially lost for words. That *has* to be a first.'

Alex ran his fingers through his hair, making it stick up at a million ridiculous angles.

'Look, Laura, I meant every single word I've ever said to you. You *have* to believe that. And I didn't ring her, she rang me.'

'But you slept with her?' My voice was low and urgent as the ache of his betrayal surged through me again and again and again. 'Didn't you?'

Alex turned away and dumped his car keys back on the mantelpiece. There was a ghastly pause.

'Did you sleep with her?' I persisted, unable to raise my voice much above a whisper.

I had to know the truth; I *had* to.

Alex turned back towards me but was unable to meet my eye.

'No,' he said at last.

For a split second the pain abated. Was Isobel lying? Had I somehow managed to get hold of the wrong end of the stick? Was there a chance we could rescue something out of this unholy mess?

'But I did agree to meet her, and if I'm being honest with you, the time we spent together wasn't entirely platonic. It might have gone further, only however much I tried I couldn't get you out of my head.' He stared miserably at his shoes. 'Laura, I know what this makes me look like, and I haven't forgotten what I said about being in love—'

'Who with?' I snapped. 'Her or me?'

Alex walked over to me and took my hand in his, but

I snatched it away angrily. I was aware of my chin jutting out defiantly in a way that made me think of Mel.

'How could you, Alex! How could you think I would never find out? Are there any more guilty secrets you've got hidden away? Any more members of my family your dad bankrupted? Or perhaps yet another relationship with a smug leggy blonde? Go on, spit it out.'

Alex flushed red and glanced away. I bit my lip: that had been way below the belt.

'I didn't think I stood a chance with you.' He looked utterly miserable. 'Especially after your mother's little speech. Then you yelled something about wanting the lot of us to clear off, and I assumed that was mainly meant for me. I was so totally gutted I spent Saturday lunchtime in the pub. After I'd had about six pints, Isobel called *me* and thanks to my beer goggles it seemed like a good idea to go along with it. I suppose you could describe what happened next as a bit of a comfort snog – on my part at least. Anyway, that's the reason I didn't return your calls: I was desperately trying to work out how the hell I was going to explain it to you so that you would forgive me.'

Our eyes met and I could see my own turmoil perfectly mirrored in Alex's beautiful face. This was as hard for him as it was for me, or maybe harder, because he obviously believed himself to be the author of all this destruction.

'Laura.' He looked away once again and fiddled with the keys on the mantelpiece. 'Is there anything I can say – anything at all – that will make a difference to how you feel about me?'

For a moment I wavered: my behaviour on Saturday morning had not been without reproach. If I'd been in Alex's shoes, would I too not have fled thinking it was all over bar some pretty energetic shouting? My feelings for him were strong, that was not in doubt, but were they strong enough to overcome *this*?

Then, as if from nowhere, the naked vulnerability swept over me once again and I shivered. Being with Alex would be like nothing I had ever experienced before: it would be honest, intense and scorchingly intimate, and if it failed, I didn't fancy my chances of getting out unscathed. Did I want to risk all that for something that had already proved so very fragile? Would that be the sensible thing to do?

I met Alex's gaze unflinchingly.

'Not if what you've just told me is true,' I said. 'It's too hard; there's too much at stake.'

The pain frightened me and I wanted to be shot of it as quickly as I could. I was only going to do that if I told him it was over.

He looked away. 'I know,' he replied.

Somewhere in the flat, a clock struck one.

'Please stay.' He was almost pleading with me. 'Whatever you think about you and me – even if you're truly convinced that we are over – *please* don't go back home and risk being pulverised by a bunch of nutters.'

The emotional turbulence of the past twelve hours was taking its toll, and I suddenly felt crushingly tired. Despite every ounce of rational opinion telling me it was a bad idea, I nodded my assent. He was right: it would be madness to trek all the way back to west London at this hour of the night with the very real risk that my nocturnal visitor would return together with his chums and a couple of outsized crowbars.

'Alex,' I sank back down on to the sofa, feeling unbelievably small and alone, 'hold me. Don't read anything into it, please; just hold me.'

Without a word he sat down beside me and gathered me back up into his arms. I put my head on his chest, still damp from my earlier tears, and closed my eyes. Isobel or no Isobel, I needed the solid reassurance of another human body next to mine – and if Alex's was the only one available, then it was going to have to do.

'Do you mind if I turn that light off?' asked Alex after a long pause. 'Only it's shining right into my eyes.'

'Be my guest.'

Uncurling one of his long arms from round my shoulders, he reached behind us and clicked the switch on a little lamp standing next to the sofa. The darkness fell comfortingly across us like a blanket and we sat in silence, our breathing synchronised, our bodies folded into each other like a piece of human origami. This was how it should have been, I reminded myself grimly: me and Alex cuddled up together in the orange twilight of a London night. But it was simply impossible. Whatever it took, I had to get him out of my system and move on.

'I arsed up, didn't I?'

'What?' In the warmth of his embrace, I'd fallen into a doze. 'Yes. Yes, you did.'

'I'm sorry,' he murmured.

'I know you are,' I whispered back. 'And so am I. But the chances are that it would never have worked, Alex; we might as well wipe the slate clean and forget about it.'

Alex tipped his head and rested it on top of mine; then, for good or ill, we lay semi-prone in each other's arms until sleep arrived and claimed us as his own.

13

I became aware it was morning mainly because a loud clattering noise somewhere above my head woke me up. This was followed by a heavy 'whump', some thud thud-thudding and then a bit more clattering for good measure. I groaned softly and went to turn over but found I was held fast by a pair of arms. The owner of the arms shifted slightly and I felt the warmth of his breath in the nape of my neck.

'It's the newspapers,' he grunted. 'Bloody paper boy insists on dragging his bloody bike along the bloody railings. One day I'm going to find out where he lives and go round at five a.m with a couple of dustbin lids to see how he likes it.'

'What time is it?' I tried to sit up, but remembered too late that I was on a sofa and nearly fell off on to the floor. Luckily Alex's embrace held fast.

Oh, bugger.

Alex.

I had a hazy recollection that we'd been fighting like a couple of hungry lions over the last gazelle in town. What had the row been about? Me going home? No, there had been something *after* that. Me being a fathead? A thought filtered down through my sleep-fugged brain and a dark, empty pain tugged at my heart – Isobel. We had had a screaming row about Isobel. Or at least *I* had screamed. Alex had simply looked as miserable as sin and kept on apologising.

'Dunno.' Alex was responding to my earlier question and rolled over to squint at the clock on the mantelpiece. 'Six ten. God, I feel knackered. What time did we get to sleep last night?'

Against my back I could feel his chest rising and falling, and with every breath I could feel the gap between what I wanted (Alex) and what I *could* have (not Alex) pulling me apart just that little bit more. This morning was not going to be any easier than last night.

'Not sure,' I said, wriggling my way out of his clutches to perch on the very edge of the sofa cushion.

Alex closed his eyes as though he was summoning up the courage to say something deep and meaningful. I felt my heart turn over as I registered the long black lashes that fluttered down on to smooth, clear skin spattered with a few tiny freckles.

I looked away.

I'd made my decision and I had to stick to it. He'd failed to tell me about my father and he had failed to tell me about Isobel. This was not what I needed at the start of a new relationship.

'About Isobel,' he began, reaching out to pull me back in to him. 'I think she might have given you the impression that we were closer—'

I leapt bodily off the sofa.

'Please, Alex, just leave it,' I said firmly. 'We've been over that and we ended up shouting at each other. I don't want another row.'

'We always row,' Alex reminded me.

This was true.

'But in a good way,' he added, giving me a strange sideways glance.

This was also true: arguing with Alex, even over a subject like Isobel 'Boyfriend-Snatcher' Norland, felt bizarrely honest and open. Despite the fact that we let rip with some truly awesome firepower, there was a weird sense of respect in my dealings with Alex that made it possible for me to say what I felt *and* acknowledge where he was coming from; and I realised with a pang of regret that I had never experienced such open acceptance in a relationship with another human being in my life before.

Not that I could allow that to alter anything.

'I know, Alex,' I replied, the thought of dragging my body into another day without him making my limbs feel like lead. 'But this isn't Friday night; everything's changed. And right now I have a million things I need to do – like getting home and sorting out the mess Mel has landed me in.'

Alex looked at me for a moment, his face completely impassive; and then threw off the rug and planted his feet on the floor.

'Right,' he said, 'of course. Do you want a shower while I put the kettle on?'

After coffee and a bite of toast, he drove me home. Even though neither Isobel's name nor my father's business was mentioned, they hovered in the air like the proverbial black cloud, making the pair of us twitchy and uncharacteristically reticent, and I wondered if it would have been better for me to take a cab after all. When we arrived back in Hammersmith, however, I found I was pathetically grateful for Alex's presence. I lagged behind him as we walked up the path to meet the locksmith, and then, when the front door finally swung open, I ran my fingers lightly along the hem of his jacket, drawing strength from his nearness as I stepped over the threshold.

Fortunately there were no bloodthirsty loan sharks

hanging around inside, sharpening their disembowelling cutlasses and waiting for me to return. In fact the flat was exactly as I had left it. I took off the coat Alex had lent me for the journey home, cranked the heating up and went to ring Mel – only to hear a key in the lock and see her curly head poking round the living room door moments later.

She looked from Alex standing awkwardly by the window, to me in my pyjamas, and a grin spread slowly over her face.

'Well, well, well,' she said. 'Quite what Mum is going to say when she knows you're still knocking off the bloke who ruined the family fortunes I don't know, but I expect you'll be able to see the sparks from here!'

Given the circumstances, I think she'd have been hard-pressed to come up with anything more likely to light my fuse.

'Do yourself a favour and don't push it,' I replied tersely. 'I'm not in the mood.'

Mel's grin decreased, but not by enough for my liking.

'Come on, sis. It's quarter to seven in the morning, you're in your PJs and Alex looks guiltier than an MP claiming a second home allowance.' She gestured at my pyjamaed figure. 'Are you honestly expecting me to believe there is nothing going on?'

The profound longing that something should indeed be going on between Alex and myself zapped through me like an electric shock, but I pushed it away.

'Believe me, Mel, if you think you're about to be murdered in your bed at midnight, you don't really care if you end up sprinting down Fulham Palace Road in your slippers.'

Mel looked as though someone had hit her hard on the back of the head with a plank of wood.

'Whassat?' she gawped. 'Whatdjusay?'

'I had a visit from some of your pals last night,' I said, thrusting the note into her hands. 'Make Alex a cup of tea, and when I've got some proper clothes on, I want you to tell me what the bloody hell is going on.'

I was only out of the room for five minutes, but whilst I was absent, Alex seemed to have done most of the heavy work for me. By the time I came back, I was confronted by a sobbing Mel, a pot of tea and a large plate of chocolate biscuits.

'So,' I said, sitting down on the sofa, 'tell me the truth, Mel. What are we looking at here?'

Mel blew her nose on something I recognised from Middle Temple as being Alex's handkerchief.

'Gobshite needed some extra cash,' she managed in between gulps.

'In addition to the nine thousand you'd already spent on your credit cards?' I asked.

Mel nodded and blew her nose again loudly.

'I didn't tell you the full story, but there was this chance of a recording contract, you see,' she said, 'and the band needed to do a demo, a proper one on to CD, so Fat Andy and Creepy Dave's mate Psycho Pete—'

'God, Mel, listen to yourself,' I interjected. 'Does it surprise you you're up the creek? They hardly sound like characters from a Jane Austen novel.'

Mel gave me a look that said 'just leave it!' and continued.

'Anyway, Psycho Pete knows someone who used to do A and R stuff for Metal Spike Head Death in the eighties, and the lead singer has a farm out near Bath with a recording studio in it. He said they could use it but it was going to cost.'

'So you borrowed the money from some loan sharks.'

Mel nodded. 'Only I didn't know that was what they

were. Gobshite said it would be cool because they were friends of Psycho Pete's, and they were great about lending us the cash, so we promised them free tickets to Gobshite's band's first stadium gig . . .' Mel's voice dissolved into a high-pitched whimper.

I put my head in my hands, unsure whether she was demonstrating the boundless optimism of youth or plain, thick-headed stupidity.

'They were probably great about lending you the dosh because they knew they were stinging you for sky-high rates of interest and if you didn't pay up they *also* knew your address so that they could come and rearrange your kneecaps for you.' I paused and wrenched my mind back to the nitty-gritty practicalities for a moment. 'Just so as I know where we are, Mel, what was the interest rate?'

Mel looked at the floor.

'Thirty per cent,' she muttered.

I sat back and allowed myself a tiny sigh of relief. Whilst that was more than four times the rate on the Chiltern standard credit card, it was only ten per cent over and above some of my store cards.

'A week,' added Mel.

'Hell's bells!' I exclaimed. 'How much did you borrow?'

'They're after me for a full grand – plus the interest.

'And how much if you add in the interest?'

'About another grand on top.'

I put a cushion over my face to stop myself screaming out loud.

'This is extortion, Mel,' I cried (once I'd removed the cushion, obviously). 'How could you do this to yourself – and whilst we're on the subject, how could you dump this on *me*!'

Mel gave me a look that could scorch holes in Teflon.

'Oh, right,' she spat. 'So it's all about you, isn't it? The fact that I had to leave my home because a bunch of thugs want me to cough up money I couldn't get my hands on even if I lived to be eighty doesn't matter!'

'I don't think you should leave off paying till you're eighty,' Alex interjected, taking another biscuit and dunking it in his mug. 'Assuming we're talking about compound interest here, you'd end up shelling out . . .' He screwed his face up with concentration. 'Oh, I don't know – shedloads.'

'Yes, thank you, Carol Vorderman,' I replied. 'I think we've worked that one out for ourselves. Now listen to me, Mel – this is your fault. You ran up this debt and you can't simply expect me to bail you out yet again. You are an adult, a *grown-up* – and if you ask me, it's about time you started behaving like one.'

Mel leapt off the sofa. Her eyes flashed and her lip trembled in a way that made me unsure as to whether she was going to cry or yell.

It was the latter.

'Shut up!' she screamed. 'Shut up! Shut up! Shut up! All my life I've had you and Mum – and yes, even Dad when he's around – going on and on and on about how fucking perfect you are and I am SICK of hearing it. Do you think I liked living in a dive in Bristol with Gobshite's rancid mates and having a dead-end job throwing sawdust on the Friday-night vomit down at the Black Dog? Do you think I had any option other than to borrow money from Psycho Pete's mate?'

'Oh please!' I wasn't buying her sob story. 'It's not as though someone held a gun to your head and said, "Mel, if you don't spend the rest of your life being a total loser then I'm going to kill you"! You're bright, you're talented; you could have done anything you wanted but you chose not to. Did you hear that? It was *your* choice.'

This only seemed to fire her up even more.

'With you as my sister there wasn't much point trying! By the time I got there, you'd already done it with bloody bells on. Eleven plus? Laura romps home. GCSEs? Why bother turning up? I didn't go to art school because I kept being told it wasn't as good as Laura McPerfect's university degree. I even thought about getting a job in a bank.' She gave a hollow laugh. 'But guess what – you sail right into a graduate traineeship and no one at home can stop talking about how brilliant you are.'

I was stunned.

'I had no idea,' I protested. 'I only took the job at the Chiltern because it seemed like the sensible thing to do. It's dull, Mel, but it pays the bills. It certainly wasn't some sort of master plan to make you look stupid.'

Mel gave another snort of sarcastic laughter.

'Well, to listen to Mum, you might as well have been the Messiah of Parental Expectation, come to fulfil her dearest wishes. Whatever you want to say about Gobshite, at least living with him I didn't have to put up with being compared to YOU twenty-four hours a day!'

I shifted uncomfortably on the sofa.

'I'm sorry,' I said. 'I wasn't aware of any of this.'

Mel bit her lip.

'I know,' she said. 'I'm sorry, I just snapped. I'm scared, Laura, really scared.'

I took her hand.

'So am I, Mel, and this time Super Laura really doesn't know the answers.'

Our moment of entente cordiale, however, was destined to be short-lived.

'What I'd like to know,' Alex fingered his chin thoughtfully, seemingly unaware of the hostilities that had been going on around him, 'is how they knew you were here, Mel. I wouldn't have thought they'd be able to track you down in a city the size of London.'

Mel went red. Then she went very, very pale.

'Melissa,' I dropped her hand, 'what have you done?'

Mel swallowed. Hard.

'You know your diary,' she began.

'You read my diary!' I gasped. 'After I told you not to?'

'I'm sorry, I'm sorry,' placated Mel, 'I couldn't help myself.'

'I'm just going to get myself another cup of tea.' Alex excused himself from the theatre of war and crept off into the kitchen.

The thought of what she must have read, the intimacies to which she was now privy, made my blood run cold. She knew all about Alex and the depths of my feelings for him; she knew about my precarious situation at work; she would even have read the entry relating to Isobel – it was excruciating.

'Listen,' I hissed, in a voice that spoke of a painful and lingering death if she did not do as she was told, 'if you ever, ever repeat any of that stuff – and especially the bits about me and Alex – I personally will make sure your life is not worth living. So keep shtum or you're going to wish Psycho Pete's mates had caught up with you after all.'

But Mel didn't reply. Instead she hung her head and shuffled one of her feet slightly.

'I think I may have put it up on the internet,' she said at last.

For a full ten seconds I stared at her, speech completely beyond me.

'Anyone for a refill?'

Alex, with worse timing than a broken stopwatch, stuck his head round the door and grinned cheerily at us.

'She put my diary up on the internet!' I screeched,

finally regaining control of my vocal cords. 'She put it on the bloody internet. Anyone can read it.'

Then a terrible realisation struck me.

'People *have* read it. Tom knew I'd kissed you and that's why he came over all alpha male and punched my boss at the dinner – he got you mixed up with Will. Ohgodohgodohgod! You and me, Alex, last Friday night – that's all up there; and my mum and Gerald, and Polly and Archie, and' – I curled up into a tiny ball on the sofa and clutched a cushion protectively to my chest – 'a whole load of stuff about SunSpot.'

I buried my face in my cushion, words failing me yet again. I think I would rather have mud-wrestled Isobel in the middle of Trafalgar Square than dealt with this. Even considering the somewhat startling events of the week so far, this pretty much took the biscuit.

Actually, make that the whole *packet* of biscuits.

'Why, Mel?' Alex asked, seamlessly picking up where I had been forced to leave off.

'It was an accident.' I almost hear Mel squirming as she replied. 'I was trying to get to the next entry and my hand slipped and hit the 'upload' icon.'

I removed my cushion to grab some much-needed oxygen.

'And couldn't you have un-uploaded it? Deleted it? Done anything other than leave it up there for the whole frigging world to read?' I cried.

'I thought I might make it worse.'

I peered at her over the cushion's tassled border.

'How could you make it worse? Unless you're about to tell me you sold it to the *News of the World* or had it broadcast live alongside the National Lottery.'

There was a pregnant pause.

'You didn't, did you?' I asked.

'Of course not,' snapped Mel, 'but it must be how

Psycho Pete's mate knew where I was. He saw my name, saw your name – and bingo.'

'But I haven't put my address in any of my diary entries.' I felt as though my brain was struggling through a slick of porridge.

'Just your name is enough for someone to trace you. Electoral roll, marketing data – all sorts of stuff,' Alex supplied. 'It's quite easy if you know where to look.'

He held out his hand and hauled me to my feet. Mel cleared her throat and stared at her shoes.

'I'm sorry, Laura,' she said.

But I wasn't interested in her apologies. So far this week I'd dealt with Isobel, a break-in and now *this*. I was quite a long way beyond the end of my tether.

'I'd like you to leave, Mel.' I said, making sure my voice remained calm and level.

'You mean go? Go now?'

'Yes, now. Take your stuff and find somewhere else to live.'

She looked as though I'd just slapped her round the face.

'But Laura, I couldn't help it – it was an accident!'

For a split second I wavered, but I found I was clean out of second chances.

'No it wasn't, Mel. It was stupid, selfish and destructive, just like you. You are the biggest waste of a life I have ever come across, and right now I wish you had never been born.'

The little colour that was left in Mel's cheeks drained away.

'Do you really mean that?' she whispered.

I nodded. At that moment I think I was angrier than I had ever been before in my whole life. And possibly more than a little irrational.

'You sponge off me, you lead a bunch of thugs into my home and you put my private diary on the internet.'

'But I'm your sister.'

I turned my back on her.

'Not any more you're not. The gravy train stops right here, Mel; this is the end of the line. Now go on, get off.'

'Alex!' Mel's voice was pleading. 'Alex – say something. She'll listen to you!'

There was a terrible pause as I waited to hear which way Alex was going to jump.

'I think it might be best if you do as your sister wants, Mel,' he said softly.

'But I don't have anywhere to go!' Mel protested. 'I can't keep on crashing at Karen's – it's far too small!'

'Look.' There was a rustling noise as Alex produced a piece of paper from somewhere and the 'click' of a biro lid being removed. 'Call this number and say I told you to ring.'

Mel went to her bedroom to pack, leaving Alex standing awkwardly a couple of feet away. He tried to slip his hand into mine but I pulled away: he might have sorted out Mel's accommodation problem, but that didn't mean he was entitled to any sort of physical contact.

'Are you going to be all right?' he asked.

'Yes,' I replied stiffly.

What else could I say? I would have to be all right. Unlike Mel, I didn't expect other people to spend their lives bailing me out.

'Do you – do you want to stay at my flat for the time being?' he asked. 'At least until the police get their hands on Psycho Pete?'

I shook my head. My job was to build a life without Alex in it, not start chipping in with his milk bill and arguing over whose turn it was to buy the loo rolls.

'Okay,' he started to put his coat on, 'if you're sure; but the offer remains open – any time, day or night.'

He gave me a rueful-looking grin.

'I'm sorry about dragging you into all this, Alex,' I said. 'I'll sort it out – I'll delete the whole bloody thing. It was just silly adolescent scribbles in a pathetic diary – only please, *please*, don't go online and read it.'

'I won't,' he promised. 'You have my word on that. But let me ring you later. I want to check how you are and what the police have to say.'

'I'll be fine,' I said loudly – as much for my own benefit as his. 'And please make sure Mel steers clear of me, or they'll have a murder on their hands.'

I turned away and made a great play of staring out of the window until I heard footsteps in the hall and the front door close behind him and my erstwhile sister. Then I sank, exhausted, on to the sofa and waited for the rozzers to turn up.

14

By the following day, despite the fact that I had been putting in a fair few hours of tossing and turning during the night, I was beginning to feel cautiously optimistic that I'd done all I could to exorcise the various hideous scenarios that had been visited upon me.

After Alex and Mel had left (and once I'd phoned Will and lied through my teeth as to why I wasn't going to be in that day), I finally plucked up the courage to go online and face up to the internet presence from hell that Mel had so considerately created for me. With the help of a big button helpfully labelled 'edit', I deleted the various entries one by one.

Next the police materialised, looked very disappointed that I hadn't been beaten up and left for dead, took a statement and pushed off again. Then Alex rang to check that I was okay, and inform me that not only was Mel safely installed in Jules's apartment as a temporary measure but that, miracle of miracles, she had also managed to land herself one of the jobs she'd been interviewed for. I thanked him for taking her under his wing and apologised for my earlier outburst. He repeated his offer to put me up at his place and I too reprised my earlier refusal and instead paid my locksmith the GDP of a small developing nation to call back and fit a mortise lock on each of the front doors and a further lock on every window. Finally, after making her swear on Archie's wedding tackle that she wouldn't tell a soul about what I'd written, I recruited Polly (who was a bit of a techie whizz on the quiet) to get rid of the last remnants of the blog and try and hoover up any references to it that might still be floating round the ether.

I was aware, of course, that eliminating the blog did not mean my problems miraculously vanished. It had been up there for goodness only knew how long (there were even a few enthusiastic-sounding comments tagged on to some of the posts) and Polly had been honest in warning me that she might not be able to eradicate it entirely from the blogosphere. The thing that scared me most, though, was not the thought that my intimate escapades might still be hanging around for people to 'ooh' and 'ahh' over, but that some of the SunSpot material would still be available. Because if it was, and someone who understood what they were looking at stumbled across it, my troubles could be only just beginning.

Since the idea of going into Will's office and confessing to hacking into his firewalled accounting records then sticking the whole lot on the web didn't sound like anything I would include in my Five-Year Career Development Plan, I decided the best course of action would be to hang fire and see if anybody did actually pick it up and run with it. With luck, people would be so busy gawping over the various comedy stunts that comprised my love life that they wouldn't even notice the references to the accounts.

When I arrived at work the next day, all seemed thankfully quiet on the Western Front. There were no banner headlines in the financial press about accounting anomalies at SunSpot and no journalists on the phone demanding interviews with me as the Chiltern's whistle-blower. Beginning to feel as though I might have got away with it, I did a bit of work; spent an hour and a half in a telephone training session (I kid you not); and then, before my brain actually atrophied with boredom, lied about having been double-booked into another meeting and slipped into the kitchen on my floor to make myself a mocha latte.

I pulled out my BlackBerry and checked the markets for any hint of trouble, but it all seemed mercifully calm. The FTSE was up fifteen points; the pound was looking good against the dollar; and God was in his Heaven and all was right with the world. I breathed a sigh of relief and flicked on to the performance of the banking sector. Barclays, RBS, Lloyds, HBOS – all fine and dandy. Now for the Chiltern . . .

My fingers froze where they touched my BlackBerry. Then my hand went numb.

My arms, too, felt as though they had lost all sensation as I stared at the tiny screen in front of me. No, that couldn't be right, it just couldn't – the figures were red and falling faster than autumn leaves in a force-ten gale: we were down a full half of our share value.

I stood next to the coffee machine as it hissed and spat boiling water in my direction, scrolling through the headlines and trying to find out exactly what was going on. A shudder ran through me: *Rumours about the liquidity of the Chiltern Bank send share price plummeting.*

Holy Nora! It was out! Someone who knew what they were looking at had picked up my post about the accounts and published it! What the hell was I going to do?

In a blind panic I ran out of the kitchen, across the office and through the door into the corridor beyond. I heard it slam heavily behind me as I pressed my face against the cool solidity of the reinforced glass wall and gasped.

Normally I loved the view afforded by the corridors

that ringed the Screwdriver like layer upon layer of glassed-in balconies. Staring down on the vista of the City as it opened up before me and sensing the thrum of a million people doing deal after deal after deal and shifting trillions of pounds round the world with the click of a mouse usually made me feel as though I was some sort of tiny neuron in a huge, lightning-paced collective consciousness.

But today it was different.

Today it felt as though everyone else in the Square Mile was staring up at me, leaning out of their windows in the Lloyd's building, the Gherkin and Tower 42 and pointing me out to their friends and neighbours: there she goes, they were whispering to one another, the woman who broke the Chiltern; the person who single-handedly brought down a three-hundred-year-old financial institution in the space of a day by blogging about it on the internet.

I unstuck my flaming face from the glass and looked back down at the screen of my BlackBerry. Opening up the page on Bloomberg that contained the story about the bank, I forced myself to read the article so I knew exactly what I was up against. It was rather vague and insubstantial, but from my point of view that was good. Most importantly, it didn't mention blogs or the internet.

That meant I had a degree of breathing space.

Swiping my card through the security scanner, I took the deepest of breaths and pushed open the door into the office. To my utter relief, there was no sign of panic amongst my colleagues – much less any cries of 'traitor' as Sophie Spink rugby-tackled me to the floor and shoved my P45 into my hand. As I watched, I saw people anxiously keeping an eye on the figures ticker-taping around the bottom of the television screen, but essentially getting on with their work.

I knew that I should simply do what everyone else was doing and sit down at my desk and crack on.

But I couldn't.

I was far too jittery to tap away at my keyboard and coolly glance up at the financial news from time to time. So on the pretext of dropping back some paperwork, I made my way down to Will's office to try and find out from the horse's mouth what was going on.

As I approached, the door was closed but the slats of the blinds were open, allowing me to see that Will was on the telephone having a rather heated conversation. I raised my hand in order to knock on the door, but he beckoned me in with a curt wave and I took this as my signal to enter.

'Well, ring me back when you *do* know,' I heard him say before he slammed the receiver back into its cradle.

'Bad news?' I asked.

'Fucking Bently's want to take their fucking money out.' He ran a hand through his hair, and for a moment it took on the same sort of trajectory as Alex's. 'They've invested with me for years – before I ever joined SunSpot – and they were biting my hand off to get on board Dresda. Now they've just told me that not only are they *not* going to be investing in Dresda, but they also want their money out of three other funds as well.'

Bently's were a large-scale corporate investor, one of the biggest in the mighty pack that hunted with Will and his traders. They were adept at sniffing out the highest-yielding funds and had been rolling on to their backs with their tongues lolling out as soon as they had heard about Dresda. The fact that they now wanted to get out completely was bad. Very bad.

'But they can't just demand their money back, can they?' I asked. 'Isn't there a two-year lock-up term in SunSpot investment contracts?'

Will wiped a hand across his brow and nodded.

'That's what I told them,' he said. 'But we need people like them in on the ground for Dresda. Once it gets round that Bently's are quitting, you and I are going to be crushed in the stampede for the exit. You know that.'

He was right. I did know that.

'I saw the headline on Bloomberg,' I said.

Will shot me a look.

'What d'ya want – a medal? We've all seen it and we all know what it means: share price down, confidence faltering, investors pulling out, so the share price falls even fucking further. Vicious circle doesn't even come close – suicide circle more like. Did you see this?'

He hit his computer keyboard with such force I was surprised the key-tab didn't fly off into the air.

'E-mail from Dave Headly in the bonds department – *bonds*: I mean, how safe and boring do you wanna get? – to say they've lost three institutional clients already this morning and he has meetings lined up to try and salvage another two. We're haemorrhaging investors, and if it doesn't stop soon, we're sunk.'

'Does anyone know the basis of the fall in the share price?' I asked tentatively.

'Rumours.' Will turned his back on me, shoved his hands in his trouser pockets and stared moodily out of the window once again. 'Pathetic, baseless industry tittle-tattle about losses no one should even know exist.'

My heart jumped into my throat and stuck there. I swear I could feel my pulse reverberating out through my jugular.

'Losses?' I asked, trying unsuccessfully to make it sound like a statement.

'Jesus H. Christ, Laura – where have you been? It's all over every TV station on the planet. Yes, losses – in our currency dealing sector apparently. I pay you to know this shit.'

'Of course,' I said, relief rather than terror now pumping through me like the bass line on an R and B track. 'I'm afraid I've been rather tied up this morning.'

Will suddenly removed one of his hands from his pocket and thumped the wall. Luckily not too hard, or it would have gone right through the plasterboard, which was all that separated us from the main office outside. Even so, it was enough to make me jump.

'I think you're mistaking me for someone who gives a fuck,' he said. 'You need to keep ahead of the game or you're out – and whilst I'm on the subject, get on your knees and start praying this thing doesn't get any worse, or we're all screwed.'

He was right. As I knew to my cost from the Davis Butler episode, rumours could grow into super-rumours that in turn could cause entire banks to collapse in the blink of an eye. In the City, confidence was the Elixir of Life – without it, you might just as well pack up and go home. The only tiny saving grace was that it hadn't been me who'd been the epicentre of the stories now rocking the Chiltern and its subsidiaries like a shift in the San Andreas.

At least this time.

'Fine.' I nodded sharply – message received and understood. 'So do you want me to carry on with Dresda?'

Will shook his head.

'No, get on to these rumours and find out what you can, and then let me know. I've got a conference call at eleven with a high-net-worth private client and I want to be able to tell him that any worries about SunSpot and the bank are bullshit. Even if they're not, that's what he's going to be told, so I need to get my cover story together.'

I stared at Will: he was going to *lie* to the client.

He eyeballed me back, his gaze as hard as titanium-coated nails.

'I do what I need to do. You will give me the information I need to make any problems at the Chiltern look like commercial advantages.'

I nodded again. 'You'll have it by quarter to eleven.'

'Ten thirty.'

I bit my lip. I suddenly had an overwhelming desire to ask him about the accounts I'd found; to know once and for all if everything was as it should be. A sixth sense whispered urgently in my ear not to be such a fool and to keep quiet.

I turned on my heel and made my way over to the door. As my hand clamped itself round the handle, however, I swivelled back round to face Will.

'I ...' The words caught in my throat and I found myself half choking.

Don't say it, pleaded my brain. *Please don't say it!*

'Just get the fucking stuff from the currency clowns, will you?' barked Will, scowling. 'If I go down, you do too. Think about it.'

That did the trick.

I went back to my workstation and booted up. I opened my inbox and then, checking no one was watching, opened a fresh window on to the internet and logged on to the blog site. Thankfully Polly had done her stuff: it had vanished.

With a sigh of relief, I focused on getting the stuff from the currency clowns.

'Share price just stabilised!' Archie yelled from across the floor, and a cheer went up. 'No – better than that, we're up three pence. Financial News Today has traced the source of the rumours back to Hong Kong overnight and they are erroneous. I'm mailing round a clip from one of their economics team.'

The e-mail with the link appeared in my inbox as he spoke, and I clicked on it. I was suddenly presented with a picture of Alex, his mouth open mid-word and a large white arrow and the words 'click here to play' stamped across his face. My hand shook so violently that I knocked a cup of water off my desk and on to the floor.

'Share price up thirty pence,' Polly yelled, and there was a general murmur of relief.

I deleted the e-mail.

I handed Will his research at ten thirty, relieved that he was not going to try and swindle someone into investing in a house of cards. Then, like an iron filing drawn to a particularly forceful magnet, my mind flipped back once again to the accounts.

My gut instinct told me that things were not right – but the problem was, I didn't know *how* not right they were. Was this a trading issue? A management issue? Or were we going the whole hog here and talking large-scale financial corruption?

I shivered.

The thing was, I simply didn't have enough facts to back up my suspicions. If the anomalies in the accounts were genuine mistakes, then there was nothing to worry about, but if Will was somehow massaging his trading figures to look profitable when in fact he was clocking up loss after loss, then he was guilty of fraud.

And me – what about me?

Could the very fact that I knew about it but had done nothing to remedy the situation be enough to make me complicit? (*Go directly to jail; do not pass go, do not collect two hundred pounds.*)

My hand hovered above my desk phone. Like all big banks, we had an internal compliance officer on the staff whose job it was to make sure we toed the financial line.

Maybe I should tip him off before something serious happened (like, oooh, someone inadvertently putting the figures up on the internet and the media getting wind of it?).

But if I was going to start talking about the rogue trades. I was throwing up a whole host of issues, including whether or not I should have been using Will's password to go rooting round in the bowels of the accounting system in the first place.

I allowed my hand to drop back into my lap.

As I saw it, I only had one real option. What I was going to have to do was go back into the accounts, take some careful notes of dates, times and figures and then make an informed decision as to what I was actually dealing with. Only then, with the evidence secure in my hot little hand, would the time come for involving a third party.

But I needed to act fast.

I knew Will was due to fly to New York late that afternoon, so I waited until he left for the airport then, muttering something to Melody about loading a new spreadsheet on to his computer, snuck into his office and shut the door behind me. I knew that IT could track down which terminal had been used to access which sets of data, and I wanted to make myself as inconspicuous as possible by logging on to Will's.

So far, so good.

I flexed my fingers and typed in Will's opera password. Next, I opened a window and began inputting the stuff I'd need for my cover story in case Melody barged in and started asking awkward questions. Then, with half the data on board (and after I'd checked that Melody was busy altering her status update on Facebook), I opened the SunSpot accounts.

Huh?

One of the current funds, Adriana, which last week had been resolutely making a profit, was now in the red. How could this be?

I swivelled Will's chair round and stared at the ice-blue spring sky.

It didn't help.

I focused on a bunch of pigeons fussing round on the windowsill outside.

They too had very little to add.

I decided to cast my eye over the last few days of trading to see if Will's team had crashed and burnt their way into minus territory – but no: from the day-to-day trading accounts it all looked pretty normal.

This didn't make any sense whatsoever.

I rotated back round in my chair and had another good look at the pigeons.

There were only a limited number of possibilities: the first was that I had made a mistake last week and confused the accounts with something else. This was possible, but I was confident enough in my own abilities to know that I would remember the names of the funds I had been looking at. Secondly, there was the risk that I was going crazy – which *did* seem unlikely but, given the events of the last few days, not entirely out of the question. Finally came the only remaining option. The one I hoped and prayed and crossed my fingers it wouldn't turn out to be: that there was something dodgier than Dodge City going on and only me and Will knew about it.

I swung the chair back to face the desk, intending to have another good look at the Gisela figures but (rather like my errant sister before me, I thought grimly) my finger slipped and I mis-clicked on an icon buried somewhere near the bottom of the screen. In an instant, the trading accounts had vanished and a blank screen demanding yet another password had popped up in front of me.

Bugger!

Glancing back up at the door to double-check I wasn't being spied on, my fingers darted over the keyboard and I pressed return. *Please let Will be like the rest of us and only ever use one password – pleaseplease please!*

To my utter astonishment, it worked.

A new window sprang to life in front of my eyes. It too contained a list of names – but there wasn't a single one I recognised. In fact, the various monikers before me bore no relation to the cosmological epithets favoured by SunSpot. These had strange, almost random names. Names that didn't make me feel particularly easy. Names like Reaper and Sidewinder, which sounded as though they would be more at home in a horror movie.

I stared at them and felt my breath catch in my throat: they were all showing losses. Massive losses.

I scanned down the list, my eyes growing wider by the second as my brain tried to absorb the scale of what I was witnessing. Whilst Will's profits were generally considered stunning, these too were equally mind-blowing – but, I promise you, not in a good way. It was as if I had stepped through a portal into an alternative dimension where SunSpot was not a City darling but a sort of financial black hole, capable of sucking us all into oblivion with the force of its gravitational pull.

For a moment I simply sat and stared at the screen, aware of not much more than a growing sense of physical sickness.

This all had to be some appalling mistake, some piece of complex accounting that I simply didn't understand. SunSpot was one of the most profitable companies in the UK; it couldn't carry losses like that and yet keep soaring up the FT 100 share index with the trajectory of the space shuttle.

With shaky hands I found the mouse and clicked on the unattractively titled Impaler. The total losses it contained literally took my breath away: it wasn't just millions, or even hundreds of millions. The figure for this particular fund or entity or whatever it was ran to well over a billion.

This couldn't be happening; this simply couldn't be happening – and the fact that Will had access to it all through his private password simply made it worse.

A sense of utter revulsion swept over me: just looking at the figures made me feel tainted, as if I was somehow responsible for them. I quickly exited the program and shut down the computer. Then I went back to my own desk, put on my coat and made my way out of the building, anxious to put as much distance between myself and the Screwdriver as I possibly could.

15

I spent most of the next day trying to put the horrible scary loss thingy out of my mind. I'd tried several times to pick up my mobile and anonymously text the compliance people, but when the moment came to actually do the deed, the idea of it all being traceable back to me, Laura McGregor, proved too much and I'm sorry to say I chickened out. However, on the plus side (in as much there *was* a plus side), I'd double-checked the bank's profits, assets and share price and it did seem that, even if push came to shove and the figures I'd seen *were* current, both the Chiltern and SunSpot looked to be secure.

Just.

Phew.

I still wasn't a happy bunny; and then, to add to the general weirdness of my life, at about six o'clock I had a phone call from my mother wanting to talk about, of all things, Alex.

'Laura?' she'd asked tentatively. 'Can I have a word? It's about the Hodder boy.'

'I suppose so,' I replied warily. 'If you insist.'

'I do,' replied my parent. 'I can't stop thinking about him.'

Join the club.

Despite being determined to shove my feelings in the

emotional equivalent of a large concrete block and bury it deep within my psyche, I couldn't get him off my mind. I wasn't helped by the fact that he had rung twice the night before (ostensibly to make sure I hadn't been nobbled by any Bristolian loan sharks), and each time I had heard his voice, a wave of longing broke tsunami-like over me. A rebel part of my mind had even begun to wonder if I had done the right thing in refusing to give him another chance. Yes, he should have told me about my dad, and yes, he certainly shouldn't have gone off snogging Isobel – but as far as the latter scenario was concerned, I wasn't entirely blameless; and as for the first, was it really a good thing to run the quarrels of my parents' generation on into ours?

I found myself wavering.

'I just wanted to say,' my mother continued, 'that if you did want to get together with him, then I for one would be happy for you.'

There was a 'crump' noise as my jaw hit the floor. Had I heard her right?

'Pardon?' I said.

'You and Alexander Hodder; I think you'd make rather a nice couple.'

'What?'

It was a shame we didn't have any windows up there in my office because I'm sure if I'd looked out of one right then, I'd have seen a squadron of pigs zooming past with flying goggles on.

'I've been mulling things over since Saturday, Laura; not just about Alexander but also about me and your dad.'

'Oh?' I truly had no idea where any of this was going.

'Well, you know that things didn't work out for me and him . . .'

'Um, yes,' I replied, hoping that I wasn't in for a

lecture about letting opportunities for love slip through my fingers.

'To be honest, the divorce is something I really regret. It was a difficult time, a stressful time, and in many ways I wish I could turn the clock back and do things differently.'

I boggled at the phone. This was definitely news to me.

'Okay,' I said slowly, as the import of her words gradually sank in. 'But what does this have to do with me and Alex?'

'Well,' my mother took a deep breath, 'seeing him there in your living room took me rather by surprise, and, frankly, I didn't react very well. I'm sorry about that – there is no way I should have allowed a little thing like Tony Hodder's cheque get to me after all these years.'

'What do you mean, "little thing"?' I protested, now more certain than ever that she had either gone insane or had spent the ten minutes before she phoned sniffing photocopier fluid. 'At the time you made it crystal clear that the Hodders were the root of all evil and responsible not only for our family problems but probably world hunger and global warming into the bargain.'

My parent let out a sigh that spoke of a lifetime of care and suffering.

'I don't really blame the Hodders, dear, no more than I blame you or Mel. Yes, it didn't *help*, but even if the money had come in on time, I suspect the outcome would have been the same. Tony was just a handy scapegoat. So – you and Alexander?' She continued. 'Any chance?'

Another wave of Alex-longing surged over me.

'I don't know,' I stuttered. 'We'd have a lot to work out.'

'Well, think about it. Your dad reckons you would be good together. He said he always liked Alex – sensible head on his shoulders.'

'You – spoke to Dad?' Now I was *sure* I hadn't heard her correctly.

'Mmmm. I rang him when I got back from London and he said he was just about to fly over. We had dinner yesterday and talked quite a lot about the pair of you. Anyway,' Mum suddenly sounded a bit agitated, 'he's coming round here in – oh, damn – five minutes. I've got to go and get ready. Byeeeee!'

And she hung up, leaving me staring at the receiver as though it had just tried to bite me.

Huh?

'Everything okay?' Polly materialised at my desk, her coat on and a large brown internal mail envelope in her hand.

'Fine,' I said, 'except for the fact that my parents have been abducted by aliens, who have replaced them with a pair of rational, sane human beings who have dinner together.'

Polly grinned. 'Maybe they'll want you and Mel to be bridesmaids at their second wedding.'

'I don't *think* so,' I snorted, and threw my coat on prior to accompanying her out of the building. 'This is my parents we're talking about. I give them a week at the outside before they resume their previous hostilities and start sending Semtex through the post to one another.'

'Oh ye of little romance,' Polly chided and held the brown envelope out towards me. 'I'm sorry to do this to you, Laura, but internal mail delivered this to me by mistake. It should have gone to Isobel Norland, and I *would* give it to her myself but I don't know where she sits and I'm supposed to be meeting Archie and his sister in five minutes. Could you be a sweetie and drop it off on your way out?'

'Archie's sister, eh?' I would rather have chopped my arm off than voluntarily go anywhere near Isobel, but Polly's welfare had to take precedence. 'This *is* getting serious.'

Polly blushed and nodded whilst I relieved her of the envelope and shoved it into my bag along with a large roll of duct tape I'd swiped from the stationary cupboard to cover up a mousehole behind the telly at home.

'I think you could be right.' She grinned. 'Maybe if you don't get to be bridesmaid at your parents' wedding, you could do the job for me.'

I stared at her. 'You're not? I mean – already? So soon?'

She shook her head. 'Not yet, but I can't help wondering . . . Anyway, I'll see you tomorrow. Cheers m'dears for dropping the mail off.'

And she was gone.

I buttoned up my coat, threw my bag over my shoulder, and if I'd known what 'girding' actually meant and had happened to have any girds on me, I think I'd also have taken the precaution of girding my loins.

You see, after Alex's confession to me that his reunion with Isobel had been nothing more than an unhappy drunken fumble, I assumed that he would have done the decent thing and disabused her of any fantasies she might have been nurturing about destiny and love and the pair of them punting up the Cherwell in the twilight, etc. etc. The only problem was, there was no way this news was going to be well received by Isobel. It didn't matter whether he mentioned my part in the whole unhappy scenario or not; sooner or later she was going to find out that it was me who had stolen the love of her life away from her, and I didn't think for one second the consequences were going to be pretty.

Especially if I did what my wavering mind was now urging me to, and gave Alex the second chance he had asked for.

Holding on to that slightly scary thought, I made my way down to the twelfth floor and sought out Isobel in her lair.

Unlike my own cluttered workspace, her desk was completely empty apart from her computer, a bottle of Chanel nail polish and an antique glass perfume atomiser (did she ever do any work?). The woman herself was sitting on a chair that looked almost as luxurious as Will's, and frowning with concentration at the pages of a glossy magazine. She looked up and nodded approvingly at me as I entered.

'Ooh, Laura,' she purred, tapping a pencil against her chin, 'just the person I wanted to see. Would you say that I was: (a) Flexible and willing to compromise; (b) Firm in my beliefs but happy to discuss another person's point of view; or (c) Conflict-averse and unwilling to commit myself? Hmmm, it's either (a) or (c) but I can't make up my mind which.'

I bit back my instinctive reply that Isobel was probably the least conflict-averse person since Mussolini, and tried to see which publication it was that she was engrossed in.

She caught my eye, and a flicker of something strange ran across her face.

'It's a quiz about whether or not you've found your soulmate,' she said slowly. 'I can't stop doing these compatibility tests, you know; I'm simply *addicted* to them.'

'Really?' I said, feeling as though someone had just given the floor under my feet an almighty tug. 'And have you?'

'Have I what?' A smile flitted across her face. She was enjoying this.

'Found your soulmate?' I repeated.

I had to know. This wasn't just idle curiosity – she was talking about Alex, I could *feel* it.

Isobel's lazy, cat-like smile traced itself over her features and she put down her pencil.

'Well,' she drawled, 'let's just say that after what happened yesterday, I have every confidence that he and I are going to be extremely happy together.'

I think at this point my heart actually stopped beating for about thirty seconds. It was either that or time literally stood still as the full import of her words sank in. After the near-grovelling terms in which he'd spoken, the effort he'd put into convincing me he felt nothing for Isobel, I struggled to imagine Alex ringing her up and suggesting that they would be *extremely happy together* – but what other possible explanation could there be?

'Good for you,' I managed at last. Whatever trauma I was going through internally, I refused to be cowed by a woman whose most pressing daily concern was whether to match her lipstick to her shoes or the other way round.

I carefully placed the envelope Polly had given me on Isobel's desk.

'This was sent to Polly Marchant by mistake; she asked me to drop it round,' I said, pretty coolly, actually.

'You know,' Isobel put her magazine down and leaned over to pick up the envelope, a concerned expression etched deep into her flawless face, 'there are always winners and losers in these matters, Laura; but I want you to know that I harbour no hard feelings whatsoever towards you.'

'No,' I said, clenching my fists deep inside my coat pockets so that she wouldn't see. 'No hard feelings.'

'Good.'

Isobel smiled at me and picked up the envelope. As she flicked through its contents, her previously smug expression vanished and was replaced by one of pure horror.

'They've brought the meeting forward to tomorrow!' she squeaked. 'I've got a whole presentation to do before the morning!'

She tried to switch on her computer, but nothing happened.

'Damn!' she exclaimed. 'The system's down.'

I smothered a weak grin. Maybe there was a God after all.

'Shame,' I said. 'Essential IT maintenance, I think. Anyway, have fun. Hope you hadn't arranged to see him tonight!'

The look I received in return wasn't pretty, and for about a nanosecond I felt very sorry indeed for Alex. Then I got a grip, told myself he knew exactly what he was getting himself into, and bestowed a dazzling 'I-don't-care-who-you-date-honey' smile on Isobel.

Then exited with what I considered an impressive amount of dignity.

Outside, however, my feelings surged unchecked as I stomped down the road to the tube station. To my astonishment, I found tears blinking into the corners of my eyes and I brushed them away angrily. Why had I allowed myself to believe that Alex and I ever stood a chance? I might be able to excuse him not telling me about the business debt; I might *even* be able to brush his first drunken dalliance with Isobel under the carpet. But this – *this*? The man was obviously a pathological liar – either he was lying to me about his feelings, or he was lying to Isobel. Well, it had to stop here, and it had to stop now. If I'd got shot of Tom with little more than a wave goodbye, shouldn't I be able to do the same for Alex, a man I'd only known for about two milliseconds?

With my head thumping, I stopped, pulled out my BlackBerry and typed in a text with so much fury that the machine was in danger of short-circuiting.

Heard news from Isobel. I stabbed at the keypad. *Stay away from me.* And I pressed 'send'.

As it whirled off through the ether to Alex, I doubled my determination to ensure that whatever I felt for him ended immediately. There was no way I would be able to survive Isobel dropping verbal cluster-bombs about what a *simply maaaaaarvellous* relationship they had unless I took drastic action and eliminated Alex from my life completely. It had to be a clean, surgical incision that cut away all residues of feeling I had for him once and for all.

And my time starts – now!

I swallowed hard to get rid of the lump that was threatening to form in my throat (*he's not worth it!*) and clattered loudly down the steps of the tube station, taking out my frustration on the concrete underfoot and hoping that if I walked fast enough, I could outpace the feeling of aching emptiness that had once again returned to haunt me.

As I emerged from Hammersmith station, my BlackBerry beeped and I fished it out without breaking stride.

It was a message from Alex!

My heart pumped wildly. Did I open it and see what he had to say for himself? Or did I just hit the 'delete' button and send him packing once and for all? My finger hovered from one button to the other . . .

Delete.

There, the deed was done. Alex was consigned to the past and I could now walk forward into my future unburdened by the baggage of unrequited love.

I sniffed twice, picked up my pace again and turned into the warren of little residential streets behind Fulham Palace Road. I stopped at an offy for a bottle of wine (Chateau Dutch Courage, if I wasn't much mistaken) and then stalked down the road that led home. The only thing I was sensible of was a cold, empty, aching feeling that started in the pit of my stomach and spread out through my veins to the whole of my body. So all-encompassing was it that it seemed to hover in the air above and slide between the shadows down the street behind me.

I had allowed Alex to take my heart and beat it into a pulp, and then – just when I thought it was safe to think about giving him a second chance – he'd done exactly the same thing again. Once bitten, twice as stupid. Well, never again, Alex Hodder – do you hear me? Never again!

My mind was full of black thoughts and tiny hot tears were pricking into the corners of my eyes as I rounded the corner to my own little street and saw something that made my heart not only miss a beat but stop entirely.

There was a figure lurking outside my flat.

And when I say lurking, I don't just mean 'hanging around waiting for someone to open the door' or 'trying his luck to see if I wanted to change my gas supplier', this was full-on, scary lurking, with the lurker in question pressed right up against the front wall of the house and peering round behind him in what could only be described as a suspicious manner. He was thin and wiry and looked as though he featured members of the weasel family among his recent ancestors.

I ducked out of the fuzzy orange glow of the street light and slipped back into the shadows. There was a stumpy old tree a couple of steps away from me that had been pollarded almost out of existence and I sidled up towards it. My efforts at subterfuge were nearly foiled when my foot came down heavily upon an empty crisp packet and the subsequent 'pop' made the Lurker glance wildly about him.

Damn! Damn! I flattened myself up against the tree in a manner reminiscent of Shaggy and Scooby Doo, then cursed again as the plastic bag containing my wine bottle crashed against the trunk and the Lurker jumped a full three feet in the air.

Taking some consolation from the fact that he seemed to be even more on edge than me, I watched as he sidled over to my front door. He turned his back on me for a nanosecond and I used the time to scurry down the pavement to the next tree along, this one situated directly outside my house. I watched as the Lurker tried first the living-room window, then my bedroom one, but both held fast – thank God for the window locks. He fumbled round in the pocket of his hoodie and pulled out a phone.

''Ello, Dave?' he said in a broad West Country accent. 'Yeah, s'me. No, oi can't gerrin. It's locked.'

At the sound of his voice, my heart decided not to bother pumping any blood round my body and simply froze. Those couple of sentences told me all I needed to know: this was Mel's loan shark, all the way from sunny Bristol.

The Lurker/Loan Shark wandered back to the window and gave it a desultory tug.

'Oi'm tellin' yer it's locked,' he whined into his handset. 'An' there's some sorta bolt on the front door. Any'ow, oi knackered me credit card tryin' to gerrin last time, an' oi ain't doin' that again whatevver Tony says.'

There was a pause, presumably while the person on the other end of the line added their thoughts on the subject.

''Ee don't scare me,' the Lurker went on. ''Ee's only

saying that because it gets the shits up that gobshite Gobshite. That's how we know where his bird's bin hangin' out.'

My breath caught in my throat. So it hadn't been Mel's meddling on the internet that had led them here after all; it had been Gobshite with the shits up him (a thought I certainly didn't want to dwell on).

The Lurker was now standing on the steps outside the door looking up at the house.

'Orl right,' he conceded to his accomplice on the other end of the line, 'but if that don't work oi'm goin' off down the pub.'

Behind my tree, I swallowed hard. I was completely on my own. Both my flat and the O'Linehans' were in darkness, and apart from me and the Lurker, there was no one else out on the street.

Then things started to happen.

The Lurker stopped standing on the front steps staring up at the house and began walking backwards down the garden path, his eyes still firmly fixed on my front door. He hadn't seen me and had no idea at all that I was watching him, even though my heart was beating so loudly they could probably hear it in Chelsea.

I held my breath: he was now almost within spitting distance. He took another step, and then another, until he was walking through the gap in the garden wall where the gate should have been. Suddenly he stumbled on a patch of uneven ground and I saw my chance.

'You nasty little shit!' I screamed, running at him with all the speed I could possibly manage. 'How dare you break into my flat!'

And I sent the plastic bag containing my bottle of Jacob's Creek Shiraz Cabernet crashing into the back of his neck. He emitted a strangled cry before swaying gently and pitching forward face first on to the pavement.

To my great joy, I saw that he had coincided heavily with a big pile of dog poo.

I leapt on to his back, pulled his hands up behind him and scrabbled in my bag for the roll of duct tape. Holding it in my teeth, I wrapped tape round his wrists (and took the opportunity to grind his forehead down a bit further into the doggy doo-doo as I did so). Then I repeated the same trick with his feet and rolled him over on to his back, standing with one foot perched on his stomach ready to kick him in the cojones if he tried to get up.

He stared at me as though I was the scary mad one.

'What did you fuckin' do that for?' he cried. 'I'll have the law on you, you nutter. You can't go round tying blokes up.'

'Give me your phone,' I demanded.

His eyes opened even wider.

'You a mugger?' he asked, his voice perfectly balanced between terror and respect.

'No,' I growled, wrestling the phone out of his pocket myself. 'I'm Mel's sister and this is my house. Now give me Tony's number. He's Psycho Pete's mate, right?'

My captive nodded dumbly before adding helpfully, "Is number's in me phone book under Mad Dog.'

'Fabulous,' I said, dialling and hearing the connection click through. 'Good evening, is that Mad Dog Tony?'

A voice on the other end confirmed that it was indeed that particular gentleman.

'Good,' I said, almost beginning to enjoy myself. 'Because I'm Mel McGregor's sister Laura and I've just caught your colleague . . .'

I covered the mouthpiece.

'What's your name?' I hissed.

'Wayne,' my captive replied.

'. . . Wayne trying to break into my house. Anyway, I've immobilised him and he's currently lying in the street in a pile of dog excrement. Here he is, he'll confirm it for you.'

I held the phone a few inches away from Wayne's mouth.

'Yeah, mate, it's me,' muttered Wayne. 'she's got me tied up – no, don't laugh, she's a fucking loony, mate. She knocked me out wiv a bottle and now oi've got this tape round me arms and legs and oi caan't move.'

'Right.' I checked that none of Wayne's dog-poo face pack had made its way on to the handset and put the phone back up to my face. 'You two are going to tell me who exactly is behind this, and if you don't—'

'If we don't – then what?' I could hear the sneer in Mad Dog's voice. 'What are you gonna do about it?'

For a moment I panicked. I had no idea what I *could* do, short of handing Wayne over to the cops, and something told me that was not going to be enough to get him out of my life. It had to be something worse than the strong arm of the law – something to freak them *both* out so much that they steered clear of me and Mel forever more.

Then I noticed the answer to my problems poking out of the top of Wayne's T-shirt.

I went back into my bag and pulled out the little manicure case my mother had given me one Christmas years and years ago. As far as I could remember, I had only ever used it once, when I needed an emery board to smooth down a splinter on the edge of my desk. Now, however, it was about to come into its own. My eye ran along the various instruments until it alighted on the tweezers. I pulled them out and snapped them together a couple of times so that Wayne could see them.

'Whatya gonna do wiv them?' Wayne bleated, correctly deducing that whatever it was, it wasn't going to be pleasant.

By way of reply, I dipped down towards the neck of his T-shirt and plucked out one of the protruding chest hairs.

'Arrgggggghhhhhhhh,' he responded gratifyingly.

I flexed the tweezers smugly and fixed my gaze on Wayne's chest.

'Whaddaya want to know?' he said quickly.

'Your full name, please, Tony,' I replied.

There was a slight hesitation, so I dived in and grabbed another hair.

'Tell 'er mate, tell 'er,' begged Wayne. 'She's killin' me!'

Thankfully Tony didn't need to be told twice.

'Anthony Kevin Marshall,' he gulped. 'Twenty-four Riversea Gardens, Portishead.'

'Is that right?' I asked Wayne.

He nodded.

'Please don't do it again – it bloody hurts!' he begged.

'Good,' I said grimly, scribbling this information down on the back of an old supermarket receipt. 'Then you'll understand I mean business. Who are you?'

'WayneDrewslipfifteenCranburyRoadWestburyonTry mBristol.' He was practically in tears.

Tony quickly confirmed that this was, indeed, correct.

'Now, which one of you actually lent Mel the money?'

There was silence from both Wayne (although he did a bit of whimpering) and Tony. I waved the tweezers in Wayne's face.

'Tony,' he bleated. 'It was Tony that lent them the money. Nothin' to do wiv me!'

'And how much was it?'

'Five 'undred to 'im and five 'undred to her,' he said.

This was something I didn't know.

'So why did you come after Mel for the full amount?' I asked.

'Tony thought she'd scare more easy than 'im,' bleated Wayne, 'and corf up.'

'She hasn't got any money,' I told him. 'If she did, do you think she'd have come to you pair of con merchants for a loan?'

'Gobshite made 'er do it,' replied Wayne. 'She told me she'd rather eat dirt than borrow from scum like us.'

Maybe my sister had a bit more sense than I generally gave her credit for.

'Right,' I said, getting out my chequebook, 'here is five hundred quid in full and final settlement of all claims on my sister. You are reducing the interest rate to nil as a gesture of goodwill because of the prompt repayment of the debt.'

'Well I dunno about that . . .' Tony began.

I yanked out a third hair and Wayne's screams rent the frosty spring air in two.

'Okay, okay,' Tony muttered.

'But it's already been paid off,' said Wayne, looking askance at the tweezers still in my hand.

'Shut up, you silly bastard!' yelled Tony in my ear. 'She didn't know that!'

'I was just coming round to give you the receipt,' Wayne continued.

Receipt? It was almost touching.

'It's in the same pocket as me phone,' he said.

I delved in and duly pulled out a handwritten docket:
Mel Macgregor has payd five hundred quid sined Tony Marshall all debt is payd off.

'Thank you,' I said, pocketing it along with my unused chequebook. 'Now, Wayne, do you think I should ring the police?'

He looked terrified.

'Well, let's see – there's breaking and entering, threatening behaviour, harassment, lending money at extortionate rates of interest. I think the rozzers would love to meet you, don't you?'

'No! No! Please! If oi get arrested again they's goin' to activate me suspended sentence and send me to prison.'

'What about you then, Tony?' I turned again to the man on the other end of the line. 'Why shouldn't I go straight down the nick and drop off your names and addresses to the cops?'

'I don't really care,' he replied miserably. 'Can't be worse than what that other bloke said he'd do to us if we didn't clear off.'

'Other bloke?' I asked.

'The same one who paid the five 'undred quid,' chipped in Wayne. 'He was scary. Tall and a bit mad-looking with a big black coat and a scar on 'is face. Quoit put the frighteners on me, oi don't mind tellin' yer. Oi knows yer won't believe me, but oi'm leaving you McGregor girls well alone after this.'

I stood up. Jules must have paid them a visit – but how? Why?

Whatever the reason, something in Wayne's desolate tone and the crappy little receipt told me they weren't planning on bothering us again.

'Okay, well I've reported the break-in to the cops, and I'm giving them your names and addresses: I'd be a mug not to. But as long as you steer a bloody long way clear, we'll just keep it at that, shall we? A little insurance policy for me and Mel.'

'Don't worry,' said Wayne. 'The pair of you are fucking barmy and so's your mate in the big black coat. He scared the crap out of me.'

'Good for him, Wayne. Right, nice talking to you, Tony – I hope I never have the pleasure of doing so again.'

I placed the phone on the pavement not too far from Wayne's head.

'Night night, Wayne,' I said as I turned to walk up my garden path. 'Don't hesitate to sod off out of my life, will you?'

'Aren't you going to untie me?' he cried.

I paused.

'Let me think . . .' I placed my index finger contemplatively on my chin. 'No, I can't be arsed. Goodbye.'

And fingering my receipt, I went into the flat and bolted all the doors very carefully behind me.

16

Friday and then the weekend passed quietly, with no hassle from Wayne, no word from Alex and no further upsets at work. Polly casually mentioned that a stockbroker friend of Archie's would like to ask me out for a drink, but despite agreeing to meet up with the three of them on Sunday evening, I found myself ringing Polly at half past five on Sunday afternoon to cancel: my heart simply wasn't in it. However, on a happier note, I slept easy in my bed for the first time in ages, and despite a couple of strange dreams in which Isobel stalked through my flat holding a large clipboard and took all the furniture, fixtures and fittings back to her own house, I awoke on Monday morning feeling reasonably rested.

This was good – because Will was due back today and I needed every possible ounce of energy I could lay my hands on to tackle him over the accounts.

My dilemma, essentially, was this: if the figures I had stumbled across *were* the truth, the whole truth and nothing but the truth, then I was in the territory of a financial fraud and the authorities needed to be informed. *However*, if I did turn whistle-blower, I knew I risked ruining my entire career. I had followed the stories of other City workers who'd broken the news about their companies' wrongdoings, and not only had a fair few been fired for their pains, but they had then found it hard to gain alternative employment. I had to be one hundred per cent convinced not only that a crime was being committed, but also that it was serious enough to risk losing my job over.

The more I mulled things over, the more certain I became that, despite the fact that his password unlocked the various databases containing the dodgy figures, Will wasn't at the heart of this. It simply wasn't his style. He was a worker, a grafter, and I knew he wouldn't get any satisfaction from cheating his way to success. Something fishier than bouillabaisse was going on, and I was going to find out what.

Emboldened by having sorted out Wayne and Tony with nothing more than my bare hands and a roll of duct tape, I walked up to Will's office on the dot of seven thirty and peered through the glass wall.

It was empty.

I knew that Will, in authentic Gordon Gekko style, thought that sleep was for wimps and was legendary (amongst much else) for being at his desk by six. True, he was due to have flown in on the red-eye from New York that morning, but if he didn't do sleep, I felt it unlikely that he was going to do jet lag, and so I peered in again, unable to believe that he hadn't already put in a good couple of hours.

And then I saw it.

Or rather, I *didn't* see it: there was a huge gaping hole on his desk where his computer with its multiple screens had been situated. I squinted through the tunnel of my cupped hands, trying to see if anything else had gone AWOL, and was amazed to note that the walls were bare and that the floor was covered with a number of large cardboard boxes.

Exactly the sort of boxes they give to people who have just got the sack so that they can pack up their office.

As well as hearing on the office grapevine how Sophie Spink and her Execution Squad dispatched the likes of me, I had also heard rumours of how the high-level firings worked: basically the firee didn't have a clue until the bombshell was dropped; then, as they were having their fate explained to them in a tiny room by the Spink, a team from IT was busy disabling their computer, and if the information they held was sensitive or important enough, their belongings were packed for them and sent home by courier. I had even heard of dismissals where the subject wasn't allowed to bid farewell to their colleagues, but was escorted by a security guard straight off the premises as soon as their meeting with HR was over.

So I knew what this meant – and it was enough to virtually stop my heart: for reasons as yet unknown, Will's short stint at SunSpot was over.

I looked round for Melody, thinking that much as I disliked the idea of voluntarily initiating a conversation with her, she might have some insider information on Will's fate. But her desk, in the otherwise busy office, was vacant.

I was almost at the point of making my way over to one of the trading rooms and enquiring there, when my BlackBerry went off. Without thinking, I grabbed it out of my pocket and slammed it against my ear.

'McGregor,' I said.

'Laura? Hi, it's Alex. Look, I hope you don't mind me ringing you . . .'

It was a measure of the shock I was in over Will's disappearance that I didn't freak out immediately at the sound of his voice.

'I can't speak right now,' I said automatically, looking over my shoulder just in case Sophie Spink was standing there. 'Something's happened.'

'I know. Look, Laura, there's something I need to tell you.'

Suddenly my whole body stiffened. The thought of Isobel waving her compatibility quiz round in my face like some sort of victory salute slammed into me with the force of a sixty-tonne freight train. No! I was going to sever the link between me and Alex. Whatever he wanted to say would have to be put on hold.

Preferably for ever.

'Alex,' I replied icily, 'I've spoken to Isobel and I know what the score is. Now if you'll forgive me, I have better things to do than listen to you justify why you're shagging her.'

'This isn't about Isobel,' he persisted. 'Or at least, there *is* something I need to tell you regarding her – but something else much more important has cropped up, and for reasons you'll understand in a minute, it's imperative I speak to you *now*.'

The old empty, aching pain welled up again inside me and for a moment I felt real despair. Was I *ever* going to be rid of my feelings for this wretched man? I had tried denial, I had tried forgetting him, I had even agreed to go on a date with another bloke! What was it about Alex Hodder that he should become the infuriating, indelible red-wine stain on the carpet of my life – and why couldn't he take the hint and *stop bloody ringing me!*

With a shuddering sob beginning to build in my fast-constricting throat, I took the hurt and the frustration that had been smouldering inside me and flung it back at him.

'I HATE you – did you hear that, Alex? I HATE you! I hate the fact that you stopped me leaving the meeting room because you wanted to ask me out; I hate that you knew I'd like Turkish food even though I'd never tried it; and I hate that you wanted to see me home safely after the Middle Temple farce – and do you know *why* I hate all those things? Because they are what made me fall in love with you! Only as soon as I did, you went and threw yourself into the arms of that self-satisfied, husband-hunting tart – and then spent most of Tuesday night lying to me about it! So don't you DARE ring me up and pretend to be all concerned, because as we both know, the truth is you couldn't GIVE A SHIT.'

I stopped to draw breath and glowered at the other people in the office, who were, without exception, staring at me with their jaws hanging open.

Alex used my pause to leap into the conversation.

'That's not true!' His voice was rising too. 'If you would just give me a minute to explain—'

'It so is true! You tell me on Tuesday you're in love with me and then you waltz right on back to Isobel and tell her exactly the same thing! Well it's cruel, it's selfish and I'M NOT PUTTING UP WITH IT ANY MORE! Do you hear?'

'That's Isobel Norland in Marketing, by the way,' I said, turning to my eavesdropping office-worker audience, who gasped gratifyingly.

'But – but you said I didn't stand a chance with you!' Alex sounded bemused; I could almost *hear* the furrows in his brow as he tried to work this one out.

'Like that makes a difference!' I snarled back.

Illogical, yes – but hey – this was love we were talking about, and I was fast learning that logic didn't come into it.

'Now, Laura,' Alex wasn't giving up, 'please don't do anything that you might regret later . . .'

I laughed a mirthless laugh.

'Like what, Alex? Finding you attractive? Trusting you not to hurt me? *Sleeping* with you?'

My listeners-in emitted a little ripple of 'oooooh's at this last revelation.

'Laura,' Alex thundered down the phone, 'for the last bloody time – you are a stubborn, opinionated, feisty woman; you drive me out of my fucking mind; and I meant what I said: it's *you* I want – not her!'

His voice was angry and honest and something in it tugged painfully at my heart – but what he might have wanted on Tuesday night and what he now *had* in the slender shape of his ex-girlfriend were two completely different things. I wiped my nose with the back of my hand and shot back:

'Let me assure you, Mr Hodder, that even though I am in love with you now, this is only a temporary aberration, and normal non-Alex service will be resumed shortly – and do you know why? Because I am worth more than a one-night stand; I am worth more than you are prepared to give me; and most importantly, I am worth a *hundred* Isobels – and if you can't see that, then that means YOU are not good enough for ME!'

There was a cheer and a bit of sporadic clapping. I almost felt as though I should take a bow.

'For God's sake, Laura,' Alex still wasn't giving up, 'for once in your life, please work with me here – I do need to talk to you about Isobel, that's true; but there is something else.'

There was a pause, and I knew in the marrow of my bones that I wasn't going to like what was coming next.

Alex took a breath so deep it must have been drawn up from the tips of his toes.

'I know you told me not to,' he said, 'but I read some of your diary.'

'You did *what*?' I shrieked, making everyone else in the office take a step back.

There was silence on the other end of the line – presumably as Alex yanked the receiver away from his ear, waited for the pain to cease, and then put it back to continue the conversation.

'I know, I know – you have every right to be angry with me, but you also need to believe me when I tell you it was totally unavoidable.'

My head was reeling. His betrayal of me was complete: he had substituted me with Isobel and then stabbed me in the back over the diary. He'd chewed me up good and proper – all he needed to do now was spit out the pips.

'Good God, Alex! How on earth could it be unavoidable? Did someone Sellotape your eyes open and wave a printout in front of your face? Did they kidnap your entire family and tell you that unless you read the same personal, private journal I had expressly told you not to, they were going to murder the lot of them? You really are un-bloody-believable.'

'I appreciate what it looks like, Laura, but *please* listen to me. One of my colleagues was researching a story and sent me a link to check out, and—'

With the tears choking up my voice box, my reply was never going to win any awards for elegance, but the vehemence of it took even me by surprise and drew another round of applause from my enthusiastic audience.

'You still bloody read it, though, didn't you? You can say what you like, Alex, but I'm never going to listen to you again! In fact, as far as I'm concerned, you can GO TO HELL. Have you got that? Sod off, get knotted, sling your hook – because if you don't, I think you might actually drive me mad!'

And without ever finding out what he had actually called to tell me, I hung up on him.

Then, wiping my face with the back of my hand and allowing myself one large, gulping sniff, I ran out of the office and into the nearest ladies', where I locked myself firmly inside one of the cubicles and proceeded to howl for England.

After a little time had passed (and I'd staunched the flow from every single facial orifice except my ears), I heard a noise. At first it was so quiet that I thought I'd been mistaken – but then it came again, a faint but distinct 'tap, tap, tap', and looking down, I recognised the toes of Polly's shoes through the space under the door.

'Laura,' she whispered, 'are you in there?'

I eased myself off the toilet seat, threw the last remnants of my soggy tissue into the tampon bin and unbolted the door. I couldn't have been a pretty sight, but Polly, bless her, didn't care: she folded me up in her arms and let me rest my mascara-stained cheek on her shoulder.

'Are you all right?' she asked before sharply correcting herself. 'No, of course you're not. You wouldn't be crying in the bogs if you were. What I meant was, what's up?'

My tears had subsided but my breathing was still coming in huge, shuddering gasps, so I confined myself to merely shaking my head, making sure I didn't smear too much eye make-up on her jacket in the process.

Polly pulled a tissue out of a box near the washbasins (the Screwdriver had posh loos) and wiped my eyes with it.

'What's wrong?' she asked again. 'Is it to do with SunSpot?'

I helped myself to another tissue and blew my nose vigorously.

'No,' I gasped.

'Thank God for that,' Polly replied. 'I was really worried that you'd had bad news and came to find you. There's been some rumour doing the rounds in the past half-hour that something's up with SunSpot and Will's got the boot; I thought for a moment you'd been told you'd lost your job too.'

Her words were like a slap round the face: instantly the gulping stopped and the power of speech was restored.

'You're kidding,' I gasped, my hand holding a tissue frozen halfway between the box and my nose. 'They really and honestly fired *Will*?'

Even though I'd seen his office full of boxes, I still hadn't quite believed it. Polly's eyes narrowed.

'Well, nobody from head office has actually come out and confirmed it; but equally it's not been denied, either – and you know what that means.'

I did indeed. City institutions, always sensitive to the old 'confidence = share price' equation, were usually keen to head off any rumours that didn't have a firm basis in reality. Anything that was left floating about usually had the ring of truth about it – including the time Jason, one of our senior executives, had surprised the world of finance by allegedly turning up for a meeting in a pussy-cat-bow blouse and asking everyone to call him Dolores.

'But *Will* . . .' My sentence trailed off into silent incomprehension.

Even though I had no reason to doubt Polly's news, it still seemed incredible. Will was the Golden Boy; the star of the show. The reason why people – incredibly rich, influential people – got out their chequebooks and started giving us money with large numbers of noughts on the end. Without him in the driving seat, I didn't want to think about what might happen.

Polly regarded me with dark, serious eyes.

'I know,' she said. 'I thought you might have some inside information.'

'Sorry.' I shook my head again. 'He flew to New York

for a meeting on Wednesday and I haven't seen him since. But . . . but . . .'

Once again I struggled to find the right words.

'If Will goes, then SunSpot goes too?' Polly read my mind with uncanny accuracy. 'I hate to say it, Laura, but I think you're right. And what sort of impact is that going to have on the rest of the bank?'

We stood for a moment in silence, contemplating not only Will's fate, but our own destinies too.

'Don't worry,' I said, brushing her arm with my hand in a gesture of solidarity, 'it'll be fine.'

She bit her lip and nodded at me, forcing herself to look slightly less suicidal than she had moments before.

'You know,' she said at last, 'if I turned the light off, we could do some actual whistling in the dark.'

'Or we could go and check the news,' I suggested, 'see if there's been some sort of official announcement.'

Polly paled.

'There was something else,' she said, 'something that came up on the Financial News Today network just before I came to find you. One of their journalists has dug up some dirt on SunSpot; he was on telly saying that some of the funds aren't making the profits SunSpot claims they are.'

For a moment I thought I was actually going to be sick. I leaned over the washbasin and waited for the inevitable – but thankfully it never came. I stared into the mirror in front of me, my face the same colour as the bleached white paper towels piled up next to the taps, and my eyes met Polly's.

'Which journalist?' I asked, hoping against hope that she wouldn't confirm my worst fears as my stomach continued to lurch and roll like a ship in high seas.

Polly scrunched up her forehead in concentration.

'Hodder,' she said at last, 'Alex Hodder.'

I closed my eyes and forced myself to take big, calming breaths.

That must have been why he was ringing: he was warning me he was about to go public with the stuff he'd found in my diary! Even allowing for the fact that the man had fewer scruples than a recidivist cockroach, this was impressive stuff. All that bullshit about me being the one he wanted, when in reality he was about to raid my private life for everything he could get and use it to get his big fat face plastered over every television screen from here to Tokyo.

'Where are you going?' called Polly as I pushed past her and raced for the door.

'The office,' I yelled back over my shoulder. 'This is an emergency.'

As I pounded back up the stairs with Polly behind me, my phone went again. I whipped it out, and after checking that the number on the display did not match up with any I had for Alex, accepted the call.

'Hello, Laura?' The line was bad, and it was as much as I could do to make out the words, let alone decipher who might be speaking. 'It's Will.'

I almost dropped the handset.

'Bloody hell, Will – what the hell is going on?'

'I resigned yesterday,' he said, the line badly distorted by crackles. 'I won't be coming back to SunSpot. I couldn't stand it any longer.'

I lowered my voice as much as I could.

'I know about the false trades,' I whispered.

'I know you know,' he replied. 'You didn't cover your tracks very well. I guessed it was you from the log-in times on the pages you opened.'

I could have kicked myself: of course! One of the security features on the system was to record the time and date a particular page was accessed. Will would easily have spotted somebody else snooping round his accounts.

'Oh shit!' I breathed.

'Relax,' Will told me. 'No one else is going to realise it wasn't me; your secret's safe. However, the problem's bigger than that. SunSpot was dependent on the money coming in from new investors to keep the returns up. Bogus trades were used to drip-feed the money into the funds before siphoning it off again later.'

My breath ground to a halt in my chest as I remembered how the fund I'd looked at had suddenly plunged from profit into loss, and I choked out the words:

'God Almighty, Will, were you running a Ponzi scheme?'

'I hate to call it that, but yeah, basically that was what was happening. Only – and you've got to believe me on this one – I didn't start it and neither did I benefit from it by so much as one penny. It was established way before I got there, and I actually put in all my profits and about half my salary just to keep the figures up. The problem is much higher up the food chain than me. Try asking the chairman of Chiltern where he found the money for his executive bonus this year.'

'Will,' I said, glancing around to make sure no one else was within earshot, 'why are you telling me this?'

'Because you need to get out. Go now and start looking for something else. I've already spoken to the regulators on Wall Street about the American arm of the business, because I do not want my name associated with this sort of scandal; this is not the way I operate. It took me a while to figure out exactly how big this was but, as soon as I did, I made my position clear to the powers-that-be that *no way* was I prepared to put up with this on my watch; however, I was then told that if I breathed a word, I would be implicated up to my eyeballs. It's taken me a couple of months to safeguard my own position before going after them.

'Are you telling me the bank is using SunSpot to hide massive losses?'

'I don't know what the losses relate to. I don't wanna know, but they run into billions and there's no way siphoning money off a few hedge funds is going to pay them off. This is only the tip of the iceberg. What I'm saying is for God's sake look after yourself – you're under no obligation to anyone else.'

'Okay.' I tried to digest the import of what I'd been told. 'Will, does this mean you'll go to gaol?'

Will did a plausible imitation of a carefree laugh. If I hadn't known him so well, he might almost have convinced me.

'I can take care of myself,' he said. 'I was careful about what I saw and I'm making damn sure the regulators get everything I can give them. It's survival of the fittest, Laura – and you know how hard I work out at the gym.'

Despite the bravado, there was the tiniest wobble in his voice that told me he knew he was in trouble. It was like hearing Captain Oates telling his comrades that he was just popping out into the blizzards of the South Pole for a mo, and not to hold their breath waiting for him to get back.

'Oh, and Laura . . .'

'What?'

'Two things: first up, if you need it, don't forget the opera. And second up, if you're over here, call me and I'll take you on that date we had to the Met.'

And he rang off, leaving me staring at the phone and thinking that this was not the time to be gabbling about opera as Rome pretty much burned around us.

I looked up the flight of stairs to where Polly was

holding open the door that led into our office. She beckoned me.

'Now,' she called, 'you've got to come now. That Hodder bloke is on and he's saying that SunSpot have been operating some sort of fraud. It'll be why Will got his ass fired. Come on!'

And I pounded up the stairs after her, praying that my ass wasn't the next in line.

17

As I walked through the doors of our normally buzz-ing office, I was in for a shock. The room had the energy level of a morgue – and not a zippy, go-getting sort of morgue either. In fact, I swear the temperature dropped by at least five degrees as I stepped over the threshold.

People either stood at their workstations or huddled in small groups, but unlike last week, when they had been gamely getting on with their business in the face of the unfolding crisis, they were stock still: the only thing that moved in the entire room were the pictures on the television screen on the far wall and the twenty pairs of eyes watching them.

Polly ground to a halt a couple of feet away from the door and stood chewing her nails.

'Oh shit,' she breathed, wiping flakes of French polish off her tongue with the back of her hand.

I looked up at the screen and immediately concurred with her assessment. Oh – and indeed – shit.

'It's not just Will,' whispered Polly, just in case the ability to read had momentarily deserted me. 'They're saying that the news about SunSpot has caused the Chiltern's share price to collapse and – oh my God, look!'

I followed the direction of her chewed-up fingers and watched in horror as the picture cut away from the anchor lady and focused on – no! It couldn't be! The shot on screen was of the Chiltern branch just down the road, and there was a long, snaking queue of people standing outside it. A red ticker ran along the bottom of the screen carrying the words: *Breaking news: as Chiltern Bank share price collapses, customers start to besiege branches.*

Someone with a remote control whacked the sound up.

'. . .and the reports that we are getting in across the country tell us that the situation is pretty much the same in every major town and city,' said an on-the-spot reporter jovially. 'Let's just see the scene in Manchester . . .' The shot cut to one of identical-looking people standing outside a red-brick building in the rain. 'Cardiff . . .' Ditto. 'And finally Edinburgh.'

If anything, the Scottish bunch looked the most fired up of the lot. Even though there was no sound feed, you could almost hear them rattling their walking-sticks and muttering angrily about the imminent collapse of civilisation.

'But,' I began weakly, 'how? Why?'

Polly pointed to the words now coming round on the bottom-of-the-screen ticker:

Evidence of fraud was leaked by an employee to a member of the FNT news staff. Chiltern Bank bosses are refusing to comment.

At that particular moment I would have inflicted severe physical damage on Alex had he been in the vicinity. The bastard had raided my blog and shoved the whole lot on national telly. The fact that this had then caused the bank's share price to collapse meant that it could very well destroy the Chiltern, destroy my life and destroy the livelihoods of every single one of my colleagues. He might as well have aimed a tactical nuclear warhead at the Screwdriver and taken us all out that way – it would have been more humane.

I collapsed into a chair, my body completely and utterly numb. The implications of what he had done were almost unthinkable. Will was already toast, and I fully expected to be shoved under the grill myself any second. I didn't know whether or not the powers that be had tracked me down as the source of the leak yet, but surely it would be only a matter of time before my name came under discussion in the plush stuccoed boardroom on the thirtieth floor.

And losing my job was only the start of it. There was also the question of legal proceedings – could I go to gaol for not reporting what I knew to the appropriate authorities? Would I be sued by the bank for breach of confidence for the stuff Mel had put up on the net? I had no idea.

I was beginning to wonder if I should simply slip unobtrusively down to the staff toilets on the ground floor, climb out of a window and sneak home, when I glanced over at Polly's face and watched as she rubbed her left eye, only to have a stray tear trickle out of her right one and roll down her cheek.

'Oh, Polls.' In a complete reversal of our earlier positions, I put my arms round her. 'It's going to be all right – you'll see.'

Polly shook her head.

'There's no way it can be all right – no way at all. There's going to be a run on the bank and we're either going to be taken over or closed and . . . and we're all going to lose our jobs.'

'No we won't.' I hugged her again. 'We are the third biggest bank in the UK. There is no way the government will let us go bust.'

'The Royal Bank of Wales is making a bid to buy out

the Chiltern!' yelled Archie, breaking the deathly silence that hung over us like a shroud.

'Not the Royal Bank of Wales!' cried a fresh-faced young chap who'd only started the week before. 'They took over the Preston Northend Building Society last year and sacked every single one of the existing staff.'

A collective whimper ran round the room. The cull at the Preston Northend had become the stuff of particularly bloody legend.

'The Prime Minister says that because of the Royal Bank of Wales offer, the government won't be backing a rescue package for us!' shouted Archie as yet another breaking story ran across the ticker at the bottom. 'He says there's not enough money to keep bailing banks out indefinitely.'

A gasp of horror surged like a Mexican wave round the room.

'Enough!' I marched over to my desk and turned the computer on.

'Hey!' hissed Polly, momentarily distracted from our collective woes. 'What are you doing?'

'We're panicking,' I said, suddenly feeling energy surge through me and knock out the numbness. 'We are panicking over something that might never happen.'

Polly stared at me as though I'd offered to make her a porpoise omelette with a side order of whale fries.

'Excuse me,' she replied, 'but it *is* bloody happening – the bank is going to fold and we're all going to lose our jobs.'

And I couldn't deny she had a point.

The bank that wants to make you smile had somehow transformed itself in a matter of minutes into *the bank that wants to make you panic*. Over by the potted plants in the corner, Georgia began to cry and Claire blew her nose loudly on a tissue; even the normally jovial Archie was looking as though someone had hit him over the head with a length of lead piping. It was almost enough to make me grab a magic marker and scrawl the words 'Abandon Hope All Ye Who Enter Here' above the double doors.

But not quite.

Because the emotion currently swirling through my veins was not despair but pure, powerful, vengeful anger. I was buggered if Alex Hodder was going to get away with this.

But if I was going to outsmart him, I needed evidence.

I booted up my computer and within seconds found my way into the SunSpot accounts. Immediately the password box popped up. Damn! The first thing they would have done was disable all of Will's access codes. I typed in 'Verdi', and sure enough 'Access Denied' flashed up on the screen in big red letters. I took a deep breath: I couldn't spend the rest of the afternoon trying random password codes; I simply didn't have the time. Every second I wasted staring at a computer terminal was a second during which our share price dropped further and the Royal Bank of Wales got closer to a takeover.

I took a deep breath and typed in 'Traviata'. From Will's burblings on the phone, I would have been willing to bet my shirt that this was his personal code. In fact, it wouldn't have surprised me if he'd set up the access himself without our IT department knowing anything about it. I waited for what felt like several millennia as the server checked out my authorisation, and then . . . bingo! I was in.

I went straight to the SunSpot accounts and spotted a few more bogus trades that had been added in to pass off the new investors' money as profit. Next, I found the list of losses contained within 'Impaler' and its cohorts.

I sent the relevant sheets to the printer.

Then I re-examined the figures I'd already pulled out about the Chiltern's current securities and assets, scribbled them down on a piece of paper and shoved the whole lot into my bag.

Right: I was ready to go.

I stood up and began to make my way silently over towards the lift. No one else in the room noticed; they all had their eyes glued to the TV screen – apart from Polly and Archie, who had disappeared into the kitchen for a comfort snog as their world collapsed around them.

As the lift shot downwards, my legs suddenly acquired the strength of old knicker elastic and my stomach began heaving like the Atlantic Ocean in a force ten. My focus, however, remained resolute. I was no longer Laura the Ostrich; I was Super Laura, Laura the Brave, and I was going to show Alex he couldn't dump me in it like this. By the end of the afternoon, he was going to wish he'd never been born, or at least that he'd phoned in sick today.

I slipped out of a side entrance and skirted round the throng of TV reporters and journalists who seemed to have materialised out of nowhere to besiege the steps of the Screwdriver. As there had still been no comment from the board of directors – or indeed anyone from inside the bank – they were mostly looking bored or doing pieces to camera with the phallic protuberance of my place of work looming over them in the background. In addition to the reporters, there was also a small but very vocal group of sixty-something ladies waving a large placard with the words 'Don't Trust the Bankers' written in black marker pen. As I passed them I quickened my pace, keeping my gaze fixed determinedly ahead and refusing to make eye contact with them in case the words *Chiltern Bank employee – thump me now* flashed up across my pupils.

I was heading for the Financial News Today offices, which were a couple of streets away, hoping to beard Alex in his lair. It wasn't far as the crow flew, but it took me ages to fight my way through the sea of people. Two steps – another two steps: I could just about see the corner of the street in which the studios were situated. Another two steps and I was almost through the heaving mass of journalistic humanity. Three more steps – I was about to cross the road. Another step, and then—

Something slid out of my pocket and landed on the pavement.

'Oh look,' one of the militant banker-hating ladies (who was clad in a pink velour jogging suit) bent down and picked it up, 'you've dropped this.'

In slow motion I turned round and stared at the object in her hand.

It was my security pass.

Moreover, it was my security pass with my name, my job title and the words: *The Chiltern – the bank that wants to make you smile!* emblazoned across it in large red letters.

'She works there!' shrieked the lady excitedly. 'She's one of *them*!' And she brandished her placard at me as though it were an offensive weapon.

I looked round wildly for escape but found myself hemmed in on all sides by an unholy combination of angry elderly ladies and bored journalists. I was stuck like a wasp in a jam-jar trap and the mood amongst the ladies was starting to turn distinctly nasty.

'We're going to lose our savings and our pensions – and it's all your fault,' one of them snarled.

'But I'm not a fraudster – I'm an analyst,' I explained, trying to remain calm and reasonable.

But the ladies weren't interested in being calm or reasonable.

'Don't try and be clever,' cried one with bleached blonde hair, tight jeans and a glittery T-shirt. 'The bank is about to collapse and I need to know whether my money's safe!'

'It's safe,' I said. 'The first fifty thousand pounds in all UK accounts is guaranteed by the government, and in any event, the bank is not going to collapse.'

Suddenly, before she could open her large, overly red mouth to reply, a small gap opened up in the crowd and I knew I had to make a dash for it.

'Anyway,' I said brightly, 'hope that answers your question – nice talking to you, and goodbye!'

I went to disappear, but the ladies weren't having any of it.

'She works for the bank! Stop her!' one of them yelled.

And my cover was blown.

Every single journalist within a one-mile radius (and right then that was a heck of a lot of journalists) stopped drinking coffee and stared at me. It was one of those terrible moments where nobody moved and nobody spoke – apart, that was, from a man wearing a sandwich board proclaiming 'Money is the Root of All Evil' (a point of view with which I was rapidly becoming sympathetic), who pushed his way through the crowd and stood looking blankly at me.

A fraction of a second later, the tension broke and all hell was let loose.

I was bumped and jostled on all sides, journalists shoved microphones, tape-recorders and camera lenses in my face and I lost my breath as someone's elbow collided with my solar plexus. Something that looked like a dead hamster on the end of a fishing rod dangled in my face – and I almost dropped all my papers down the drain. Then, in the midst of the chaos that was enveloping me, I felt an arm round my waist, and I was steered firmly and swiftly out of the maelstrom and back up the steps towards the glass doors of the Screwdriver. I looked round to see who my saviour was – and got another nasty shock.

'I told you to stay away from me!' I hissed, and pushed him angrily. 'I mean it, Alex: nothing you can possibly say can change my mind about you, so just get over yourself and scram!'

I turned to face the sea of people, all staring up at me expectantly. They were being held at the bottom of the steps by a group of big, burly policemen, and further down the street, I could just make out the silhouettes of yet more police, this time on horseback and holding large, scary-looking shields.

My legs suddenly turned from old bits of knicker elastic into mayonnaise, and my breath came in short, unattractive gulps. Of all the things I didn't do, impromptu public speaking in front of a crowd who would rather like to lynch me was pretty near the top of the list – but I couldn't sit back and let the bank fold when there was a chance I had the information that might just save it.

'Are the rumours true?' yelled one of the reporters.

'No!' I yelled back. 'At least most of them aren't. There is nothing wrong with the bank. We are not about to go under.'

'What's that?' asked someone a metre or so away. 'Did you say the bank is definitely going under?'

A worried murmur flowed out across the crowd like ripples on a pond.

'No,' I shouted at the top of my voice, desperate not to make the situation any worse than it already was. 'It's all fine! Safe as houses. Nil problemo!'

'Then why are there thousands of people queuing at branches all over the country to get their money back?' asked the old lady with the bleached hair, carefully folding her arms to show off her tattoos to their best advantage.

'Speak up!' yelled someone at the back.

One of the policemen tapped me on the shoulder.

'I think you're going to be needing this, miss. The Riot Squad down the road thought it might be helpful.'

He handed over a large grey megaphone, which I tentatively raised to my lips. Further up St Andrewgate a group of black-clad mounted police waved cheerily at me.

'Er, hello?' I began.

The sound of my own voice booming out across the road almost knocked me over. However, it had the desired effect, and the crowd stopped murmuring amongst themselves and fixed their attention one hundred per cent on me. Then, just so that I knew where he was, I looked round for Alex. Our gazes collided and I scowled at him; to my satisfaction, I was convinced I saw him wilt slightly.

Then I lifted the megaphone to my mouth and started to speak.

'I'm Laura McGregor,' I said, 'and just like the rest of you, I am not entirely sure why everyone is panicking so hard.'

'A representative of the bank has just admitted that they have lost total control of the situation,' one of the reporters gabbled enthusiastically into his microphone.

'No!' I replied, fixing him with a stare as deadly as the one I'd just inflicted on Alex. 'That is *not* what I said.'

The man took a step backwards and clutched the microphone protectively to his bosom. I continued.

'The reason *why* I do not understand the panic is because it has nothing to do with the real financial position of the bank. It has been entirely manufactured by people like you in the media to get a good story.'

The reporter went a bit red.

'But you can't deny, can you, Miss McGregor,' Alex's

voice rose above the babble of the crowd, 'that a serious fraud has been perpetrated at your place of work?'

My heart pounded and I could feel heat rising up into my cheeks and spreading across my face. At that moment I hated him; I hated him very much. And most of all, I hated it that to feel so intensely, I must care about him very much indeed.

'And you, Alex Hodder,' I said with as much dignity as I could muster, 'frankly you are the worst of the lot.'

'With respect, Miss McGregor, I think you should stick to the matter in question rather than make personal allegations about me – especially when you are not in possession of the full facts.'

Yeah, *right!* What other facts could there possibly be? He was back on with Isobel and he had raided my diary to find a big fat juicy story – as far as I was concerned, there was no room for ambiguity. I glowered at him again but was disappointed to note that this time my cutting stare didn't have the same effect: Alex was obviously developing nasty-look antibodies.

'I know all I want to know about you, Mr Hodder, thank you very much; but to return to the Chiltern, I agree it does look as though there was a fraud committed,' I replied calmly – raising my hands to diminish the cacophony that arose from the crowd the moment the words left my lips, 'but whether there was or not, the point is that the amounts involved in that fraud are small enough not to affect the overall viability of the bank. It is quite capable of remaining as a healthy going concern – or it would be if this media circus hadn't resulted in the share price plummeting.'

Alex was leaning against a pillar with his arms folded; something that could have been either concern or annoyance was etched across his features.

'And you have this evidence, do you?' he said. 'The

board of directors entrust you with their intimate secrets?'

I hesitated for a moment – was he giving me the cue I needed to make all of this public? Was he actually *helping* me? I shook myself. No, that was impossible. Alex was only in it for what he could grab with his greedy little paws – and even if he wasn't, I didn't *need* any help from him.

'I have more than enough information, Mr Hodder.' I waved my papers in the air and a few flashbulbs went off to capture the moment. 'The *alleged* losses – and we have to remember that nothing is proved – amount to no more than five billion pounds.'

There was a gasp from the crowd.

'I know,' I said, 'it sounds like a lot, but as of yesterday, the bank had far, far more than that. The Chiltern doesn't have any bad debt, we didn't buy any of those sub-prime loans and we have more than enough money in our reserves to pay everybody's savings and everybody's pension. However, if low-life, irresponsible scaremongers like Mr Hodder here keep talking the share price down and we can no longer function normally, that situation might change. It's that simple.'

Alex opened his mouth to protest but quickly closed it again. I seized the opportunity to keep on talking.

'These figures here,' I waved my papers in the air again, 'clearly show that whatever losses may have been hidden were clocked up years ago. Money from the SunSpot hedge funds was being siphoned into paying them off – that's the fraud – but it doesn't mean the bank will go under.'

I turned to Alex.

'Did you know how much the losses were?' I asked.

'Our source didn't reveal any amounts,' he said stiffly.

For a moment I was caught on the back foot. Alex had said he'd read my diary, and the figures were all in there. Surely *I* was his source – why was he denying it now?

'The Chiltern employee who broke the story to me is not a British national,' Alex continued, his voice cold and emotionless. 'Then I stumbled across some information on the internet that seemed to substantiate our whistle-blower's allegation. It was a quote from a blog that was subsequently deleted, but I didn't go seeking it out.'

My mouth gaped open.

Sweet Lord! Alex *hadn't* gone trawling the blogosphere for my diary. His source had been Will. He must have phoned Alex and broken the story directly to him, and then Alex had run up against some corroborating evidence online that happened to be a quote from my journal. He wasn't quite the rat fink I'd had him down as.

The hand holding my megaphone dropped limply to my side.

Alex's cameraman tapped him on the shoulder and he turned away from me to do a report for his viewers. I watched him as he checked his earpiece and tested his microphone and then began to speak confidently and assuredly to the waiting camera. Was it my imagination, or was there something unforgiving about the slope of his shoulders and the angle of his neck? Then he spoke my name, and there was a quality to his 'Miss McGregor' that made a shiver run all the way down from my neck to the base of my spine.

'Why should we believe you?' demanded a voice.

I looked down and saw the woman in the pink velour jogging suit standing at the bottom of the steps with her hands on her hips.

'For all we know, you're just saying the bank is safe so that you still get your fat-cat salary.'

'I'm saying this so that an institution we both depend

on doesn't disappear,' I replied through the megaphone, which suddenly felt as though it weighed a ton. 'And anyway, I'm not a fat cat so much as an anorexic kitten.'

A ripple of laughter skittered through the crowd. I glanced back at Alex. As our eyes met, his expression softened slightly but his smile did not return.

'Excuse me!' shouted another television reporter, and I heaved my focus back on to the crowd in front of me. 'Can you confirm that the Chiltern is in a better position than most other high-street banks?'

'Yes,' I nodded confidently, feeling that I was at last on home territory, 'even with the hidden losses, we will not require a government bail-out – just so long as our share price doesn't crash, other banks continue to do business with us and there isn't a run on customer deposits.'

'Chiltern share price up fifty pence!' yelled someone from the crowd.

'Sixty!' shouted another reporter, who had been studying his BlackBerry.

'Seventy!'

'Chiltern shares now trading at six pounds seventy-two!'

My legs and arms began to shake visibly with relief. I had done it. Somehow, somewhere, someone in the world's stock markets had listened to what I'd had to say and the share price was on the up.

'Chiltern shares back up to yesterday's level and the customers are leaving the branches!' called out somebody else.

I handed the megaphone back to one of the policemen and shrank behind a pillar, leaning against the comforting honey-coloured stone for support. Thankfully, all the journalists (including Alex) were enthusiastically doing 'breaking news' pieces for their own networks and no one paid me any further attention.

The sheer enormity of what I had done began to sink in. Yes, I might have transformed myself into the mouse that roared; yes, I might even have saved the bank, but I had almost definitely lost my job. Apart from the fact that I had more or less confessed to sticking my nose into the SunSpot accounts, I had then gone and deliberately shared that information by appearing on billions of television screens around the globe. You could forget the blog – even allowing for the fact that I had done it from the best of intentions, my TV debut was enough to get me fired a hundred times over. I knew far too much to stay on.

I glanced over at Alex, who was still on air and gesturing enthusiastically at a bunch of police cars that had pulled up by the edge of the road and begun to disgorge plain-clothes officers, presumably from the Fraud Squad.

Even though he was a matter of mere feet away, I had an overwhelming sense that I was utterly disconnected from him. His tone, his manner, the way in which he had articulated my name in the piece he had just recorded made me feel as though I had been somehow cut adrift and was now being pulled along on a current taking me further and further away from what we might once have had together.

I wrapped my arm around the cool solidity of the pillar and watched as Alex handed his microphone to the sound-operator and went round to the back of the camera to watch a replay of the footage. My gaze must have been burning into him, because he looked up and met my eye. He signalled to his cameraman to stop the film and took a step towards me – but I turned my back on him and moved pointedly away to the other side of my pillar. I didn't need to wait for the fat lady to warm up her vocal cords to realise that it was over; even if I had been mistaken about him raiding my diary, he had still made his decision over who he wanted to spend his life with – and had plumped for Isobel. Could I really blame him? Almost since the moment we'd first clapped eyes on each other in the meeting room, I'd been telling him to sling his hook, and unsurprisingly, he had gone and done just that.

Only now, with the anger trickling out of me, I discovered it wasn't what I actually wanted.

Slowly, very slowly, I turned back towards the doors and made my way inside. A familiar and very welcome figure was waiting for me by the reception desk.

'You were marvellous.' Polly enveloped me in an enormous hug. 'You saved the day and we love you.'

As I sank into her arms, my eye caught a brown cardboard box resting on the top of the marble reception desk.

'What's that?' I asked, even though I already knew the answer.

Polly didn't reply immediately. Instead she gave a bit of a sniff and wiped her hand over her face.

'Bastards,' she hissed, 'bloody HR bastards. After what you did to save their arses, they go and fire yours.'

'P45 in the post?' I asked, feeling amazingly calm.

Polly nodded.

'I got your bits together for you,' she said. 'I'm not even supposed to speak to you but I couldn't just let you go – you're my best mate!'

She sniffed again and I looked in the box. It contained papers, Post-its, pens and a framed photo of Tom that I'd forgotten I even had. Strangely, none of it felt as though it actually belonged to me. They were the possessions of another Laura who had worked for a bank a long, long time ago.

'Come round tonight,' I said. 'Bring wine.'

Polly gulped and tried to force a smile.

'And chocolate,' she said. 'Chocolate always works well at times like these.'

I kissed her on the cheek, feeling truly thankful that I could count on someone like her to be there for me. Then I pulled away, did up the buttons on my coat that she had brought down for me and put my bag over my shoulder.

'Don't you want your stuff?' Polly looked confused.

I shook my head. My work, the bank, the fast-track training scheme – none of it was me, the real, essential me, and I didn't need its trappings any more than a snake needs a skin it has just discarded.

'I know this sounds weird, but it's part of my past; it doesn't feel as though it matters any more.'

'Laura,' Polly was now looking worried, 'are you all right?'

'No,' I said honestly, 'I'm not. And at the risk of sounding even weirder, it's nothing to do with my job.'

Her face was clearly saying 'cannot compute', so I took a deep breath and elaborated.

'It's to do with that man on the telly. Alex Hodder. I discovered about three minutes ago that he's the one I want to spend the rest of my life with, and I also realised, more or less simultaneously, that I never will. Believe me, the bank doesn't even come close.'

Polly rubbed my arm sympathetically.

'Never say never, mon amigo,' she cautioned. 'You don't know what's round the corner.'

'I think I do, Polls,' I whispered, 'and if I went on to tell you that I want him so badly that right now I would be sacked ten times over if it made any difference to how he felt about me, it would just make me sound sad and desperate – so I won't.'

Polly looked as though she was about to burst into tears on my behalf.

'Tonight,' I said. 'Bring wine, chocolate *and* tissues. But for now, bugger off and have a coffee, snog Archie, do anything – but for God's sake cheer up a bit.'

There was the clack-clack-clack of heels behind us and we both looked round.

'Hello, sweetie,' smarmed Isobel. 'As soon as I heard the news, I just *had* to come and say goodbye. *Such* a loss to the company you going.'

'Yes, it is, isn't it?' I replied, squeezing Polly's hand and preparing to leave.

'And I just *had* to show you this before you went; it might be my last opportunity to let you in on the good news.'

Isobel waved her left hand in front of my face. There on the third finger was a ring. One with a solitaire diamond so huge nestling in its setting that I was amazed her knuckles weren't actually dragging across the floor.

This was presumably the other thing Alex had been going to tell me when he phoned.

'It's only going to be a short engagement,' she informed me smugly. 'I don't want any fuss; just me and him and a couple of close friends at the registry office. Well, you know how it is when you are in love.'

She over-emphasised the last two words deliberately.

I was too punch-drunk from the events of the last half an hour for her news to have its desired effect. I already knew I had lost Alex. I had lost him completely and for ever, and nothing Isobel could say or do would make me feel any worse than the knowledge that I had to suffer the rest of my life without him.

I nodded towards her.

'I hope you will both be very happy,' I said, and found I meant it.

I wished with all my heart and all my soul that Alex would, indeed, not live to regret his marriage. My hatred and anger had gone and I cared too much about him to wish him any ill.

Isobel looked thunderstruck. Presumably her plan to send me off the premises sobbing into my cardboard box had backfired.

'Er, thank you,' she said awkwardly.

I turned to Polly.

'Seven?' I asked.

'Seven,' she confirmed.

And then, without a backwards glance, I strode across the marble floor of the foyer and out for the last time through the revolving glass door of London's most iconic building.

18

I am sitting on a banquette in the horse-brass-bedecked saloon bar of the Rose and Crown in Bournebridge, Wiltshire. To be honest, the place hasn't changed that much since I used to sneak in here for a Malibu and Coke after A-level revision sessions, and despite it changing hands at least three times, the only visible sign of the passing years is that the ceiling has ripened to a darker shade of mottled, sticky-looking brown and you can now get chicken-tikka-flavoured crisps, which down in Bournebridge is pretty much the cutting edge of gastronomic experience. Heston Blumenthal wouldn't last five minutes.

It is lunchtime on a sunny April day. Outside, the first green of spring is dusting the fields and hedgerows, but as I don't feel particularly sunny or spring-like, I am huddled away in the gloomy interior trying to get my head together. On the table in front of me is a half-consumed pint of Scabby Pony real ale from the local microbrewery and three chewed-looking beer mats. The beer mats are looking chewed because in between sips from my pint, I am picking at them with my fingernails. This does nothing for the beer mats, but it gives my hands something to do as I readjust to the seismic events of recent days.

As I'd expected, I received my P45 in the post the next day. Strangely, however, I wasn't actually sacked. Instead, and in return for a media gagging clause, I was offered redundancy and a small lump sum. Not enough to pay off my debts or my mortgage, mind you, but better than the slap in the face I had thought was heading my way. Of course, I made sure that all the information about the SunSpot Swindle (as the red-tops are calling it) was passed on to the SFO – I wasn't going to be colluding with the fraudsters on the Chiltern's board of directors – but I don't intend to issue any front-page exclusives for a while.

After two days of kicking around disconsolately in the flat and hearing from recruitment agency after recruitment agency that there was nothing doing on the jobs front, I packed my bags, jumped on the first train out of Waterloo and – get this – came home to Wiltshire to think things through in peace and quiet.

The relief that fell from my shoulders as the train click-clacked out beyond the dank grey perma-grime of south London was immense. It was as if my job and money worries had floated upwards into the smudge of pollution that circled the City skyscrapers I was leaving behind. Only an empty, gnawing ache right where my heart should have been told me that total escape was impossible: Alex – or rather the loss of him – was going to be with me for a very long time to come.

The heavy mock-medieval door on the other side of the Rose and Crown's saloon bar opens, letting in a spike of sunlight and interrupting my thoughts. I look up and see a small, blonde-haired woman wearing Russell Brand's jeans and a long black trench coat stepping over the threshold. She looks at me, and as our eyes meet, I see a shimmer of uncertainty pass over her otherwise supremely confident face. She takes a deep breath and juts her chin out defiantly – and I note that I am doing exactly the same.

'Hello,' says Mel, making her way over to my table and pulling up a massively over-upholstered stool. 'Mum said you'd be down here. Lunchtime drinking, is it?'

I can't decide whether this is a cue for an invitation to join me or a thinly veiled slight, so I raise my eyebrows and say nothing.

'Refill?' she asks, half rising from her stool and fishing a purse out of one of the trench coat's pockets. 'I think it must be my round.'

I'm tempted to say 'Who are you and what have you done with the real Mel?' – but I don't.

'You don't have any money,' I remind her.

'I'm working.' She shrugs. 'Besides, it's not really a drink – it's more of an apology.'

'All right then,' I reply. 'I'll have a half of Coke that is really, really sorry for meddling in its sister's business.'

Mel gives an appreciative half-smile.

'And what about a packet of crisps that wants to make amends for not telling you about some dodgy Bristol con merchants?' she suggests.

'Less of your lip, young lady,' I say. 'That's my mate Wayne you're talking about.'

'Wayne's on police bail,' says Mel, 'but they're keeping Tony banged up till the trial.'

I take another sip from my pint.

'I know,' I say. 'The rozzers want me to give evidence.'

'Me too; I've said I will.'

I stare at her. This is not like my scaredy-cat sis who ducks out of any and all difficult situations. Mel risks a glowing, if slightly self-conscious, grin.

'Jules will be there,' she says simply. 'He'll look after me. Salt and vinegar, was it?'

'Cheese and onion,' I reply, 'and what's all this about Jules?'

But Mel, now with a definite twinkle in her eye, is over at the bar putting her order in and – I swear to God – getting a crisp twenty-pound note out of her purse to pay for it.

'I said,' I repeat as soon as she is reseated on her stool, 'what's all this about Jules?'

Mel looks away and blushes slightly while I have a Psychic Polly moment.

'You're sleeping with him?' I hiss over the table.

Mel nods and her cheeks go redder than a sunburned tomato.

'We're together,' she whispers. 'Alex took me round to his flat after you and I had that big row. Jules said I could stay for a bit till I got myself sorted, and then we – then we sort of fell in love. God, he's gorgeous.'

She takes a restorative draught of her gin and tonic, and a thought flashes through me.

'That's why he sorted Wayne out for us?' I ask.

Mel nods.

'He and Alex tossed for it and Jules won. Besides, Jules's great-grandfather came over here from Sicily, and let's just say he made them an offer they couldn't refuse.'

Despite the fact that the mention of Alex's name makes the black hole at the centre of my chest pulse painfully, I nudge Mel's knee under the table.

'Good for you,' I say. 'It sounds like it's been a bit of a life-changer.'

'More than you can guess.' Mel grins again, winding a blonde curl round her index finger. 'I'm even off to art school in September: time for me to put my money where my mouth is and actually do something with my life.'

I chink my glass with hers.

'Congratulations,' I say. 'I look forward to receiving a faked-up copy of the *Mona Lisa* that I can sell for millions.'

Mel delves into another pocket in the trench coat and hands me a small rectangle of paper: a cheque – for two hundred pounds. In return I give her a disbelieving stare (old habits die hard).

'It's cool,' Mel shrugs, 'and it won't bounce either. I'm paying you back – every penny.'

I put the cheque into my purse. The way the job market is looking, I may well be depending on Mel's repayments to keep the interest-only-mortgage wolf from my door.

'Thanks,' I say, 'but why are you here? And please don't tell me you've taken time off work simply to hand me your hard-earned cash, because then I *will* know it's time to ring for the men in the white coats.'

Mel looks at me as though I'm a few fairy cakes short of a tea party.

'It's Easter,' she says simply. 'Today is Good Friday. You know, one of those bank holiday things: no work-o, no problemo.'

I stare at her. Easter? Now? Here? So soon? I thought I was pretty much on the ball – but it turns out I hadn't even clocked which festive season it was.

Mel pats my cheek.

'Earth to Laura!' she laughs. 'Dad's coming to Sunday lunch, remember? It's the Great Parental Rapprochement plus chocolate eggs. What's not to like? Mum's even had her roots done.'

'Has she?'

Mel's face contorts into a worried frown.

'Laura, are you sure you're okay?' Her voice is low and I feel her hand rest on mine for a second.

'Of course,' I reply. 'I've just had a lot on my mind recently.'

'You know what,' Mel's knee nudges mine again, 'I thought you were bloody brilliant on the news. I cheered when I saw you telling that nasty little journo where he could stick his media hysteria.'

'You mean Alex?' The connection in my mind is instant.

'No.' Mel frowns again. 'Alex isn't nasty. He – I think he really regrets what happened between you, Laura.'

'Yeah, fine, whatever.' I turn my face away and focus hard on *not* thinking about Alex.

I'm at the point where I can sometimes go for two hours at a stretch without him popping into my head, and I don't want Mel to make me relapse. My sister drains her glass and pushes her stool back. Her butterfly hand rests for a moment again on mine.

'Okay, but we talk later, all right? You've done a lot for me, Laura, and I owe you more than a pile of cash.'

I smile at her. I could get to like this new, emotionally aware Mel.

An envelope is produced from one or other of the trench-coat pockets and slides across the table towards me. Mel shifts awkwardly from one Converse-booted foot to the other.

'Open it after I've gone,' she says. 'You'll probably hate me, but I had to do it.'

Anxiety stabs through me – is it a letter from Alex? I glance at the franking mark, my heart pounding: *Esterman Publishers Ltd*. It means nothing to me. I slide it under a beer mat and nod at her.

'I'll open it in a minute,' I promise and glance at my watch. 'I won't be long – tell Mum I'll be back in half an hour.'

Mel smiles, opens the door and is promptly swallowed up by the spring sunshine.

I pick up the envelope and shake it: nothing.

I run my finger along its base and gauge its weight: it gives away none of its secrets.

I put it under my nose and sniff it: I am still none the wiser.

Finally I decide I might as well meander home, so I manoeuvre my way round the table and raise a hand in cheery farewell to mine host. I push open the door that leads into the stunningly euphemistic 'beer garden', consisting of a battered-looking picnic table covered with bird poo standing in the car park next to the bins, and am just about to turn left on to the main street of downtown Bournebridge when—

ARRGGHHHHHHH!!!!!!!!!!!

A figure steps forth from behind the shadow of the wheelie bins and blocks my path.

I close my eyes and tell my beating heart to get a grip.

Then I open my eyes again and—

ARRGGHHHHHHH!!!!!!!!!!!

I realise that the figure is Alex.

A couple of heavily tattooed locals smoking round the other side of the bottle bank pause mid-drag and eye us suspiciously.

Alex shifts nervously, but whether this is to do with the said heavily tattooed locals, who are now eyeing him up as prospective punch-bag material, or whether the pangs of a guilty conscience are weighing heavily upon him, I have no idea.

'Laura,' he begins – and then stops.

My heart is pounding as though I've just finished the London Marathon and my stomach is doing its best to climb out of my throat.

'Alex!' I say. 'What on earth are you doing here?'

'I'm fine,' he says – and then we both realise he's answered the wrong question.

'Are you – are you down here for Easter?' I ask politely.

After all, why would anyone come to Bournebridge –

apart from a three-line whip to spend the holiday with their family?

'Um, that's right – the old spring visit to the parents,' he replies with cringeworthy jocularity.

We succumb to a silence that feels as though it lasts into the middle of next week.

'Right then!' I say, my voice as bright and breezy as a children's TV presenter. 'Have a lovely time!'

And before he has time to react, I dodge past him and make for the high street, leaving him staring thunderstruck after me.

I look round and watch as one of the super-sized locals finishes his ciggie and stubs it out on the tarmac with a steel-capped toe, then hoists up his trousers and stares at Alex in a manner that suggests he's ready for action. As a journalist who has reported live from riots, war zones and natural disasters, Alex knows when it's time to make himself scarce – and comes haring after me.

I walk faster.

So does he.

I break into a steady jog.

Alex does the same.

I stifle a scream: *why* does this *always* happen with Alex? How come, at any significant juncture in our lives, we end up looking like an out-take from the Keystone Cops?

'What do you want?' I throw the words over my shoulder and keep going.

'To talk to you.'

Well that's just plain ridiculous! Of course he doesn't want to talk to me – the last time we coincided, up on the steps of the Screwdriver, I insulted him and he could barely keep the disgust out of his voice. Talking is the last thing he'd want to be doing.

Then I take two more steps and reality slaps me round

the face. Oh bugger! He's come to do the decent thing and tell me about his wedding.

'Isobel not with you, then?' The words are out of my mouth before I can stop them.

Alex looks horrified and glances behind him as though he expects to see a willowy blonde figure closing in on us.

'No,' he says nervously, 'no, she's not.'

'Congratulations,' I offer. Tersely.

I might want him to be happy, but the same doesn't apply to her.

Alex stops dead in his tracks and does a good impression of someone suffering from terminal bewilderment. *Oh for goodness' sake – do I have to spell it out?*

'Mr and *Mrs* Hodder,' I reminded him, beginning to wonder which one of us has lost the plot.

'Er, my mum and dad are fine,' he replies warily, 'but thanks for asking.'

'No,' I say, pulling to a stop a few yards ahead and conscious of a flush of annoyance spreading over my cheeks, 'I'm talking about you and Isobel. For richer, for poorer.'

Alex's face continues to have a horrified '*huh?*' written all over it.

'The wedding!' My teeth are so gritted they can barely part to let the words out. '*Your* wedding!'

Then the penny drops with a clang so loud they could probably hear it over in Swindon – but his reply still doesn't make any sense.

'Isobel *is* married,' he says, 'but not to me.'

'Oh don't be ridiculous, Alex,' I snap. 'Of course she is.'

'Um, no she isn't.' A shiver runs through him at the very thought. 'I think I would have noticed.'

Now it's my turn to do the *non comprendez* routine. For a moment I think I'm about to topple over in shock, but as I would have an uncomfortable landing on top of a memorial bollard dedicated to Mrs P. Anstruther, parish councillor for forty years, I decide against it.

'Isobel *is* married,' Alex repeats the words slowly, as though he is very unsure of my reaction, 'but her victim – I mean husband – is Tom. She sent me an invitation to the ceremony at Chelsea Registry Office but I told them I was washing my hair that day and couldn't go.'

I grip Mrs Anstruther's bollard for grim life. *Tom?! Isobel??!*

'Bugger me!' I say loudly, all pretence at maintaining an internal monologue beyond me, adding: 'Oh, hello, Reverend Tibbs!' as the vicar comes out of the village shop right behind me.

'I told Isobel the Tuesday after I met up with her that she and I were a no-go zone,' Alex continues. 'And I *also* informed her that the reason for this was because I'd met someone else, someone I had very strong feelings for – in fact, the person I might very well want to spend the rest of my life with. I did try to tell you this vital piece of information on a number of occasions, Miss McGregor, but as usual, you wouldn't let me get a word in edgeways.'

Alex gives me a nervous glance.

'I know you told me you never wanted to see me again, Laura, but I couldn't just leave it like this. You drive me nuts – in a totally good way – and I reckoned it was worth one last shot.'

He looks at me expectantly and takes the ten steps necessary to come and stand next to me and the bollard.

'So,' he says, 'with Tom and Isobel out of the picture, that sort of leaves you and me – if you've changed your mind about hating me, that is.'

I do a sort of gulping swallow thing.

'Hate you?' I echo, the memory of that phone call

feeling rather blurry and distant. 'No, I don't hate you. I thought *you* probably hated *me*.'

Alex's lovely brows draw together in a puzzled frown. 'Why on earth would I hate you?'

'Oh,' I shrug, picking at a blob of paint on the bollard, 'just one or two reasons: because I yelled at you; because I said I never wanted to see you again; because I called you a low-life, irresponsible scaremonger on national telly. That sort of thing really.'

Alex starts to grin. An irrepressible, contagious grin that starts at his eyes and ends up spreading all the way over to my face and pulling the corners of my mouth back into a big beaming answering smile.

About a billion different emotions are surging through me at this moment: relief, love, hope, fear, regret and complete unabashed bewilderment. Are we really going to be given a second chance – or will fate yet again step in with its size nines and kick us into touch?

'Except,' Alex continues, running his fingers across the lumpy surface of the bollard and grasping the corner of the letter I'm clutching in my left hand. 'Except there is something else I have to tell you.'

Immediately my heart plunges back down to the depths. Of course there would be a catch: this is Alex and me we're talking about; the course of *our* true love runs about as smoothly as an old banger with three wheels and no suspension. Why did I even bother getting my hopes up?

I'm vaguely aware of Alex tugging the envelope out of my unresisting fingers and fidgeting with it.

'I'm afraid I'm not going to be in London for much longer, Laura; I'm going to New York. That project Jules and I have been working on – well, we've got an opening in the US and I'm flying out for six months to see if I can make a go of it.'

'Oh.'

So that's our final great stumbling block. He didn't love Isobel after all – but he's emigrating to a different time zone. Great. Well, so long, Alex, and thanks for letting me know.

'And,' his hands continue to fidget nervously, 'here's the thing, Laura: I was wondering if you would come with me. I know this is all a bit sudden, but I just can't bear the thought of us being apart any longer. I've waited ten years as it is. Please say you will?'

I look down and realise he's shredded the edges of my envelope. I quickly grab the letter out of his hands and it flutters a bit in the breeze. Alex just keeps right on babbling.

'I know you've got issues with work and there's your flat and things, but I thought that perhaps you might consider it a sound move to leave everything you've ever known and fly halfway round the world with a comparative stranger.' (He is nothing if not optimistic.) 'Laura? What do you say?'

I'm not listening, however; I'm staring at the letter. Very slowly, with my mouth moving silently, I read it again.

'Laura,' Alex says, 'Laura – what is it?'

'It's an offer,' I reply, unable to take my eyes from the sheet of paper batting about in the spring breeze in front of me, 'an offer of a book contract from a publisher. Mel sent them extracts from the blog before I could take it down – and they loved it. They want to pay me to write a book based on my diary.'

I hold it up for him to see, the tremors in my hand making the paper shake even more than the wind can achieve.

'Fantastic,' he says. 'Wonderful news.'

But I don't believe him. His face is pale and there is

something that looks suspiciously like despair in his dark brown eyes.

I fold the letter up, put it carefully in my bag and smile at him.

'Yes,' I say.

Alex frowns at me, uncomprehending.

'Yes,' I repeat, 'I *will* go out for that drink you suggested ten years ago – only perhaps we'd better make it Manhattans, seeing as that's where we're going to be living.'

Alex stumbles backwards and almost falls over the bollard.

'You're coming to New York?' he asks incredulously.

I nod. 'I can write just as well there as I can in London, and besides' – I lean over and kiss him – 'I wouldn't be able to do *that* if we were on different sides of the Atlantic.'

'No,' it's a point he seems happy to concede, 'you wouldn't. Besides, I have a feeling you're going to love America.'

I wrap my arms round his waist and pull him as close to me as the bollard allows.

'I think you're right,' I say, 'but probably not as much as I'm going to love you.'

little black dress

brings you fantastic new books like these
every month - find out more at
www.littleblackdressbooks.com

Why not link up with other devoted Little Black
Dress fans on our Facebook group? Simply type
Little Black Dress Books into Facebook to join up.

And if you want to be the first
to hear the latest news on all things
Little Black Dress, just send the details below to
littleblackdressmarketing@headline.co.uk
and we'll sign you up to our lovely email
newsletter (and we promise that we won't share
your information with anybody else!).*

Name: _____

Email Address: _____

Date of Birth: _____

Region/Country: _____

What's your favourite Little Black Dress book?

_____

How many Little Black Dress books have you read?_____

*You can be removed from the mailing list at any time

You can buy any of these other
Little Black Dress titles from your
bookshop or *direct from the publisher*.

FREE P&P AND UK DELIVERY
(Overseas and Ireland £3.50 per book)

TO ORDER SIMPLY CALL THIS NUMBER

01235 400 414

or visit our website: www.headline.co.uk

Prices and availability subject to change without notice.